1 9 8 8

D1474875

The Book of Seeing
With One's Own Eyes

SHORT STORIES BY

Sharon Doubiago

GRAYWOLF PRESS   SAINT PAUL

Some of the stories included in this collection appeared previously in periodicals, whose editors are gratefully acknowledged:

"Ramon/Ramona" appeared in *Country Woman* and in *Alchemy.*

"Raquel" appeared in *Arts and Entertainment Magazine,* published by the Mendocino Arts Center.

"Chappaquiddick" was published in *Alcatraz.*

"The Art of Seeing with One's Own Eyes" appeared in both *New England Review and Bread Loaf Quarterly* and *The Pushcart Prize, Volume X.*

"The Whore" was published in *New England Review and Bread Loaf Quarterly.*

ISBN 1-55597-101-6
Library of Congress Catalog Card Number 87-81373
CIP Data and song permissions statements on back page

9 8 7 6 5 4 3 2

The cover art is *Delusions of Grandeur* by Rene Magritte, and is reproduced by permission of Hirshhorn Museum and Sculpture Garden, Smithsonian Institution. Gift of Joseph H. Hirshhorn, 1966.
The painting is © 1988, Charly Herscovici, Brussels, Photo © 1988 ADAGP.

Publication of this book is made possible in part by generous contributions to Graywolf Press from the Jerome Foundation, the National Endowment for the Arts, the Minnesota State Arts Board, and other corporate, foundation, and individual donors. Graywolf Press is a member agency of United Arts, Saint Paul.

Published by GRAYWOLF PRESS,
2402 University Avenue, Suite 203, Saint Paul, Minnesota 55114.

Contents

FOR DANNY AND SHAWN

To see
is to forget
the name
of
the thing
one sees.

Paul Valéry

If the eye were an animal, sight would be its soul.
Aristotle

If the doors of perception were cleansed,
everything would appear to be as it is, infinite.
William Blake

THE BOOK OF SEEING
WITH ONE'S OWN EYES

Part I

Beauty and the Beast

HELEN

All Greece hates
the still eyes in the white face
the lustre as of olives
when she stands
and the white hands.

All Greece reviles
the wan face when she smiles
hating it deeper still
when it grows wan and
white
remembering past
enchantments
and past ills.

Greece sees unmoved
God's daughter, born of
love,
the beauty of cool feet
and slenderest knees,
could love indeed the maid,
only if she were laid
white ash amid funeral
cypresses.

H.D.

Ramon/Ramona

The days are hot, but nights we wear first strapless bras, full starched petticoats, our hair in pony tails, slow dance in this old farmhouse beneath eucalyptus. Seventh grade is over, now we are eighth graders.

Through the whole party the Penguins sing "Earth Angel." Chuck and Nadine are dancing, her head rests on his tall shoulder, a couple forming that will be together all through high school. They will be all that the rest of us will want to be. I am dancing with Ramon. When we break at the end of each song I feel regret and everyone is making comments about our being in love. I don't feel in love. I feel his body against mine. I feel the slow moan of the music moving our bodies together. Over his shoulder I watch Chuck and Nadine dancing around us as we dance, *earth angel, earth angel, will you be mine?* and I want this, this body dancing with me, though I have no words for it. Not *love*. Is this how it begins, the long fall? I look into his face that is looking into mine. Fear tremors through me. He is strange, foreign. Indian, he says. Mojave. *Not* Mexican. He says this last like spit. When I get home my blond hair is dark and oily from his oiled black hair.

Every day I walk the three miles to Ramona, down the granite hills, along the dirt roads, the temperature always over 90, sometimes as high as 120. I walk past the field where last summer, my first summer in Ramona, Jesse's father was digging a well. Jesse was dark, handsome, full-grown like me, though only fourteen. He came to my house on horseback, riding twenty miles over the mountains from Poway into El Valle del Ángel. I went on my first date with him, to Ramona's Wedding Place in San Diego. He played the guitar and sang the songs of the Sons of the Pioneers. *All day I face the barren waste without a taste of water. Cool clear water. . . .* He showed me the diamond used for drilling. He pulled me down into sage on the dry riverbed and I saw his face for the first time, the intention of something in him. His eyes had too much light, the same blue light as the summer sky behind them. A cloud floated like a river over his body, like the river this land never knows, and I saw something in him that I loved. But when we weren't kissing I would lose him behind his pretty words, his dramatic gestures, the important role of himself he was always acting. I grew bored.

The summer is dark and green here in Angel Park. Ramon and I have been swimming, our bodies alive from hours in the cold water. We come down the hill beneath eucalyptus, sycamore. He says let's sit down here for awhile. We lie in the deep cool grass, within a half-circle of pink and white oleander bushes. We are talking, words we don't hear. I am lying on my belly. His hand is moving between my breasts and the grass. My surprise is deep, real, both in that he has done this and in the way it feels. I have prepared for years not to be seduced but this isn't what I thought it would be. I'm prepared in my mind, in my will. This is different. This is my body. His fingers on my breasts feel like rivets, the reverberations cutting deep down through me. The nipple grows like a small tower. I'm afraid he'll quit what he's doing. Ramon. I know nothing about female orgasm, but across the park I am moving deep into the ground, vaguely aware of a figure walking down the tree-lined path, praying no one sees us, until the green of the park has become the color of the sun setting, corals and pinks, streaks of violent red and my pounding insisting heart trying to reach through to his fingers, to push the tower the blood the trees myself through to him, Ramon, Ramon, trying to drown with my blood forever the enormous and boring time of childhood.

I don't fall in love with him. I fall into his body, into his copper color and thick Mojave bones, his teeth so shocking white and straight in the dark vortex of his face. I fall into his story, his life, its strange alienation from others. A foster child. He doesn't know his parents. He lives on a small farm with an old couple who get money from the county for him. He works for them. No ones seems to like him, not even our classmates, though he has lived here all his life. I am new to Ramona. In school I am smarter than he. I suspect he can't read but he is more interesting to me than anything in a book.

My father is angry with me. He accuses me of not loving him. He accuses me of not liking Ramona because I don't like him. He accuses me of sitting around thinking up ways to hurt him. He accuses me of avoiding him. On my thirteenth birthday, three weeks after moving to Ramona, he hits me, a blow that throws me across the garden space he is plowing, and something in me closes to him. Now we fight all the time. He hits me and the strength of his body shocks and angers me even more than the injustice I feel, more than the horror of the mistakes he is making with me. I swear I'll always tell him what I think. I swear I'll never hesitate before his stupid brute strength even if it kills me. I can understand his screwed-up heart. I can't understand that might makes right, the murderous venom in his arms.

But it's true. I hate Ramona. It is slow, hot, old, dead, the people ignorant and small. We left LA because they were afraid of my growing up there. They made me leave my best friend, Sarah, and my heart is broken for her. My old junior high was fifty percent Mexican with a high delinquency rate. There were weekly marijuana raids on our lockers. They were afraid I'd fall in love with a Mexican. Watch out, my father warned me in the sixth grade. Mexicans love blondes.

On my first day of school in Ramona a slimy condom is thrown at me, hitting me in the face. The delinquency here is worse than in the city, I cry. It's crazier. There's nothing to do here. The kids come to school drunk. In the city you never see the kids after school, or the houses they live in, or their parents, what they're like. Here there's no place to hide. Everyone knows everyone else and everyone is afraid. Everyone is bored. There's nothing to do but gossip. Everyone is watching, gossiping about you. Everyone is afraid of the gossip about themselves. The hills are barren, dry. There's no place to hide. Except in the boulders where they go to drink. And fight. And drag their cars looking for something. Freedom, Ramon says.

Daddy builds a drive-in restaurant: *El Angel's Heavenly Hamburgers*. My mother, my sister and I work as the waitresses. My father is the

cook, my brother the janitor. Sometimes on weekends when I'm working Ramon gets drunk. He drinks with the older Indians, with the
sailors who come up the mountains from San Diego. From inside the
drive-in I can see him weaving down Main Street through the twilight
eucalyptus. I beg him not to drink. My feelings are confusing. I know
my plea is not just for his welfare. I'm jealous of the experience, of what
goes on between him and the others, of what he knows and where he
goes inside when he is drunk.

In the eighth grade the girls go swimming in Nadine's reservoir. They
take off their clothes but my breasts are so much larger than theirs. The
way the nipple shrivels in the cold air is embarrassing. I don't know if
this is natural. I wear my bathing suit. Disgusted, they make fun of me.
Still, there is the first time I find myself wanting to undress in front of
Ramon. For no reason but to show him my body.

On Saturdays when everyone is gone Ramon comes to the house. I
stay home on the pretense of cleaning it. Before he arrives I vacuum.
The radio plays the thrilling songs of a man named Elvis Presley. With
such an ugly name I think the singer is forty-eight years old, fat and
balding. It doesn't matter. He's my favorite singer, his voice breaking
through the artificial boundaries, the enforced boredom of the world.
Ramon comes and we lie on my bed for hours kissing and caressing
each other. The heat is intense but our bodies get beyond that, desire
moving us through hours, explosions like strings of firecrackers rip-
ping through me. I see my reflection in the mirror and understand why
he loves me without clothes. I love him without clothes, his penis a
deeper copper than the rest of him. But though we are naked together
we never have intercourse. My will is impenetrable. No amount of passion is greater than my determination not to get pregnant, not to be
one of the girls in Ramona publicly humiliated, forced to get married. I
don't want to ever be forced to do anything. Freedom is my most important word. He seems to understand and accept. Sometimes he
leaves me and goes into the bathroom. I sense that he's ejaculating
though I hardly know what that is. Loneliness like none I've known.
Sometimes Daddy is suddenly in the house and there's no time for

Ramon to get away. I hide him in my closet, the temperature there another ten degrees higher than the already one hundred. Talking to Daddy. Cleaning the house, my body sweaty and shaky from Ramon. My hair oily and dark. Sneaking glasses of water to Ramon in the closet.

The great citizens come to the drive-in late at night to talk to my father. You should keep your daughter away from that Ramon. He's no good. Can't you see, man? Your daughter is beautiful. He's an Indian. An orphan. A drunk. A thief.

Sometimes I wonder if they know things about him that I don't. But it doesn't matter. I know him as no one else does. I keep silent when I hear what they say, riding great waves of scorn. *Indian. What difference does that make?* I keep silent because to utter the words is to give credence to the whole stupid town. *What about Ramona?* I want to run down Main Street screaming, the white girl who eloped with a Temecula Indian? *What about Ramona?* the girl this town is named for.

My father makes me date other guys in order to date Ramon. At least he knows better than to cut me off from him altogether. Probably he thinks Ramon such a loser that the encounters with others will draw me from him. The phone rings all the time. Sailors, marines, college and high school boys from San Diego, Ramona high school boys, men twenty years older than me. They drive up the hill on motorcycles, horses, in sports cars, pickup trucks. But like Jesse, most of them seem transparent, their motives obvious, their self-interests, while feigning interest in me, great and boring. I like Ramona high school boys the least because they all seem alike and they gossip. Dating one is like dating the whole school. I like the sailors best because they come from faraway places and tell me about them. They bring me presents from those places. Always they tell me I'm beautiful. But then very quickly they tell me I'm not. They seem offended. You're not so beautiful, they sneer at the oddest times. I think they want to beat me down.

I'm in the sports car of a twenty-year-old boy from La Jolla so that I can go to the dance with Ramon on Saturday. He has been telling me how rich he is. He has a scrapbook with newspaper clippings and photos proving that he is an international tennis star. As he is pointing out how great he looks in one of the pictures he swerves too sharply and we land nose-down in a ditch. When he takes me home we are still shaking. He sneers at the shabbiness of our house. Is this the way most men are? Oh, Ramon, where are you? I love you.

Daddy raises rabbits. He takes Jason, my nine-year-old brother, out to watch them mate, to teach him the facts, he says, of life. I dare not ask to go with them but I want to.

The night in Ramona is so silent Daddy says he has trouble sleeping. I lie in my bed unable to sleep, unable to get used to this strange place, to the strange things happening with my body and with Ramon. My anger at Daddy. Tonight there are the strange noises of the Santana Wind. The night is vast and deep with stars I've never seen before. The silver-granite hills swim in the clear deeps of their light like dangerous animals. The pepper tree sways, then scrapes violently against the window. In a quiet between gusts comes the eerie yelping of coyotes as they run in packs over the hills. Today I saw Lobo. He lives right behind our hill. A man with dark hair and a beard to his waist. They say he roams the hills at night pretending he's a wolf. I think he's in the pepper tree looking at me and my sister, Bridgit, sleeping. Like the Peeping Toms used to in our backyard in LA. I worry about Ramon respecting me. Mama has been telling me for so long that men don't respect women who have sex with them. Men love virgins. Well, at least I'm still that. I read everything I can find about sex, but nothing explains the explosions. Like that rifle hammering away across the valley. First you know something way off, calling you. You only begin to pay attention. But then it comes closer and closer, until soon your whole body begins to fill with it. It floods you until it is a roar and then an explosion of many smaller explosions, exploding, exploding, exploding. It will be three years before I read about female orgasms.

Mama talks about the beauty of Ramona. She says it is the reason we moved here. That and what happened to Daddy last fall. It was right after Grandma, his mother, died, and he was on a fishing trip in the Sierras. After hours of walking up hill, as he rose up over another one, he had a religious experience. Suddenly, he saw the land. Suddenly, it came into his body. He was thirty-seven years old, had been born and raised in the mountains of Tennessee, but he had never seen the earth before. His body had been closed. All his life he had been unhappy. Now he understands something. It changed him. Mama looks at me and my new anger and seems to ask me to understand the land, to love Ramona. I don't. I feel new things in my body but they are not the land. If the land is so great, I want to say to her, why then are the people here so narrow-minded? Even as a small child when we went for our Sunday rides I always wanted to go to the ocean. They always wanted to go to the mountains.

North, in the mountains, where most of the Indians live, are the reservations. There are more reservations in San Diego County than in any other county in the country. Barona, Santa Ysabel, Mesa Grande, Los Coyotes, Inaja Cosmit, Capitan Grande, La Jolla, San Pasqual, Rincon, Pala, Mission, Campo, Manzanita, La Posta, Cuyapaipe, Sequan. Giant boulders, arroyos, barrancas, and snowy mountain tops: the southwest corner of the United States, the last place the Indians could be pushed. Penelope, the most popular girl in high school, the head cheerleader, has married Ramon's cousin, the only relative he knows, and has gone to Mesa Grande to live. One night in a bar in Los Tules he is castrated by six other Indians because he made love with one of their women. I don't believe the story until Ramon visits him at County Hospital. I can't believe something so horrible could happen to a person. I wonder about the rest of his life. I wonder that he was unfaithful to the most beautiful girl in high school. I wonder what she will do.

On Saturdays when Ramon comes and we are on my bed he tells me of an underground river which flows beneath our house and comes all the way from Canada. I try to imagine it, longing as I do for water, *cool clear water,* for pines, for ferns, for the cool rushing sound of water. Sometimes I'm determined not to make out with him anymore. Sometimes I'm bored and want to do something else. In the window the pepper tree is unmoving in the summer heat. But then his hands and tongue are on my nipples.

At night he calls me. He confesses that he does it to his cow. He can't help it. He hates himself for it, has to get drunk afterwards, talks of killing himself. He says if I will do it with him maybe he can break the habit. I try to explain to him that it doesn't seem horrible to me. I can think of a lot worse things. It leaves me breathless to think of it, and even jealous, but I think the cow must love him too.

Sundays. Mornings, evenings, I attend church. I do this in order to see Ramon. There was a long time, before Ramona, when I was very religious. Then Jesus came nightly to my bedside when I prayed. He hovered over my bed, listening to me, sharing with me His Love and Knowledge. I prayed to Him about everyone I knew. The nights were transparent, matter and time, His vivid face, the glow around His body, the unmistakable goodness of it. Hours in the dark with Him, wandering over the earth with Him, sharing the people's suffering, seeing the real intent in people's motives. Always, He pointed out to me, the intent is love. Even with the worse deeds, the initial longing is for love. I wonder now that the intensity of Him is gone, yet I know He lives within me and I understand instinctively the truth of cycles. Now is simply not the time of His outer manifestation; He is within me. I am He. He is me.

We make our love across from the church, in the deserted halls of the grammar school. A stucco atrium to the main office becomes our place, the one we can always go to, our bodies swimming like fish toward the mysterious mouth of the river home, until I'm exploding three, four, five times, hours, with the want to mesh forever with him, to find myself in his skin, my bones growing in his body. I'm aware of not only Jesus being here, knowing this of me, but my grandmother also. In death I know there are no space or time barriers and sex is good.

Beyond our sounds I hear the cars of the high school kids dragging Main Street, the sad clanging of the band in the high school gym playing the dance we have left to come down here to make out. A part of me regrets our having left, like I'm missing something. I never lose sense of where I am, not even when the explosions come. Sometimes it's like I'm watching myself, like I'm Jesus and Grandma watching, like I'm marking time, waiting. I don't know what I'm waiting for. I walk through Ramona wanting to break out of something. Everyone around me, everything—my parents, the people, the land—tells me to calm down.

During school when I walk by this place I see the small children and stuffy teachers swarming. They have no idea of what we do here. How strange life is. I look closer to the stucco walls of our corner where his body finally pushes mine into this world, trying to penetrate the mystery. There's no trace of us. I look in the same way at the bodies of my girlfriends. Are the explosions happening to them too? How strange, I think, the body in space and time. How strange, I think, history is, that places bear so few marks of what went on in them. Where is the evidence of the people here for thousands and thousands of years? How strange the land—silent, unmarked, ungiving witness to so much.

I walk along the road thinking of our dark Indian children. I think in four years we can marry. On the one hand I don't want to marry Ramon; I feel trapped. On the other I am too deeply committed to see any way out. Sometimes there's a smallness about him that surprises me. A smallness in regards to me.

I like to read but it's hard to find anything interesting. The librarian seems unhappy when I walk in. She sneers like I'm a whore or something. Everyone whispers that I'm pregnant. It hurts but I'm beginning to care less about what they think. My so-called reputation. I read *Ramona* by Helen Hunt Jackson. I follow Ramona and Alejandro everywhere on the map—Temecula, Pala, San Diego, San Pasqual—in their flight from the bloodthirsty whites. She has a baby. The baby starves. Alejandro loses his mind. They end up on top of Mt. San Jacinto, the highest point in Southern California, 11,000 feet. There the whites gun him down. After he's already dead, in Ramona's presence, they blow his face off.

I read *The Diary of Anne Frank*. I read a book about Jedidiah Smith, the man who made the first recorded journey from the Missouri River to California in 1826. He camped a week with the Mojave tribes on the

Colorado River, who then guided him across the desert to San Diego. From there he went north to the Stanislaus River, across the Sierras and the Great Desert back to Utah. He then led eighteen men down the route of the previous year. They camped another week with the Mojaves who by now were Smith's favorite Indians. The book talked of the good-humored bare-breasted Mojave women who felt it an honor to ask white men to sleep with them. In Mojave society the women were free and equal to the men. So they slept together, made love, feasted, built rafts to cross the river. But midstream, without warning, the Mojaves ambushed the whites. Ten men died while Smith and the others escaped into the desert to the west.

We are walking the highway to his house from church. I'm wearing high heels, nylons, a pink sheath dress. He takes me out to the shed, built down and into the side of a hill, and his cow he milks and screws. The afternoon is hot but it is cool in here. We lie in the scratchy hay. Through the rise of our rhythm I watch the mysterious cow standing heavy and large above us, her belly rising as we rise, great flops of shit coming out of where I think he must put it in. I wonder about semen in a cow. Then it is the first time I see semen. The spill of it all over my bare belly. Suddenly I'm afraid. I have to keep myself from crying because he is crying. It's okay, Ramon. The smell of hay and shit. The smell of his whole race on my belly. I wonder who is in it. What they know. Oh, Jesus, I pray, *please* don't let me get pregnant.

He walks me home. Though I have walked the road now every day this summer he knows Ramona in a way I find incomprehensible. He has always lived here, roaming and playing in her granite and sage. He talks about the hills with a seriousness that awes me, I who move through them to get beyond them, the hot thorny arroyos with their rattlesnakes, tarantulas, black widows, scorpions, lizards. The whining coyotes, the old men who live in crumbling hot trailers propped against the boulders who buy him liquor, the other Indians, the strange laws of the reservations in the mountains where he goes. Lobo with his long hair and wild eyes. I think of the weird woman who comes to the drive-in sometimes, a tall thin white woman with a limp who is married to one of the chiefs. He is fat and always drunk, Jesus' cross tattooed on his cheek. She is the dirtiest person I've ever seen, her hair matted, her face bearded, her hands tattooed. Ramon says she's on dope, many Indians are, but they think of it differently than we do. She has many children, lives in a teepee in the winter, outdoors in the summer, does all her cooking over an open fire, that's why she's so dirty. I stare at her, trying to comprehend why she stays with such a man and lives in such a way. Why do women submit to so much for a man? I think she's found the land alright, like Mama says, and look what it's done to her. Yet something in the woman draws me to her.

As we walk along he points out Ramona to me. You can see her, he says, over the whole Valle del Ángel. I have never been able to see her before, but now, suddenly, I do. She lies on her back, perfectly formed by the southern granite mountains, her gravelly hair spraying out behind her head, her arms and shoulders, her breasts, belly, and legs against the blue sky. The mountains behind her hair are in Mexico, Ramon says, and Ramona is her white man's name. We can't tell what it really is but someday she'll get up and when that happens the land will be ours again.

He traces for me the course of the underground river. It flows directly under your house, he says. How can you tell? He becomes fierce like I've insulted him. *I know!* I know this land. I've slept over it. The river is enormous. I can hear water falling through granite hundreds of feet below. They shouldn't bring water from the Colorado. It's wrong. There's water right here, right under our feet. Plenty of it. But no one will believe me. I'm just an Indian. He pulls me down in the eucalyptus grove and beyond his face I see Ramona in the skyline of the mountains, an angel caught in earth, and think the world is an underground river of semen and vaginal fluids. I think I want to live in Northern California where I've never been, but where I've read it's cool and foggy, with plenty of water on top of the land, making everything lush and green.

The well is dry. We spend most of the summer without water. Daddy's tomatoes, corn and squash wither in the garden. The only hope is to deepen the well, which is expensive. But we have to do it. The thirty-foot well is drilled thirty more feet through granite. No water. Then thirty more feet, sheer granite. No water. Down a hundred feet. There's talk of giving up. All of Ramona is watching, waiting. *Whatcha gonna do when the well runs dry?* Fats Domino wailing down Main Street from our juke box. Ramon says tell them to keep going. There's a huge river under there. He stops by the drive-in to tell my father to keep drilling. My father won't talk to him. The well is drilled deeper. One hundred and fifty feet. Two hundred feet. Sheer granite, no water: these words on everyone's lips. At two hundred and fifty feet the drilling is stopped. The expense is too great, the prospects too hopeless. Ramon spends the afternoon walking the underground river with the welldigger, Jesse's father. *Oh, Dan, can't you see that big green tree where the water's runnin free and it's waitin there for you and me cool clear water.* . . . Jesse's father brings a water witch to the site. The dowsing rod almost jumps out of the man's hands. He offers to drill the rest of the way at his own expense. His livelihood is at stake. At two hundred and sixty feet water is struck, water shooting all the way through granite to the sky. An artesian well. Ramona is saved.

One Saturday morning in my bedroom he is depressed and angry. He says his foster parents are going to get rid of him. Then suddenly my mother is home and he flees through the window and down the pepper tree. My mother and I are in the living room when I look out the window and see Ramon walking down the middle of the driveway in full view. Luckily my mother doesn't look up, but I'm frightened and don't understand. When I ask him about it he says he just doesn't care anymore. I'm shocked. What about me? If my mother had seen. . . . I would never let you down like that. My sense of betrayal is very great. My father would have killed me. Maybe he thought my mother could save him, but *I* knew that she couldn't, even though she was an orphan herself. She has to stick by my father. No matter what.

The sheriff is looking for him. He's been gone for days. The sheriff, his probation officer, my parents threaten me. I don't know where he is. In the hills, in some dry oak canyon. What's wrong with that? He loves the hills. He likes to run them at night beneath the moon. That's crazy, they sneer. He's no good. Something is wrong with him. In the fight

Daddy's blow sends my body thirty feet. I know it's thirty feet because Mama is always talking about the length of the living room, planning when we'll have enough money for carpeting. I hate him. I hate him.

Past midnight there is a tap on my window. Ramon is in the pepper tree crying, the moon full behind him, its light glistening in the water on his face. I open the window to the screaming of coyotes, the smell of pepper tree, the smell of sage and semen on his unwashed body. I muffle him with blankets so my sister sleeping three feet away and my parents behind the thin wall won't hear his sobs. Aren't you afraid out there? I whisper. Nothing separates me more from him than the land, which is inaccessible to me. No! he cries. Yes! I don't know. I *am* afraid. Something's out there. It wants me. I have to go. I belong out there. Not here. Not in the city. When I'm running in the hills I can forget this town. When I sleep out there I remember my dreams. They tell me great things. I don't belong here with these people. Out there I'm like a star shining in the dark. I can follow the voice of my dreams.

I don't question him, not even when he is accused of stealing an old man's car. Everyone questions him and he doesn't have the words, and though there is so much I don't understand I do understand night, and almost, the need to be crazy. Something in Ramona, something in the daylight is missing. Somehow Ramon finds it in the very land I hate. The land I hate, the boulders, the brush, the sun withering my pale skin, the monotonous, hellish limits of the people who live here, their spirits dried up and discarded like the skins of rattlers everywhere. If I had been an Indian in the old days, I think, I would have killed myself. Or been the tribe's whore. Following him always into more dirt and rock, the only relief being the liquid softness of his body, its cool shade, and then it doesn't matter where we lie. Tarantulas, black widows, rattlesnakes aren't frightening. They're alive. It's the dry suffocating stillness of the land that terrifies me. The danger of dying while your body keeps living. The danger of your soul being castrated. Ramon/Ramona. I hate you. I love you. El Ángel.

There is fire in the mountains. Sage flaming from the heat of sun alone. Flames surround Ramona. There's talk of evacuation. His Mojave eyes over me like rain clouds, so dark with storm I can see the flames, the

Santa Ana flames whipping down the canyons, ashes the size of sycamore leaves smothering us, the black hot soot, roasting my white body dark for his, this rock bed we lie on. Air drafts suck in fire, explode where safety has been sought, the firefighters backed into a granite box canyon, *Inaja Cosmit*. Eighteen Indian prisoners burned alive. Marjorie's father dead. Her dark skin turning white with the news. Ramon/Ramona in the skyline, the granite left in ashes. Earth angel, earth angel, I love you. I hate you.

Mojave. It is a word on the birth certificate. It means orphan. A mother who was taken from the reservation and then disappeared in the streets of San Diego during the war. Mojave. It is dark pigment of skin, the black shiny hair, the white teeth, the mystery of alcohol, of the mountains. *Ramona, when day is done I hear you calling.* Running in the dark dreaming hills with the liquor of old white men.

He keeps telling me his foster parents are going to make him leave Ramona. They're going to send me to the city. I don't believe it. I think he's feeling sorry for himself. He drinks. He gets crazier. I tell him they won't do it. How could they? They've had you since you were a little boy. They love you. They must. Some. Besides, they need you for the farm work, the money they get from the county. But one day he is moving. Moving to San Diego. He sobs in my arms. "You are the only good thing that has ever happened to me."

I am sitting at his bedside at County Hospital. My mother in a rare gesture has lied that I am sixteen so that I can visit him. I am fourteen and I am sitting here in an all white room watching Ramon toss and moan dreamless beneath the anesthesia. Under anesthesia, I've read, there are no dreams. The ward is full of other men, ripped apart and broken, sick from car wrecks and knife fights and knife surgeries. They say he is an alcoholic so they took his gall bladder. I am fourteen. I know nothing. I don't understand the hate in the world but I find myself knowing they cut him open because he is a ward of the county and they can get money by taking parts of his body. Someone cut him open for the money and he let them do it because he feels sorry for himself. I sit in the room, waiting for him to wake, reading a pamphlet I've brought him about the Mojave Indians, about a man named Kroeber who studies them, an old man who follows the Colorado River to find their stories and their beliefs. Everything it says sounds like Ramon. The way they look. The way they think. It says they are natural geographers with a deep interest in the landscape. It says that the heart of their society is geography and dream. The source of all their religion, tradition, ritual song and shamanistic power is individual dreaming. In dream the hidden stories and trails of the land are known. Suddenly I see before my eyes Jedidiah Smith and his men being ambushed midstream the Colorado, and I see why, what he could never figure out. The women, when they took the white men to their beds, realized what kind of friends they really were and in the night their dreams told them even more, the future days of white men coming without any honor for them at all. And suddenly I realize something else, that Ramon and I have been intentionally separated. His foster parents got him out of Ramona as a favor to my parents. Like Ramona and Alejandro. Like Romeo and Juliet. Everything falls into place, including my mother's lying about my age. She feels guilty.

I sit here beside my first love as he tosses and moans beneath white man's medicine, beneath his knife, in a room full of wrecked men, and suddenly I am knowing the world. I love you, Ramon, but I'm different than you. No one's going to cut me open, no one's going to destroy me. It says you are a geographer of the far borders of the land, a geographer of the far borders of consciousness. So get up. Don't let them kill your dreams. Let's go down to the Colorado River, Ramon, and make love. I'm here, Ramon, Ramona running with you to the dark dreaming of the Colorado River.

A doctor and a nurse come in. Looking directly at my breasts the doctor orders me to step aside. They pull the curtain around Ramon, but I can see through the crack. When the nurse pulls the sheet down his penis is erect. The nurse sneers in disgust. The doctor slaps it with his hand. They do nothing else. They walk away, laughing.

Later, much later, after the Colorado River has been dammed and drained west into Southern California, Scripts Institute of Oceanography announces the discovery of a large underground river that flows all the way from Canada to the sea at San Diego, its main course through the Valley of the Angel, beneath the town of Ramona.

Raquel

We move to Ramona the first of April, three weeks before my thirteenth birthday. On Friday night I stay with Sarah. Her twelfth birthday. Our last night together. I'm full of anguished love for her. I don't want to move. She is so beautiful. Her long legs, her thick blond hair, the depth of her being I fall into. She has pubic hair, the first person my age I know of, other than myself. In the sixth grade she was the smartest kid in school. I was second smartest. In the seventh we entered enormous Rancho Los Amigos Junior High School and became lost from each other. This night we come back together, renew the bonds of our souls. We vow to always know each other. We still do.

On Monday afternoon my brother, sister and I are enrolled in the fourth, sixth and seventh grade classes of the Ramona schools. Los Amigos Junior High in the Los Angeles School District had three thousand kids, Ramona Junior High has one hundred. Do they wear lipstick here in the seventh grade? Will they get the wrong idea because I do? I don't dare go without it now, I'm so plain. The principal, Mr. Nordahl, looks across his glasses from Bridgit to me and says, "Good!" His eyes fall to my breasts, the same size as my mother's. They've been growing since I was nine. "You, my dear, will be our Miss Angel when you are sixteen.

"And Bridgit, I see that you are the brain of the two." He looks up from her records. She is eleven, two years younger than I, but only a year behind in school because in the second grade her I.Q. registered 182. She doesn't have breasts yet. "We can use you, too."

Then he focuses on my little brother. "I see, Jason, that you have neither brains nor beauty." He makes a funny sound with his tongue. "What's a fellow gonna do with two older sisters like these?"

We leave Jason in the fourth grade, the teacher looking like the witch who ate the little brother. "Can't read? Jason, you could be with me for years."

Then the four of us follow the principal through the dust of the playground over the dry arroyo that separates the elementary school from the row of four classrooms that constitutes Ramona Junior High School. At the end of this day, on the bus ride home to Olive Hill, I will hear how last week a seventh grader raped a first grader in this arroyo. "I hope Jason will be okay," Mama frets. This annoys Daddy and the principal.

I'm afraid, my body too large around us. Mr. Nordahl and our parents disappear into Mr. Silverman's sixth grade glass, leaving me and Bridgit in the open corridor looking out on the desert. We will learn later that Mr. Silverman is the smartest man in Ramona. Also the cruelest and most evil. His greatest disgust is dumb kids. He persecutes them. He's Russian and that's probably why he's hated. Now I see that he may have been Jewish, but that was a concept I didn't encounter until I was an adult so I can't say for sure.

"In this school," Bridgit suddenly announces, her voice echoing down the hall, "I am not going to be smart. I am going to be average. From now on, I will get Cs."

I look at my sister alarmed. I die in humiliation, in the prison of my limitations. My mind seems capable of learning anything, but my ability to move myself into the world is so blocked.

"Why?"

"Because," she says very firmly. "Boys don't like smart girls."

Suddenly, Mr. Silverman appears at the door. The longest eyebrows I've ever seen. At least two inches, shining silver in the sunlight as if coated with Vaseline, like I use to thicken my eyelashes. They stick straight out from his forehead, shading his deep-set, gleaming, silver eyes.

"Welcome, Bridgit." He shakes her hand as if she's a man. "I see here from your records that you are a brilliant student. My class is most fortunate to have such a student come along at this time. Welcome to Ramona Sixth Grade."

And the door slams, taking my little sister, newly embarked on the road to averagedom, enveloped in the brilliant Mr. Silverman's arms, with it.

My sister and I usually have the same perceptions of the world but I don't understand her declaration that boys don't like smart girls. All my life I will think they only like perfect girls. The most beautiful, the smartest, the most graceful, the kindest.

The principal and my parents leave me at the door of the seventh grade. So I walk in. All eyes turn. Three or four whistles crack the air, wolf whistles, cat calls, the boys out of their seats, leaping from their desks. Is *she* stacked! The teacher, Mrs. Williams, is meek, bored, uninterested, ill or something. I keep hearing an obscenity I've only heard hissed from Peeping Toms in LA, or read on the walls at Los Amigos. *Fuck*. One boy, taller than me, is balanced on one hand, swinging around the top of his desk, screeching *whee-whee-whee!* Another is on top of Mrs. Williams's desk chanting *Blondie! Blondie! Blondie!* I stare at the linoleum in front of me while Mrs. Williams announces my name over the din. The white dark-stained thing lying at my feet is a used Kotex. She leads me to the desk next to the monkey boy, who is now moving an unpeeled banana back and forth in his mouth singing my favorite song, *I am the great pretender*. The girls stare at me, still and sullen. One growls as I walk by her. After I sit down a condom blown up like a balloon shoots across the room, hits me in the face, then lands on my desk, deflated, saliva, snot or something spilling out of it. Everyone roars with laughter. "It's a rubber," the fat girl in front of me whispers. There's a motherly tone in her voice. She tells me not to worry. "It's just a joke." When the bell rings for recess she says "Stick with me. I'll protect you." In those last cruelest months of seventh grade, Judy is my only friend.

Everyone in town says I will be Miss Angel when I'm sixteen. "You're the most beautiful girl I've ever seen," the grocer says the first time I shop in his store. Wherever I go someone says this. I want to hide. They want something from me. I would give it if I could, but when they look closely they see the truth. Then I'm just a big disappointment. Worse than that because I've aroused their hopes. *"Smile!"* they beg. "You're too serious," they complain. It's hard. Nobody can see their own face. You can't see yourself walking down the street.

Bridgit and I attend the Miss Angel Beauty Pageant held in the Ramona Theatre, which is owned by a man named Hugh Hefner. Everyone knows his name because from Ramona's sister theatre in Escondido, eighteen miles down the mountain, he has just launched a new girly magazine, *Playboy*. Now he's moved back to Chicago and the Ramona Theatre is in disrepair. The glamorous high school girls parade in bathing suits across the stage beneath the screen, which in the glaring spotlight, is torn, has coke and beer stains. We eat popcorn and agree on the girl we think the most beautiful. But she doesn't even place. The winner is Pat Dawson. In our few weeks in Ramona we already know about her. She's the school whore. Judy explains, "Out-of-town judges don't know reputations or real personalities."

It's our first experience with a small-town scandal. All Pat's term the whole town chokes and gags about the whore Miss Angel. My mother, however, uses Pat as one of her examples in her on-going lectures about the great and secret power, the power of positive thinking. We are all in the car, Jason who has just failed fourth grade sitting between me and Bridgit, driving around the hills, exploring, as we always do on Sundays. Mama and Daddy are telling us again. "Jason could learn to read if he put his mind to it." "Of course Pat's not beautiful. Anyone can see that." We all laugh with Daddy. "But for that night, for the purpose of winning the Miss Angel contest, she thought herself beautiful. And so she won."

The winners of all the small-town contests in San Diego County proceed to the big contest, the Miss Fairest of the Fair Contest at the Del Mar Fair. The winner of this contest then enters the Miss California Contest. Because I'm told that this contest is my destiny and that if I think myself beautiful enough, if I work hard enough for the next three years I will be Miss California and then Miss America and then Miss Universe, I follow the contests in the paper. I know it is true, as my mother says, all I need is to want it badly enough. It doesn't matter that I'm really ugly.

It is June, my first in Ramona, in the country. The temperature hovers in the mid-eighties. Most days are overcast, breaths of steam rising off the giant boulders. I descend the path through the sagebrush, down over the granite slabs that cover half the hill, down to Olive Road, the one olive tree shaking insecurely like a grey old man on a cane in the sunset. The smell of the sage and the granite is pungent, wild. As the sun goes down, the full moon rises. *I hate Ramona.* I long for asphalt, traffic lights, city kids. My parents took me from my birthplace; they took me from Sarah. They say over and over it was too dangerous. They were afraid of the Friday marijuana raids on the lockers at Los Amigos. They were afraid when Linda Allen had a baby at twelve. I keep trying to tell them it's wilder in Ramona, the boys in my class are already alcoholics, they think only of sex. I can't convince them. My parents think people in the country are innocent.

The rocks, as I walk down in the twilight to get the evening paper, breathe and twist and discover me. When they do this I lose who I am, I lose my hatred to a beauty that's turned around from all I'm being told is beautiful. The smell of the land is stark like courage. I don't want to be Miss Angel. I want to be this road I'm walking now, this sudden drop from Olive, down past Giant's Grave, the mound-shaped hill Mama always says she could make disappear if she had faith as a grain of mustard seed, if you have faith the mountain shall be removed, nothing shall be impossible, and then she'd have a view of town. Down around the tight snake-loops curling the spilled granite, past Mrs. Henderson's, a woman who lives alone in the grove of pepper trees. Why are old women who live alone frightening? I'm bored, I know so much more than anyone wants me to know but there's nothing to do with my knowledge. The sage, not so thick as on the hill, but more fierce, seems in need of me, a need which as I pass is less and less. At the paved crossroads, a mile from the house, I get the newspaper from the mailbox.

MISS LA JOLLA WINS MISS FAIREST OF THE FAIR! Her photograph is in the left-hand corner of the front page of the *San Diego Tribune.* She is at the center of her royal court, a dark girl in a white ruffle gown. Her princesses surround her. Pat is not one of them. Her name is Raquel Tejada. She is seventeen and a senior at La Jolla High School.

I start the climb back in the hot twilight. Venus, the one star I know, is setting; the full moon, though it is still not dark, is rising behind my shoulder, behind Ramona, the granite woman lying as the mountain horizon who will rise again they say, and with her, the Indians, whose land this is. Behind her, Mexico, always purple, when visible. And Raquel. Raquel Tejada. The Queen.

I've been studying the photographs of beauty queens but they keep meshing into the same woman. This photograph is different. A white rose behind her ear, her long, dark curly hair. I wonder who she really is. Is she like Pat? Is she a real queen? The photograph pulls me like the sage pulls me. I'm thirteen, I'm awakening in the deepest part of myself to the world, what it wants, what it thinks, sage, soil, rocks, sky, people, society, stars. I'm trying to understand the politics of beauty, how it works, the steps: from *here* you must go *there* to be acclaimed the Fairest. The path is open to me if I want to take it, my mother's instructions in the power of positive thinking is a great advantage, but I'm in excruciating pain for my ugliness, my ugliness greater than my faith, *ugly, ugly* as an old witch. Sometimes I catch myself in the bathroom mirror and I *am* beautiful, like the body of Marilyn Monroe on the calendar that hung over Daddy's workbench in the garage in Los Angeles. Sometimes I catch myself in the bathroom mirror, climbing out of the tub, and I am an ugly old woman, uglier than Snow White's cruel stepmother. At school I read *The National Geographic*. The Chinese bind women's feet, the Ubangi's stretch their lips, the West Africans stretch their necks, the Incas their earlobes. Some people make scars on their bodies to be beautiful, and tattoos, and some people think fat is beautiful. One day you wear a flannel shirt and they don't see you. You can stand a long time in the grocery line before he waits on you. The next day you walk in wearing the clothes you've bought from your first job, your new lipstick, or you can just laugh in your old flannel in such a way that the grocer will be rude to the middle-aged man in front of you, or anyone, your mother, the school principal. It is so clearly a game, one all people in their choice of being ugly, beautiful or in between, must know. But then there's my mother, so beautiful, but so apart from this game. She does nothing to be beautiful. She just is, herself, what she is, no exaggeration, no effort to exist outside herself. Is there real beauty, I keep wondering, apart from what we learn? Is there real ugliness?

In the moonlight Raquel Tejada's features are hardly visible. It's not her beauty I'm fascinated by. There's something in the photograph itself. When I get back to the house I study the picture in the dining room light.

Daddy builds a redwood drive-in stand. He designs and constructs it himself. Everyone in Ramona says we're fools, we'll never succeed. But we have positive thinking, we open on a day in August, *El Angel's Heavenly Hamburgers.* Nineteen cents. We're a success! The drive-in is on the south end of town within a grove of old eucalyptus trees, instantly, the teenage hangout, the tourist stop. The tourists driving up from San Diego on a Sunday to see the mountains, in fall the colors, in winter the snow, in spring the wild flowers. I don't know why they come in summer, in the unbearable heat. But they do.

The first day. I'm nervous, self-conscious. What if we *are* fools, no one comes by? The Pepsi man is installing the tanks. He keeps staring up from the floor at me. My father is sulking behind him, scraping down the new grill. I'm wearing my new white waitress uniform, my red-checkered apron. The Pepsi man tells me of his son. He's 26, he's already a regional manager for Pepsi in San Diego. "I think you'd be perfect for him. Would it be alright if I give him your phone number?"

Daddy explodes. "She's only thirteen years old, man!"

It's always like this. Working at the drive-in, I come in contact with all sorts of men, not just the junior high boys who make me so uncomfortable. Even when we are much older these particular boys make me nervous. They come to the window and sneer, "What's so hot about *her?*"

I swim every day between seventh and eighth grades in the small public plunge in Angel Park. When I climb out of the water to dive there is always a great uproar from the boys so I learn to stay in the water. Just as I did when I was five I pee right in it.

Sometimes older guys building the houses across the street, stand outside the chain-link fence staring that strange way at me, calling for me to get out of the water. Walking down the hill after swimming all day, through the oleanders and eucalyptus they are hiding in the bushes with their pants down. Playing with their stiff penises which fascinate them. "Hey, Blondie, look at this!" Once, inside the dark, damp Ladies bathroom in the center of the park a sweaty man without a shirt grabs me. I get away and never go in that place again, no matter how badly I have to pee, but I will feel his wet shoulders in my nightmares forever.

But sometimes I enjoy the attention. I study myself in the mirror of the dressing room. I can see it is true, I have a beautiful body. Sometimes I want men to see it. It seems to make them happy. And sometimes, deep inside, my body is thrilled to be walking by them. My body makes *me* happy.

Toward the end of summer Ramon is often in the pool. Our legs touch, then wrap around each other's. We slip below the surface. We sink beneath their jeers, *are you blind, Blondie, can't you see he's an Indian?* He kisses me with his warm, wet tongue. There is nothing like the compulsion I feel toward him beneath the water. Only if I look at him in a certain way do I see he's an Indian and then I love him even more. In him I know beauty no one has told me of.

When you are told you are beautiful, you know that you are ugly. Women considered beautiful are always the most insecure. You are valued as an object but you know only too well the ways you are flesh and blood and mind and spirit, the ways you cannot satiate a lonely, materialistic world.

My shoulders slump. Everyday Mama says, "Hold your shoulders up, honey. What are you ashamed of? You have beautiful breasts."

Orlon sweaters and straight skirts are the fashionable clothes. To compensate for my bad posture, which I can't seem to help, and to not disappoint those who seem to gain so much pleasure from my tits, I stick them out when I wear one, when they yell *"sweater girl."* By the end of the day I'm exhausted, the strain on my diaphragm. I can't breathe. So I wear something unrevealing for a week. "Hold your shoulders up!'' everyone yells. ''You are beautiful, can't you see that?'' But the opposite is always the truth.

Ramon has to talk to me. ''It's important.'' We hide in the dusty arroyo where the seventh grader raped the first grader. I'm wearing my baby blue sweater I worked weeks at the drive-in for. ''It's hard to tell you this,'' he says, looking down the rocky cut where it goes under the road. ''Let's go down there.''

We can hear the cars rumble over us. I'm afraid of the rattlesnakes. But his hands are on my breasts, his penis against me. At first I resist. At night I pray to resist. I know this is wrong. But then the tide starts deep and back inside, wildly building waves that make life worth all the pain, that have to crash on the shore. Even so I don't let Ramon enter me.

He's helping me to hook my bra when he says, ''It's Chuck who says I have to tell you this. For your own good.'' He sighs, then angrily grabs me by the shoulders. ''*Why,* when you wear sweaters, do you stick your tits out so far? Don't you know everyone laughs at you? The guys can't stand you for it. They say you're cheap, you're teasing them.''

I want to die, lie down in the gutter, let the rattlesnakes have me. I can't even let Ramon know, my pride is so devastated, I have to hang onto something. The waves of shame, of public humiliation wash through me for months. I will never wear a sweater again. Though they are my best clothes, though they are the wonderful fashion.

Daddy teaches me to drive. Swimming, learning to drive. I can't get a license until I'm sixteen, but because they're always working at the drive-in they let me take the car home and back for errands. As long as I take the back roads. I love being in the car alone. Now the waves are of freedom, of exploration. I take two-wheel-rutted dirt paths off the back roads, back into the hills among the giant boulders, onto the reservations, into places of Ramona I never knew before, rock n roll blaring from San Diego. I come to flash streams running across the road. I plunge right in and pull out the other side. When the water stops me, my parents' Ford stuck midstream, I wade out, walk home all night in the dark. I'm afraid but curious too about the land, the can-

yons and valleys, the mountains and rocks and dams. The night. I feel
the coyotes, the mountain lions, the jackrabbits watching me. I'm
afraid of the oak trees because tarantulas nest under them. But then
when I touch the gnarly trunk I know every person who has passed
here through all time. Sometimes I know I am the first to place her foot
on this rock. When I finally get home Daddy screams and screams. I'm
grounded for weeks.

To graduate from eighth grade in California, to get into high school,
every student must pass a history test with emphasis on the Constitution of the United States. I'm terrified of another public humiliation.
For the whole year I study. I buy No-Doz pills and stay up nights
studying under the blanket so my parents won't see the light. My class
is noted for its high number of intelligent students. At the end of the
year, when the scores come back from the state, I'm told I passed.
Everyone is raving about Neal Hopkins, one of the three boys in my
class with genius I.Q.s, how high his score is, one of the highest in the
state. His picture is in the *El Sol*. On the day of graduation, I see the
scores. Mine is a half point beneath his. I was a close second. I don't understand why no one said anything about it. My speech for graduation
is entitled "Freedom."

I write my first stories in the eighth grade. I write science fiction. I
write a story about a beauty contest called "Universe," an outer-space
competition of creatures from all the galaxies, creatures of bizarre and
spectacular shapes and sizes. I don't call it *Miss* Universe because in the
universe such a competition would not be limited to one or even several genders and of course it wouldn't be limited to the unmarried. It's
clear to me that these are provincial ideas of the little part of Earth I live
on. Miss Earth this year is a deer. She competes with enormous star-
shaped flower creatures, flaring mole shapes, a beast from Revelation,
kings like strange fungi I've seen in the oak groves, glowing white. The
winner is from Venus, a being shaped a little like an earthling, except
for the green iridescent husk that robes its body and its noseless face.
Everyone has an ugly nose. If you came from a world without noses
you'd think we were deformed with our knotty protrusions.

I write another story about the last couple on earth after the Bomb. They drive from town to town across the United States in the cars they find strewn everywhere. In their lifetime they will never run out of gas, which seems like heaven. But they worry about the future. Who will know how to make gasoline? Though there is no one to marry them, their obligation to have sexual intercourse is very clear.

Mama reads about an art class offered Saturday mornings in Angel Park by a world-famous painter. Mr. Gavinsky, eighty-three, showed at the World's Fair in Chicago in 1933. She encourages me to take the class because I keep a sketchbook and draw all the time. Drawing, I've discovered that all objects are animate. But it's the pleasures of following the lines of the human body that I especially love. Mr. Gavinsky is crabby and his paintings are not interesting to me, muted landscapes of oranges and browns. To me the land is electric, *fuchsia, indigo, silver.* Still, I'm excited about learning something. But he ignores me, talks only to the middle-aged women who comprise the rest of the class. On the third Saturday he asks me if I don't think I should drop the class. "A girl like you couldn't possibly be interested in what I have to offer. Besides, you are distracting."

I leave quickly, walking towards town. Fighting the tears. Inside I'm screaming. *How dare you think you know who I am!* But anger is something a girl like me cannot show. As with so many feelings that give away the heart. The privacy. It's all you have.

"You are too beautiful for your age," the president of the Board of Education says when I enter the essay-speech contest on democracy to win a trip to the United Nations in New York City. My grade on the essay on which our names are not printed is fifteen points higher than the grade of the skinny undeveloped boy who wins.

When Bridgit enters high school she tries out for cheerleader. Just as Mama has fretted, there's no trace now of her former brilliance. "Bridgit thought herself average and so now she really is average." Our mother bemoans the power of thought. But Bridgit is very popular. She used her magnificent brain to achieve that, I figure. And her breasts are far from average. Suddenly they are much larger than mine, *much much* larger. They call her Jayne Mansfield, Anita Ekberg. I'm sure they're the results too of the power of her thought. As a little girl, big boobs, as she called them, were her greatest dream. She'd sneak Mama's brassieres from the dresser drawer, fill the D cups with water-filled balloons, put on Daddy's white T-shirts and for whole days parade around the blocks, jugging, it seems now, into her future body. It's a surprise when she isn't voted cheerleader.

Late that summer we are secretly informed by the student-body president, a good friend of Bridgit's, that in fact she was voted head cheerleader; she received more votes than any other girl. But Mrs. Deal, head of the English Department and the committee that counted the votes, put her foot down. "I will not stand for that girl to be out there bouncing up and down before all of Ramona, no *sireee!*"

I'm fifteen. A glamorous couple has moved to town. They are unlike other adults, they don't have children, she's on TV a lot, commercials for Johnson's floor wax, Kellogg breakfast cereals, chocolates for losing weight. Liz Carter. She was Miss Chicago. She was fourth runner-up in the Miss America contest. She opens a charm school, Liz's Charm School. I take my paycheck from the drive-in, sign up. I know only too well how uncharming I am. She instructs, "You must learn to walk with your knees bent so that you glide, as if on roller skates. When I won the Miss Chicago crown the judges debated whether I had roller skates on beneath my gown. Before they crowned me they sent someone backstage to check me out."

She takes us to see the movies *Picnic* and *The Man with a Golden Arm.* Liz was best friends with Kim Novak before Hollywood discovered her. Liz says Kim is really a fat slob with black hair and pimples. Just look what she has managed to do for herself. The beauty business will be your best investment.

Liz isn't beautiful to me. She's too old, as she herself always says. She's twenty-six, a fading beauty, her life of glory gone. She talks incessantly of the war to stay beautiful and "alive" for her husband, to keep him happy. All she can really do is to try and help us, to share what she learned when she too was young. Thirteen lessons, thirteen weeks.

She teaches us how to sit, how to walk, how to wear clothes, how to put on make-up. Every week she urges me to cut my hair. "I had hair as beautiful as yours, as thick. Only . . ." a tone now suggesting hers was superior because "it was black." "But long hair causes you to slump your shoulders, it makes you stick your head out in front of your body, to lead the way. It looks like your brain weighs too much."

She takes us to the Miss North Island Beauty Pageant sponsored by the U.S. Naval Station in San Diego. Terry, the first girl, leaps from the side curtains, struts out before the audience of hundreds, sailors and San Diego dignitaries, her chest and her smile expanded. She teases and flirts and winks at the judges, sashaying her high little ass beneath its ruffly skirt at them, juts her bottom lip, drops her eyelids, hands on her hips, for the boys in the front rows. She throws us all big tongued kisses. The place comes down in a roar, the pandemonium of the seventh grade. None of the twenty other girls is able to match her exuberance, her strut, her blatant sexual-fun strut-tease.

But now the bathing-suit competition. Terry is called out again, the obvious winner. There's the roar again, these guys love her. Again the seventh grade: they're panting at the mouth, they're close to jacking off collectively. But in her metallic-green one-piece, Terry is timid. Now she doesn't strut or prance, she hesitates, head bowed, the triumphant smile gone. She takes the obligatory turn-arounds, then walks out the ramp, tripping slightly in her high heels. The roar of the boys, deafening when her name was called, is diminishing with each stringy step until there is only embarrassment in the hall. She is *skinny,* everything, legs, bottom, chest, arms, the bones protruding from the base of her chicken neck. "If only she had strutted in her bathing suit," Liz instructs, "she would have won. We would have seen her triumphantly thin, a model with a boy's body. But she *thought* herself skin and bones. Beauty is an illusion. If you want to be beautiful, you must become a great actress."

The next year Liz's husband, Eddie, coming up the canyon from the beach at Del Mar, drives his convertible right off the five-hundred-foot drop into dry, boulder-filled Lake Hanson. Liz, in her grief, prepares to receive the insurance settlement. But then the insurance company declares his death a suicide. There weren't any skid marks. Liz's Charm School closes. She loses the war to be beautiful, to keep her husband happy.

One day in my sophomore year Cal Johnson from the Ramona Chamber of Commerce and Pilgrim Fellowship, the Christian teenage organization I used to belong to in order to get out of the house on Sunday nights to be with Ramon, drives up the hill to our house with the Miss Angel application. He asks me about Ramon who's been sent to the San Diego County reform school. "I don't know how he is. We broke up." Mr. Johnson is delighted with this news. "He was never good enough for you."

He helps me fill out the form. Weight: I lie; ten pounds less. Hobbies: I've quit drawing so I can't say that. Talent: "I always wanted to play the piano but we could never afford one." Career plans: marriage. "You can't say that. They want you to be domestic, but not that domestic." *Yeah, they want you to be a virgin forever.* Maybe I'll write *sex* under hobbies. Color of eyes: Mama says they change to whatever I'm near. Measurements: 38-23-35. Measurements is easy because I know my answer will make the judges excited and it's not a lie. "Talent," Cal says, "is the most important thing next to looks. You have to have a lot of that. And personality."

I have neither of these. Everyone says "you're beautiful but you don't have any personality." Bridgit has the personality, the brains.

"But you're head majorette. You can twirl the baton."

That's true. I'm head majorette for the Ramona High School Band. But I've never had any lessons or teachers or even examples of what a majorette is, except for the Rose Bowl Parade every New Year's Day on TV. This isn't talent, just hard work. I figured the baton out, twirling the silver bar for hours all the summer before the tenth grade. I found twelve girls, taught them what I'd taught myself. I designed our uniforms, drove the forty miles to San Diego to buy the material, sewed every blue sequin on the thirteen white corduroy bodysuits. Now I haul the girls off almost every weekend to march in five-mile parades behind palominos whose shit we strut in, choreograph (a word I don't know) every football and basketball half time. My favorite is my

Indian routine. We tie colored scarves to our ankles and light the ends of our batons with fire. The drums thump out the beat, we howl past the feathers in our braided hair. Against the cold, dark night beneath the blinding lights of the Ramona Stadium during half time in which the Ramona Angels are always winning, we are wild savages before the civilized crowd.

"Well," Cal says, "baton seems to be your only talent. You better put it down."

The week after the Miss Angel contest he enters me in, Cal Johnson disappears, leaving his family, the church, his insurance business. Everyone fears foul play or that he's dead at the bottom of one of the steep canyons. At church we pray for him. In my prayers I never forget him. He was the most beloved and respected man in Ramona. But then two years later the police find him in the desert in Calexico, remarried and re-established in the insurance business and the church. All the forms of propriety, or perhaps it was insurance, didn't reveal Cal's true self either.

The man I want to marry is a sailor at sea. Sergei. He's a Russian from New York, he's as tall as Ivan the Terrible on whom I am writing a paper when we meet. Six feet five inches. Nineteen. We've known each other only three weeks when he is shipped off for seven-months duty in the Pacific. I have the map above my bed. I follow him, Honolulu, Yokohama, Hong Kong, Taiwan, the Philippines. We write every day. I date a different guy at least every other day. Mostly they are sailors. I like them because they come from other states and contrary to their reputation, to mine for dating them, they are gentlemen, I don't even have to kiss them. None of them is able to make me forget Sergei.

For the Miss Angel contest each girl is required to have an escort. Sergei arranges to have his best friend, Gino, drive up from Miramar Naval Air Station to escort me. The gesture is gallant but I wish I was with anyone else.

A strapless, peach formal. Expensive. Layers and layers of net and taffeta over a rented hoop skirt. The gown was Bobbie Sue's, my nineteen-year-old cousin recently killed in a car accident. When Gino, in his dress blues, walks into the long living room that opens onto the whole Valle del Ángel, I'm standing alone, watching the sun go down, waiting. He bows, "I crown you Miss Angel."

In the twilight, the color of my gown, I do feel beautiful, though tight, that terrible awkwardness when I feel social expectations. I can't possibly fill the need, though I pray to. I love the world. I want to do something for it before I die. At the last minute I put on the mustard-seed necklace my mother gave me for Christmas. Faith. We drive down to the town in his '54 Ford hardtop convertible. He's my boyfriend's best friend. There can be no electricity between us. There is nothing to talk about. Later I think if he had been a potential boyfriend, if there could have been energy between us, the outcome of the night might have been different.

This year the pageant is held in the Ramona Town Hall on Main Street. Old photographs line the walls. Main Street, 1889. Main Street, 1900. *Nuevo,* Ramona's original name, written in white ink across the buckboard in front of the Pioneer Market, the first Miss Angel in her gown of turkey feathers. Ramona is the turkey capital of the world.

The hall is jumping. Television crews from San Diego's three stations, one from Los Angeles, a hundred miles to the north. The three judges, two men and a woman, are escorted in with much pomp and applause. One of the men is a well-known TV personality for Channel 6. The current reigning Miss Angel, Annie Alison, stands benevolently with everyone. Her mother, Miss Angel, 1936, is wearing the antique gown of turkey feathers. She was the last queen required to wear it. The Los Coyotes Reservation band plays its savage mix of Catholicism, patriotism, school songs, San Diego Back Country Blues, swing of our parents, be-bop jazz of our older brothers and sisters, Mission Indian tribal stomp, Tijuana Mariachi, our very own rock 'n'roll. I hold onto my escort's big arm, his Navy stripes. People move aside as we walk up the steps. But not their eyes. They stare as they never have before, as if this event finally gives them complete rights. I guess it does. We hover with the other girls in their formals, leaning on the arms of their escorts. The smell of Evening in Paris and aftershave. The lights of the hall spark off their eyes. They are more beautiful than I realized. They have their real boyfriends with them. It is awkward that Diane Smith is with the wildest, most terrifying Indian of the whole county, Lincoln Quintarra, thirty years old.

"Do you recognize the lady judge?" Jennifer asks me. Jennifer is the one I think should win. "It's Miss Fairest of the Fair from three years ago, Raquel Tejada. Remember her?"

Raquel Tejada is moving among the dignitaries, the adults. She is very small. In her photos she always looks large. I remember the strange compulsion I felt toward the first picture I saw of her. I can't really see that it's the same person.

"Can you believe? She just had a baby—two weeks ago!" Jennifer says.

"She sure got her figure back quick," Susan says.

"Yeah, but her boobs are *still* small," Diane says. "No bigger than mine." Everyone laughs.

"When did she get married?" I ask. I want to be married. I want to be an adult. I want a meaningful existence before I die. I want to sleep all night with the man I love.

"Well," Jennifer snickers. "Of course she *had* to. Her name now is Raquel Welch."

Raquel Welch is wearing a strapless full-length gown too. Ice blue. She isn't as pretty in real life as her photos but she holds my attention. The other judge I recognize from the women's page of the *Tribune*, Don Juan, a famous figure of San Diego high society. I still don't understand the concept "society" except that where he goes, it is. He's always being photographed with a celebrity family of blondes, mothers, daughters, cousins. He escorts them in parades, many of which I've marched in, to charity balls and museum openings, down to the docks to meet important ships from across the seas, big Gabor lips across everything, the Captain, the sea, the newspaper, Don Juan.

Raquel makes her way across the crowded room. Don Juan rises from his seat. He wears a white Mexican tuxedo, a red cummerbund around his small waist, a sombrero with tassles around the brim. She is being introduced by the TV host, *Mrs. Raquel Welch, née our very own, our favorite ex-Miss Fairest of the Fair, Miss Raquel Tejada from La Jolla*. Though the *Don* has often announced his preference for blondes, and though she is an ex-queen, married, two times a mother, for this night he will be the gracious escort, like Gino is mine, for this damsel in distress. He removes his sombrero, a grandiose gesture, sweeps it behind his back as he bows, and, holding out his hand, into which she slides her small fingers, he bends, very deliberately, the upper lip lined in a pencil-thin moustache, and kisses them. The Indians finger the strings of their guitars. A little snare. *God. What will I do if he does that to me?*

The contest begins. Lily, Susan, Jennifer, Ella, Nadine. Jamie's dream is to run her own business. "I know I can do it," she says, "but it will be like climbing the tallest mountain in the world." Diane says she's going to be an airline stewardess if she can just make it to twenty-one. Everyone laughs. For the first time I realize Diane has personality.

And now, for our only blonde in the contest. The spotlight blinds me. I can't see anyone. But I'm smiling. I'm smiling till my face hurts, the bilateral sides of my face. People always complain that I don't smile enough. I'm determined not to lose the contest for that old fault. They said the crash was so sudden Bobbie Sue still had a smile on her face though every bone behind it was broken. The host is so stupid I don't know how to answer his questions. A TV camera zooms in. Under hobbies I finally wrote *"drawing."*

"Oh," he jokes, his grin omnipotently large, the camera moving into my aching mouth. "I bet you really mean *drawing men.* "

The room roars and something rushes through my face. I guess so. *Relax.* Relax, the last thing Gino said as he shoved me forward. *"Relax!"* Cal ordered. "The Chamber is counting on you. We'll never win unless you relax."

Relax. Relax. The chant up and down, my strapless falling down. The smile on my face will kill me. *I'm in the second grade and my parents take me to an office on Sunset Boulevard. A Hollywood movie agent. He has seen me in two school plays, one in which I star as the diphtheria germ and the other in which I'm an old woman. As Diptheria I wear a bedsheet dyed with black spots to symbolize the lethal germs, I loom and hover evilly around the world. As Granny, my hair is brushed with cornstarch, turns silver. I rock, cackle, make witty, sarcastic remarks to all the young ones. It's magic to step into another's body. I love the stage, the audience watching. But ever since then I've been cast in straight roles, always the pretty innocent girl, a role I can't play. The dark-suited movie agent pulls on his cigar, leans way back in his swivel chair and demands, "Alright. Let's see how cute you are."*

Recite nursery rhymes. I don't know any. Mirror Mirror on the wall. They bore me. The only verses I can recite are from the Bible. Who's the Fairest of them all? Can't you be cute and coy like you're supposed to be? Like a seven-year-old. Like a sixteen-year-old.

It's awful to disappoint him. And my parents. I don't know how to be cute. I have no personality. When I try to be as they want I embarrass myself. Mama always blesses this day though. She says the nature of Hollywood is contrary to mine. From then on she applies herself very seriously to the task of making sure I don't grow up to be a movie star. Letters from agents, the agents themselves come to the house, telephone, but she never lets them talk with me. So why am I here now? When I leave the spotlight, my oldest name is hissed at me, *Blondie, hey Blondie!*

During the balloting we crowd together into the restroom to refresh our make-up, comb our hair, consult Liz. To rest my face from smiling. In the huddled group I lose myself a little. I feel like one of them, a part of the human flux, a feeling I love. Once I read that an artist's collage of a thousand faces makes the most beautiful face anyone has ever seen. But then suddenly this old sense fills me with alarm. Tonight I'm in competition with my friends. I'm to be the most visible.

"Oooh! Just imagine! One of us will soon be Miss Angel!" Diane squeals in the center of the swarm. A wave of embarrassment sweeps through us. Her lust to win, as with so many things about Diane, is undisguised. But light irradiates her large eyes. She's beautiful. I never thought so before. She's an F student and her reputation is horrible. Probably none of us is without sexual experience, but she makes no effort to hide hers. Somehow she's related to Ramon, a cousin. Like his, her Mojave mother disappeared after her birth. The Mojaves are superstitious about half-breeds. The county is always taking her away from her white father, the local car mechanic who never got over his penchant for drunk reservation women. He disappears for days at a time into the local reservations and Diane runs from her newest foster home. That's what she's doing with Lincoln Quintarra. She runs to older men.

I move out of the bathroom, into a dark corner behind the throng of people. The band is playing "Mood Indigo." Raquel Welch is standing in front of me. She's just standing there in her ill-fitting blue gown, small and unglamorous, thinking no one is looking at her. Light doesn't spark off her as it does the girls in the contest, as I can see it coming off me. The nostrils of her thick nose flair with each breath. She really is, as everyone sneers, Mexican. But I love the dark, the earth. She had a baby two weeks ago. Her second baby. She has milk. I'm sucked into her as into a cave, the hole so visible from the recent birth. Why are you wearing a dress that's too large? Maybe you almost died.

Bridgit comes through the crowd to take a picture of me. She recognizes Raquel and takes it of her instead. "Raquel Tejada!" she emotes with the flashbulb and instantly the dark sullen figure becomes sparkling light.

But too late for the photograph. And before world fame. Before plastic surgery, age and film make you large. Before silicon, before Italy, before the starry debut. Before the great actress. You stand in front of the old photographs of my hometown, a stage coach on dusty Main, the army with Kit Carson the day before the massacre, *Nuevo* printed in white ink above your head. I'm a white ghost behind you. Miss Angel in her turkey feathers. Your hair is cropped, your head too small. You are too small, sinking, the deadly vortex, your mother a wetback maid for the rich. Into her you must sink, be a fading beauty at twenty, acquiesce to anonymity, live on this earth through the lives of your children, be smoke, not flames. Postpartum blues. You are a woman being removed from the world.

Along with her camera Bridgit is carrying a copy of *The Valley of the Dolls* by Jacqueline Suzanne.

"Are you reading that book, too?" Raquel asks.

"Oh, yes! I can't put it down!" My sister can be chums with anyone.

"My mother gave it to me while I was in the hospital," Raquel says. "My mother's so dumb she thinks because it shows Hollywood in a bad light I won't want to be a movie star. It just makes me more determined than ever."

"Me too!" Bridgit exclaims. "But I can't even let my mother see I'm reading it."

They both laugh, talk about some scene or character they love. I've never read that book. Someday I must. I'm sure I'll learn some basic things that have always escaped me. But I still have the photo my sister took of me and Raquel that night. It's as important as another one I carry, of Marilyn Monroe and Jayne Mansfield. A detective friend took it on a studio lot about the same time Bridgit took hers. The two famous sex queens are standing in very high heels and very low-cut dresses, facing the camera. Monroe has one arm around Mansfield's deeply indented waist, the other slid into her enormous left breast. Mansfield has one arm around Monroe's shoulders and the other plunged up her dress into her crotch. Both blondes are laughing uproariously at the joke, their big joke on the world. They are consummate comedians. When I think of their deaths, Jayne's like my cousin Bobbie Sue's, I think they were murdered. Someone, the government, despite the world's insistence on the Dumb Blonde, got wind of how smart these women were.

And Raquel. In my sister's photograph you can see the birthing of a person who must become an artist of her own body, personality and being. She is deciding in the very moment to become the world's most beautiful woman. She will pay any price for this. You can see, any price is worth it. Years later when I can't remember the girl this story is about, when the world will have changed so much, I'll zip past newsstands in supermarkets and drugstores all over Los Angeles, past two or three, sometimes as many as a half-dozen covers of Raquel's midsection: the famous flaring navel, her trademark, (there was the letter to the editor of *Playboy* magazine in 1975 celebrating her navel as the most beautiful ever created, bemoaning the fact that no other woman's belly button could make the writer as horny), the wide-winged shoulders, the flaming bones of her face. THE MYSTERIOUS RAQUEL. WHO IS RAQUEL WELCH? Photographers know she's had children from the marks on her famous belly (pregnancies being the cause of her stretched navel) but where the children are, where she has suddenly come from, how old she is, who her husband is, will remain manipulated mysteries for years. I will always be sorry she didn't come on as Raquel Tejada, a name more beautiful than Raquel Welch, but in shooting for Hollywood fame in racist Southern California she obviously had to erase her Latin American heritage, which in fact is

Bolivian, not Mexican. In Southern California anything south of San Diego is Mexican.

In a short and sweet presentation, Miss Congeniality, "the girl who is easiest to get along with and helps the most," is awarded to Lily Walker. Then the real announcements begin. By order of placement, the top seven that is, the Queen's Royal Court and then the Queen. As each name is called a squeal comes from the girl and then the slow dawning that she isn't Miss Angel seems to overtake her as she arrives at the front of the room to receive her tiara and sash. Princess Six, Princess Five, Princess Four. When there is only the Queen to be announced and my name has not been called I know she is not me. I look across the faces of the four of us who remain. Diane explodes like a Fourth-of-July firecracker, each successive explosion more beautiful than the last as she jumps, cries out, stumbles ecstatically, tears falling in the spotlights and camera flashes, toward her robe and crown. The band is playing, *"Ramona, I hear your mission bells ringing. . . ."* Annie, last year's Miss Angel, as she forfeits her crown, is bawling.

The three of us, Ella, Susan and myself, the three of us who have not placed, are just standing here wondering what else is expected of us. Cal Johnson runs up, "Now girls! Don't be bad sports. Go up there and congratulate the new Queen and her Court."

Mechanically we start doing as we are told, when Cal grabs my arm. He looks into my eyes. "Do you realize you came in *last. Last!* When are you ever going to learn to smile?" I'm bobbing for apples the last church Halloween party at his house, how sexual it is, nose and teeth in the water with the boys'. "And didn't you promise me you'd have your hair thinned?"

"It's just that the judges couldn't see your pretty face, honey." Cal's wife is suddenly beside us, she who is about to be deserted, her tone more gentle. "We're so embarrassed for you."

The minister of the Friend's Church says, "You were holding your shoulders up just fine, and then halfway through the interview you let them slump again. I prayed you were over that old problem." I haven't been able to stomach him since I heard him preach that any man who thinks he can worship under a tree on Sundays rather than in a church is a sinner.

I'm looking around for Gino. Mr. Nordahl, the school principal, stops me. "Your answers were just too deep, dear. It's a disgrace you came in last, a disgrace that *Diane* is our new Miss Angel. *Heavens!* You should have *thought* more about your answers."

A lady from the Eastern Star has tears in her eyes.

"For next year's contest," Liz is saying, "you must let me cut your hair. There's nothing wrong with the rest of you. Everyone knows you have a good face."

I nod to them all. I will not be Miss Bad Sport on top of Miss Last Place, Miss Ugly Angel. But there won't be a next year for me. I watch Raquel Welch leave the Ramona Town Hall on the arm of Don Juan.

I'm on the train from San Diego to Los Angeles. It is the week before my sixteenth birthday and the day after I place last in the Miss Ramona contest. I'm going to Sarah's for Easter vacation. I'm wearing white three-inch high heels, a lot of make-up. Much more than in the contest. A pale mint-green suit: straight skirt and soft sweater, dyed-to-match. My first sweater since I was thirteen. The train, used mostly by businessmen commuting between the two cities, races along the beautiful coast, the tracks lined in yellow and fuchsia ice plant. The men keep saying you are so beautiful. They keep buying me screwdrivers and saying you are the most beautiful woman I've ever seen. One who sits awhile with me says, "I know you are a fashion model, anyone as beautiful as you are has to be." But I am not cute nor coy, nor do I drink their drinks. My old strangeness, my inability to be anything other than deep, the physical ache too much smiling brings my face causes them all to leave me shortly. I see my face in the hot window speeding along the ocean, the water beginning to well up in the eyes that change to whatever they're near over the glary light of the aqua-blue-and-white-ribboned sea. *Last place.* But the tears of humiliation I will not let fall. The day is beautiful. The hills wild with the flowers of spring. And so am I.

In July I meet Sergei's aircraft carrier, the USS *Hornet,* home from the Orient. I design and sew a beautiful red dress for him. He takes a picture of me with his new Japanese camera standing among the thousands of other loved ones on the dock. I want to be an adult. I want control of my destiny. I want to make love to him every day and night.

On the road up to Ramona he confesses his Japanese prostitutes. It is a pain different, deeper than any I've known. He says they are a different kind of girl than me, I have nothing to worry about. Losing the war and the Bomb made them that way. He helps my father dig the hole for the new swimming pool. I watch the two men I love the most from the window, digging. I feel dug into. If I have nothing to worry about, if she is so different, so dismissable—*why?* I see her naked in the large room of mattresses, Japanese on top of him. *Why were you with her? I stayed a virgin for you.* In a week we are secretly engaged.

On the day we buy our rings, in downtown San Diego, we drive up to Del Mar, to the San Diego County Fair. Diane has not placed in the Fairest of the Fair Contest, though next year, Susan, one of the three of us who came in last, will become Miss Angel, Miss Fairest of the Fair, and place second in the Miss California contest. Ella disappears for ten years. I meet her one day on Telegraph Avenue, a Berkeley radical with a Ph.D. in Russian Studies.

Don Juan is strolling the promenade with two princesses on his arm. A fat Indian woman dressed in purple silk guesses age and weight for fifty cents. She guesses me fifteen pounds under my weight and ten years older than my age. I win a beatnik doll.

We have our portraits drawn by a chalk artist. As I sit a crowd gathers. He asks me my hobbies. I say drawing and sewing. In his picture I am drawing men, that is, luring them.

We watch the horse races, my head nestled into the armpit of my tall sailor. I love to listen to him talk, his sexy New York accent. We walk around the agricultural exhibits. We gasp over the fat hogs, the ridiculously groomed sheep, the unabashedly randy bulls.

In a lighted case near the exit, the year's score cards for all the county's animal competitions are displayed, including the beauty contests. I refuse to look, but Sergei does. He discovers that from the scores of the two men judges I would have been Miss Angel. But Raquel Welch gave me zero in every category.

Part
II

King   Kennedy

The only human value of anything, writing included,
is intense vision of the facts.

William Carlos Williams

Chappaquiddick

There are things that happen to you that take a long time to tell. It was 1969. So many were leaving the country. We decided to look for it. My children were eight and five. The man was the man I would love for a very long time. My parents, heartbroken over the murder of Robert Kennedy and my living with Maximilian, were "letting me go," but they had given me, when I began graduate school at Cal State Los Angeles, a 1960 Falcon station wagon. The four of us fit well into it. David, my eight-year-old, slept on the front seat; Darien, five, in the back with us. Sometimes they traded places. We slept outside as often as possible. The Falcon was our home for six months.

We went east out of LA, across the grey desert. It was the beginning of April. We stayed a week on Lake Mead while I recovered from an abortion, and he, he said, from the politics of the decade. Recovered? Did I ever? Politics? For all our effort, the efforts of so many, the war raged unabated: the killings, and Watts now would always be the place, besides the riots, of our aborted love. Even LA County couldn't stop the bleeding. Dark-suited men with notepads hovered around my bed. *"Was this abortion artificially induced?"* The man scraped and scraped without anesthesia. I was too weak, too grief-stricken to protest. "April is the cruelest month." I remember his face between my legs, his green smock. I remember understanding through the greatest physical pain I am sure I will ever have to endure: *he's enjoying this.*

I sat on the rim of that ugly man-made lake, the world gravel and dammed water for as far as I could see, and read Sartre's *Nausea*. I read with the stupidity of an M.A. student, in sheer defiance of any intuition leaking through my psyche that the book or the place could be a deterrent to the healing process. Existentialism. There are no connections. I was thankful I hadn't been born an Indian, into a culture that had no books. To have only the land to read: the boredom, I was convinced, would have destroyed me. I sat there in the waste, amidst boulders, still bleeding, and hated Nature. I felt as if I was on the moon.

When I was stronger we toured Hoover Dam, which is also known as Boulder Dam. Hoover was the original name but during the Depression that president fell into such ill-favor with the people that his name was discarded, until 1948, for boulders. We descended beneath the water, the Colorado. Colorado means red, the color of blood. I had drunk the water of the Colorado River all my life. Boulder Dam, water and light for Southern California, for Ramona, my hometown, for the control of floods in the Imperial Valley.

A Shriner's convention was taking place in Las Vegas and a group was on the tour with us. Max kept referring to them as the "wobblies." He was not being political or historical; he was ridiculing them for being old, which annoyed me. But then one of them, a drunk old man with a green tassle bobbing around his grinning head, reached out and pinched my left nipple as we passed between the eight generators. I screamed at him, started bleeding again. The engineer, another beady-eyed old man, cackled at the sight and pulled a switch. The place roared with rushing water. I thought I was encountering a contemporary version of Charon, the ferryman to the Underworld. I could feel tons of water over us. I could feel the flood out of control within me. I heard again the Mojave prophecy for the Colorado River. I felt a sudden rage at Max, the first I had known. There is one photograph from that week. I am sleeping on the ground, my son is fishing the Las Vegas Wash, my daughter is sitting beside me, staring at me. I look as if I'm gasping for air. I look very old, the color of gravel.

But when we left there early Sunday morning, after showing the kids the spectacle that is Las Vegas, something rather unusual and fine happened, which I see now was the beginning of healing. Crossing the northwest corner of Arizona, between Nevada and Utah, we found a Shivwits Indian burial ground. We would not have seen it, hidden from the highway as it is, except we stopped for the kids to pee. I noticed smoke coming from behind a low hill. Curious, I walked around it, making my way through the thorny desert growth. The small cemetery was enclosed in chicken wire. A rock marked each grave. The smoke was rising from a black sooty patch on the ground. Over the broken gate hung crude wrought-iron letters: *Land of the Sun.*

How to say what happened to me there? In 1969 I was over-whelmed with the dead. The dead of the war. The dying of the earth. The death of art. The death of hope. The first death of our love I carried now in my body. Before leaving LA, waiting for the abortion to take effect, we had toured Forest Lawn in Glendale, again, it seems, in defiance of anything psychological or spiritual that might have been happening to us. But it was more than this. In our six-month sojourn around the country we sought out the cemeteries of every town and city we visited, some in extremely remote places, the graveyards of ghost towns. I think that we, Los Angelenos, were looking for the past, a history, the country we knew so little of, for the education nei-ther of us had received in all our years of schools. With the kids we sat over graves and imagined the lives and deaths of the occupants. Forest Lawn was our first tour. We spent that afternoon walking around reading the outrageous headstones, me with a catheter jammed up my cervix, waiting for oxygen to kill the foetus. It took two weeks, three tries. The life in me did not want to die. Now the simpleness, the beauty of this crude burial ground of the Shivwits, after the ostentatiousness of Forest Lawn, brought to me the first feelings of joy and correctness I had known in a long time.

And so I did something there for the first time, in the *Land of the Sun,* that I continued to do as we traveled around the country, some-thing done in reverence, not desecration. It became a ritual, a private ritual of transformation for my desolate spirit, a way of touching the land as I couldn't seem to in any other way, a way of leaving part of my self with the land and the dead, a way of touching the dead, who so haunted me. A way, in fact, of honoring my own body, the dead in me, of loving the least honorable aspect of it. And, finally, a way of touch-ing the comic spirit of the universe that so evaded me. I searched out

and found the right place. How to tell what I did? Perhaps quoting
from a poem I later wrote, one of my first:

I squatted in graveyards all over this country!

On the great plains of Kansas
in the little towns of the South
in the gothic plots of New England, the dead of the 1630s
and in New York City
at the end of Wall Street
facing Europe.

I squatted over the graves of Revolutionary and Civil War soldiers.
I shat on the wars of Europe, the Philippines, Korea, and Viet Nam.
I showed my ass and cunt
to the founding fathers of our country
and to burned witches, hung
murderers in the weedpatch boothills of Montana.

I shitted on uptight judges and society ladies
on the Unknown Soldier in Richmond, Virginia

       though he is guarded by "Memory"
       a fifty-foot white angel
       "symbolizing the womanhood of Virginia"
       who bows her head to the eternal
       "Torch of Liberty"
       and 10,369 Virginia names.

I squatted over three Presidents, the graves of
Unknown Women, Blacks,
Chicanos, Indians, Asians and
movie stars,
young boys in Arlington, unknown
young girls,
over the grave of Henry David Thoreau
and high over Denver, Buffalo Bill
and, in Abilene, over even
Eisenhower.

Hiding behind the widest cross
in the middle of a little Tennessee town
giggling to commit
(my children pretending I am not their mother)
shit into the Holy

> *I memorize the names*
> *I meditate on the dates*
> *I come to know*
> *that beneath*
> *is human*
> *coming to Stone*

It was the beginning of my love for Nature, including a begrudging appreciation of the terrible dissolution back to the Mother.

We spent a month in Moab, Utah, with an old friend from Los Angeles. Una was born a "Jack Mormon," but she had become in the time of our friendship a devout Mormon, moving back to the place of her birth, the home of her church. She had been divorced from the father of her four children but as part of her conversion she remarried him in the Temple — for Eternity. Our visit was a true reunion; she had ended our friendship when I fell in love with Max who was in prison for refusal to be inducted into the army and for use of marijuana. Part of her leaving LA, going back to her husband and the church, was her belief that the Latter Days were upon us, that the race riots and counter culture movements were the beginning of the Civil War prophesied a hundred years before by Joseph Smith. This Civil War is a major Mormon prophecy: the Red Hordes will invade from the Pacific, the U.S. Government will be destroyed and the Saints will found the new Capitol in the Rockies. But now Una met Maximilian for the first time, and for all his hair, outlandish clothes and talk, she loved him instantly. Two of a kind: mavericks! He was most impressed I think with her two-year food storage, which every good Mormon has, a survival system of wheat, salt, honey, powdered milk and canned goods. One year supply is for the family and the other year is for the non-Mormons who will flock to the Rockies refusing to fight their brothers and sisters. "I'm getting ready myself," he said, his sky-blue eyes twinkling at her through his black curls, "for the Civil War." "You look just like Jesus," Una responded, pulling on his ragged headband, his halo of thorns. Una decided that pacifist hippies must be the non-Mormons of the prophecy.

Nineteen sixty-nine was a watershed year for many people of many different beliefs. During our visit Una, thirty years old, fell in love with a nineteen-year-old Cherokee student in her Sunday School class, a Lamanite in Mormon racist terminology. When the Lamanites—and all other people of color—are redeemed, their skins will be washed clean, that is, white. I had argued with Una so much in years past over Mormon doctrine with the only effect being the loss of our friendship, which had broken my heart like civil war—I *loved* her—that now I kept my mouth shut, knowing that a nineteen-year-old Cherokee would wash *her* soul clean. I loved her falling in love with him. For the courage. It was going to get ugly when her husband, the Church and the town found out.

Johnny Lookfar was a giant—six feet, six inches tall and almost three hundred pounds. He worked in the mines, had mystical knowledge, both Indian and Mormon, of the land. We spent most of the month exploring it with him—Monument Valley, the La Sal Mountains, Deadhorse Point, Arches National Park. The four of us walked along the Colorado River to a hidden beach with petroglyphs where Una had once tried to kill herself because the Church doesn't believe in divorce. "To be married to him in this life, well, I can handle that. But when I think of Eternity . . .!"

In Boulder I took the last exam for my degree. I had passed the first two parts of the all-day test with "brilliance," but had failed the third part miserably. The disparity between the two was so great that the English department made a rare exception: I had to repeat only the part I had failed. Such extremes in performance were typical of my school career. I called Cal State Los Angeles the week before the tests and explained that I was in Colorado with my two children, that I couldn't afford to return. Could it be arranged for me to take my exam through the University of Colorado? During the week I studied in the ivy-shrouded old brick library—ivy and brick! just as the legend goes about Eastern schools—and Max and the kids explored the area. At night we went up into the mountains, slept on the banks of Boulder Creek. Boulder was a cultural oasis in the middle of the country, a great relief for us after two months of straight people and strange land. There was a festive, near explosive, tension in the air; the students looked and obviously thought like us. On Saturday the chairman of my English department, who had once raged that my hippy style of dress was inappropriate for a graduate student and reflected poorly on his whole department—I don't think he realized who it was on the phone, his department being so large—called the test question to the chairman of Boulder's English department at the exact moment my fellow M.A. Candidates were sitting down to it in LA. This eliminated any chance of the question being leaked to me. Of the multiple choices I chose to write on the epic characteristics of T.S. Eliot's *The Waste Land*. "I will show you fear in a handful of dust." Within the first hour I knew I had my masters degree of English.

Now we truly came undone from our lives, what they had been—my preparation and study, their waiting for me. We were far from home and all we had ever known. There had been a moment in Utah, turning east a little north of Panquitch, heading down that lonely mountain, then desert, road across the world to Moab, when I had a similar feeling, a small hysteria at leaving everything, going so ignorant and alien into the unknown. There's a photo of the kids that day: the churning sky and Sevier River churning around their little bodies still seem to portend this.

We slept on Buffalo Bill's grave in the mountains high above Denver and then, the next day May 22, headed east, descending into the great central plains, the Heartland. We spent seven days crossing eastern Colorado and Kansas, a straight line to Missouri. It was a major effort to stay on the old road. Every time we asked directions we got directed back to the interstate. All the way we sang the old song, "I'm going to Kansas City." Through the boarded-up farmhouses high on the slight rises, through yellow and green fields like giant checkerboards, beneath dark blue skies, the land growing flatter and flatter. We moved through Russian settlements (*fleeing the army*), German settlements (*fleeing the army*), Swedish settlements (*fleeing the army*). We followed the tracks and the history written on rocks of the Union Pacific. Down every Main Street of every town: teenage kids cruising. We visited a sod town. Over three million people lived in sod houses, 1865–1935. We lost another hour.

In Grinnel, Kansas, running through a wheat field, we became fascinated with the mystery of wheat to flour, studied closely the grains, ate them raw with milk and honey. *Wheat goes through one hundred and eighty different processes before it's ready for bread.* And so rich is this country, it rots in storage bins. "So it's dumped into the sea," Max explained capitalism to the kids, "rather than fed to the hungry." We toured "the wildest of cowtowns," Ellsworth, could see the train passengers shooting at the immense herds of buffalo, the carcasses left to rot in the engine's trail of smoke, and the famed dance-hall girl trotting down Main Street on a white stallion in the costume of Lady Godiva. We visited every free museum, fort, library in our path, using the bathrooms to bathe in. We lost each other in a prehistoric burial pit with the remains of a hundred and forty-seven Pawnees. Six-footers, not the seven-footers of Coronado's myth. We visited the Eisenhower homestead and library and the replica frontier town of Abilene that comically borders the property. We spent two days following the Civil War in Kansas, the Pro-slavery cause, the Free-State Clause, John Brown's Body and his Broadswords. And the Emigrant Tribes pushed here all the way from the Atlantic Seaboard, Wyandot, Shawnee, Pottawatomie, Ottawa, Miami, Chippewa, Delaware, Kickapoo. We stopped to look for wild marijuana growing, according to California legend, along the highways. Into churchyards Darien threw our seeds. David screaming at the cows as we come down Highway 40, land of so many kinds of cows.

We could hardly believe the state-run liquor stores in every town, the prim and proper little old ladies standing hypocritically before rows and rows of glittering bottles. "For the job you must sell your soul," Max explained. We turned around and went back to check on anything we couldn't quite believe we'd seen. A turtle, or was it a rock, crossing the road. David saying there are no rocks in Kansas; Darien saying once or twice I saw a rock. And flaming rivers leaking from the sun in the west, the farms growing smaller, closer together. Max saying I can dig it. Raising your kids here. Sitting on your porch taking long strolls through your tree-shaded town. Then low rolling hills started appearing on the horizon, the flint hills. We tried to make fire, like the Indians, by rubbing flint together. An old man working at that rest stop warned us, "There's lots to do in Kansas City. It's wild!" He said it was meadowlarks making that song. The kids were into it—history, geography, social studies, ethics and morality they would have hated in school.

Once we slept in a park. Early in the morning before light the town's high-school graduation party arrived—crazed, drunk, scary and scared seniors leaning against the car, sitting on the hood, banging on the roof. Most of the boys were leaving for the army the next week. Viet Nam. I wanted to jump out of the car, beg them not to go. Instead, afraid of them, we lay perfectly still, hardly breathing, holding hands. Those drunk kids never realized we were bedded down behind the paisley curtains, heart of their party, their last high-school night in Hayes, Kansas.

In Kansas City we hunted down all the streets for the address in the song, "I'm going to Kansas City, Twelfth Street and Vine." We couldn't find it. The closest we could get was Twelfth Street and Wyandot— Wyandot perhaps slurred and slanged to Wyan. Everyone seemed perplexed and amused that we would take the address in the song so seriously. The kids were delighted that there are two Kansas Cities. (We checked both towns.) As soon as we crossed the Missouri River from Kansas City, Kansas, into Kansas City, Missouri, the dates jumped back fifty years. The land, even the air, seemed older.

I began keeping a journal. Months before, one of my last days on campus, I had taken a vow never to be a poet. In graduate school I had come to see the parallel between the Law and Order of Poetry and the

Law and Order of the Army. Fascism. I had taken this vow, yet now I found myself rather mindlessly keeping a travel account, jotting down the images from the streets and countrysides, parts of conversations overheard, of my kids, of the locals, things I encountered that disturbed me until I wrote them down. I was particularly caught by the way people looked, different than Californians, as if place has physical influence, and the way they talked, the syntax of their sentences, their colorful poetic idiomatic phrases—Una's from Moab had always put me in a spell. The writing in this journal is barely English, hardly legible; certainly, not "poetry." Poetry's law and order could never encompass what moved me to write. I wasn't interested in being "creative." I wasn't interested in writing like a diarist, about myself, or even about my family. I wanted the truth—the energy, the facts of these new places, myself, my lover, my kids: the Unknown—to speak through me. Not for me to speak to it. As a teenager I had photographed everything for the same reason: trying to see and then to hold, somehow, the present. The historical markers in Missouri were compelling too: the writing style, *what was regarded as history*. We stopped at every one as we crossed the state so I could copy it down. Then in Columbia, Missouri, I met an old man who turned out to be the writer of these highway signs and the founder of the Missouri Historical Society. I was intrigued. I didn't know what I was doing, really, or why. It took five years of this kind of journal writing before I understood that *I am a writer,* in fact, *a poet*. In school I had missed entirely the notion that a writer, first and foremost, is one who writes. I had confused writing with publication, good grades, degrees; that is, product and approval.

In opening this first journal now the most prominent entry is glued-in pages of the *St. Louis Globe-Democrat*, an article entitled: THOSE WHO HAVE DIED IN VIETNAM DURING THE LAST YEAR

> Here are the 397 Missourians who died in Viet Nam since last Memorial Day. There are slightly more casualties—425—during the same period ending last Memorial Day. There have been 167 Missourians killed in the war since Jan. 1 this year. 418 in 1968; 309 in 1967; 174 in 1966; 33 in 1965; and 2 from 1961 to 1964.

Beneath this is twenty pages of photos of the Missourians dead in a year's time from our country's undeclared war in Viet Nam. And other photos: of the mothers, wives, little brothers, headstones, flags, cemetery trees. *Dickens, Freddie D., Mrs. Ora L. Dickens, Poplar Bluff (wife); Slaughter, Philip, Mrs. Philip Slaughter, Kansas City (mother); Smith, Maynard Lee, Troy (no survivors)*. . . . The names go on and on. As a child I believed in Jesus. In 1969 I was an existentialist. There are no gods. No connections. At least between heaven and earth. We are alone. But I did believe in something. I believed in learning, living in the present, acting from first-hand experience rather than blind custom or habit, and I believed that there are connections between us. In the fact of the Viet Nam War, in the horror, despair and helplessness I experienced, I came to reflect again, or so I tried to write, on what Jesus had meant when he said to me as a child, *I am with you. I suffer your sins. I give my life for them.* I sought to know the pain of others, particularly the pain of those who suffered from the war. It seemed to me that the only possible alleviation of pain in the world was in consciousness—that in knowing the suffering of the Other, one eases, in the simple comfort sharing brings, some of the pain. In a fundamental way I wanted to know every person. The individual throwing against the prison walls of the self—the "fleshcase" I wrote then, a word I'd gotten from Joyce's *Ulysses*—in the longing to tell its story, its pain, is part of the world's collective pain. I believed also, I still believe, that in the manifestation of the Golden Rule, *do unto others as you would have them do unto you,* lies the eradication of evil.

We camped a week on an Indian's land in Missouri. Mingo Onago was a Modoc Indian, in spiritual exile, he said, from Northern California. He owned forty thickly-wooded acres in the farm center of the state and had advertised in a national magazine for "counter-culture" people to camp on his land. Even before meeting him we felt a strange trepidation. We arrived at dusk, drove around his fenced, thickly-wooded plot. He was expecting us within the hour but we retreated back down the dirt road and spent the night in a small churchyard. In the morning we drove twenty miles back to town to telephone him. Dressed all in black, he came down the road to the churchyard on a black BMW with a sidecar. He told us right off that the famous Modoc, Captain Jack, was his grandfather, that he had just returned from the United Nations where he had presented a plan for five states to be returned to the Native American organization of which he was president. The group was demanding Idaho, Wyoming, Montana, North Dakota and Florida— far-off Florida for military strategy. He led us down the road, as in a procession, to his woods. We set up our camp on the creek, planning to spend several weeks.

But early one morning Mingo brought a portable record player down to our campsite and played an old 78 record of the Nuremberg Trials. When Goebbels is asked if he is guilty or innocent of the crimes of which he is accused, he spits on the courtroom floor. The sound of Goebbels's spitting greatly excited Mingo. "Did you hear it? Did you hear it?" We hadn't. He picked up the needle arm, placed it back on the record so as to replay the section. He did this again and then again, becoming, each time the SS man spit, more agitated. Another time, while strolling with him through his idyllic woods, he suddenly informed us that we should never eat candy bars from Chicago. Chicago candy, he said, is manufactured by Jews who use as a main ingredient Negro sperm. The intent is to make white Americans complaisant and passive "like coloreds." Another time he showed us pictures of his mother and his grandmother, Captain Jack's wife, to prove, he said, that they were blond Swedes. Mingo's land and the way he lived on the land were very attractive and new to us. The forty acres were entirely overgrown, the only woods in the county. "The way nature meant it to be," he said. He farmed one acre at the center. He had built a log cabin in the Modoc fashion of stacking trees vertically, "as they grow." I milked my first cow under his guidance, "Jersey," who wandered free through the forty acres and from whom I derived an inkling of what it means to be ruled by Taurus, the Bull. But by the end of the week we had become so paranoid of this man that we fled in the middle of the night. We were convinced that he was really a deranged, perhaps self-appointed undercover agent from the nearby air force base.

We headed directly south into the Ozarks of Arkansas, crossing Norfolk Lake by free ferry. That afternoon, on a warm foggy beach, while the kids fished and we watched from an opening in the woods, never taking our eyes off them, Max inserted his long fingers inside me in such a way that I had a series of vaginal orgasms stronger than any I had known. It felt like I could go on with them forever, like the whole lake was gushing from its source inside me. "It felt like you were turning inside out," Max gasped afterwards, looking with awe at his fingers. The new Women's Liberation Movement was being predicated on "The Myth of the Vaginal Orgasm," as "proven" by the newly published Masters and Johnson's *Human Sexual Response*. I read the report, I read the women, dismayed. The long, deep interior of my vagina, supposedly a nerveless muscle, incapable of feeling, had always been the center of *all* my sensate experience; it's my dominant memory of kindergarten. Pages of that first journal trying to describe the differences between clitoral and vaginal coming. *Clitoral orgasm is the breathless sweet high pitch of the violin, but higher, more shrill, the color of brilliant rose, a clarity that takes you to the screaming/singing angels in the hierarchical chain. Vaginal orgasm—deep, low, yin, like flying off a cliff and hitting the beach below, the incessant moaning of a foghorn, the sound the earth makes as it turns on its axis, the groan of all forms coming into being, the color of earth, brown dirt. Vaginal orgasm is so low, so deep, so broad, so guttural as to seem to be the feel or consciousness of the body's organs as they function—move, pump, spill forth, diastole, systole—deeply, darkly, independently. The whole sense is of* OPENING. Combating denial of my personal reality was an old event, is perhaps the oldest psychic movement in the preservation of the self in any creature, but the absurdity of liberation based on a definition of woman as less than I was—was maddening. Science, objective study and the medical profession were all losing credence with me. While I could understand the need to liberate the female from male sexual dependency, this hailing by women of a study based solely on masculine principles—lights and cameras inside my vagina inside a lab might make even mine play dead—still brings a bitter taste to my mouth, a rebellious throbbing to my cunt. How many years I wasted having to refute this simple but dangerous lie. It prevented me from seeing, in my own life, the crucial issues of feminism.

We went east to the Mississippi River, then south on I, the road that borders the eastern levy of the river all the way to New Orleans. This was real descent, going down into a world as mythical to us, as steamy as dream. We had been involved all of the sixties with the Civil Rights Movement, knew it in our lives as the historic catalyst from which all our liberating consciousness emanated. Now, mile by mile, the real thing: the poverty, the heat, the unpainted shacks, the black people bent to the immense fields, none of whom would acknowledge our presence—then, every few miles, the mansion, if not antebellum, 1950s rancho, a plane parked in the drive. We told the kids all we knew, from Africa to the present. We were driving the road on which Bessie Smith was injured in a car accident. The injuries weren't serious but no hospital would admit her. She bled to death. We were singing her songs and others from our visit to a jazz and blues museum in Memphis and we slept that night under the Mississippi Bridge just like W.C. Handy when he wrote *I hate to see that evening sun go down.* We were trying to give our country a chance, to see for ourselves the truths beneath the charge of the Civil Rights, Anti-War and Student Protest Movements: that Capitalism is inherently, unavoidably, evil; that for money, human beings are bought and sold and taught to hate and kill. Everywhere we went the hypocrisies and injustices were even more glaring than we had expected. We spent an afternoon in a Greenville drive-in watching robust white kids in their cars buying pops and cones, playing the juke box: "Lighter Shade of Pale" and "You Don't Know What It's Like." *To love somebody. To love somebody. The way I love you.* My emotional despair with my country was funneling deeper and deeper into love of Maximilian, our life with him on the road. This man who had put his life on the line, who chose to go to prison rather than to war.

It was in Kansas and then Missouri that he first noticed that David was taking an unusual interest in Civil War cemeteries. There are pictures of him at the mounds of Union soldiers on which he has strewn wild

flowers, kneeling in a manner close to prayer. One night we found ourselves locked inside the extraordinary Civil War cemetery in Vicksburg, Mississippi, "the final resting place of seventeen thousand Union
soldiers." We bedded down between two enormous angels and listened to David tell in detail and with pathos the major battle fought
there. We couldn't imagine where he had gotten the information. He
still couldn't read. It was Max, so scornful of any "mysticism," who
kept pondering David's past life.

In New Orleans we continued our pattern for a few days, watching,
trying to take in everything. Then we counted our money. Just enough
to get back home. Or get jobs. We left town, driving west into the
soggy sun, rather than answer the *White Only* ads. But a few miles out
we turned back. Within two hours I had a job as a bar maid at the Mississippi Delta Lounge. I worked two shifts a day for three weeks
straight until we had enough money to continue. The one good thing
about the place was the air conditioning; outside the air was steaming
water. Most of my customers carried guns. There was prostitution upstairs. Occasionally news from the outside world leaked in—angry talk
of People's Park in Berkeley—but I was too lost in the timeless fog of
their alcoholism, horniness and our mutual exhaustion to pay attention. Workers are stupid because they're exhausted! But environment
is part of the mix too. In the dry Nevada desert I had felt emptiness and
meaninglessness in the universe, an absence of all spirit, absence of
God; there seemed to be only matter, little bits of grey gravel. But
Louisiana seemed *all* spirit, the cosmos as hideous demons ready to
grab you, fate your life. One unbelievably hot and humid morning
Max and the kids were driving me to work. As we rose up over the Mississippi a car coming in the opposite direction suddenly stopped at the
crest of the bridge. A woman jumped out of the passenger side, ran
over to the opposite railing and threw herself off. By the time we got
parallel to the stopped car, the driver, a man, was leaning over the side,
bewilderedly looking into the river, police sirens were wailing and already a Coast Guard boat was coming across the water from the docks.
Right beneath the spot from which she had disappeared a huge tanker
was slowly revealing itself from under the bridge. My customers talked

about it all day, going into great detail about the rip tides and currents of the river, how she was dead as soon as she hit. That night the hints that I work upstairs were unavoidable. I didn't go back the next morning.

From New Orleans we went east along the Gulf Coast to Mobile, then north up the interior of Alabama. Now we were in the land of the grandparents. Max's mother and my parents were from old Southern families. All three had fled the South before our births. People were physically familiar: my mother in the grocery line, my brother working on the road, my father drinking his morning coffee next to me in the cafe, his thick wrists and fingers, my sister pushing her babies down the street. For the first time I could appreciate and accept the fact that I *do* look like Daisy Mae just as I had always been teased, as the men in my family look like the strapping Li'l Abner.

Janis Joplin was giving a concert in Atlanta. We didn't attend but got caught in the traffic jam, experienced some of the wild energy. We visited the library in Charlotte, North Carolina, disappointed that the old one where my parents met in 1938 had been torn down. We found Max's mother's childhood home near Salisbury, found the old paths she walked in the woods when she ran away from school, before she ran away from the place and her family forever. First she fled to Washington D.C. where she found herself pregnant with Max, deserted by his father. When she found herself pregnant and deserted the second time she fled *everything,* the East, all emotional and financial security to raise her sons in dignified privacy—in the slums of downtown LA.

So many palm readers along the road from Atlanta to Danville. In the art museum in Richmond, Virginia, we kept seeing in the classical art the art of porn mags and I discovered the Egyptian myth of Isis and Osiris. So then as in the myth, the pieces of his body strewn across the land, we moved up the Jefferson Davis Highway, into even deeper layers of time and people, the Revolutionary War beneath the Civil, into ancient peoples, colonial peoples, pioneers and armies moving south. Even the kids said they could feel them, see them. We traveled from headquarters to headquarters of Lee's army from 1862 to 1864, the Confederates moving southeastward, the Union Army crossing here, the spot where Lee and Grant faced each other, over the road Sherman made his raid on his way to Richmond. *"While Lee and Grant were fighting at Spotsylvania ten thousand Union cavalry filled the road for several miles,"* the battlefields like chessboards. And Stonewall Jackson's men, the birthplace of George Rogers Clark, the kids' and my distant ancestor and *"conqueror of the Northwest." "Here the Iroquois by a treaty of 1722 agreed to deliver up runaway slaves." "Here on Little Hunting Creek Margaret Brent, secretary to Lord Baltimore* (on whose ship our family had come) *and first woman in America to demand the vote, patented land in 1663." "Near here was the Indian village Petomek where Pocahantas was kidnapped." "Washington slept here on his way to visit his mother." "Uncommon valor was a common virtue":* the Iwo Jima Marine Memorial near Quantico, Virginia. The night before we entered Washington we slept on the side of the road and were awakened by a cop, his flashlight in our faces. "This here is the colored section. You folks better move up past that light yonder."

And in a trash can at a rest stop the next morning Max and I found a large stack of glossy girly magazines, all April and May 1969 issues. These magazines had one theme: pudendum, vulva, female crotch, genitalia, pubis, beaver, cunt, quim, pussy, pink, whatever the word is. "God's Terrible Eye," Max offered. He had shared a lot of pornography with me but this was the first time either of us had seen such photos. It was the first time I knew for certain I was normal. In one magazine there was a review of a book by an editor of the *Village Voice* about Robert Kennedy, the last five years of his life, how his brother's death affected him. *"He changed from a Camelot style to a Camus style, from the knight in shining armor to living and acting only from experience."* I quoted extensively from this article in my journal, wrote nothing about the photographs. But for a long time I saw the vulvas of those women across everything.

It was very hot when we arrived in Washington D.C., the place of Maximilian's conception. We found a parking place beside a shady park. When I opened the car door I heard singing coming from the busy street. A bread truck, the kind with open sides, was slowly passing

our car. The driver, a young black man, was standing at the wheel singing the old Sam Cooke song:

You-oo-oo-ooh, se-nd me. Darling, you-oo-oo-ooh, se-nd me . . .

The tune and words lifted off the ninety degree heat, floated out of
the smelly, noisy traffic. I don't know why but I have never heard that
song since without recalling this uneventful, yet somehow out-of-the-
ordinary moment. I could almost see the song drift by us over the
green grass and waft through the treetops to the west.

We sat on a bench and made peanut butter and honey sandwiches. A
sloppily dressed, white-haired man approached us. His white, short-
sleeved dress shirt had yellow stains down the front. He wore white
suede loafers and on his briefcase was the bumper sticker: MAKE
LOVE NOT WAR. As he talked at us I saw that his clothes
were expensive, just soiled and crumpled as if he had been sleeping in
them. He wanted to know if he could help us find our way around,
that—and this came in the same breath—his son was one of the sixteen
expelled from Harvard that spring for protesting the war.

This man, so congenial, almost excessively human, was an exception. Washington seemed mostly a city of marble and granite statues.
Dead men caught in stone; ugly, grey block architecture that seems to
affect the whole flesh-and-blood populace. While the kids played on
the steps of the Supreme Court I counted ninety-eight pillars. The National Gallery of Art is the largest marble structure in the world. We
studied the long, troubled history of the construction of the Capitol.
And there are slums two blocks from it. Where they are rioting. This is
the sixties. After days of sightseeing, my five-year-old threw herself
down outside the Library of Congress and cried, "No more boys! I
don't want to visit any more statues of boys. Don't they make girl
statues?" We were both stunned. As much as we had been trying to be
newly conscious, particularly in terms of their education, we had not
realized that all the statues had been of "boys." So we sought girl
statues. We could find only one: the Jane A. Delano statue in Red
Cross Square. Delano organized the Red Cross Nurse Corps. She
looked like the Virgin Mary, or perhaps the fifty-foot white angel,
"symbolizing the womanhood of Virginia," who guards the Unknown Soldier. On the marble base was inscribed a verse from the

Ninety-first Psalm: *"Thou shall not be afraid for the terror by night. . . ."*

We spent a day in the Smithsonian. I copied all of one of Martin Luther King Jr.'s speeches. *"I believe that unarmed truth and unconditional love will have final word in reality. . . . I still believe that one day mankind will be crowned triumphant over war and bloodshed, and nonviolent redemptive goodwill proclaimed the rule of the land. . . . I still believe that we shall overcome."* We witnessed the emperor of Ethiopia, Haile Selassie, land by helicopter on the White House lawn. The city's Ethiopians turned out in native costume. The U.S. Army, fully armed too, turned out. There's a series of snapshots of David sneaking up on the whole affair with his toy gun and helmet.

We visited Arlington National Cemetery, an important one in our fascination with graveyards. In my journal I've written from some unnoted source: *"At first the residents around Arlington were startled, surprised at how fast the cemetery was suddenly filling up with boys from Viet Nam, but now they've grown used to the many daily burials."* We walked, the four of us, through the crosses, the plain, identical, small white crosses, hill over hill over hill. Darien and Max did cartwheels. David played far to our left, hiding behind the crosses in the great Civil War of his own. As I walked I could feel each man, *alive,* beneath my feet, trapped in the ground. Viet Nam veterans have said to me, "You can't know, as a woman, how bad it was." I know that this is true, but not because I didn't try. I promised I would never grow used to it, as the Arlington residents evidently had. As a result of my effort I entered my own hell. *Waste. Boys. Grief. Parents. Mortal. Gone. Ashford, Bill, St. Louis. No survivors. No connections. The Dead. The graveyard that is my country.* I walked through the crosses crying. Instead of the ritual I had come for, tears. Tears of rage. We found the Kennedy graves. The eternal flame was out. As we walked away, I began reading the long letter I had gotten that morning, care of general delivery, from Una in Moab. She was being threatened with excommunication.

We decided to visit the Senate. I followed the kids and Max down the street as I continued to read her letter. Three black guys seemed to be following us. Max was telling the kids again about poverty, about racism, about thieves, about tourists. We were parked again by the park of the first day. He fixed them sandwiches. I couldn't eat. I sat on the grass and thought about Una. I lay down and looked at the blue cloudless sky between the trees and saw a Viet Nam village on fire. The bread truck passed again, very slowly, the driver still singing:

You-oo-oo-ooh, se-nd me . . . O, darling, you-oo-oooh. . . .

Yes. You always do. But Sam Cooke is dead. He was raping a girl. The motel manager, a woman, shot him. Maximilian and Darien were jumping rope, one end of the rope tied to a tree. David was behind a tree shooting at people with a broken tree limb.

We cleaned up, locked the car, took off down the street to get our passes to the Senate and House. People turned to stare, as they had done all across the country, admiration, disgust, confusion playing across their faces. Our hippy beauty was great. I was walking in a cloud, detached at last from the world, from the dead, living inside with Una, how long I had loved her, how much had happened to us. We were in a crosswalk, waiting for the light to change when Max touched me and said, "Look. Here comes Gene McCarthy." We stepped into the street. Gene McCarthy started from the other side. We met in the middle, the cars whizzing by, a gust of wind. He was smiling at us, from ear to ear, looking exactly like one of his posters, the one in which he is grinning and his hair is blowing. *A Breath of Fresh Air. Gene McCarthy for President!* I remembered that he'd been a priest, an English professor, a poet. I wanted to wrap my arms around him to show my gratitude for him hating the war enough to break, however little, from the Establishment. He looked at the four of us, shook his head as if at something not quite believable, as if at something that greatly tickled him, and laughed.

"Hi!"

And we said hi back, our grins as large as his, and passed him. I looked back and watched him walk down the street, past the Senate Office Building. When we reached the curb we were greeted by a cop laughing at us. I said, "Yeah, well, *I* voted for Eldridge Cleaver for President!" Walking away I added under my breath, "Which asshole did you vote for?"

A Quaker group was sitting on the steps of the Senate. A very old man was reading the names of each boy dead in Viet Nam. In the crowded elevator I read another page of Una's letter. The Senate was debating the A.B.M. Army plan to install nuclear rockets around every major U.S. city. Goldwater's stiff, spindly legs surprised me. He looked like an impotent old man rather than a powerful political figure. *"We could win the war if we could just go all out,"* he was saying. The senator from Maryland was giving a speech against the war, *"Forty thousand casualties since Nixon took office, thirteen thousand last week... American boys, Vietnamese children... those responsible... the Army incompetent...the growing militarism of the government."* "It's wrong!" he summed up. But the senators weren't listening. They were reading their newspapers, smoking cigars, tapping their fingers, walking around, coughing loudly, showing their disdain for the Maryland senator and his pleas. Dirksen kept taking his teeth out. *" ...those of the generation who want everything done yesterday. ...."* I looked around. We were the only ones listening. It was hard to keep from screaming CRAP! They addressed each other as *Honorable.* They were second-rate clowns at a circus. To calm myself, I took the letter from my back pocket. Max pointed to a sign NO READING IN THE GALLERIES. Down on the floor many of the honorable senators were reading the morning newspapers. The headlines of the *LA Times* spread across the kitchen table, the Puerto Ricans shooting from these galleries when I was a child. I wanted to throw something, *shit,* down on them. They were so full of it. "The Honorable Senator Tower from Texas. ...." The Maryland Senator was addressing him between his quotes of body-count statistics. How could he address these men as honorable when he knew what he did? He was playing the game, the honorable murderers game. He didn't *feel* what he was speaking. He was *debating.* The honorable tradition of debate. The immoral tradition. I had to fight to keep from spitting. I saw myself being carried off to jail for spitting on the senators and the absurdity of that stopped me, though to sit here unprotesting was to play the same game as the Maryland senator. The whole scene, including myself in it, was disgusting.

Max whispered that the man sitting in front of us was Dan Rather. I didn't know who Dan Rather was, but I was intrigued by the ambiguous name, *rather.* Then a very attractive woman, a blonde, entered the press section, the narrow aisle in front of us, and with much commotion, girlish smiles and whispers, chose the seat next to Dan Rather. She wore a bright yellow mini-skirted sundress. Her arms were firm and golden. Her thighs, knees and calves seemed pumped full of the first hormones of puberty. Yet she was not that young. At one point she moved across the aisle. She had to press between the railing and someone sitting in the first seat. Her ass barely gave with the pressure of the rail. I still didn't realize who she was. She was so much more beautiful than her photographs. Only now, as I write this story and read of Ted Kennedy's campaign through the years for the presidency do I learn why Joan Kennedy looked so extraordinary that day. She was pregnant. Pregnant with a spirit fated not to survive. She would miscarry the following week.

Then Kennedy entered the room. "There he is," someone whispered. Her body quickened. She leaned forward. I leaned forward. *If there's anyone who has the power to stop the war.* . . . I could see that he had it. He wore a dark blue, beautiful blue, suit. A dark blue tie. As with her, his physical beauty was great, so much greater than the news photos. I remembered Una telling me of seeing his brother John in 1960. "They had been using the word *charisma,* but until I saw him in person I didn't know what they meant." Then he left. Then he was back. The Senate Whip. Everyone in the galleries whipped forward. He made several motions. Dan Rather wrote something down. How straight he held himself. His broad, blue back; how tall, blue and elegant he seemed. He looked as you would think a rich man should, not effeminate as most do. I didn't remember that he wore a back brace due to a plane accident. His hair was dark, thick and curly. The words "shock of hair" shot through me. Suddenly I saw his head fly apart, a bullet shattering it. I looked away. I took a deep breath. Max glanced at me. Then I looked again. I saw him in water. Water falling on him, his body falling through water. Again, I tried to come to the Senate floor. *This is the Ninety-first Congress.* I found myself in the shower with him. I looked at him and he was naked. I saw him making love with the woman in front of me whose perfume I was drowning in. Then we were in the water, making love. I kept trying to come back, emerge to air, make sense of what I was seeing. My attempts to restore logic to my mind simply put us in something like a shower stall together, inside an enclosed container, rather than in the chaos of the open sea. I was taking a shower with him. He was masturbating. I was going down on him. The water was falling all around us. He was afraid he was drowning. I became afraid I would drown. I became afraid of him. He was in my arms. Understand me, my brother died just a year ago. You have the power to stop the war, can't you feel each life you could save? I saw that he could. I saw that his tragedy is in knowing the killing and knowing that he will do nothing to stop it.

Max was watching me. He pointed to the sign N O D E M O N S T R A - T I O N S I N T H E G A L L E R I E S. For someone who had been to prison three times he was so conservative when it came to me. I frightened him. But he had no idea what was really happening to me. And though I longed to share it with him I knew, as with so many things important to me, he would not let me. So I was whispering in the man's ear I love you. You could save us. Stop the war. *Now!* Before another life is lost.

But after awhile I lost interest in the Senate Whip. He wasn't going to do anything. I left him, despairing, my feelings spreading through the room. I could hear the roll call of the dead coming from the Quakers outside on the steps. Nixon was raised a Quaker. Now his mother disowns him. The Whip started to leave the room. He stopped near the back entrance, turned around and looked up, high into the galleries. He must have been looking for her but she had left. Our eyes met. We floated in water. I reached out for him. He stared at me. How can you stand there while so many are dying in your name? Then I looked away. I was afraid. It is hard to look a murderer in the eyes. When I looked back he was still staring at me, motionless before the door. Then he looked, puzzled, to my right, then to my left, and then back at me. S T O P T H E W A R! He said something. He gestured slightly with his right hand. Then he went out the door.

"Let's go to the House," Max said. We left the Senate Chamber, moved down the corridor lined with the marble busts of all the vice presidents. The hall was crowded with senators, reporters, tourists. We were stopped by the crowd before an enormous mural of *The Battle of Lake Erie*—life-sized dead bodies floating around their hero: Someone, Whoever, a Man. A huge crystal chandelier dominated the center of this room. Money enough, I kept thinking, to feed how many of the poor just two blocks from here? *"I have the audacity to believe that people everywhere can have three meals a day. . . ."* We stood at the railing. I was trying to calm myself, but now Max was exploding, *Those fuckers!* I could hardly hear him. I was trying not to hear him. I was afraid of what I might do. The violent emotions churned my stomach. I have my children here. *Right temporarily defeated is stronger than evil triumph.* But all I could think of was finding a brick to throw at the gaudy chandelier. A good lesson for my children. One they wouldn't forget. The violent emotions became violent joy whenever I looked at them, touched them. They guided me into an elevator instinctively, knowing their mother. I took the letter from my pocket and began reading. We came to the House of Representatives just as Una was describing her four-day sit-in before the twelfth floor door of the Apostle of Bindings in Salt Lake City, petitioning for divorce. I sighed, knew joy, *knowledge of this woman is one of the great blessings of my life.* On the fourth day he admitted her. I knew she'd succeed. Such spiritual courage she has. It doesn't matter how different our lives are, that we both abhor the trappings of the other's path. We recognize each other. Anarmed, unconditionally. Again, the sign NO READ-ING IN THE GALLERIES. I put the letter in my pocket. We entered. They were discussing the oil spill in Santa Barbara, a bill or resolution to provide federal aid for the emergency. Max was cursing, *"The oil companies should pay!"* But I could feel very little of it now. My psychic involvement had peaked, was silly and useless I knew again—again and again through those years the despair—as I started coming down. I'm a fish floating in oil. I am left here with just my body. I'm a drowned creature washed ashore, just the fetus of our love. I felt another burst of love for my kids who had been so quiet and attentive. I saw Mingo's beautiful land, the cow Jersey. I wanted to find such a place for them. I remembered how fucked up Mingo was, the men in the Mississippi Delta Lounge. How fucked up we all are in this country.

Now a woman was sitting to my left. She was blonde too, another version of myself. Except her whole persona was "proper." I was chewing my fingers, wearing cut-off levis. Her nails were long and polished.

She wore an expensive but colorless linen dress. Her shoulder-length hair was pulled neatly off her forehead and neck. She was taking notes—a sort of writer, a legislator's aid, perhaps—on her job, making money. What was it that happened in my life that has blessedly kept me from being her? Moral compromise as the dance of each day of your life. With my Master's now I could do that, make some money, buy a farm, buy the kids things, send them to good schools, sacrifice the present for the future, what all parents say you have to do. But *fuck! Blood money is blood money!* There are no jobs, careers not paid in it! To truly love my children, to raise them not to be soldiers, whores, mindless workers—that's the task. To teach them about money, about genuine honor, about real beauty, to show them their country, the land and its people beneath its corruption, stupidity, its genocidal history. I had to grasp the railing, put my head down between my outstretched arms. My uterus cramping. Sea life, unaccountable numbers destroyed. I watched the murderers through the frame of my long hair, smoking cigars, chatting to one another. Their guffaws floated up in the polluted air. I'm a California gull trying to fly to Utah to my mate, but my wings are pinned down in oil. I'm the rejected lover, the woman jumping from the bridge, my cunt scraped across everything. The child of our revolutionary love a pool of blood in Watts. I stared at my thighs, bare in front of my face, somehow in that moment more me than any other part of me. My fat thighs, Mama's thighs. I'm a good swimmer. But oh, Max, even when I knew for sure I was against abortion. Abortion is murder. The soft blond hairs glistened in oil. I was going to disappear with the kids so that you wouldn't be forced to marry me. Or desert me. I'd spare you everything. Even making a decision. I'd have our child, my unconditional love, though I might not ever see you again. It happened that first night on your mom's floor, after moving all day out of our apartment to go on this trip, you punched a hole in my diaphragm, your cock, your dick you call it, so long, too long, those weeks at your mother's, getting ready to leave, waiting for my period, I began to see her, Sonia, her life, the already-run movie of what mine was about to be. Her god-awful life on Arapahoe. Fuck, whatever happened to the Arapahoe, were they ever in LA? Your mom fleeing everything, for *what*? For love of a man she would never see again. Your father you'll never know. The scars on you, Max, on her, on your brother, are terrible. A repetition of that story in your life would be evil. *You,* now, the unknown, longed for father. God I started seeing sex and gender at the heart of everything. I can't explain it Max but I *know* it's true, *Viet Nam is about sex!* So finally I told you, I'm pregnant. You said it instantly, what I'd not thought of, abortion, started making the arrangements. I just got out of prison, I have to be free. I've helped support my mother and brother since I was eight. You took me to your corners where you sold the *LA Times* at rush hour, told me the terrible stories. It's crucial to keep this revolution going, it's wrong, the murder of both our futures for the sake of an unformed foetus, the accidental exuberance of our fucking. That's what's always gone wrong with couples. I began to see your point, for me to take all the consequences is wrong. To have your baby against your will is wrong. The life is equally both of ours. Both of us must alter our age-old patterns. The female's physical martyrdom, the male's disassocia-tion are basic in the polarization of the sexes. The Revolution is our love lives. I have to learn to be a man, you have to learn to be a woman. And so though I loved our child inside me and knew it as murder—I would not be so cowardly as to abandon the truths of my old con-sciousness, I sought to be more conscious—I finally agreed. I moved into that state like an Indian making prayer to the animal or enemy she is about to kill. I believed you were doing this too, making the gender leap into me as I was making it into you, your whole life such leaps. You went to prison rather than obey them, your moral integrity and courage is the reason I love you. Though you can't even say those words, *I love you.* So afraid. Your lost father. I know you're looking for him Max, Maximilian Rainbow, down there on the chamber floor.

I pulled Una's letter out then and continued to read. I'd take a chance, at least on this, of getting kicked out of the United States House of Representatives, to finish it. Permission for the divorce was granted. I began to calm. I took a deep breath. Emily Dickinson's line came to me *"After great pain a formal feeling comes. . . ."*

1969. It seems a little unbelievable now that Chappaquiddick and the moon landing were the same weekend, that Woodstock occurred three weeks later. In little over a month Everett Dirksen would be dead and we would be back in Los Angeles when the Sharon Tate murders would occur, and a week later we would be camped on a beach at Big Sur with members of the Manson family, who, unbeknownst to us, were on the run. It would be on that beach that I would read the first news leaks of My Lai, in the *Berkeley Barb*. And doubt, even I, the veracity of the account, wonder on the nature of sensationalism. 1969: drugs or no drugs, the country was on an acid trip.

We spent the rest of that week in New York City. Each day was hotter than the one before. We found the kids' Russian great-grandmother out on Long Island. She was the lost side of their father's family—lost, though all four of us bear her name. She turned out to be a writer and a mystic, her work a fusion of the two. We tried to sleep one night in the car on something like 95th Street near Riverside. I kept opening my eyes to a man seated, beyond the colorful, all-night sidewalk throne, in an armchair at his open window reading *Siddhartha* by Herman Hesse. About two a.m. we gave up, drove up to the Bronx where we found a dark churchyard to sleep in. On all the walls of the subways were posters announcing the concert to be held at Woodstock. As with Janis's concert in Atlanta, we didn't consider going. A year and a half before Lyndon Johnson had come to Century Plaza Hotel in Los Angeles and we had taken David and Darien. It was one of our first dates. It was a mistake. The panicky crowd, the helicopters overhead with machine guns pointed at us, the rioting, the beatings terrified them. I didn't think they were ready yet to handle large crowds again.

We went up the coast, New Haven, New London, Providence, Boston, Salem, towns two hundred and fifty years older than California towns. On Friday, July 18, the hottest day of the year, we drove out to Cape Cod. We visited Hyannis Port, a quaint little village. I bought candy in a little store for the kids. On the wall were photographs of John Kennedy home from the White House on a Friday afternoon, buying candy for the neighborhood kids. A policeman stood in the middle of the narrow, tree-lined street turning cars away from the compound.

We looked for a beach. We were excited. Our first night to sleep outside since Vicksburg. We had slept in the car all through the South: the heat, the bugs, the rain, the fear of snakes, the cities, the fear of rednecks. The movie *Easy Rider* wasn't released for another month but we had heard the stories. We scouted one beach that looked back onto the Kennedy Compound. I was filled with a sudden loathing. I didn't want our night under the stars to be tainted by the sight. After almost giving up, we found the perfect beach, far enough away from everything to not attract the police. Grass, hills, sand dunes, low tide, exposed rocks, a small hotel a mile away, the sun setting over the land, the moon coming up over the ocean. How backwards that seemed to us Californians! The kids marveled at it. I studied the map. We were facing south toward Martha's Vineyard. We put our bags between the mounds of two sand dunes, up from what we estimated was the high-water line. We built a fire for dinner, roasted marshmallows afterwards. The three of them fell asleep early. But I was excited with the sea, with the night, with the stars, with my new awareness of the constellations, with an odd sense that I was learning to read the land, with the first time to myself in weeks. I pulled a T-shirt over my bikini. I walked a long way in one direction, digging my feet into the warm sand, dancing back beneath the moon in the low melodic tide. The Atlantic Ocean! I was born in Seaside Hospital on the Pacific Ocean! I ran. I sat on top of a sand dune and wondered in which direction the tide ran, facing the east, facing south, and watched the moon climb, quartered, cloud-teased. *There are men headed for it! Soon they will land.* My period started, the warm, sweet blood, the show on my fat thighs. I was so late. Is it because men are messing with the moon? When I remembered the abortion, I walked into the dark sea. A bath. I need a bath. I'm a good swimmer.

But the climb out of the cold water was hard with the contraction of the uterus and all its tendrils into the thighs. The small of my back ached. I lay in my bag. I watched the moon. *There are men headed for it.* The Eagle ship on the Apollo mission. Falling asleep. Deep down, then up from water. Dunes. The quarter moon. In Virgo. Men are entering. In Salem we had visited the custom house that Nathaniel Hawthorne wrote about in *The Scarlet Letter.* A red "A" for adultery. We walked on a wharf built before the Revolutionary War to outfit pirates.

They stole fortunes. Now they're the country's oldest, best families. Old Salem town where they burned women. *Here lies Judge Sewabe of the Witch Trials. Shit! Here is the House of Seven Gables.*

Then I was awakened. Something. Something was calling me. Something out in the water. Something very sad. I was dreaming of a drowning baby. But there was a strange double sense about the dream, the sense that someone was really drowning while I merely dreamed that a baby was drowning. In the dream I must wake up because someone is trapped alive in a large container under the water. A double sense, a container of air deep in the water. There is time to save the person. All I have to do is wake up and go to the water. I sat up. I looked out to the sea. The water was like glass though the tide was coming in. The moon had gone to the west. I was only dreaming. I felt sorrow and a lot of fear. Go back to sleep. It's just one of those dreams.

I lay back in the sand dune. *Thou shalt not be afraid for the terror by night.* . . . I turned on my side. Now I dreamed of a glass toy that has fallen into a plastic swimming pool beneath the elm tree in the front yard of my girlhood home. It was the elm tree I always climbed to see into the neighbors' backyards, to see what was happening on the other side of the railroad tracks, to see the ocean fifteen miles away. From the branches I saw a girl trapped inside the glass toy. She was banging on the glass trying to get out. She saw me watching her. She called to me, pleaded with her eyes. How can you lie there and let me drown? Her anger was terrible, that I could see her drowning and do nothing about it. She curled into the foetal tuck, floated in her amniotic sac. There is still time. Please. You must wake up and save me. Please . . .

Again I rose in the sand dune. *Who is it?* My inadequacies, my fear, my sorrow were unbearable. *You have the power to save me?* How? What must I do? *You have the power to save me because you can see. Hurry! Before it's too late. Can't you feel how I want to live?*

Darien had kicked off the top of her bag. I covered her. My sweet mysterious girlchild. The moonlight glowed on David's gold curls. And Maximilian, my man. I am so in love with you. But where is our baby? Do you love me? I stay with you because you fuck so well you said the last time I broke and asked you that. And I answered that's as holy a reason as any. You said you needed a place to store your things.

You'd be on the road most of the time. You couldn't commit yourself to a relationship, a woman with two children. But here we are, two years later, on the road together. There's no such thing as love you said another time. Then I'm a drowned creature for loving you, our baby dead. Why even live? I lay back down on the Cape Cod sand dune. I'm sorry. I don't know what else to do. Maybe you're just the men in the space capsule swimming to the moon. The menstrual moon. They must be in trouble. What does life mean anyway? What does anything mean?

All the next day as we continued up the coast the kids and Max sang *"We all live in a yellow submarine, a yellow submarine . . ."* The dream with its double urgency and terrible double images would return to me. I told them of it, wondering at the coincidence of this song they had never sung before, but they maintained that they were singing about our life in the Falcon. From that day, though the Falcon was blue, Yellow Submarine was its name. While Max drove and they sang I sat in the back seat and wrote the dream into my journal, *"Friday night, July 18, on a beach near the Kennedy Compound."* In Gloucester I looked down all the streets for Charles Olson. I knew I'd recognize him. His poetry had given me hope. The fog came in and while Max and the kids had hot chocolate in Dunkin' Donuts I walked to rid my-self of the dream's images. Instead, Olson's words, that I didn't know I knew, came to me. *"Offshore, by islands hidden in the blood, jewels and miracles, I, Maximus, a metal hot from boiling water. . . ."*

We spent Sunday on a beach in Oqunquit, Maine. Max almost got busted for changing into his trunks behind the dressing room. He kept screaming in California they don't charge money to change your clothes. Somehow the three of us appeased the cop. We piled into the Yellow Submarine, drove north three miles to Wells Beach, and then, for the first time in almost three months, headed west.

Around six that night, we stopped for gas in a little Appalachian town between Maine and New Hampshire. I walked back through a filthy, dilapidated garage to the bathroom. The radio was on. The moon broadcast. I looked into the cracked, greasy mirror and remem-bered the dream. I had quit wearing make-up on the trip and I saw for the first time that I looked good without it. I put in a tampon. At the pump I asked the old woman attendant if they had landed on the moon yet. First she said yes. Then when I questioned her closer she said, "They've only set the thing down."

"When will they land?"

"Tomorrow morning. But then, you know, it's midnight where they are."

"It's midnight on the moon?"

"No. It's midnight in Houston, Texas. So they may start the moon-walk *anytime*. There's six hours difference, you know, between here and Houston."

Driving away, even the kids laughing that it couldn't be midnight in Texas, their having learned that much about time and the country, driving all night through New Hampshire and Vermont, I kept wondering, *what time is it on the moon?* Three days later, in Ohio, coming out of a Stucky's Restaurant on the Interstate, the four of us licking ice cream cones, I glanced for the first time in weeks at the newspaper headlines. The newsstand. My thighs went weak. The blood again. *Some things take a long time to tell.* But it was true. She was drowning.

The Art of Seeing With One's Own Eyes

It is the need to enter what we loosely call the vision to be one with the Imago Mundi, that image of the world we each carry within us as possibility itself.

Robert Creeley

Only off in the West is the glorious light of the setting sun telling us, perhaps, of light after darkness.

Edward Curtis

I remember the night as Halloween, the night of the Dead, Halloween as in "holy person, hence saint," the dictionary explains, but looking back in my journal I discover that it was the Autumn Equinox. At any rate, it was Vermont in fall and harvest was greatly upon us. The first frost had come, we had brought in our garden: root-stringy, dirt-clodded green tomato plants hanging upside down on our apartment walls. *Allende dead,* my notes say, *Victor Jara's fingers cut off, Agnew may be impeached.* An *I Ching* quote: "*Superior man on the decline. Inferior man on the rise. A time of this.*" Someone coming up the stairs. A knock on the door. A young woman, a Jehovah's Witness, walking in with pamphlets: THE WORLD IS COMING TO AN END IN TEN DAYS. Me in my nightgown. "We are canvassing all of central Vermont. We are trying to give nonbelievers a chance."

All week at Goddard, the local college, the Stan Brakhage Film Festival had been occurring, the filmmaker himself hosting the event. Stan Brakhage's affinity with Charles Olson, the first poet to inspire me, made his presence in town exciting. "*The sentence as an exchange of force rather than a completed thought,*" the journal notes exclaim. "FORM IS NEVER MORE THAN AN EXTENSION OF CONTENT!" My journals from those days are dominated by Olson.

At 7:30 P.M. we dropped windowpane acid. We had done some the week before, a trip that was wondrous. It had been my first acid in a year and a half, our first in Vermont, a warm, emotional experience of great love between Maximilian and me. We spent that Sunday canoeing around a beautiful lake in the Northeast Kingdom, a lake named Eden. Of the many lakes of the Kingdom we picked Lake Eden because Eden is my maiden name. The photographs of that day are my favorite photographs of us. We are floating over an enormous mirror of giant flaming maple trees that line the shore, through a brilliant red, orange, maroon and gold paradise. If lysergic acid diethylamide can be photographed in the cells of the body it is in these pictures. We look at each other as if eternity cannot separate us. Max looks like Jesus with his full beard and long black curls, his image rippling back from the water. I am wearing lace and jewelry, a rarity for me. A red and green glass-bead bracelet, which had arrived that week from Nic, a friend traveling in Guatemala, shimmers, catching the light above my oar. The smell of patchouli oil can't be photographed either but I smell it when I look at these photographs. On that day there was a big sun eruption estimated ten times the size of the earth, equal to one hundred million atom bombs. "There was a twenty-minute period after the flare reached its peak when long-distance short-wave radio communications on earth experienced a complete fadeout," the Space Warning Center in Boulder, Colorado said. "Particles ejected by the flare are expected to reach the earth's vicinity tonight or early tomorrow causing magnetic disturbances and possibly auroral displays in the low latitudes." We walked in the dark woods, the sun filtering through the autumn leaves to the ferns on the floor. The whole world seemed benevolently aflame. And then we fucked, very gently, standing up, face to face, while a soft rain fell on us. We lay on the shore and stared into each other's eyes a long time. "What is this?" he said, in a momentary flash of his normal embarrassment at intimacy. "A love trip?" That night we saw our first Brakhage film. I wrote *"Infinite parts/The Body/The Self/floating in infinite directions./The myth outside/The stars inside./We are caught in the bodies of others."* On our walk home from Goddard we stopped in at friends who were watching the movie *Tora, Tora, Tora*. "Tora, Tora, Tora" was the Japanese code for the bombing of Pearl Harbor. I was struck for the first time by an understanding of the great difference between persons born before World War II and those born during or afterwards. The difference bombs make on the new psyche. We stayed up all night. The neighbor living below us said later he knew we had dropped acid when he woke at four in the morning and we were still giggling.

But tonight, as soon as we dropped, the phone rang. Max answered it. I heard him explain that we were on our way to a movie but that yes they were welcome to come over for about fifteen minutes. They were two friends of Passing Cloud, an old LA friend now living in Taos, New Mexico. Passing Cloud had given them our address when they left New Mexico for Montreal on an important business trip. We regarded Passing Cloud as one of our craziest, least-reliable friends—we had many in those days—so we prepared ourselves for the possibility of a screwy encounter. Or so we must have thought we prepared.

We were prepared for hippies from Taos. The two men who entered our apartment looked like Chicago gangsters, at least as they are portrayed in old movies. They were sturdy middle-aged men in dark suits, black silky dress shirts, white ties and identical Panama hats beneath which twitched pencil-thin moustaches. They seemed charged with a great conspiratorial air. When they removed their hats the glisten and smell of hair oil and the exposed skin around their ears and necks were shocking. This was 1973; this was not the current look. No one in their right minds, I thought, looks like these guys. Certainly no one I knew. Perhaps they walked in just as the acid started coming on.

We were as cordial and friendly as possible, engaging them in the usual questions of first encounters and explaining where we were going. We told them how to get to the theater in case they were interested in seeing the film. I couldn't imagine that they would be. Such men as these could have little interest or patience in the art of Stan Brakhage. I was already a little hung-up on trying to figure out who they were. I was afraid of them and did not want to leave them in our home. In a while our children would return. They said they would walk around town and perhaps attend the film later. When we left the building we noticed their car: a highly waxed and polished black antique limousine with New Hampshire license plates. Again, I had the sense of gangsters, the shot of the car pulled up to do a job.

We walked the mile to the school. The film this night, culminating the festival, was to be Brakhage's current masterpiece, *The Act of Seeing with One's Own Eyes.* The hour-and-a-half film takes place in the main Philadelphia city morgue. The subject is autopsy, the technique documentation. Our program explained that the etymology of "autopsy" is "seeing with one's own eyes." It was very cold and we, native Californians, were happily bundled in our new thrift-store coats and hats. Max said he read that LSD opens the lens of the eyes wider than normal, letting in more light so that you see more of what is actually here. "Hallucination is an incorrect word. It's just that the brain, used to the old programming, can't process what the eyes are newly seeing."

I was looking forward to an autopsy film. I was curious as to how a great artist would handle such a subject. One of the first stories I ever wrote was in reaction to the autopsy report in the Warren Commission's *The Assassination of President Kennedy.* The reading of that report was for me as bad as any bad acid trip I would ever take. I found little interest in the statistics proving how he died; that he was dead was the shock. The body of John Fitzgerald Kennedy is described in graphic detail: a muscular, well-developed, well-nourished adult Caucasian male measuring 72 1/2 inches and weighing 170 pounds. His hair is reddish brown and abundant, his eyes are blue. And skewed, divergent, deviated. We are told that he has an unremarkable bony cage. His teeth are in excellent repair. We are told of old well-healed and recent incisions on the nipple line, the lumbar spine, the abdomen, the right thigh. His genitals are not described, but the cutting of the customary Y beginning at the nipple line deep into rigor and algor mortis muscle to examine his body cavities is. His lungs are well aerated with smooth, glistening pleural surfaces and they are grey-pink in color. There is an area of purplish-red discoloration. His right lung weighs 320 grams, his left 290 grams. A straw-colored fluid floats in his pericardial cavity. His heart is of normal external contour and weighs 350 grams. His coronary arteries are dissected and analysed for us. His liver, spleen, kidneys and intestines are described, as are the many hernias and lacerations and bloodclots. There is abnormal mobility of the underlying bone above the right eye caused by a sizable metal fragment. He has a large skull defect with an actual absence of scalp and bone and ex-uding from it is lacerated brain tissue which on close inspection proves to represent the major portion of his right cerebral hemisphere. At this moment in the autopsy, federal agents bring the coroners three pieces of bone recovered from Elm Street and the presidential automobile. When put together, these fragments account for approximately three-quarters of the missing portion of his skull. Then the scalp wounds in his coronal plane are extended to examine his cranial content. His brain is removed and preserved for further microscopic study. A Gross Description of his brain is given. Following Formalin fixation it weighs 1500 grams. Photographs, colored and black and white, and roentgenograms are taken of his entire body, inside and out. He is sewed back up for burial preparation.

My story is of a young woman who never fully recovers from read-ing this report. Like so many she had idolized John Kennedy. Know-ing exactly how much his brain weighed, that he had an "unremarkable bony cage," were facts demonic to her psyche, facts she found herself wishing—though she was a twentieth-century child and a full partici-pant in its glories—could not be known by anyone. She thought of how the Indians in her home town said you lose your power if you tell everything. How much does the spirit weigh? In which cavity does the personality reside? What happens to these men in the minutes they are handling John Kennedy's brain? How do you weigh the shock the na-tion experienced at his murder? Which investigation will prove who killed him? Are there "lacerating," "herniating," "exuding" residues still? In the air, in our food?

Still, I anticipated identification with Stan Brakhage's effort. If I were a filmmaker it is conceivable that I would film an autopsy. I am making such a story now. The *art* of seeing with one's own eyes. Brak-hage had built his career on seeing what our culture makes taboo. A 1957 film, *Flesh of Morning,* is "an intense, introspective and totally controlled work about masturbation." "It is so important to *see*," I said to Maximilian as we walked down Highway 2, "to see our way out of the programing of our culture."

I told him of a car accident I was in when I was sixteen. "There were five of us. I was in the back seat. We were speeding down Angel Canyon when we met another car coming up on a blind curve. Both drivers made the same, instantaneous decision, to crash head-on, rather than swerve off the five-hundred-foot drop into the granite canyon. Somehow we made it, everyone was okay, though one of our wheels was off the edge, the fenders scraped and ripped. What I was most struck by afterwards was that while my friends buried their heads in their laps when they saw the car I sat up straighter, my eyes bulging, straining to see my own death coming at me. In that moment I felt fierce about this. I wanted to *see* myself die. It seemed everything was being taken from me and all I had left in this split second of life was sight and so I would use it."

The theater was nearly full when we arrived, students and hippies come down out of the mountains for a Friday night movie. The colors and costumes and abundant hair swirled and mixed wildly with the smells of woodstoves, patchouli, marijuana. People were festive, inviting, orgiastic, the clear invitation to sex exuding from many. Open marriage was the newest popular attempt to break through our puritanical programming and many couples this night, well-known among us all, seemed ecstatic with their new daring, their new discoveries.

But I couldn't talk. The acid was coming on strong, my throat was dry, I was afraid I might throw up. I held onto Max's arm and he found two empty seats in the front row. As we sat in them, I knew instantly they were a mistake. I felt on stage, exposed. At the same time I felt unable to get up, to move through the thronging people to the back. I waited for the lights to go out to do this, for the veil of darkness. But then, Stan Brakhage was introduced and an inhibiting silence fell through the room. He began a long talk about his films. I couldn't move.

It was an evening of strange men; perhaps this is why I remember it as Halloween. Brakhage seemed a sort of triplet to the two men who had come to our house. He too was large, big boned, sturdy. He was wearing a black tuxedo. His thick black hair, with a streak of silver down the middle, was oiled and cut very short and he was clean shaven. All through his amazing lecture he would stop mid-sentence, turn his head to the right, simultaneously pull from beneath his coat tails a small silver spittoon. I could hardly believe my eyes. The arc of spit across the lights from this man dressed so severely, so strangely, so formally like the president, was bizarre. "Style," he said twice between spits, "is social manifestation of soul."

He described his films as "meditations of sexuality, meditations of light." "We are locked in creation at a certain level," he said, "and we can't get out. This is the fact of our existence. The trick is to find the key, the process is to get back to the garden, but the *purpose* of the riddle is to celebrate the mystery. My films celebrate the mystery.

"My themes are birth, sex and death. I don't know about other artists, but when I work I sweat, snot comes out of my nose. Between me and film it can't be otherwise. I have a mold chamber. I grow mold on my films. I mean, how do you keep on as a filmmaker in a field that struggles to be an art and not Hollywood escapist and I am left with the rags and tags of a Sam Peckinpah?"

I was feeling overwhelmed. Sam Peckinpah's daughter, a friend of ours, was in the room. "Max, can't we move?" I looked around. The theater behind us was full now, people lining the three walls. "The way Hollywood separates the dream sequences from reality as if they aren't the same thing." Max whispered, "There's no place to go," and then added apprehensively, "Anything you want to tell me?" My paranoia was making him paranoid. Does he think Brakhage is turning me on? I put my hand on his thigh. I thought of the letter I had received that morning from my friend, Ramona, about her brother Verne being anesthetized and manacled to the hospital wall to receive twenty electric shocks. "Reich," Brakhage was saying, "was organically insane, I mean, not functioning at the end of his life." Maniacs, I was thinking, we are all maniacs, manacled to our bodies, speeding blindly down our lonely one-way canyons. "Vision," he was saying, "is a part of our separateness. Your vision is you, it makes you separate from others. Vision is just the inside of your head. These films are just what's inside my head. Fish, bodies, sand, wagon of my childhood. The word 'vision' is elevating and idealizing, but it's just simply one's take on the world."

Max whispered, "That smile of his is a trip."

"Remember Olson. 'There are no hierarchies, no infinite, no such many as mass. There are only eyes in all heads to be looked out of.' I'm reading Pound again these days. The artist's business is to discover his *virtue,* the particularity that distinguishes him from all others. His signature.

"My goal is to photograph an angel." Suddenly he demanded from the audience, "Has anyone here ever seen an angel?" He waited for a response. To myself, I answered yes. A few in the crowd must have raised their hands. He challenged them. "I mean a *real* angel. With *wings.* Not some light around the body that looks like wings. Angels must be real or why would they be so prevalent in the paintings of European culture? Many have seen them. It is my goal to photograph an angel."

He began to prepare us for *The Act of Seeing with One's Own Eyes.* The large, dark body took on a manner and tone that was apologetic, like a stern father who must do his duty toward his children. "It should be clear that this is not a window on an autopsy room. This is a *motion picture* made up of twenty-four still shots and an equal number of blank shots per second. It is made up of different kinds of film, for a greater range of color. Color is one of the themes of this film. One should make of this film a song. It is composed as a song. Even so, my films do not have sound. Sound distracts the eyes from seeing. Any sound on a sound track is more distracting than the same sound in an audience of any situation. *Equality* of *seeing:* this is what I am after.

"There's humor in this film. Humor is everywhere. Humor of vision. Humor in sound. Humor in Beethoven. Humor of thought. Humor in nature. When you lie down in a field and notice one weed blowing faster than the others, that's funny." He arced his wad into the silver cuspidor, a funny arc of light. "Art is gentle in that images are better than the light that people bounce off reality. Art is not escapist. It is not something different. This film is like the *Tibetan Book of the Dead* in that it is a map of what the Dead experience." When he said it again, it was a command. "Art is gentle. One should make of this film a song. It is composed as a song."

The body is wheeled in on the gurney, the white sheet removed from a naked male about sixty, the saw started up. The light is glaring, white fluorescent, without shadow. There can be no secrets here. Nothing can hide from us. The morticians, Brakhage has said, are artists. He also used the word *lover.* Noguchi, LA's coroner, for so long the bogeyman of my dreams, he who did Monroe, he who brags of having written the masterpiece of our times, the autopsy report of Robert Kennedy, leaps into my mind.

In Stan Brakhage's full-length documentation we are shown the autopsies of a half a dozen bodies. It is true, one of the themes of the film is color. The shocking red of blood under the white light, the pink of lungs, the ash of flesh. I can't remember now the color of the brain, the liver.

There is a deft build-up in the drama of images. It is true, orchestration like a song. I began to hear *no, no, no*. When the second body is wheeled in and the sheet removed, we, the audience, gasp. She is young and very beautiful, a small, dark brunette. She is the star of this movie, a famous movie star without a name. The white lines of her bikini are in such sharp contrast to the deep tan of her beautiful skin, one thinks for an instant that she is wearing it. Perhaps she drowned today at the beach, so recently she bathed in the sun, walked her perfect body for us.

But this is a story of the Dead. This body is who she is. Two of them, one at her feet, one at her shoulders, lug her over to another table. She sags heavily between them. They are hard workers. I keep hearing *sorry, sorry, sorry*. The old man takes great pride in his work. He revs the saw, then grinds down her middle, counter the bikini lines. Her high-pointed white breasts unzip, then slide under her shaved armpits. Black individual hairs of her pubis blow in the saw's wind. Her perfect hips, which arch high and erotically over the perfect line of her buttocks, are chainsawed in two. Everything oozes, is slush, the myths broken in a marshland. They scoop her out. Then, they burn open her skull. Her face, which in our culture would be described as cute, falls down around the neck, then is turned inside out. Later, when they put it back on, they stretch it over the remains of her skull which they have battered with hammers, just like a rubber Halloween mask.

I've never had the experience of knowing or remembering a past life. But now I remembered being dead. I remembered being a corpse, of being handled this way. Flop me on the table, do your work. Drain my blood, weigh my brain, finger my heart, my cunt, remove everything, liver, intestines, kidneys, clitoris, muscles, my white fat, my bones.

You are so desperate to find out. You believe that you can.

I felt great compassion and grief for myself. I remembered the pain in the dead body, the same, no less, for all the so-called anesthesia of death, as pain in life. I knew the full consciousness behind the fully paralyzed body. Now the monolith. Centered. Massive. They boast of a common anesthesia used in childbirth that you feel the pain but later you have no memory of it. The cruelty in this proclamation is characteristic of our utter disdain and incomprehension of the present. We are anesthetized to the present, but our insides, our inner being gutted wide open to the world, for all time, for anyone, always knows, always remembers.

People were leaving the theater, though not as many as one would have thought. We seemed riveted to our seats. There seemed to be some test involved, a test of courage, of intellectual courage. Or perhaps it was spiritual. I looked back once and saw the two New Mexico men and a pregnant friend leaving together by the same door.

You say this is not a window on an autopsy room, that this is a song. The coroner is talking. Behind him are six headless gutted torsos, six extremely remarkable bony cages. The image is truly grotesque, shocking. The poor, poor body, rifled, sacked, emptied, an utterly empty husk. I kept hearing *cask. cage. coffin. shell.* I kept hearing sobbing, an uncontrollable sobbing. Hang me in a locker, sell me as a side of beef. Throw me in a red baggie for further microscopic study. I saw Sioux children sleighing down snowy hills in the rib cage of bison. I was afraid I'd start sobbing. No. No. No. I remembered my lover Milton. He had worked as a mortician assistant in LA and he would tell stories, like the little old lady who fell out of her casket during the funeral, fell stiff, head over heels down a Forest Lawn hill. "Like a plank of plywood, like an upright tree," before the whole family. There is humor in everything. In the story of the mother who wanted the ring off her daughter's finger, so he broke the finger off, the quickest way to get the ring. When Milton and I made love he never came, not once did he ejaculate though we spent most of our time in bed. He just stayed hard. Ramona always excused her husband for being so cold and cruel because for the first three years of their marriage he had to work nights in the Pomona morgue to support his other family.

The walk back home was hard, like coming back from the dead. I don't know what Maximilian was feeling, he was very silent, but I felt crucified. Just keep moving, I told myself, try not to see the blood the blood everywhere. The organs hanging like fruit, like pine cones, like fall-colored maple leaves, the liver, the heart, the brain, the beautiful lungs fallen to earth. Art is gentle, but reality is violent, the real dead are everywhere.

When we got to the meadow we lay on our backs, mindless of the cold. Give up the body, let the world in. Down my right side it was hard to know where I left off, where he began. Beneath us the creation, above us the reception. "Can you feel the earth spinning?" How often in our years together Maximilian asked me this. "Do you remember? This is the equinox. The day the sun crosses the equator, making day and night of equal lengths in all parts of the earth. Imagine," and he put his fingers down my pubis, "all parts of the earth."

The word equinox made me think again of Olson. I had been trying to understand his essay, "Equal, That Is, to the Real Itself," with its address to Melville and its great discussion of language using the mathematical metaphor of congruence. The corpses in the movie seemed perfect illustrations of his thesis, of "what really matters, THE THING ITSELF, that anything impinges on us its self-existence, without reference to any other thing," the corpse itself, not the spirit or soul or history of the person as it leaves the corpse. "Matter," he writes of the whale, "offers perils wider than humanity if it doesn't do what still today seems the hardest for it to do, outside art and science; to believe that things, and present ones, are the absolute conditions. . . ."

The constellations passed above us. Max quoted bathroom graffiti he had just seen. "Know your own archetype." "I'm blind Orion," I answered, "chasing the sun, seeking the eyes promised me if I can catch the light rising in the east."

"When I die," he answered, "I want to be cremated. Promise me you won't let them do an autopsy. Steal my body if you have to. Do you promise? They might accuse you of murder."

I promised. And then I made him promise the same thing. "But I don't want to be cremated. I want to be laid in the earth naked without a coffin. I don't want *anything* done to me. Oh, Max, don't let them put their hands on me then. I want to go back naturally, as it is meant, to the earth.

"The Sufis believe," I went on, "we are creating God as God is creating us." I touched him. "So we and God can see ourselves. A continuous recurrence of creation. They believe we are the *place* of God. *I am creating you as you are creating me.* They say this two-fold manifestation is the appeasement of God's sadness."

When we got up, continued our walk home, the world of the dead and the world of the living seemed a little more in balance. As we stood before our apartment building that held our sleeping children it seemed the archetypal house. The black, archetypal gangster car was still parked in front of it. The stars and planets whirled above the peaked roof that swayed on the curve of the earth into the deep blue-black night of infinity. But there is no infinity. He held me in front of him, his penis growing hard on my soft ass, my soft ass blooming erect to enclose him. The soul, someone said, is like a bucketful of water. It can be spilled.

At the top of the stairs, the two men from New Mexico, or was it New Hampshire, were waiting in the hallway. Ophelia, our neighbor who was studying to be a witch, opened her door and invited us all into her apartment. "Let us enjoy Harvest together," she said authoritatively, sweeping her floor-length purple cape in a whirl around her, leading us in. This was a relief. We didn't want to be alone with these strange men, I didn't want them near my kids. From her stereo, as we entered, The Doors were singing "When You're Strange."

She had brought in her garden too. The small apartment glowed with squash, pumpkins, the faces of giant sunflowers. Bundles of freshly cut herbs and tomato plants hung upside down from the walls, between the photographs that were a school project, black-and-whites she had taken of herself in the bathroom mirror as she cried for a lost lover. She showed me the rose hips we had collected the week before from the pond: they were now crawling with worms. The place smelled like a cave. She had made me a pumpkin pie. "For *you*," she said, staring deep into my eyes as she placed it in my hands. On the counter was the Jehovah's Witness pamphlet: *Ten Days Till the End.* "Great!" Max said. "To end with a bang rather than a whimper." We all sat down to eat pie. I could distinguish the eggs from the pumpkin from the milk from the maple syrup from the spices, ginger, cinnamon, nutmeg. I felt I was eating each ingredient separately. Congruence? Is there such a thing? Synthesis. Another of Ophelia's projects to graduate from Goddard was photographing the local townspeople who fit the archetypes of the Tarot cards. I whispered in her ear, "Who do you think these men are?" She said, "They are the Capitalists. Beware. There is no card for them yet."

The men objected to the movie. "There are *some* things you don't have to see."

"But are you saying," I answered, "that there are things you *shouldn't* see?"

Ophelia said it made her think of western medicine. "Our approach is from the dead. Our knowledge comes from the study of corpses. But in China the approach is from the living, the healthy." We had more pumpkin pie. More raw eggs, syrup, milk, vegetables, nutmeg. The windows were frosted, the world turning into the dark fold of winter. "Is it snowing yet?" Max asked to anyone in the room.

There began to be a little intimacy between us. The two men became warmer, more human. One of them rolled a joint, passed it around. They told us they met Passing Cloud at an art fair, that he makes leather belts now, paints sunsets and pine trees on them, travels from fair to fair. When we first knew Cloud he was getting a Ph.D. in clinical psychology from USC. They told of their trip here from Boston. About the road and the weather. Neither had ever been to Montreal so they were looking forward to that. They seemed to be worried about crossing the border and asked a number of questions concerning the procedure. They were such dark men against the colors and smells and glow of Ophelia's room. They hadn't removed their overcoats. I thought they must be Mafia, dope smugglers. A wave of happiness washed through me. I was happy the movie was over. Then the flashes: the face sliding off, the contents scooped out. The trunk of the girl, headless, limbless, gutted, washed ashore, ribs of what once was a canoe clutching mud at low tide.

The two men were consulting each other. They looked so much alike I asked if they were brothers. Just business partners. They decided they could trust us with the great secret they were harboring. That they were harboring a great secret was apparent in everything about them. They asked us if we would like to see something "incredible."

They left the apartment. The three of us listened to them going down the stairs on the side of the building to their sinister car and then coming back up. "Do you think I should get rid of them?" Max asked. I shrugged my shoulders, even though I saw them coming back with submachine guns to kills us. "I don't think they are a danger to us," Ophelia said in her wise way. When they entered the room one of them was carrying a box of large envelopes, the other a heavy wooden crate.

They had us sit in a circle on the hardwood floor. They asked us if we knew who the photographer Edward Curtis was. None of us did.

Suddenly, Indians burst into the room like irradiated light, like pieces of shrapnel. They slammed against the walls, a thudding *boom-boom*. A wind off the ocean, the smell of iodine, blew through. Ophelia moaned. Max said nothing but sank deep into his body, cross-legged, in Indian fashion. God. They're looking at us. In a cold sweat, fighting nausea again, I eyed the path through the pumpkin-flowing, worm-crawling kitchen to the bathroom.

"These are old copperplate photogravures," the smaller man explained, as he passed large, antique pictures to us. "That's why they glow." All the drama of the evening was climaxing in photographs of Indians. Light exploded from Ophelia's tears on the wall. I heard a high-pitched chant like women calling, like coyote yelps. Just one of the portraits would have been an aesthetic, spiritual shock, but these men seemed to have an endless supply. They were, truly, incredible. I was falling into a face, the texture and smell of the rough skin as powerful as a lover's, falling shattered through the large pores like windows when another face was handed to me. The heart pounded in each body, the thudding *boom-boom* that kept up all night. These photographs were a different kind of autopsy report. These people were as alive as the people in the film were dead.

"This Ed Curtis," the larger man was saying, "dedicated his whole life to photographing all the tribes of North America, except Mexico, before the old ways vanished. He had the endorsement of Teddy Roosevelt and financial support from J.P. Morgan. Morgan wanted to produce the finest book since the King James Bible."

I remembered then the Bible says you can't look on the Face of God and survive.

"Where did you get these?"

"Would you believe?" They both laughed crazily. "We found them in a basement in Boston, hundreds of them. Gold tones, copperplates, photogravures, unpublished negatives, it's Curtis's original collection. For some reason they were stored there years ago and forgotten. Can you imagine what it was like for us to *find* them?"

"We'd never heard of Curtis either," the smaller man said. "But we recognized their value instantly."

"Yeah," the larger man said. "Like being hit over the head with a brick."

"It took Curtis thirty years to complete the photographing," the smaller man said. "But only a few sets were ever produced."

"The original cost in 1906 for twenty volumes was $3500. It was too large a project. And Morgan died."

"I think they were too painful," the smaller man said. "It was too soon. Some of the people who bought them had made their money killing Indians."

"Yes," the larger man said. "But now enough time has passed. You and I . . ." he looked at his partner in the way Ophelia had looked at me when she handed me her pie, "will never have to work again."

Many of the photographs I saw that night I've never seen again. The popular reprint of Curtis's photographic epic, *North American Indians,* published a short time later, possibly from this collection, does not, even remotely, compare to the originals. *Hopi, Apache, Mojave, Navaho, Tiwa, Zuñi, Southern Cheyenne, Sioux, Apsaroke, Mandan, Piegan, Northern Cheyenne, Cree, Sarsi, Assiniboine, Blackfoot, Walla Walla, Nez Percé, Flathead, Spokane, Yakima, Chinook, Hupa, Klamath, Pomo, Yokuts, Miwok, Mono, Cahuilla, Suquamish, Skokomish, Lummi, Quilcene, Quinault. Bridal groups at the totem poles, clam diggers on the beaches, wedding canoes, whaling boats, wickiups, sweathouses, tepee camps. The Sundance of the Piegans, the purification of the soul, the flame-riven mists of the Northern Seas, the cliff-hanging Alaskan villages, the Navaho's*

Canyon de Chelly. Hopi Snake Dancers, Mojave water carriers, prairie buf-fulo chases. The faces. The faces. The vanishing race? I remembered the belief common to all traditional peoples, that the camera captures the soul. It was obvious that these photographs were of actual souls.

"Curtis's expeditions into the secret lands of the vanquished Indians were dangerous," the smaller man said, "and his camera supplies and equipment cumbersome. Sometimes it took months for the Indians to trust him, even though he sat in their tepees and beside their fires"—he said this with an air of reverence—"not as a suppliant or a master, but as an equal being. Curtis saw the Buddha in everyone."

"And he didn't make any secret about his purpose," the larger man continued. Obviously, they had done research on these photographs, the new formality in their presentation sounding not unlike the open-ing of a sales pitch. "He told the Indians they were doomed to perish from the earth. All of them, their young and old men, women, and their children. But with his camera, he told them, he could record their stories in imperishable form so that they would live through the ages. Slowly they were won over. Having witnessed the death of so much they could believe that they were doomed."

"And so before the strange and inanimate focus of the camera," the smaller man continued, "they allowed their dances, games, array of battle, smoking of the pipes, so much that was intimate, occult or ac-tive in their lives, to be recorded on these plates so that other people in future times might know what a great people they were. They did magic things, sometimes unbeknownst to Curtis, to protect them-selves, like performing dances backwards, but all in all, the attitude was if we are doomed then we will give ourselves."

Yes, I thought, they gave that which cannot be destroyed or stolen, the soul. *"My whole body is covered with eyes,"* an Eskimo sang.*"Behold it. I see all around."* I thought this is what a real American looks like, this is what thousands of years on this continent creates for a face. The wide cheekbone structure seemed like geography, faces like rain-beaten stones, a geo-historic diffusion forged by a time utterly lost to the world. *I am all the forces and objects with which I come in contact. I am the wind, the trees, the lakes and the darkness. My eyes are two hawks perched on the peaks of the mountain range. The holy road to my mouth is to the other country. Our bodies are spiritual events. I take place out there. You take place in here.*

As the passing of the pictures continued they formed a wide glowing circle in the center of the room, and gradually as they were propped against the walls, they encircled us. The faces stared up at us and from behind us, into our backs, through the human aura of skin. Have you ever seen an angel? Brakhage asked. Ophelia dropped some of our windowpane, saying "We are the dead place between heart beats." The two men said they didn't need any.

"You are correct in being so secretive about your mission." She prophesied, "It is a dangerous mission." She looked at them in her Russian Jewish way to suggest they probably had no idea of just how dangerous. "The power plays, the intrigues, the behind-the-scenes maneuverings of dealers and collectors will reach monumental proportions."

The smaller man, sitting directly opposite me, winced. From behind him a Blackfoot woman said "I see through your eyes. I remember."

"Yes," the other man said. "There is a race on already among a small group of people to acquire as much as possible of Curtis's work. We've been a little concerned about reaching Montreal."

"Like a hold-up," the smaller man said.

I wondered if they had stolen the photographs themselves. They mentioned keeping them from Caspar Weinberger. I assumed they meant the government wanted to destroy the photographs for security purposes.

"Caspar is a ghost himself," Max mumbled, his first words since the showing of the pictures began.

"Caspar Weinberger wants them for their monetary value. He's the new secretary of Health, Education and Welfare."

"You could make a killing on dead Indians," Max said, finding his old comic resiliency.

I held Geronimo in my hands. "He's unpublished," the smaller man said. "He's our good-luck piece. He's the one we'll never sell."

Geronimo is dressed in war regalia, war cap on his head and a feathered staff in his hand. It is the day of the famous 1905 inaugural parade for Teddy Roosevelt. The Chief's face is exceedingly grim but I swear, *twice,* the old coot winked at me.

Everyone was speaking at once on the wonders of photography, of film. "Souls stolen in this century by photographs surround all of us," Ophelia said, "anxious to possess our beings." As she said this I saw the Saigon police chief blowing the brains out of the peasant-soldier, a famous photograph of the time. I had always thought the puff coming from his head was the impact of the bullet, fragments of his brain beginning to fly. Now I saw that it was his soul.

"Some people are photogenic, like Jacqueline Kennedy Onassis, Marilyn Monroe," she said. "They always say of Jackie she is not as beautiful as her photographs. And Monroe they say was rather ordinary until a camera was pointed at her. Then she came alive."

"I'm afraid of cameras," I said. "I take awful pictures." I was surprised to find my voice. "Sometimes I think it's because I grew up in Hollywood. All that sun, the scouts everywhere looking for you. My soul hides, though, so often, I've wanted to give it."

"Curtis died in Hollywood," the larger man said. "He was the still photographer for the *Ten Commandments.*"

"You have to have the kind of charisma the camera can capture," the smaller man said, who only now I saw had a severely pockmarked face, "to become famous in the twentieth century. It's the century of film." I remembered how I photographed everything when I was a teenager, driven by the need to capture the present, to save it. It was, along with baton twirling, my first art.

I felt the chemical surge in Ophelia and as it did it came on to all of us. The faces glowed at us. *My face is your mirror, my ancient face before mirrors, before self-consciousness.* A Cheyenne dressed all in white, tall as trees, in the moon dust that flew, waited for his lover. The paint on a child's face came off in my hands. Cottonwoods, clumped in a river, flickered their petals across Max's face, then shimmered in the thousand mirrors of the room, pale air and pale water. Ophelia's narcissistic tears for her lost lover splashed from the walls onto the people as they washed the wheat, as he snapped the camera, Antelope and Snakes at

Oraibi, Zuñi girls in the river. How we come through this cold song, we three Apaches, the rock, the sand, the cactus. I am trying to find my daughter, Angeline, across the Sound, but she is lost in the dirty streets of her father's village, Seattle, who proclaims *"White men will never be alone. We will always surround you."*

Stunned, we decided to stay there all night with the images, to wait for the sun to come over the New Hampshire mountains, the Winooski River that flowed behind and beneath our building. Occasionally, the movie reeled through the room. Then the two men would be angry. The smaller, pockmarked man said, "Why this fanatical drive to *see* everything? The Indians say you lose your power if you expose all your secrets."

"There are ways to honor the dead," the older, more sinister man said. "Like Irish wakes."

"That's right!" the smaller man said, "Irish wakes are as much fun as Catholic weddings."

I thought of *Finnegans Wake*. I wondered if they were Black Irish.

"They put the corpse at the head of the table, pour it a drink, dance it around."

I asked who they were. As soon as I said it they hid again.

"I'm a saxophonist," the small man said. "It's good to believe in God for no other reason than as a safeguard against the possibility he's real. If you don't have a soul, then you're just a piece of dead meat."

"A piece of dead meat," I flared, "if you lay it on the ground disintegrates back to the earth. I *want* that experience. Who knows what it might be like. This country... , we're so anti-materialistic. We hate matter. I don't want to be burned. I don't want to be embalmed, preserved, trapped in plastic and steel. They dug up that six-year-old girl last week for that trial, the one in Philadelphia. It's been twenty years since her death and she's perfectly preserved. The rose in her hands was still fresh." I probably screeched it. "What the fuck for?"

"So the earth can't be renewed," Max answered.

"Autopsy," Ophelia said, "is like Manifest Destiny. It's God's will for the Indians to be swept aside. It's in the interest of science to weigh your heart. Our technology has destroyed the Goddess."

"Did you know?" the smaller man mused. "King Tut's pyramid was built for him before he was born." He added emphatically, "And don't forget, it's his tomb."

"Form is never more than an extension of concrete," Max said, winking at me.

The larger man dug into his files and pulled out a brown-toned textured photograph of Sioux burial. A storm, this one from the Plains, blew through the room in all directions like a whirlwind, rain and snow in its heart. The body is placed on a platform on cottonwood poles in the middle of the prairie, and left there. A small red bundle on a scaffold. To go back to both, sky and earth. Bird and animal. Night and day. On the posts hang the playthings she loved: a rattle of antelope hoofs strung on rawhide, a bouncing bladder with little stones inside, a painted willow hoop. On the scaffold, tied on top of the red blanket, is a deerskin doll, the beaded design that comes from far back in the family of her mother, Black Shawl. When you fall face down beside the body of your daughter you let the sorrow locked in your heart sweep over you, the rickety scaffold creaking a little under your weight. In the sky over you a few small clouds float white as swans on water. The wind dies in the sunset of that day and rises again with the sun's returning. An eagle with his buzzards following circles the far sky and over a low rise a bunch of antelope come grazing. Seeing the scaffold, they lift their heads and run down that way, circling a little, but coming closer in their curiosity, until they catch your man smell. Then they bound away, their rumps showing white. After a while a wolf comes along a little ridge, tail high, his nose in the air. He too gets the scent of you and with a leap is off over the prairie. And when it is night again a little mouse comes creeping up a post to sniff at the bundle of cloth, stopping, listening to a slow sound that comes and dies, and comes again. Suddenly the little animal leaps down and flees away into the grass, frightened that in the smell of death there was the thing of life, the breathing. The next daylight brings nothing of the sun, only grey clouds and a drizzling of fog closing in around the scaffold. When even the earth below the posts is lost, there is one pale flash of lightning and a fog-softened rumble of thunder. This you hear and you know it is time to go.

I stared into the face of Crazy Horse, the light-haired Oglala who was never photographed. *"As the dead prey upon us, they are the dead in ourselves."* I saw Ahab chasing the whale.

The smaller man said again, "See the Buddha in everyone."

How different, I thought, that is from Brakhage, who says it is the artist's business to discover the particularity that distinguishes you from all others. Your virtue. Your vision that makes you separate from others. I remembered that he quoted the poet Robert Duncan. "Soul is not universal. It is a created-creative event."

"We're a soulless people," Max said, staring into the black, small starred windows. "Misshapen, miscolored, the mixed blood of murderers without soul."

Ophelia agreed. "We are the broken hoop of the nation, the body gutted, without honor or land. This is why we hurt so badly. We killed the lover when we killed these people."

The eastern sky slowly streaked with blood, then a color like flesh, the second day of fall. She read an Oglala prayer from one of her books. "So the God has stopped. Everything as it moves, now and then, here and there, makes stops. The bird as it flies in one place to make its nest, and in another to rest in its flight." She said we are at a stop now. "We are shaped by what we have seen. We have seen the dead. Now we are shaped like the dead."

In the instant the sun rose and hit the room like a flashbulb I saw us as a photograph of the dead family recently discovered in New Hampshire. From the coroner's report and from the neighbors the story was pieced together.

It appears that Cecelia, 84, died of natural causes two years ago. Her husband and the two others dressed her and laid her on the couch so that she could remain part of the family.

Her husband, George, 85, died a short time afterwards in the rocking chair facing his wife. A vase of white roses, still fresh, was arranged on the coffee table between them.

Grace and Roland, 76 and 72, continued living a normal life. But they were reclusive and shunned company. They did all their shopping at night and even mowed the lawn after dark. Roland died around a month ago and was asleep in his bed at the time. Grace left him there and tried to continue her life, but found she could not. She lay in the same bed as Roland and died a few days or weeks later. A bag of groceries was found on the kitchen counter, unpacked.

The description of Crazy Horse at the burial scaffold of his daughter is adapted from Crazy Horse, the Strange Man of the Oglala, *by Mari Sandoz.*

The Whore

The week would end with Johnny Lookfar dead in a car accident in Utah. Perhaps that is why I remember the days preceding as a story, though actually a story of minor significance compared to the story of the accident, the suddenly completed story of Lookfar's life, the tragic new chapter in the life of one of my oldest friends, his wife, Una, and the story of what it meant in our lives. When Johnny Lookfar died, I know now, Maximilian and I did too, though it would take two years for us to come undone from each other. So I'm not sure why this little story haunts me. It seems like a private masque, a diversion, the warm-up act before the main show. "The soul is made of mirrors," my current lover is fond of saying. In reply I am still fond of Heraclitus, "The self begins to disguise itself as it approaches self-revelation." When the news came—after the long drive from New York City, as we pulled up to our friend's house in Vermont where our children were staying and Joan was there on the passenger side as I got out saying your friend in Utah wants you to call, her husband's been killed in a car accident and the ground was coming up in my face in a black wave so that I had to push it back with my hands, NO!—Max still maintained the stupid fight we'd been having all week, he still would not speak to me. We'd been in New York for him to attend the annual library convention and for me to explore the city. We stayed at a friend's apartment on 95th Street. His anger at me began when I refused to stay in the area near the car in order to move it every hour or so to avoid parking expenses, and to walk Cinderella regularly. In the past this would not have been as unreasonable as it sounds. There was a lot of meaning, even triumph, in our finding ways to live well without money. I would have become intimate with the neighborhoods in which the car was parked and the dog walked in ways I wouldn't have ranging further out, and there would have been little expense. But he had a good job now, the job was the reason we were in the city, and while I hated how it was taking him from me—I wanted him and our life, not money—if he was going out I was going out in new ways too. We could afford parking, Cinderella, like any good city dog, could hold it and a week in New York City was clearly something one should not deny oneself if given the chance. My goal that week was to have typical New York City experiences. To have a crisis in one's relationship over parking is, I suppose, a typical New York City experience. I joked about this. But nothing opened him. I'd come home from the adventure of each day expecting his mood to have changed, for him to love me again. He was so warm and humorous to our friend I doubt she noticed his behavior toward me. We were experts at hiding the true nature of our relationship from our friends; we were considered the ideal couple by most of them. Together, the two of them would walk Cinderella, share a joint. I'd stay in the apartment, study her *I Ching*. At night we'd sleep side by side on the hallway floor in the middle of that tall building, behind five locks on her door, in the middle of that fabled island and he wouldn't speak to me. I was in the habit of these long silent treatments but was just learning not to let them interfere with my own time. He was in control and all I could do, I thought, was to take care of myself as best as possible, until he came back to me. The burden of trust lay on me, the whole thing a test by which I proved my love. He would see if I loved him, no matter what. And, of course, if I loved him no matter what I would understand, at least accept, his behavior. Each day we'd meet for lunch outside the Americana Hotel where the convention was being held. He'd eat the sack lunch I had packed that morning. We'd sit there on a cement planter, shoulder to shoulder, in beautiful New York City in July, the temperature in the eighties, all the beautiful city people swarming around us, and he would not speak to me. Maybe he was worried about my floating around so freely in such a place. But this was confusing, contradictory, something he would never express or allow to be suggested, because the opposite of this fear was also true: he wanted me to fly free, to have other lovers, to bring back to him fuck stories. Every time we made love he fantasized, he confessed, my fucking other men, he begged me, how much he wanted me to confess I had, or at least had fantasies of doing so. In terror and lust he shared with me these elaborate ever-occurring sexual fantasies of my encounters with strangers. His fear of me, mainly that I would betray the trust of this baring of his soul, was enormous, but, I came to know, part of the thrill too. On the other hand, the betrayal of me in these fantasies was not at all an issue, not even for me, consciously. (To have thought this would have been a betrayal of him.) Now in Vermont, with the news of Johnny Lookfar, I thought I'd lose my mind. This was the death of *my* ideal couple, the death of the only great marriage I knew. We were with Una in Moab, Utah, when she fell in love with Johnny, a nineteen-year-old Cherokee in her Primary class. She was thirty, a devout Mormon wife and mother of four children. She always said it was the example of our love that gave her the strength. She had been shocked when I first fell in love with Max—he was in prison for marijuana—causing the only real break in our long friendship. But later, when she met him, his beauty, his oddball personality, humorous and deadly serious at the same time, and the clear improvement of my life from the heartbreak of my first marriage presented what she called "a living testimony." She called Johnny Lookfar "my Lamanite." For two years they were on the verge of excommunication from the Church, the tenets on which they based their love: *they were as One in the Beginning, they pledged to live righteously through Time and the King-doms so that they would be blessed with the greatest and rarest of blessings: they would be Latter-day Saints, they would find each other in the Ter-restrial Kingdom.* Max and I hitchhiked from LA for their civil wed-ding in Moab, one of our own truly memorable adventures. Just two months before they had finally obtained, after five years and two babies, Eagle and Lightseeker, their Temple Recommend: they could begin the two-year process that would enable them to be married in the temple for eternity. Johnny had also just gotten his B.A. and was enrolled to study Indian law at BYU in the fall. All month they had been calling us to come to Utah. The oil boom was on. Maximilian and Lookfar would work in the oilfields, live in their camper. The kids and I would stay with Una and her six in Provo. With all the overtime we'd be rich by end of summer. When we didn't come, because I refused to put money first, to live without Max in Provo, Utah, for three months—I was afraid, from everyone's example, that once we started sacrificing for money we'd be forever confused about quality, priorities—and because he had his library job, Lookfar found another partner, a fellow BYU student. Friday, after working a seventy-hour week, they were returning to Provo. Coming around Strawberry Reservoir on Highway 40, the partner fell asleep at the wheel. Head on into a station wagon. The partner wasn't scratched. The driver of the station wagon, a woman with two kids in the back, got out screaming and cursing, then drove on. Lookfar's six feet six inches, two hundred and ninety pounds was lying on the white line in the middle of the road. He was looking up at the blue sky. Somehow his giant form had been catapulted through the front window of the VW. Even though he was too large to drive it, to relieve his exhausted partner. I'm okay, he said. He died twelve hours later. Johnny Lookfar was named for a chief of his tribe. The stories Una told me when I called, the details, I'll never get fully free of. When the doctor came down the hall saying "I thought Johnny was going to be okay, but, Una, I'm sorry, he died," her uterus contracted, doubling her to the floor. They had already taken his eyes—the doctor asked for them in the same breath he told her he had died and she gave the permission as she was collapsing—the life-support systems unhooked, when they finally let her in the room to him. Instantly she understood. She ran back out, grabbed her bishop, pulled him into the room, locked the door behind them. "He's still here. He's waiting. Bring him back!" The bishop objected. She composed herself. "Look. I have the faith. You have the power. Johnny is waiting. Together we can do it." Even the problem of his missing eyes was nothing to the faith she had in her God, in her church, to the knowledge that Johnny was still in the room, waiting for them to bring him back. "Can't you feel him? He's here. He's waiting for you to act." She wouldn't let the bishop leave. He told her she was sinning. She knew this was the greatest test of her marriage. But then she was made to see that the bishop had been wrongly ordained, that he was a simple man without power or faith. She will always blame the finality of Lookfar's death on the impotence of her bishop. That night we slept on Joan's living room floor. I was exploding in the dark: shock, grief, horror and awe of the sudden disappearance of Johnny Lookfar from the world, rage and enormous hurt and disbelief at Max's sullen, sleeping form beside me turned so deeply, so purely into himself as to be complete, that is, dead himself. I left the house for fear of waking both families, my kids asleep with the others upstairs, for fear the screams that were wrenching my body to the violent chorus of some inexorable cosmic mechanism would break through my last barrier, silence. It wasn't the first time I walked the night hills and notches, the village streets, the cemetery of Plainfield out of rage and helplessness, but it was the first time I allowed myself to consider the futility of my relationship with Max. For the first time I saw through him. He *can't* love me. But I had no bishop to blame for the failure of my faith, my love. I spent the day of the funeral on my back in our Falcon station wagon parked in Great Woods outside the library unable to do anything, paralysed, crazed by Johnny's last words which every bird was screaming, *"Oh God, somebody help me, please somebody help me."* Una had said several times the past year, "I think the suffering is finally over for me, I've paid my dues. I deserve this love." She had said to me on the phone just the week before, "We are such boobs for each other. He drives the two hundred miles every night so we can sleep together." At one point I went into the library, past Max's office—he looked away when he saw me—and found a Utah map, found Dechesne, Strawberry Reservoir, tried to see the accident, stared at Springfield, tried to see him dead, Una putting him in the ground. I tried to write a poem, one of my first. I couldn't. The death was the death of marriage, of love. Later Max defended his behavior. "The minute I heard I knew it was Una's fault. She worked him too hard. She drove him to his death. That was my first thought. If he hadn't married her he'd still be alive." Max's consistent horror of marriage. A woman is dangerous, love is impossible, a wife will destroy a man. I suppose his reaction is no more illogical than mine that Lookfar was killed by White Man, by Viet Nam, by the oil wars, by highways crossing sacred land, by the twentieth century. Psychologists say some people can't love. It is not only, as I believed of Max, that the mask of indifference won't drop, the mask is everything, the mask is the soul itself. Psychologists define my behavior with men, with Max, as masochistic. The relationship: sadomasochism. But in my love for Max I didn't derive pleasure from his sick behavior, I tried to understand it. Struggling to grasp his preposterous blame I saw that he himself felt responsible for Lookfar's death. If we had gone to Utah, if he had been driving, it wouldn't have happened. Maximilian would never have fallen asleep on Johnny Lookfar. Understanding this I could forgive him.

Does not the very condition of our lives, sadistically hung on the grid of death, on the line of time, seem masochistic? Is there greater love than the love of inflicting pain, the love of receiving pain? I believe there is.

Is my belief *masochism?*

I went prepared for the oppression New York City had been for me in the past and instead found it easy, expansive. Everywhere people were kissing, in the streets, in the parks, inside the windows and entrances of buildings when I walked by, the women looking like *Cosmopolitan* magazine covers. For me—well, it was 1974 and I was still dressed as a hippy. As the week wore on I became more and more self-conscious. My clothes were ragged, faded and, for the first time I saw, a part of something that had gone past. I had hoped the clothes revolution of the sixties a permanent one. I had worn Levis and T-shirts, or some variation of this, for years. There are three photographs of that week, two are of me, the third of Maximilian on his thirty-fourth birthday. He sits in the window of the apartment on West 95th, shirtless, look-ing sullen, mean, sadistically beautiful. My Lover, the Cancer. In one of the photos of me I am standing in the train tracks outside Brooklyn, an Indian bag made of broken mirrors slung over my shoulder. I look bored and very leery. My sister, who took the pictures, says I look younger now than I did then. I remember how the Plainfield astrolo-ger interpreted my natal chart the week before we went to New York. "The native is a Taurus but she has spent a thousand lifetimes in Cancer."

I met my sister at La Guardia Airport. Bridgit was flying in from Hollywood for a secret rendezvous with her lover, a famous actor, and also to spend time with me and her oldest friend, Janie. "Imagine," she laughed on the phone to me in Vermont, "the two of *us* in New York City!" On Wednesday evening we met in Janie's apartment and after a festive, giggly dinner during which she told Janie all about her affair, swearing her to secrecy, the two of us walked to a street on the Lower East Side that the movie company had taken over. Bridgit had been involved with the actor for over three years but I still had not met him. I was beginning to make jokes about my avoidance being reverse snobbism, the reverse of the groupie syndrome. I would have met any other lover she might have had. I just could never figure out how to genuinely meet someone who is met by everyone just for his fame.

The insurance cost of using the actual buildings was so high that a whole new row of slum buildings had been constructed in the lots burned out from the riots of the sixties. I fought my social consciousness—another difficulty in meeting the man. As we came around the corner to the crowds he was coming down the lit-up street—it was supposed to be daylight but I would have recognized him in the dark—to the surprise encounter with his ex-lover, a famous star also. They stood facing each other perhaps a whole minute, unbelieving, their whole painful history playing across the screen of their bodies, and then fell into each's arms. But then she pulled back, feeling the gun at his ribs, looked into his face like she didn't know who he was. Someone shouted *"cut!"* and they turned back in the directions from which they had come to repeat this scene. This was all done deep inside the bustling circle of the crews and their equipment, the make-up and costume people, the camera and light people, the directors and food caterers, the huge droning trucks and motor homes on the outskirts. A familiar-looking man and woman wandered through and around the encampment in a trance. Bridgit whispered their names, unfamiliar to me, said they were the supporting actor and actress going over their lines for the next scene. If they ever get to it. This scene may take all night. Camera! Action! Roll . . .! The sudden hush, he's coming down the street, she's coming up the street, they come around the corner: the wound of recognition, the saying of their names, the drone of the generators through the night like the sound of time passing, his face huge across all the world kissing hers equally huge and I couldn't help but see him kissing my sister and then fucking another in an old movie, saw him killing her. I thought the scene perfect but the director yelled cut again and again they started over. I remembered the many stories Bridgit had told me, felt the delicious thrill she must know all the time in the secret of her relationship to him. He'd gotten his start as a White House aide to John Kennedy. It was his job to pick up the Hollywood actresses who flew in two and three times a week for midnight rendez-vous with the president. He'd return for them at 4:30 and the three would have breakfast together in the servants' quarters. This was be-fore Kennedy's habitual affairs with Hollywood actresses—following in the footsteps of his father, falling back to the source of the family money—were known to the public. Certain nights were reserved for certain stars. For instance, Tuesday nights were Marlene Dietrich's, Wednesday's were Marilyn Monroe's. When Monroe sang "Happy Birthday, Mr. President" at Madison Square Garden so erotically that their secret was in danger of being guessed by the public, the presi-dent's brother, the attorney general, tried to persuade Monroe to end the relationship. There were photos and wire taps of their love trysts in the hands of both the mafia and the F.B.I. But then the whole plot took an even deeper turn. Robert Kennedy fell in love with Marilyn Monroe. My sister's lover was relocated to Beverly Hills not only as the aide to their liaisons but also as her bodyguard. Twentieth Century Fox fired her within two weeks of the Happy Birthday incident. As that machiavellian summer of 1962 proceeded and Marilyn turned more and more to him for help, fear grew in him for both their lives—in regards even, to her lovers, his employers. Bridget told me that once when he was very drunk he had called her Marilyn, then broke in her arms, sobbing about a conspiracy so great, so evil, as to be a constant threat to his sanity. He sobbed about his own guilt too, said he possessed items he took from her house the night she died, *talismans* he called them, the proof that he had tried to save her. He even implied that he had the famous red book she kept of her meetings with John and Bobby, discussions she'd overheard like the plot to kill Castro, a war in Viet Nam. In those days my little sister did bear a striking resemblance to Monroe. When the actress died she wrote me from Rome, "Everywhere I go Italians collapse at my feet crying I am the ghost of Marilyn Monroe. They call her the Goddess. They say in a hundred years the church will make her a saint." Bridget always ex-plained that the actor fell in love with her because she was an outsider to the Washington-Hollywood power structure; this is why their affair was a secret. "Did you know," she was fond of saying, "that Ronald Reagan was the commanding officer of the army man who took the first professional photographs of Marilyn in 1945?"

When the shooting was finally over we snuck around to his motor home dressing room. I felt him scrutinizing me through the warm greeting. *It was barely a month after Monroe's death that he landed his first role, a leading role.* But despite my disdain I hugged him. He's my sister's great love; his movies do soothe the world. It was either just after this moment or just before that Bridgit took the third photograph of that week. I'm wearing something of hers, appropriately glamorous, a backless halter dress. We both have our mouths open. We look like a couple in one of those magazines like *National Inquirer* or *People,* stunned, annoyed, but giving ourselves utterly to the world. Then there was a lot of commotion outside, a banging on the door. A guard informed him that a fan was refusing to leave because she claimed that a year ago he promised her in a letter that he would see her when he came to New York. He went immediately to her rescue. He returned with a very fat, very made-up, whimpering woman. "Wait for me," he said. "We'll just be a minute." He led her down the hall to the back room. "Poor thing," Bridgit whispered. "I know how she feels!" If I had a picture of Bridgit from that week I wonder what I would see now. A broken heart. A woman in danger. But in those days we loved each other by not looking too closely. I could feel concern for his wife easier than I could for my sister. To question what the other was doing with her man/men, to even *feel* concern for the other would endanger *our* relationship, not the relationship with them, whom we were loving, as our mother loved our father, unconditionally. When the fan and he emerged from the back room she was holding her cheek where he'd kissed her, tears were spilling down her hand. In the other she was holding an untouched drink. "I don't believe it, I don't believe it!" she was crying as the guards led her away. He showered then, returned in his bathrobe, drinking vodka. His famous penetrating eyes were glassy and he seemed very tired. From somewhere across the empty set a song was playing from the sound track, another tune about our dying for love. Then we were in a black limousine inching up Broadway, then through Central Park. The driver/bodyguard, Bronco, the man who'd been with him the longest, was enormous, his swollen fat bottom lip catching the shine of the street lights. My sister's lover was slumped in the corner of the passenger side in his bathrobe, nodding at every mundane thing Bronco said. He was so nice. He was so far away. Bridgit and I sat in the back, in silence. Once he put his arm over the seat and gestured for her hand. I wish I could have reached for her hand the rest of the time. Maybe it's not just a tune we sing over and over. Maybe it is our souls crying out. We could live forever if we loved.

But what happened two days later is the story I want to tell. I was at the corner of 57th Street and Seventh Avenue on my way to meet Max for our customary silent lunch when I was approached by a tall flamboyant man saying something to me in a heavy accent. I smiled, acknowledging his gesture, pulled free of his hand on my arm, walked briskly on. I didn't comprehend his words until I was sitting on the planter in the plaza waiting for Max and realized he had said, "I'll get us two beers and meet you in the plaza." I had acknowledged *that*. It was noon and people were pouring out of the offices. The man was now sitting cater-corner to me on another planter, talking at me. The sun was hot and I ignored him, already bored with the display of himself he was finding so fascinating.

I was learning to watch myself in that period. I'd been such a recluse in my love for Maximilian. Now I wanted to enter the world. I was trying to get to know New York City, to understand the Eastern mentality. I was depressed but so crazy in love as not to be able to think clearly about myself, what I should or could do. Long ago I had abolished the self-boundaries that separated me from him. To find them again presented an awesome task. The way seemed to be to move out of myself, to become more objective. I had always thought I was so much more in touch with my emotions than he but I was beginning to see that I was just in touch with the ones he denied, while—*could it be?*—he was in touch with ones I denied.

All week with so many men approaching me I had considered the possibility of another lover, but my fidelity was painfully strong. I wanted only Max. Besides, I assumed all men treated women the way Max treated me. You either accepted this, became a lesbian or did without. I had told him once, if I have another lover, naturally, I will love him. If we have other lovers, naturally, we will do it differently, we'll do it in our own ways. My emotional involvement will be stronger than yours while the numbers you fuck will be greater than mine. That seemed a fair balance, though the bad taste stayed in my mouth and I wondered why we had to go through such crap at all. Now as I sat there in the sun realizing that he was late, and slowly, that he wasn't coming at all, I felt wide open and passive and accepting to anything and everything. I seemed to rise a little higher from myself to watch New York from a place of suspension, free, without needs, no conscious goals other than "experience." I thought of my sister's famous lover spaced after the hard work of acting. At some point I smiled, looked at the guy on the planter across from me. Instantly, he was offended, as offended by me as I was by him. He moved to my side. Max's place. He was about forty with stringy silver-streaked black hair which kept falling into his eyes. He seemed tired even though very much on the make. When he spoke I heard only the accent. He handed me a can of beer. I made out that he was "from a lonely Greek island in the Mediterranean." I recognized Nicolas in him, Max's oldest, closest friend. Maybe the characteristics that so frustrated me about Nic were Greek characteristics. Was my difficulty with Nic racial? He so obliterated me in his arrogant "male bonding" with Max.

"And *you* must be from a commune in Vermont," he said with scorn and loathing. He gestured at my cut-off Levi miniskirt. I laughed, flapped my rubber thong against the sole of my crossed foot, took his question as clever, witty.

"That's close," I said. Then I looked hard at him. "And *you* must be a Capricorn."

The look he gave me was hate. "I'm a filmmaker. What are you writing?"

I was writing, as I usually did on such trips, a journal-letter to Una, notes of my New York City encounter. As it was happening. But I said, "I'm a writer," to balance his "filmmaker."

The Greek flared instantly, something about "the inherent inferiority of women writers." I looked at the undulating glass slab above him. The Americana Hotel, the brochure said, is the tallest hotel in the world. "Name a woman writer," he challenged, "who can compare with Henry James."

"Henry James?" I thought he was being funny.

"Joyce. Lawrence. Miller. Mailer. *Those* are writers." He summed it up. "I despise women writers. They write confession, soap operas."

"Yeah." I was in some sun revery of laughter. "I suppose they do." I was drinking his beer.

"No woman," he said, and I recognized Mailer, "will write a good novel until a call girl writes her memoirs."

Then he said we should go to a nearby pub. "Aren't you hot in this damn sun?"

The Greek walked very fast, mumbling constantly. As the objective reporter I did wonder why him. Of *all* the men who had hit on me all week, most of them *far* more interesting and intelligent! I still remember one man and I still look for him—we talked, at most, for a half hour in the sculpture garden of the Museum of Modern Art. Now I can see that the Greek was Max, I was trying to see myself with Max. I went with him to find out who Max and I were. The Greek was my objectivity. He made me think of the Goddesses. *I am Atalanta promising to marry any man who can beat me in the race. I am Psyche wandering high and low for my male self.* Oh, this is too complex. I went with him because I love the man who doesn't love me.

He was guiding me by the elbow through a large crowd on a corner, a swarm of stunningly beautiful women. He was sneering "Hor-é! Hor-é! Hor-é!" I was thinking how beautiful is the whoredom of capitalism. Even so it took me most of the day to decipher his favorite word.

A fern bar on 57th and Broadway. Uptown, I think he said. Lots of pale varnished wood and hanging plants and skylights that beamed particles of light and dirt between us as we drank a pitcher of beer. I got very high very quickly. I wasn't used to drinking. I had never been drunk with a stranger. The giddy joy stayed with me through the entire encounter with the man.

His eyes, watching me closely, were ridiculously melancholy. He wrote his name and address in my notebook. Alex Kariopapoulas. West 91st Street. He pronounced his name for me like spit. Then he recited Henry James at great length. I recognized *The Turn of the Screw*.

He recited Mailer, the passage where he's fucking the maid in the anus, having just strangled his wife in the great American dream. In his astounding memorization of these difficult passages I supposed he was studying English, learning English/American culture, or memorizing scenes for films. He recited Lawrence and Miller, again at great length. I loved it, the exact recall of the most famous passages of all those old guys. All his recitations, sounding contemporary, almost conversational, and at the same time, archaic, classically Greek, were of unrequited love. Sentimental, pornographic soap operas. Confessions. Of bitterness toward women so great as to be comical. What a Big Apple specimen, I thought. I was a reporter with a good lead on my New York story. Joni Mitchell was singing *California, I'm your biggest fan. California, I'm coming home.*

"You have a woman?" I asked.

"She left. The bitch. I'm plotting now my revenge."

I gave him my most maternal look—sympathy, interest, concern, the one that says, Son, you've been cute, but now it's time to grow up.

"She just left. I came back one day and she was gone. I hate her. I hate women." A length of greasy hair, like rope, fell again into his eyes. "She took off with Francis Ford Coppola's dress designer. A bald, potbellied old man. She *married* him."

Oh, it gets so lonely and the streets are full of strangers.

"Why would she do that?" I would fall into him, then catch myself, pull back.

He shrugged. "When you're beautiful and skinny you want to be a star. You can be. You can get money."

I thought of Bridgit, of something that happened to us the day before. I met her in front of her lover's apartment on Park Avenue, declining the opportunity to meet her in his room which occupied a full floor near the top. The invitation seemed solely for my sake. We were walking excitedly along as we always do together in Hollywood, Malibu or San Diego, she telling me all the latest, how beautiful he thought I was, how, really, I am his type, my high cheekbones and long body and small breasts, like his wife, to which I loudly protest to the whole street, clutching them both, "They are *not* small! Only in comparison with yours!" and how they will meet next at the end of the month on Peter Lawford's ranch in the Rockies and the latest about Janie, her life as a secretary all these years since Ramona High, how still she hasn't married, had kids, figures she has years yet to do that, and we don't know it, nor does Janie, but next week after we leave she will have a mastectomy and I will never see her again because she will quickly die of the cancer, which must be another reason I remember this week, me and my sister talking along like this, actually she's doing most of the talking because I'm a little apprehensive about our ignorance of the city, that our customary abandon might lead us down the wrong street. In California it is always a freeway ride to the next neighborhood, but I can see that here it's block by block. And sure enough now we are coming down the street to a gang of Puerto Ricans draped over the iron railings of the apartment entrances and the hoods of their cars, drinking beer. She keeps talking as if she hasn't noticed. It's too late to turn and run, they are all looking very ironically at us, I'm sure the blondest, bustiest, ballsiest creatures to hit their street—in a few weeks anyway. Me in my levi miniskirt and rubber thongs, braless in a tank top, she in her new stacked foam-rubber heels that she had so gleefully shown me in the turnstile of La Guardia as she came off the plane, *ooh, they're so comfortable,* my sister, the Pisces, ever concerned for her feet. It is too late to turn and walk back the other way, that would invite trouble for sure. *But we are walking headlong into big trouble,* the hippy blonde, the Hollywood blonde. She hasn't changed her style, her flamboyance. I have no idea, I never do, I always forget to ask her later, if she realizes what is happening. As we move into their collective stare and silence, she blurts out before any of them makes a move, "Hi fellows!"

And then spinning around, her grin as sincere as always, "Oh, you guys look fantastic! I can't believe it, *you look just like New Yorkers!* Oh, I have to take your pictures, is that okay?"

She whipped out her camera and snapped away. I stood over to the side with one of the guys who said he takes terrible pictures. She paid special attention to the meanest-looking character, the one draped over the hood of the dark lit Chevy. She got his address to send him copies. We walked on, still gabbing loudly, to the Village. One thing about my sister, you can't put her in any bag, you never could, not for long anyway. Always there is fission and fusion, flux and flow, the unexpected. Always she breaks out of the program, the domination or submission of anything. So it always surprises me that some people actually live the clichés, like if you're skinny and beautiful you want to be a star.

The Greek was still carrying on about his bitch. "I'll get her somehow. I hate her guts."

"Tell me about your work," I sighed. "Filmmaking."

He sneered some more, shrugged it off. He was so opinionated, so boastful in his literary recitations I thought he must be either very successful or utterly failed.

"Women," he chugalugged, "are masochistic."

Perhaps it was his accent that made it difficult for me to take him seriously. He laughed again about the length of my skirt. "Are you embarrassed to be seen with me?" I teased. He made fun of my uncut, bushy hair, but then grabbed a lock, yanked it to him, his eyes suddenly swimming. "Don't ever cut it!" He jumped up and played Mick Jagger. "You're outta touch, my Baby, my poor old-fashion baby!"

"Do you want to make love?" he asked me after we had each drifted off in Janis's "Ball and Chain."

"I always want to make love," I answered, truthfully. "But I'm not going to with you."

"Well, then, let me take you to dinner."

He put on the leather jacket he had been carrying, though it was still hot. The resemblance to Nic was even more striking. Perhaps this was the fascination, the mystery, that pulled me along. It's not astrological after all, I laughed to myself. It's genetic, it's race, it's Greek! But I kept seeing the teenage Indian boy who walked away from me on a Coeur d'Alene beach three summers before after a brief conversation. I yelled after him, "May 14!" Max called him back. "When's your birthday?" "May 14." But even then I was unsure if it was astrology or ESP or what. I knew he was born on May 14th because he looked just like Nic whose birthday is May 14.

"What are you talking about now?" He was so annoyed with me. The streets were packed with people coming from their offices. We were whipping through them, he pulling me along, barely missing them, the masses, the great teeming masses. At a corner in the middle of the pedestrian traffic jam he muttered again like a curse, "Hor-é! Hor-é! Hor-é!" As we moved up Broadway I clung tighter to his arm. One miss in the rhythm, the fast dance, one false move and one would be trampled. As always the smell and sight of so many people filled me with great excitement, like love, a kind of sexual energy. And again we were suddenly in the midst of exceptionally beautiful women. I felt like a mouse in my ragged miniskirt, my rubber thongs. "Hor-é! Hor-é! Hor-é!" He shouted it now as if to dispel their power, to clear the way.

"I'll take you to the best Chinese restaurant in town." He hailed a taxi. Why not? I thought. How could one know New York without doing taxis? I had been in one, with Bridgit. When we pulled away from the curb and came to the light, the driver, another archetypic New Yorker—or am I being too kind, is the word stereotypic?— humped back his face onto his fat leathered shoulder to get a look at us, a face so snarled and smashed as to be a collage of all the faces of Manhattan taxi drivers. "Tell me, girls," he leered, interrupting our conversation. "Is it true, blondes have more fun?"

Bridgit guffawed like that was the funniest thing he could possibly have said, shoving him upside the back into his steering wheel, *"You better believe it, Mister!"* He turned around to the street and didn't say another word to us as we pulled up that long island.

Now in this cab—he corrected me when I called it a taxi—the Greek and I were speeding up Broadway, I think near Central Park. We surged through the traffic without hesitation. The speed was exhilarating. Leaving the walkers seemed like power. I was excited to share all this with Max. The Greek's arm came around me and he said something about petty female vindictiveness, about how shitty women are. His arm lay heavy around my neck and shoulders. "Women are immoral." I was feeling immoral from the beer, triumphant for being with a man I would under normal circumstances have nothing to do with. I was a reporter in search of an important story. I was a student taking a compulsory class, and to my surprise, enjoying it. Learning from it. He said the best Chinese restaurant is not in Chinatown. We got out somewhere in the eighties. We were getting nearer his apartment on West 91st.

I don't remember getting out of the cab. A side street. But I remember the walk of several blocks to the restaurant more clearly than any other moment with him. My mind became a sort of camera that rose high above the two of us, a scene that would run through me for years like a movie at which I rage at the role of the woman, refusing to see that she is inside me.

As we walked his long arm flowed around me, then jerked away. Then we were walking exactly parallel, about three feet apart, our eyes locked in each other's as he recited the memorized scene:

She stood up out of the bath, her damp, warm body the paradise of sex.

I took the ends of her hair and gently pinned her back; she moved her hands behind her back and rested them on my hips.

"Now just be you."

"Who is just me?"

"I'm going to find out."

"Are you?" A little smile at the corner of her mouth.

"Do you want me?"

"I'm dying for you."

She seemed to want me to rape her. Then very quickly she slipped away; ran to the door.

"Julie?"

I saw her pale figure against the faint rectangle. She spoke. The strangest voice; as hard as glass.

"There is no Julie."

The Greek and I were staring, trance-like, at each other. *The Magus.* John Fowles. A chill went through me. Suddenly I was afraid of him. He saw that I knew the book. His smirk grew. I pulled my eyes from him, to the gutter. The street darkened. Then he was a half-block ahead of me. I watched his arrogant, beaten back, so confident I would follow. I remembered Nic's year, like the Nick of the book, teaching in a private boys' school on a Greek island. Trying to find his roots, he wrote. All our roots. The roots of Western Civilization. I hadn't met Nic yet, then; I only knew him through his frequent letters to Max. Near the end he attempted suicide. Letters from the infirmary. The scars on his wrists. The street was suddenly much darker. Clouds going over. For a moment I came to my real self. Why am I following this jerk? I looked down an alley. Shoot down it. Disappear. When he finally deigns to turn around, you'll be gone. Just like his bitch. Just like Julie in *The Magus*. Just like normally you would do. But in looking from the alley back to him I felt a sort of sorrow for him, that he would only feel bitter, that he would only be stupid. I watched his tall contemptuous Greek back, Western Civilization, Nicolas and Maximilian. To leave him now I would learn nothing; it would only be a demonstration of my ego, my own self and story, something I had lived all my life, nothing new. To leave him now would only fuel the impotence in both of us. I was in relationship with him. Some joining. I recognized my lover. He was my objectivity. I'd always envied Alison, true hero/ine of *The Magus,* her great, decisive anger after Parnassus. I had always been more like Lily Rose, like her twin, Julie, the old-fashioned woman whose being is plastic, is the chameleon, molding itself into any situation the rigid and incapable male demands. So I went back to being drunk, to being the objective reporter, the giggly girl along for the ride.

He turned the corner. I turned the corner. It may have been Broadway. He was waiting for me three or four doors down. I followed him into the best Chinese restaurant in the city. The room was enormous, like a cafeteria, painted pale green, with mirrors, endless tables covered in white linens. We were the only customers. The starched corners of the cloths pointed like arrows to the ground. The food was good. "Without a doubt," I said grandly in the slight echo, "the best Chinese food I've ever eaten." I'm sure we had a bottle of wine. My giggles persisted.

At the end of the meal, however, his belligerence was turned on the Chinese boy who served us and once again I had a moment of coming to. He had a fit, a temper tantrum about some little thing that displeased him. This was before I knew that temper tantrums are typical New York male behavior. At the time, as with so much about him, I just found it hard to take seriously. Except that I flared for the boy. The Greek stomped out. A fifty-dollar bill lay in the tray. Enough to feed my family for a week. Enough to pay for his tantrum. Instinctively as I moved from the table I touched the boy who was removing our dirty dishes. It was an act of apology, a balancing gesture, like waving a wand, to wash our insult, to ground myself. But in the touch, which I understood instantly as patronizing, as the mirror image of his temper tantrum, the structure of my relationships rose a little higher from the abyss of my unconscious.

I was drunk, I had been so bored with myself. Now I was intrigued, by myself with him, not with him. I was in New York City and no one knew me, no one was looking, not even myself. At least the famous part, my self image. *I* was looking. That part's true. Looking for her. Hoping she'd come. Trying not to look so she could come. I was wearing rags, obviously from a Vermont commune. I was mortified by how conspicuous I was in all that Manhattan high fashion, *just a California chick,* as he said, but it was easy in his room on West 91st Street, a fifth-floor walk-up. He said he'd been in the room ten years. Imagine living in the same room for ten years. His dog, Aristotle, a large white poodle, needed to be walked. I needed to get back soon to Cinderella, my small black mongrel locked in the apartment on 95th. *"Black Cinder,"* Max called her.

I really did not think I would fuck him, or let him fuck me. I just thought I'd see his room, a New York City male's apartment. A fifth-floor walk-up. A ten-year home. 1964. Why would I think otherwise? I had never succumbed to a man under such conditions. Max always said beer makes me horny but normally I wouldn't have fucked Alex Kariopapoulas dead drunk.

He pulled me down on top of him as I made my way through the small crowded space for the bathroom, yanking my panties down my left leg and off the foot and I liked it and his skin was warm and I quickly computed the days and they added up to "safe." It had been a long time since I had felt a man's rough, shaved face. A bearded commune, yes, and I felt him inside me and I sort of loved him and I was moaning and he had come before I had come to my senses or even got my clothes off and he was asleep.

And so there I was in a strange man's apartment. He was passed out like all men after they've come, but I was more awake than I'd ever been, I was still in class and wanted to nose around the apartment. But his big, hairy Greek arm was laying over me and if I moved he'd wake and then I wouldn't be able to study the place. The shouts and engines of the people on the street rose to the window, floated around the room. I could hear the Beatles way off somewhere, *oh it gets so lonely*. I studied the dark arm for awhile across my clothed breasts. I managed to reach for a book open-faced on the floor beneath the bed. *The Magus*. *"Treat her as you would an amnesiac."* The sentence, underlined in red ink, jumped out at me. *Shit!* I shut the book, opened to another underlined passage:

> She had a certain exhalation of surrender about her, as if she was a door waiting to be pushed open; but it was the darkness beyond that held me. Perhaps it was partly a nostalgia for that extinct Lawrentian woman of the past, the woman inferior to the man in everything but that one great power of female dark mystery and beauty: the brilliant, virile male and the dark, swooning female. The essences of the two sexes had become so confused in my androgynous twentieth century that this reversion to a situation where a woman was a woman and I was obliged to be fully a man had all the fascination of an old house after a cramped anonymous modern flat. I had been enchanted into wanting sex often enough before; but never into wanting love.

Sober. My real self again. Wave of nausea. I turned the pages.

> It irritated me still that she put so much reliance on the body thing, the shared orgasm. Her mistaking that for love, her not seeing that love was something other . . . the mystery of withdrawal, reserve, walking away through the trees, turning the mouth away at the last moment.

You have to play hard to get, my mother lectured me when I was twelve. *Men won't love you otherwise.* My left hand found a pen. I continued my notes to Una on the back flyleaf—in the "objective" style of those years. *Aristotle is pacing the room. He needs to go out but his master is asleep. The sleeping master's arm holds me down. The master is Greek. His Greek come is dripping out my vagina and now down my fat buttocks. He mumbles "Hor-é" in his sleep. I'm stealing looks at his uncircumcised cock (do the Greeks not circumcise? Nic was just circumcised last year. Peer pressure, he said.)* (Soon Una would be secretly in love with Nicolas.) *and his balls, his thin greying jockey shorts rolled around his thin grey thigh. "Hor-é."* I had just lost a certain kind of virginity with this stranger.

"Hor-é." He kept mumbling the word in his sleep. Then I understood it. Hor-é! I jumped for joy! I had become one! I'd broken through something. *Freedom!* I wrote that word. I thought of how much Nicolas despised Alison's commonness, her inability to hide behind metaphor, her chronically bruised face from the hurt. How much *The Magus* is about class. Christianity. The sadomasochism of courtship and religion in the Western world, that *love is the mystery of withdrawal. To save you I die for you.* I lifted the heavy arm off me. He turned his back to me, slept to the wall. "Hor-é."

Pulling on my panties, I crept around the cluttered room, reading his messages of inspiration, looking at the posters and the 8 x 10 black-and-white glossy photos that were tacked to every wall. Starlets. Hollywood publicity shots. *To Alex, I really love you. To Alex, Forever. To Alex, My Body and Soul. To Alex, Please Never Forget Me.* A beautiful young girl, *Viva,* hypnotized me. Her eyes followed me around the room. Starlet, masochist, hor-é. Photographs of Alex *I Love You!* before the grey in his hair, his arrogant face like a knife behind the camera. His horoscope: Ios, Greece. Capricorn. December 25, in fact. 1934. There was a pile of women's clothes in the corner, purples, fuchsias, reds, golds, turquoises, the wild peasant colors I love, of material, mostly cotton, nonsynthetic, I would wear. It occurred to me that this was really someone else's apartment. Then I remembered a woman had recently left him. *She just left. I came home one day and she was gone.*

I made a list for Una of his books. They seemed clues to who he was. They were almost all about love. Perhaps they were her books. *The Art of Love,* Ovid. *On Love,* Stendhal. *The Art of Loving* and *The Heart of Man,* Erich Fromm. *The Function of the Orgasm* and *The Murder of Christ,* Wilheim Reich. *Be Here Now,* Ram Das. *Love and Orgasm, Love and Will,* Rollo May. *Human Sexual Response,* Masters and Johnson. *Talks and Dialogues,* Krishnamurti. *Love in the Western World, Everything You Always Wanted to Know About Sex, The Story of "O,"* stacks of *Playboy,* the Manhattan Yellow Pages, the screenplays for *Casablanca* and *Crime and Punishment, Tourism in Greece, Greece and the Struggle for Freedom, The Lust to Annihilate: A Psychoanalytic Study of Violence in Ancient Greek Culture. Justine. The Last Temptation of Christ, Spy in the House of Love.* I pulled one book from the shelf, a plain-covered one.

The magnifying glass from the OED lay on top of it. It was full of S&M photographs. The casual, depraved look on the women's faces. Women of all shapes and ages tied to chairs, spread-eagled on four-poster beds, their heads slumped, their tongues slung. Clothes pins on nipples. The enormous, engorged penises. Into the purple vaginal slit, into the tight anus. Blow-by-blow photo accounts of bondage, gang rape, whippings. *"The Thrills of Flagellation." "The Thrills of Humilia-tion."* I looked over at the model on *Playboy's* December cover. The air-brushed Santa-caped hormonal teenager couldn't make it in this book. The beaten-hag look—the pockmarked skin, the stretch marks cutting into the fat mounds—is the thrill, deep-shadowed stripes that photo-graph like whip marks, holes like craters on the lunar surface that evi-dence the brutal passage of God our Father through Eden. In a red pen someone had scribbled *The essence of S&M is trust.* And, *S&M deals with the pain our culture denies.*

In that moment I denied my part in these scenarios. Now, just as the scene from the street where I am following the sick man plays back to me at involuntary moments, I see the shades, the many mirrors of my-self. To eroticize one's oppression seems a small crime. To love one's oppressor the religion I once profoundly believed in. *It's women who identify with Jesus,* I wrote to Una, *crucified, naked on the cross. Not men. Men identify with God the Father who demands his child's martyrdom.* Then I added: *You'd think male homosexuality would be more prevalent, all the men who love Jesus.* "But Jesus is still the most feared of all males," my current lover says, who once studied for the Catholic priesthood. "The effeminate God, the Son, the Boy. They still assassinate the sensi-tive man. Lincoln, King, Malcolm X, Gandhi, John Lennon. They all spoke of love."

Aristotle whined. He was running back and forth on the back of the sofa against the front window. A dark oily line, the habit of years, ran the length of the glass too.

Suddenly I wanted Max. I wrote the Greek a gay little note. "Dear Alex Kariopapoulas. It was wonderful. You'll never know how much. Thanks." But on the way out I tripped over something. The apartment was so cluttered. Ten years. Aristotle barked. He called me back to the bed, pulled me down on him again, and this time, very quickly, I came, the wild fuchsia blooming, and then he did, and then he fell back to sleep.

And once again I was lying in a strange man's bed, now really missing my love and, suddenly, very sober. I tried to get up. He pulled me back. He handed me *The Magus,* which had lain between us, under us, as we fucked. "Read me the last pages."

It had been five years since I'd read the book. Another floor I slept on, waiting for my body to abort our child, Max's mother's floor in deep Los Angeles, just before we took off the first time across the country. Now I read to this stranger from whom I had twice received seed. First Alison, upon meeting him in the park:

> Whenever I am with you, it's like going to someone and saying, torture me, abuse me, Give me hell. . . .

Then Nick:

> I thought I will get her on a bed and I will ram her. I will ram her and ram her, the cat will fall and fall, till she is full of me. And I thought Christ help her if she tries to shield herself with the accursed wall of rubber. If she tries to put anything between my vengeance and her punishment. Christ help her. . . .

I read to the Greek the four terms by which she must accept him.

1. He has no money.
2. He will be adulterous.
3. He is not good in bed.

The fourth condition is about gender. *As a male I will judge you as an object. As a female you will judge me by our relationship.*
"You have no choice. You do as I say. Or you don't."
And then he lays it out, right down to the seconds she must count, the number of steps she must walk, the blow, that believe him, won't hurt her as much as it hurts him. *"I shall slap you as hard as I can over the side of the face."*
They act it out. I read it out. Two steps, four, six. Then ten. She calls

his name. *Nicko.* He stops. Turns with a granite-hard face. She comes toward him. She isn't acting. Are the Gods watching? Fifteen. Twenty. He closes his eyes. He prays. Her hand on his arm. He turns again. Her eyes are wounded, outraged. He is more than ever impossible. She is trying to delay it. Some compromise. He snatches himself free. He hits her before she can speak. He flicks his arm out, holds it the smallest fraction of a second, then brings it down sideways as hard as he can, so sure she will twist her head aside. But in that smallest fraction of a warning second she finally decides.

Pain.

They stare wildly at each other. Not in love, no name, but unable to wear masks. It is Halloween. Night of the Dead. The Gods have absconded. Mocking love, yet making it. She buries her face in her hands, as if some inexorable mechanism has started.

And as firm as Orpheus, as firm as Alison herself, that other day of parting, not once looking back, he is walking. Away.

I said to the Greek. "I heard Fowles is rewriting *The Magus.*"

It was his moment of greatest scorn for me. "Rewriting it! Don't be blasphemous!"

"No. It's true. He said it's the book of a young man. He said he didn't have the balls to pull it off. He said he lost his nerve, sexually."

He rose from the bed, cursing me in Greek.

"He's writing it now from Alison's point of view. Or maybe it was Lily Rose's or Julie's."

"You're full of shit."

"Yeah," I laughed. "Who'd ever read *The Magus* from a female point of view? They'd dismiss it as confessionalism. They'd call it soap opera."

He was yanking on his pants. I noticed again how dirty and stretched his jockey shorts were, how uncomfortable they must make him. "We must walk Aristotle."

"Did you know Nick's last name, Urfe, is a pun for Earth?"

"Hor-é," was his answer.

In the new version he will not plan to hit her, it will be neither intended nor instinctive, in cold blood or in hot, but necessary. But he will not walk away. She says I hate you, I *hate* you. But now he sees something, the something he had never seen, or always feared to see, in her eyes, the quintessential something behind all the hating, the hurt, the tears. *A small step poised, a shattered crystal waiting to be reborn,* what the poet meant when he spoke of the tipping of the scales toward life, what women know in their uteruses about life and death, what the Patriarchy will never know or survive. Over the passage of ten years, the author, in a miracle, relocates himself, finally understands her word, *love,* understands that he'll "never be more than half a human being without you." And so he will be blasphemous to the Old Order, he will take a real step. He will rewrite his masterpiece.

We descended the five flights of stairs, descended to the teeming masses. On the sidewalk we turned west to the river, the Hudson River, and sat on the grass in a long park in the late afternoon sun while Aristotle ran around in ever widening circles from us. I was very concerned now about Cinderella. Lovers, real lovers, moved by, and bicycles and garbage tows on the river. Old people. The Palisades of New Jersey gleamed with light—remote, benign, the great wall to the West, my West, my land, its elegant windows to the Gods. I could hear Joni Mitchell somewhere. *Here I am strung out on another man.* The Beatles. Strawberry Fields Forever. *Nothing to get hung about. (I am always in the back seat of that sports car with Max, those two sailors who picked us up hitching 2 A.M. on the outskirts of Las Vegas speeding 100 miles per hour across the night desert to Moab and Una and Johnny Lookfar's wedding, more dope and liquor than the wildest hippy could ever dream, the two boys just back from Nam driving from Long Beach, California to Denver, Colorado on leave which was only the weekend because the only girls they knew in the States lived there, when the news came over their Howlin Wolfman Jack station from LA the Beatles have broken up. And how we were busted as the sun came up at Crescent Junction when they stopped to let us off thirty miles north of Moab, busted by Blackie, just sitting there at the Junction, waiting for us, the man who is Una's husband now. He was even then in love with her though it never occurred to us he knew her, this was thirty miles north of Moab in the middle of the desert and he was a cop. I'd forgotten about small towns. When we told him we were going to Una and Johnny Lookfar's wedding he let the two of us go, which was very lucky because Max had broken probation in leaving California, he'd still be in the*

federal prison at Florence if we'd gotten stopped in that thirty-five miles
through Arizona, the Shivwits Indian Reservation. Land of the Midnight
Sun, but so crummy for those sailors, their car stuffed full of booze and dope,
the last time I looked back they were opening the trunk, I always worried
about what happened to them. We got the ride down into Moab in that big
diesel, so stoned, so relieved, our hearts pounding, the sun so bizarre rising on
Moab, the window arches, the red columns, the Colorado, the radio playing
nothing but the Beatles, strawberry fields forever, Moab is my washpot, all
that jiggery-pokery electronics like it was a wake not a wedding we'd come all
this way for, so I was shouting out the window the Old Testament, Woe to
thee, Moab! thou art undone! He hath given his sons that escaped, his
daughters into captivity. The trucker thought I was nuts but he dug it,
laughed, right on girl! Moab! the uncircumcised and the uncircumcised of
the heart! Nothing to get hung about! It was April 1, 1970. So then I
ranted from The Waste Land, *Moab always made me think of it, April is the*
cruellest month. . . .) Now the Palisades looked like the marbled walls of
a bank. I looked at my notes to Una. I had ripped out the last pages of
The Magus with the last two lines on it. I apologized. I asked him to
read them to me if he could, to tell me what they mean.

"*Cras amet qui numquam amavit/ quique amavit cras amet.* Who is
that?" He looked at me. I had no idea. "Ovid, maybe. It says *Tomorrow*
he shall love who never loved. No. That's not right. There's no pronoun
"he" in the quote. It could be *he, she,* or *it.* The pronoun is *qui. Who.*"

He took a deep breath. His brow furrowed, the stringy hair everywhere. He looked at the river.

"*Who never loved shall love tomorrow. Whoever loved shall love tomorrow.*
Something like that. *Who shall love tomorrow never loved.* It's hard to say
it in English. There are differences in the language, in the thought."

I asked him about *"eleutheria. Her turn to know."*

"Freedom," he said.

He offered me his leather jacket, to cover my legs. A man walking by
was looking at them.

"No thanks. I'm not cold."

A ship moved down. This island, like any Greek island, here at the
beginning of time. The thing was, the chemistry, right down to the
basalt sea on which Manhattan floats, had altered. Now he kept look-

ing at me, looking at me for the first time since the fern bar. But this look was different, this look exposed him, this look said, I'm open, I need you. He smiled a lot. Aristotle jingled up to us, then darted off. From tree to tree. "Do you really love him?" I must have told him of Max. "Are you sure?" he said, a little wounded. "You could move in with me. There's room for two people, the place really needs two people. There's even clothes there for you. I'll buy you new clothes. I'll support you. You can write."

I laughed, warmly, as I had all day. I sort of loved him. I lay my head on his shoulder, my hand on his thigh.

"I have to get back. I have to let Cinderella out. Bye, Alex Kariopapoulas. I love you. I'll never forget you."

Then I was walking. Firmly north. He would never know that he was my first casual love, my first one-night stand, in the middle of the afternoon, that with him, I had finally accomplished something that had eluded me all my life. *Fragments of freedom, an anagram made flesh.* I had broken a deep bondage. A block away, I turned and he was still watching me. I wanted to cry. I waved remembering something Una said to me when we first met as girls. "Even if it's wham-bam-thank-you ma'am and he leaves $2.00 on the nightstand something human and beautiful has been exchanged."

As I disappeared (disappeared into the great communes of the Northeast Kingdom! Into the great secret cultures all over the earth! Into the great power of female dark mystery and beauty!) feeling his eyes on me as long as he could see me, feeling him inside me, feeling my disbelief that I would never see him again, but feeling triumphant too (walking more firmly away from Aristotle and Western Man than ever before!), my heart turned again to Max. If the Gods are dead, Maximilian, if there is no such thing as love as you say, if when you rise before me you are not the One I was torn from at the beginning, if all of this has been just to bring us to our last lesson and final ordeal, our fame into the destruction of not just love but mountains too, if all of this has just been the Magus driving his wedge between spirit and flesh, culture and nature, man and woman, sister and sister, our bodies into the persecution of the Son and ten million Witches, to shatter our connection with the land, to impose the mechanistic view of the world as a dead machine, so he can own it, if this is true but there's nothing that can be done about it, as you convinced me for a while as you fucked me, you were so brilliant, I was so young, I was trying to get an education, you were trying to get some pussy, then I would stay with you, never mind that you can't love me, my love for you being the only reason for me to live. But I see now that you have fallen in love with him, you are living for him, the Guy you think is watching (*the Guys!*), a whore for his everything, this frozen moment of the late twentieth century, his theater, his private little masque, his S&M fantasy for the grand finale of his god-game, his Climax. You ram me and ram me, your vengeance and my punishment and *still* you maintain you are not breaking the commandment.

When I got back to the apartment, Max wasn't home. I walked Cinderella for almost an hour, past dark. I wondered about my sister, where she was at this moment and Janie, about her life as a secretary in New York City. I thought about Una and Johnny in Utah. There was no moon. The moon was in Aries that night, it had gone down long before the sun. Una is an Aries. I remembered the first fight Max and I had. He called me a whore. Because I started seeing another man when he continued to see other women. I remembered the shock, how it took my breath away, when he threw the word. He said it in front of my kids. I should have left then. But I was so hurt I didn't consider it. It was blackmail I was a real whore for. I dug in to prove I wasn't. When I got back to the apartment and he still wasn't there, I started shaking. I threw the *I Ching* for the first time. It was lying on the window sill. It was the moment Johnny Lookfar hurled into space. I got *Keeping Still*.

Warriors

In a while we would be broken. Now the undoing began, the small implosions, the pent-up bitterness let through the thousand little cracks present in all relationships—the cracks cemented, as long as it is working, with love.

We were in San Francisco, Max to attend the annual librarian's convention and I to attend the Small Press Book Fair. It was July 9th, the day after his 35th birthday. For reasons I was unsure of, he hadn't spoken to me since he woke on the morning of his birthday. It seems absurd now but as my "gift" to him I was trying to accept this, trying not to be angry or hurt, and at the same time, trying not to let him ruin my time in the city. His moods often debilitated both of us. To love him, it seemed to me then, meant accepting the violent emotional storms that overtook him.

Nicolas picked us up Saturday night at the conclusion of our separate events. We were staying in his apartment above the Payless Cleaners in East Oakland. "I'll show you the city," he said in a tone for country cousins, assuming the connoisseur air of one who had lived in the Bay Area off and on for years. Max sat in the back seat. When he spoke, which was not often, it was to Nic. His silence roared. We drove around the Civic Center, out to the Marina, through the Presidio, out to the Cliff House, back through North Beach, Nic sharing his week, his job of teaching emotionally handicapped teenagers in one of Oakland's black ghetto high schools. Nic and Max had been best friends since they themselves were together in a Chicano ghetto junior high school in East Los Angeles. Nic's lesson that week had been "Love." His attitude, I noted, was identical to Max's. It is an impossible word to define. It is a delusion fashioned from our romantic, capitalistic culture. Most likely, there is no such thing. The degree of one's intelligence and maturity is equal to the degree one is capable of holding this point of view. Suddenly, at the Cliff House, as we looked down from the car window to the crashing waves and then turned back to the city, our lights spraying across the crowds on the Pacific bluff, the thought of Nic arrogantly instructing emotionally disturbed children that love is a delusion shot rage up my throat with choking vengeance. This was surprising, not in my objection, but in the sudden demand my objection was making for expression. For years, with Max, I had lived with the attitude. I had found it interesting and had learned from it. Perhaps it was a way of testing my own ideas and feelings about love. I understood the attitude as a result of his LA ghetto childhood. But now, for the first time, I wondered what it was in my childhood that made me think I was being mature and intelligent in understanding his denial of love for me, his consistent eight-year response when I asked, on rare, foolish occasions, if he loved me, that it is impossible to love. Why did I accept this when I knew, with all the knowledge of my body and my experience with the world, that I loved him?

The city celebrated its balmy evening, a sexual celebration moving into the night like birth. The cars on the streets were rivers of flowing light, the sidewalks jammed with people, their colorful new clothes a spontaneous fashion show, a great breaking from the previous years that so cruelly held them. Neon gave each body a phosphorescent glow, especially the exposed, tan skin, the ripple of taut muscles. I was in love with the people too!

"Let's park the car and walk awhile," I blurted out uncharacteristically as we moved down Columbus. Normally I wanted to do whatever they wanted to do. Nic, seeming not to have heard my suggestion, said something condescending about the crowd. "The grapes of wrath." I repeated the suggestion. This time I saw that he was deliberately ignoring me. Our assignment was to study the foolish masses from the objectivity and superiority of the car. Max, behind us, was like the dead center of a tornado, silently sucking everything in.

Years I'd been driving around with these guys. I love the car too, I love driving through the world, driving in and out of situations as I please. But I had spent the day looking at books of poetry produced by small independent presses, encountering poets and editors, feeling deeply frustrated that I had no books, not even a poem, to show of my own. In agreement with Max's philosophy, I didn't "believe" in writing, never mind that I had written all my life, in journals, in long letters to my close girlfriends, as a student in English literature, five years on a scholarly work of James Joyce. Certainly I didn't believe in publication, the same thing, I thought, as commercialization, to "sell-out," to Hollywood—practically my hometown. To write is an inadequate, and therefore foolish, distillation of the spirit, to write for publication even lowlier. But now suddenly I was hungry for involvement, for *love,* the love only physical engagement can make. I was seeing for the first time the attitude of these guys as voyeurism. Writing, community, relationship, children: the ideal is to remain uncommitted. Outside. The objective observer. Mental, hip, abstract, cool. I was beginning to see too painfully that all this was identical to Max's way with me. I had learned from this stance but now I was bored. Some values had survived the ridicule test. I could feel them, *interesting,* stirring within me. "If you're not going to love them," I mumbled, yearning for the people, "you have no right to look at them." I wanted to at least park the car and walk with them. But Nic continued to ignore my request.

We did leave the car once that evening, for a disastrous meal in Chinatown. Nic boasted that unlike the tourists he knew a place to eat real Chinese food. After a half hour of searching for a parking place, he walked us down a dark alley that smelled of urine, then up to a third-floor hole-in-the-wall. Assuming the air of the gourmet Nic ordered, without consultation, for the three of us. In the light I noticed the scars on his wrists and became concerned for him. There was no acknowledging the inedible food, Max protecting his friend too. I was certain they wokked our noodles in rancid oil deliberately, served the contempt, they, the real people, had for us. In this confusion— *rancid karma,* I kept thinking—we were back in the car before I knew it. We rode up to Coit Tower, Nic telling Max how Mrs. Coit is giving the city the finger, looked at the Golden Gate Bridge, the narrow river of lights pouring across it, then back down Broadway, out Market, the distance between the back seat and the front as great as the car to the street. I hadn't eaten all day. I was starving. In wave after wave the memory of the books I had just seen filled me first with frustration, then with excitement. I wanted to make a book. *You don't have to sell out,* the Small Press Book Fair screamed the revelation, *you don't have to compromise.* The poets I had encountered seemed like lovers, vulnerable, courageous and mature in the opening of themselves to the world, in their acceptance of the awkwardness of their medium their own awkwardness in it, in their *trying* to speak from their hearts, their souls. I was feeling overwhelmed by the simple, yet for me the most occluded of truths, that writing is communication. The reader is the mate! The other half of the relationship! *The reader is the Muse. The Muse!* I'd never understood the concept of the Muse before. I'd always gotten confused in the issue of its gender. Now I saw, very clearly, my real confusion stemmed from my denial of the reader.

The reader is the Muse! I turned to share this with them. *The Lover who dictates the Word, the Lover to whom the word is dictated.* Luckily, I stopped myself. These guys would put me away if I said something like that. Nic drove with outrageous scorn, Max sulked. I was silently exploding with years of things like this I wasn't allowed to say. So I just said, "Oh, Nico. Aren't we going to get out and walk?"

As we moved through Golden Gate Park and it was apparent that we were not, I started fantasizing an old secret love, a writer whose work I was in awe of. Several people at the book fair had informed me of his arrival in Berkeley that day from the East. I could see him and his poet wife on the paths through the park, then in the crowds on the streets. As the night dragged on, as we drove around and around I looked for them everywhere, seeing myself run into them accidentally as I too wandered the streets. Accident, passivity, fantasy—I was so tired of these. My restlessness beat at me from inside while the lights of the ships made me wistful. I was working so hard not to get caught in the stale, hateful energy of the back seat.

"Shit!" I finally blurted. "I wish I could walk the streets alone! If only I had the freedom you guys have."

"Well," Nic said, suddenly responding. "That's an interesting wish." I watched him put on, like a robe, his master's degree in psychology. "*Why* for God's sake would you want to walk the streets alone?"

"*Why?*" I screamed it. "To be part of the crowd. To be on the street. To walk. To learn the city."

We rode on in silence. I didn't say, I couldn't have, I didn't know it yet, that I was sick of being with them, of being in their control. I loved Max and our life too much to deal yet with this thought.

But I could hardly stand what I heard next, the articulation of a lie I trusted Nic, by our friendship, not to, even remotely, think. "It would appear," he said, turning a corner, "you get off on being a tease." And then looking ahead, he enunciated the word very carefully. "Street-walker."

Nic considered himself a sociologist of the street. He was a man who had chosen to live in the ghetto, in an attempt, I had always assumed, to better understand his emotionally handicapped ghetto students. Now I was beginning to wonder why he had no friends, why his identity seemed to lie in being the only white person in his neighborhood. He lived in exile—again, an outsider, a voyeur.

"Are you familiar with that book by the two American girls," he went on, lost in his arrogance, "who hitchhiked across Africa?"

"Yes, but I haven't read it." I had seen it all day at the fair. Much of the text is written by hand, like an original journal. It was a bestselling small press book. *The Small Press Success of the Year,* a banner hailed.

"Well, you ought to. You could learn something. These chicks, you know, were raped by an African tribe. But they were so hip, they were so philosophical and understanding about what happened to them they accepted full responsibility for the rape. They knew they were *intruders, trespassers, outsiders . . .*" he enunciated each of these words with scorn, "*hitchhikers,* in a land where they were in clear violation of the customs."

"But this isn't Africa," I said, enunciating each of my own words. "This is my country."

"Yes. That's the point. For you to walk these streets alone would be in clear violation of the laws of the streets. *You know this.* It would seem—what else can one think?—that you want to tease men."

It was all I could do to keep from bolting from the car. *Out into the dark with the rapists!* My frustration and anger had to do precisely with my understanding and compassion, which I was newly perceiving had freighted my life with a great and possibly tragic passivity. The day before, as I followed the inexplicably silent and hostile Max, the birthday boy, around the Mendocino Headlands, the lines had come to me, *Men understand nothing and therefore can do anything. Women understand everything and therefore can do nothing.*

"You're right about one thing. Rape hasn't anything to do with real sex!" I was spitting out the words, surprised at the clarity of my understanding. "Rape is a political act. Men rape women to feel superior to them. Men rape women to feel power in a culture that has dehumanized all of us. Men rape women to affirm their so-called manhood, their selfhood, the illusion that they are different, separate, superior to something, to maintain the sense that being a *man* is a special condition. Understand rapists? When are you going to understand me as well as you understand rapists?"

But he continued to argue with me all the way across the Bay Bridge. Max sat in the back seat, silent.

Max woke the next morning, his mood changed. The sun shown spectacularly through the window across our naked bodies, burning off any fog that lingered from the day before. We made love and I put on a pastel sun dress. I even wore the high-heeled sandals Nic offered me. I hadn't worn anything like them in years. They seemed appropriate for the city. They made me laugh when I walked around in them. Or rather, on them. Max pulled me back into our room to fuck me again with them on. Standing up, from behind, bending me over, lifting my dress, our giggles, inserting his long dark penis into me.

"You should wear things like this more often."

We drove the town again, this time the east side of the Bay. High clouds floated over the gleaming water, the golden, black oak-strewn hills, and all the people, the poor and the rich, the students and the old, the children, everyone, revelling, it seemed, in the sun. Wildly dressed bodies at the intersections, housewives and tourists in the open markets, and somewhere my writer lover, my long-time fantasy, the man whose intelligence is great enough to understand me, to *want* to understand me. I kept seeing us whipping by him on the street, and I'm turning, the hair flying from my face and there he is: I see him. He sees me.

We were coming down San Pablo, finally on our way to the bookstore I had been requesting we go to all afternoon. Again, I had tried not to think Nic was deliberately stalling, his pathetic need to be director, driver, authority, teacher in control, but it was four thirty and the store closed at five. We were in the outside lane at the intersection when he began to repeat his lecture from the night before. "When you are in the ghetto it is important to respect the traditions of the street." I screamed at him. Max in the back seat laid his hand on my shoulder. "Shut up. Can't you see you're acting just like a woman!"

And I was gone. Out the door, between the stopped cars, down a block behind them, then another and then another, my anger so deep and surprising I was making sure I lost them for fear of what I'd do if I saw them looking for me. I was running along picking up stones to throw at Nic's new Toyota. In their big stupid car they didn't have a chance with me on foot. On foot I had the freedom to go anywhere, behind a garage, into the shrubs.

But now the cold reality of my situation: I didn't know where I was, I didn't know where to go, what to do. I didn't know Berkeley—only Telegraph Avenue. I found myself in a poor neighborhood, black. What was I going to do when night came? I counted my money, almost five dollars. It was near five o'clock. It was getting cold. Four hours of sun left. Suddenly I was afraid.

I found the bookstore. It had just closed. I held my face and hands to the window and saw the books, the names of writers that both disturbed and thrilled me. Disturbed me for my exclusion from a world I felt I belonged to. *Turn around and walk away.* The only way into that world is to write a book.

Walk. Walk against your longings, your fantasies. Walk this street. Now walk this one. Walk like you know where you are going. Walk like home or store or your man is in the next block. Walk, with your eyes straight ahead. Think as you fast walk. Watch where you are going. Walk against your loneliness, against being maimed in loneliness. Walk against getting raped. Walk against getting busted. Recall the time you were arrested for prostitution because you were walking down from Griffith Park Observatory in LA. "People who look like you shouldn't walk," the cop said. Walk against getting hit on. Walk against the growing cold. Walk against the coming dark. Walk in circles. Know you are a woman and therefore in danger. Ignore the

"Baby!" *when you walk the crosswalk in front of his car.* "Hey! You!" *And you never learn, you vow never to learn, you will always turn around to answer, to stay open, though it's always . . . a mistake. Walk on. Walk north. Turn the corner like you know Hearst Street. Intruder, trespasser, outsider. You are a woman. In this country you are in violation of the laws of the streets.*

At the gas station I bought a Bay Area street map. I looked up Sierra Madre Avenue where I knew my writer friend and his family were staying as guests in the home of another writer. Sierra Madre was many long blocks away, all uphill. I started walking for the Berkeley Rose Gardens just beyond Sierra Madre. Where else would I walk? Why not in the direction I most yearn? It occurred to me that I had jumped from the car to look for them.

After a while I came to a little shopping district north of the university. "Northside," the map said. Coffee shops, bookstores, boutiques. A "nice area." I felt safe for the first time. I could relax. I sat in an Italian coffee shop on Hearst Street, resting, trying not to get depressed or worried, trying not to think about Max and our relationship, watching and wondering about the Mexican dishwasher, the black mathematician in the corner working feverishly with a slide rule, a hitchhiker out on the street holding up a sign for "Anywhere." The longer I sat there the more depressed I became. The headlines of the *Chronicle* were everywhere: STALEMATE A THREAT TO TALLEST REDWOOD. I kept saying Hearst. Hearse. Heart. I kept seeing Patty. I kept seeing Max, walking way ahead of me on the headlands of Mendocino. His birthday, 35. He quit talking to me. No explanations. The black figure I love, the black coat to his ankles, the thick black curls blowing wildly across his back disappearing into the fog over the crashing sea. He was so beautiful to me, he was so cruel to me. *I followed him. I follow* him. Margaret Atwood's poem ran through my mind: "You fit into me/ like a hook into an eye/ a fish hook an open eye." In *my* tradition you stick with your man through everything. Whither thou goest I will go. You love him unconditionally. Always he will test your love. Always you must prove your love. But now I wished I could see myself on the headland turning from him, walking in a different direction. I opened my journal to a quote from F. Scott

Fitzgerald's quote was one from Jung: "When love is absent power fills the vacuum." And then one by the poet H.D. on women: "Our aware- has been the complete, fine and full-hearted selfishness and chill-mindedness of Zelda." The words were a painful description of Max's hypnotic power over me. Long ago I had made the classic mistake of thinking: if I love him enough he will love me. But the dynamic be-tween us had never changed. After all these years he seemed as ig-norant of me as he did in the beginning. This was so preposterous, so damning of him it was hard to accept. And it hurt. Beneath Fitzgerald's quote was one by Jung: "When love is absent power fills the vacuum." And then one by the poet H.D. on women: "Our aware-ness leaves us defenseless."

Shit. I closed the book. How could I ever make poetry out of such crap? I left the coffee shop, walked blocks up tree-lined Euclid. I walked right past Sierra Madre where it intersects with Euclid. I had no intention of being seen walking in front of the house, obviously looking for him. I just wanted to see the neighborhood in which he was staying, a small way of knowing him. My feet were hurting, grow-ing numb. I had taken off my high-heeled sandals miles ago. I was cold in my sun dress, my shoulders bare. Of all the ironic ways to dress! I, who always wear Levis and boots, always prepared for this.

After the packed dirt, scattered trash, dry thorny weeds sprung through asphalt and cement, what a wonder that vegetation grows so lush in some neighborhoods. The red-tile-roofed Mediterranean homes beneath redwoods—the tiles made in the tradition of Indian slaves who shaped the adobe on their thighs—so quaint in their shrouds of ivy, so comfortable, tasteful, correct, still like it was when your grandfather came west to teach here in the twenties. The benevolent aroma and light of eucalyptus, the huge pastel hydrangeas, the manicured lawns, the protected hillsides, the mysterious paths into the redwoods between the houses, the red-painted sidewalks. It made me angry. The devastating conformity, the oppressive niceness, the re-spectability built on the oppression of others. I laughed aloud when I realized I was looking for stones again to break windows. And then again when I saw that there were no stones in this neighborhood.

I came to the Berkeley Rose Gardens. I walked around the reservoir, the ball park, wandered through the roses, and then sat on a bench.

San Francisco Bay lay before me, the whole mystical city. The fog was rolling in beneath the Golden Gate Bridge, the sun dropping behind it. I could smell the roses. *Granada. Angel Wings. Summer Sun. Strawberry Blonde. King's Ransom.* Is there a rose named *Rose Rodriguez: "all sweetness and no thorns"*? I have this written in the list of names of roses and their characteristics I made as I sat there on the bench, after wandering down the rose path, my back and ass melting into what seemed a velvet sedan, my heart melting as the sun descended more and more to the horizon line. What was I going to do? The California poppies at my feet were folding shut though the sun suddenly shone right on them. Beautiful couples kept arriving in sports cars and sports clothes, so smug it seemed and secure with their homes to return to after an afternoon match of tennis, here, high above everything, the whole bay, Alcatraz, San Quentin, the Sacramento pouring in with its heavy melted load from the Sierras. The Mother Lode. I remembered reading that the Golden Gate is new, the passage to the sea too narrow to let through all that water for any great length of time. The original outlet must have been the Monterey Bay. Does anyone ever jump off the Oakland Bay Bridge? I could almost see John Berryman jumping off it, as he did the university bridge in Minneapolis, the poet waving to someone, anyone, as he falls. When I asked Nic he said yes, but it doesn't have the mystery. "You know," he said, "the end of the frontier." A Japanese woman sat down beside me. She didn't lean back, as if she was uncomfortable about me. I couldn't help but stare into her back. I felt hypnotized. I saw that we would not speak and my loneliness increased. Why is it so difficult for me to enter the world? I sat transfixed, the fantasy of turning around to see my writer friend arriving to behold the roses in Berkeley as exquisite as the sun that was setting. My blood was pounding. I wanted to whisper my new name in her ear, *I am Rose Rodriguez.* The thought made me laugh, lifted my spirits, but it never left me, the worry of getting home through miles and miles of dangerous ghetto, to East Oakland. Of course I would go back. I'm an understanding woman. All sweetness. No thorns.

When the sun was gone I realized it had been two days since I'd had a meal, tasting again last night's rancid noodles. As I walked back to the shopping district I watched a dog run frantically back and forth down both sides of the street, obviously lost, trying to smell his way home. I bought a hamburger and chocolate malt, my first meat in two years. It tasted terrible. I thought I needed it for strength for whatever was ahead. A man stared at me the whole time I struggled with the big thing. When he sat down at my table I immediately started asking him questions to make it more interesting. A Ph.D. biochemist from Iran. Post-graduate. He told me of an Arab poet I should read: *Mamud Daraweesh,* the name in a strange handwriting in my journal. A phone number. It was dark now and hard for me to think clearly, with him so attentive, about what I should do next. His car keys lay on the table between us. I knew he would love to be Sir Walter Raleigh—I mean Omar Khayyám—for this damsel in distress. It was the move I should make. Except he was so sexist in his manner, the expectation for "payment" so present, this solution bored me. Which gave me new energy —or was it the meat? I wasn't so desperate after all. I was still into the adventure. He was talking to me, ignoring my question about the body's immune system when suddenly I saw my writer friend, the one I'd been thinking about so much, his wife and host coming down the sidewalk.

It seemed I was staring at them a long while before I realized it was really them beneath the movie marquee. His wife's eyes, her self-conscious, nervous animal stare. In the flash before they walked on, the picture I think I will always carry of them, they embodied the terrible beauty an old love has. You see it all again, what pulled you, but now framed in the sorrow of its failure, the story that seems the basic sorrow of your life.

The Iranian man was saying something about leaving, that obviously I was involved in something he didn't understand. I could feel that my face had drained of color. We said goodbye, my hands shaking, my mind whirling, where have they gone? I started out into the street, then darted back inside. What would I ever say to them? Our encounters had always been fraught with confusion and, seemingly, their disgust for me. I bought another cup of coffee. Maybe I could go to their house and stay awhile. Maybe they could give me the ride home.

Finally, I wandered down the street in the direction they had dis-appeared. A steep hill in my sandals, which I had put back on to enter the deli. I looked into the ice cream shop. I went into the crowded bookstore. Then I crossed the street to the campus and walked down a path into high, dark foliage. They must have gone to an event on campus. I became afraid of the dark. I found myself on the steps of the Geology Building. From the corner a man, huddled in a blanket, snarled. I ran back to the lit shopping district. I called Nic's. It was after ten. No answer. I called transit information: four bus changes to get to East 14th and 14th Avenue, with one fifteen-minute wait in down-town Oakland. I had enough change to make it. I realized I shouldn't get on a bus—the next one would be at 10:44 somewhere near this corner—until Nic and Max were home to let me in the door. Nothing could be more dangerous than to be locked outside Nic's apartment, worse even than being stranded in downtown Oakland where there are at least street lights and crowds. I was standing there, trying to look like I knew what I was doing, aware of several men watching me, when through the corner window I saw them returning, eating ice cream cones. Without thinking, I walked right into them.

I guess I was in love with the man. In love? I guess I don't under-stand this kind of love, this kind of humiliating confusion and un-consummated longing. My fascination had to do with his deep in-volvement with poetry and writing. At thirty years of age he had sev-eral books of autobiographical prose, which led me to believe I had in-timate knowledge of him. Another classic mistake. He, of course, had not read anything I had written and tended to dismiss me as—well, once at a party in Vermont I overheard him refer to me as an LA Blonde. But I'm a very understanding woman. How could I expect him to know me as I knew him? The fact that most people in the town in which we lived as neighbors hated him, the fact that his poet wife had encouraged a relationship between us so that she could pursue her own fantasy lover, a well-known sculptor in the town, the fact, I sup-pose, that he then rejected me all added a strange fuel to my compul-sion toward him.

The man who was their host, a well-known Berkeley writer, recog-nized me from the book fair. Then the wife, then the man. It had been a year since we'd seen each other and that had been in the East. Where people are so different. Five minutes, maybe ten, we stood there, the three of them licking ice cream cones. The wife, gloriously tan, wearing an orange-striped sun dress and stylish high-heeled sandals, looking, in fact, more like an LA Blonde than a poet, tried to be cordial but was clearly impatient with meeting me again. She was worried about the cold. "Imagine meeting *you* in Boulder. Boulder? Oh, where am I? Berkeley. Yes, well, call me if you need me next week, care of the Foundation. Is that alright, Bill? We'd better go now. It's getting cold."

The host stopped her. Ice cream dripped from his nose and beard. Can we take you somewhere? No. No. Confusion and embarrassment. Do they realize this encounter isn't entirely accidental? Suddenly it seemed that all the events preceding this meeting were set in motion by me intentionally. To cover myself, I half explained my situation. "Max and I had a fight." "I thought it must be something like that," *he* said. "I mean you just wouldn't be out here like this." *Why wouldn't I?*, I almost snapped. They offered to take me down to University and Shattuck for the main bus connection but I had decided not to leave the area until Nic or Max answered the phone. I couldn't explain this adequately. It was too complicated. Understandably, their attitude toward me became like that of dealing with a naughty, difficult child, the attitude they had always had about me.

I declined their offer to take me home. When I explained it was in East Oakland they did not insist. We were not connecting, they were not connecting with me, and for all my longing for them and their literary world I could not enter a relationship with them, more than passively, without their also entering into it with me. Nothing I could ever do, I suddenly knew, could break their preconceived notion, their fantasy of me. In *my* fantasy of them, as with Max, I had given them too much credence. I had made the classic mistake of assuming that people so involved, so pleased with their own intelligence, would be intelligent with me.

It was a day of significant endings, a day when I began to act on a lifelong understanding that the inability to see the other person is the most common stupidity, a tragic syndrome perpetuated by our culture that maintains only by maintaining this blindness. I saw that I was guilty of the trait, too, in a sort of opposite fashion. I couldn't see their blindness, at least enough to take it seriously. I expected them to know me as I knew them—though I had supplied them with very little access. No books. When I walked away from them, the man and his wife, my three-year fascination and compulsion for them was dead.

I went back to the deli and ordered a beer, the first beer I ever bought for myself. It relieved me of the fatigue I was feeling. The sore throb of blisters on my feet, the men staring at me diminished as hassles in my mind. There was an answer when I called Nic's. Without speaking I hung up. I left, impatient with everything.

In the bookstore I asked the cashier if he knew the location of the bus stop. Hovering over him was a large display of my friend's latest book. I hadn't read it. Last year's bestseller. A clearance sale. I knew I'd never read it. The cashier advised me to walk down to Shattuck to save money on the connection there. Much to my annoyance I started down the hill. I was annoyed because I had automatically followed his advice, which could screw up my whole zip-zap bus schedule across town. I was questioning everything about the passivity of my nature. It loomed like a stupid, dangerous animal all around me. I just needed to move, I told myself. As I hurried down the hill in the dark, I hunted through my bag for a ribbon or pins, thinking I would be less conspicuous if my hair were tied back. This was a tactic Max was always advising. But as earlier in the day I could find nothing with which to do this. And for all my consternation, Shattuck turned out to be just a block away.

Then the long ride through the city in the dead of Sunday night, the buses full of tired and lonely people whose bodies shifted back and forth in a slow motion tug-o-war as the bus stopped and started up again, drone and whine, the rough rhythm the rhythm of their lives, the larger machine that carries them. When we arrived at the downtown Oakland stop the bus driver announced the number 80 bus would be forty-five minutes late.

And then everything I dreaded and feared began occurring. I kept thinking about self-fulfilling prophecy and then I'd be angry for assuming such responsibility. I was sick of understanding everything at my own expense.

I remember seeing, as they surrounded me, the handful of people also waiting for the late bus, backing away from us. I remember most vividly a very sad-looking man on my left and a woman carrying a grocery bag of work clothes on my right backing far away into the silver marble walls of the Wells Fargo Bank, as I heard one boy say, "I'll bet she'll talk to us when we drag her by her yellow hair into the alley."

There were six of them, young teenage boys, black, circling me. From my back one gathered some of my hair in his hand, yanked it. They circled and circled, spitting obscenities into my face. The violence in each of their young male bodies banded with each of the others, chaining me in a dance of awesome, suffocating power.

"*Sunshine.*" The name spit from the meanest looking face I'd ever seen. "Sunshine." He kept repeating it. Spit and his hot, vomit-and-booze breath on my face. He was fifteen at the most, his skin exceptionally dark, close to true black, his features smooth and drawn in a pure, exquisite hatred. I saw the black widow spider that once walked around on my bare belly. I had been fertilizing roses in my back yard and she had been hidden in the folds of the twenty-five pound sack I jostled against myself as I moved down the long row and then lay down to rest in the cool grass. When I noticed her I lay unmoving and watched her wander up and down on my naked front, then walk directly to my groin, her long black legs powerful and thick against the flimsy hairs of my pale pubis, the red hour-glass on her back too beautiful, too perfect in its contrast to the black, for nature I thought and I thought *that's what evil is,* perfection, before she moved down off the side of my hip and into the grass. At the time I did not know that black widow spiders rarely, if ever, bite women. They bite men, usually in the groin.

He spat on my bare feet.

"And when we get Sunshine back there, we's gonna pull every one of them yellow hairs out. One by one."

I was becoming grounded in an out-of-the-ordinary manner. Everything was moving in slow motion and I was struck by many little details. It seemed my salvation lay in understanding everything.

"And then we'll see how beautiful she is. Bald."

The leader moved his face, his whole body, even closer.

"Are you prejudice?"

The question was the opening I was waiting for, it made me laugh a little, gently with them, such a naive question, it made me move my body in a little dance of my own.

"No," I answered, grinning largely and truthfully at him.

I sat down on the bus bench that I had avoided earlier, before they came, as making me too vulnerable. He sat down on the bench with me, trying to regain the ground he had lost.

"And when we're through with you, Sunshine, we is gonna fill all your small holes with rocks."

I moved closer to him. I moved closer and began opening myself. I opened every hole, every cell of my body as wide, as open as I could to understand. I asked him his name. Do you live in Oakland? Do you go to school? This question made me laugh again. What a fucking hell-hole high school is! Some fucking school deserves this boy! I asked him the corniest questions. I couldn't help it. I wanted to know who he was, who this swarm of spiders crawling over me was, circling me, the flashes of their blades, their bright shirts. Why am I wearing pink? my shoulders whiter than this paper I write on, the breastbone beneath my chin as pink as his face was black, a face so dark it was like looking into starless space and I was sunshine alright, setting right into the abyss of night.

One behind me kept pulling my hair. The meanest face I'd ever seen had now become beautiful, bathed in the aura of human light you sometimes see around the bodies of strangers in a crowd. I felt admiration for him.

The fingers pulling my hair now stroked my shoulder. Someone voiced impatience.

"Let's do it."

I kept seeing that he looked like my fourteen-year-old son. I kept wanting to say it, "You're just like my son." I kept thinking of my son's fourteen years, of this boy's fourteen years, I thought of what it means to have been born fourteen years ago, of what a fourteen-year-old therefore knows that I don't. I thought of the civil rights marching I had done when I was barely older than he, I thought of such corny, silly things. I knew I couldn't say them, I knew the tightrope I was walking, but the words were in my mouth, they floated between us like some ancient chant, *you're just like my son, you're just like my son*. He's an athlete, a jock, you're a street leader, so much the same thing, a beautiful boy of high grace and energy one could only acclaim as leader of the gang, the team. I'm a poet. For the first time I proclaimed it, even though the words were not vocalized. I'm a poet. How similar is the energy, our task, the knowledge of self-greatness, at least at the beginning, in youth, before disillusionment and power corrupts the spirit, corrupts the purity of the Second Wind, the Muse, and what you play is for fame and the paying fans, and what you write is for power and money, and what you do on the streets turns too much to cruelty and the loss of heart, where you become overly masculine and you understand nothing and therefore can do anything.

"My name is Rose. Rose Rodriguez." I laughed, relaxed and grounded, moving into his body with my chummy questions. I asked them from my most sincere girl place, looking him directly in the eyes. I squirmed around a lot keeping time to my secret chant, my walking chant, my street poem, *you're just like my son, you're the Muse*. I knew danger now in being still. He didn't answer, how could he and save any face, but after awhile I began to feel some of the tension easing. The fingers were gone from my shoulders and the boys seemed to have taken stations, like guards, around us and they were silent.

Now we were all silent. I felt an emotional wave pass between me and the leader and then over us, engulfing us in weariness, now a sorrowing, mutual admiration. Sitting there with him on the bus bench I saw two warriors encountering each other in the middle of a battlefield, suddenly overwhelmed by the reality of the other. How much our lots decree we must fight. I felt myself like a camera pulling away from the scene, an aerial view of two ancient warriors surrounded by armies, his the teenage boys, mine the tired workers clutching their lunch pails and work clothes, sitting on a bus bench at midnight in downtown Oakland. Both of us now were in a sort of trance. We stared at the pavement just beyond the curb. After awhile two of the boys wandered off.

A lowered, crimson-and-chrome car filled with a half-dozen older boys pulled up to the curb in front of us, rhythm and blues blaring from their radio. They expressed great delight in seeing what their younger brothers had caught. The leader got up from my side and talked to someone in the middle of the back seat. All their eyes were on me, my bare legs in high-heeled sandals, an astonishing collective hunger sitting before me in a deep, red car. But then, as if from an order, in unison, they all looked away, the expressions on their faces suddenly of disinterest. They paid no further attention to me.

Now the number 80 bus pulled up behind the crimson car and waited for the spot. The leader opened the door, squeezed into the back seat. As the car roared off there was a split second when our eyes met again. I hadn't taken mine off him since the car arrived. Then he looked away, his face washed of all feeling.

I felt the presence of three remaining boys. The bus pulled up. The door slid open. I climbed on. They followed. The whole scene registered painfully on the driver's face, he almost groaned aloud, but for that long ride I could get no idea if he would help me if I needed it. Probably he had no idea either. He was afraid.

I sat on the right, about three seats back, the nearest available seat to him. The boys loped through the bus claiming it, swinging from seat back to seat back. I watched them reflected in the dark window. One went all the way to the back seat and sat down at the head of the aisle. Another sat in the seat directly behind me, the other behind and across from him. There were other passengers but I don't remember them. The four of us had taken over the space.

We drove east from downtown Oakland. There were many stops, people getting off, people getting on, all of them black, exhausted seeming, the bus echoing through the empty midnight streets. At one stop a boy got on and greeted the three of them. He sat on my left, directly across from me, staring, puzzled. I watched the bus driver in the mirror. Our eyes kept meeting. His expression had become one of petitioning, *please. Don't cause me no trouble.*

East 14th and 14th Avenue had always confused me. I watched the street ahead, worried that I'd miss my stop, or get off at the wrong 14. Will they get off with me? Will the door be locked? The door is always locked at Nic's. The neighborhood is dangerous. But surely this time they will have left the door open so they won't have to walk down the stairs to open it for me. A scene from a childhood horror movie was running now on the screen of the street, a young woman begging her mother to open the door while the murderer closes in. The mother is angry at her daughter for calling "wolf" too many times and so this time she refuses to open the door. I watched the boys watching me, their faces like daemon angels hovering the dark street we moved along. It occurred to me that they were escorting me home.

Finally I saw it. *Payless Cleaners,* lit by the eerie blue street light, Nic's apartment above it. I pulled the cord, giving them plenty of time to think about what I was doing. As the bus came to its dragging halt, I stood, holding my balance. Then, stepping into the aisle, I said good-bye to the driver with a little smile and wave, I said goodbye to all of them, and jumped the long step to the street. I never looked back, the bus churned on, I never knew if the boys got off, I felt them seeing where I lived, right now it didn't matter, the door was unlocked, I moved inside, locked it.

Upstairs, Max and Nic were on the living room floor among a scattered stack of *Playboy* magazines. They didn't acknowledge me.

I took a long shower. I tried to scrub away the boy's spit but it had soaked through my skin. In the furnitureless room where we were staying I shut the door and got into my sleeping bag on the floor. The light of the street lamp in the huge, shadeless window was so bright I could read. I selected a poetry anthology from the small press book pile by my pillow.

I'll never forget what I opened that book to. I couldn't believe it. A poem to the white woman who had been murdered the summer before in a Boston black ghetto. I saw the news story on Max's mother's television. The woman had been a longtime civil rights worker, a person who understood the injustices and conditions by which people are twisted into monsters. In this consciousness she and her husband had chosen a black ghetto in which to live. One evening on her way home from work she ran out of gas. A teenage gang made her pour the gasoline over her own head. They made her light a match. I remember at the time being particularly struck by her husband's words. He couldn't blame the kids, they were simply victims of our racist society.

Now in writing this story I think to rename it for one of the oldest poems, The Song of Songs: *I opened to my beloved, but my beloved had withdrawn himself and was gone. . . . I sought him but he gave me no answer. . . . I rose and went about the city and in the streets and in the broad ways I sought him whom my soul loveth: I sought him but I found him not. The watchmen that go about the city found me, they smote me, they wounded me; the keepers of the walls took away my veil from me. . . .* For in that room above the Payless Cleaners on the corner of 14th and 14th, above the ghetto of Oakland and Berkeley and all the students and all the middle class and all the rich, above the tallest redwood and a rose named Rose Rodriguez and the great Bay with its Alcatraz, and San Quentin, its ships, salmon and whales, its men and women, above San Francisco and its Golden Gate, the narrow last road west: the frontier, the Mystery, above the fantasies and the Real, the poor tired world with its marriages, its grapes of wrath and its poets, safe and alone, I held myself and at long last found the terror and came, in great jolts of nausea, undone. I fell to pieces as my mother would say, as petals from a rose, as ashes from a ball of fire burning into the abyss of our country, that floated back over the whole day.

Part III

Those Who Can't Hear the Music Think the Dancers Are Mad

. . . it is no longer such a lonely thing to open one's eyes.

Adrienne Rich

Maybe there's something happening or something happened long ago somewhere that affects my life here and now, but I can't see it because my life is too short, and my mind is too narrow; I can't, I can't see that.

Isabel Allende

Have you thought enough of Gaspara Stampa?

Ranier Maria Rilke
THE FIRST ELEGY

Now I a fourfold vision see,
And a fourfold vision is given to me;
'Tis fourfold in my supreme delight
And threefold in soft Beulah's night
And twofold always. May God us keep
From single vision & Newton's sleep!

William Blake

Jonah

I

The last time I saw him alive was one of those moments when all the universe seems to press in on the small shared space of your bodies and hum, electrically, a silver-string song: *Something is happening.* . . .

He drove the fifteen miles south to my cabin on Navarro Bluff to get the single painkiller Robin had been given by his dentist. I was sitting in the middle of my bed, my back against the window and ocean, surrounded by books and papers, working on the Wyoming poem of my book.

I watched him step down the hill, come onto the porch. The wind, as always, was raging from the three directions of ocean. In an instant, it unbuttoned his faded blue workshirt, blew it in flags around his thin trunk, and whipped his straight blond hair off his head like gulls lifted from under the bluff and scattered in every direction. I signaled for him to come in.

"Robin said I can have the Percodan the dentist gave him."

"It's right there on the table."

He reached, almost sprang, his form dipping through the air, his bony chest exposed beneath the unbuttoned shirt, his long legs, his long thin arm, his long fingers, his long skeletal New England face, a momentary ballet across my room to claim the tiny tablet. And turned to leave. That quick. That is when we looked at each other, his long skinny stare across the room to mine, and I heard the silver singing. When Jonah and I first met we looked at each other romantically, sexually, and then there were the two years we didn't look at each other, though we were often in each's company. This moment was probably the first and only time that we really saw each other. Jonah? Everything in me called except the censor at my throat. He turned, was gone. I watched him climb the broken steps, up and away.

It was Halloween. That night at the annual End of the World Dance in Elk I looked for him in the masquerade, watched for him while I danced. But if he was there he was in disguise. And though Robin was there, his presence was more visual than auditory: the seated, crazed-looking bearded man playing the electric violin like a cello, between his legs. He still wasn't grooving with his new band. He was screechy, un-sure; then, too bold. Actually, they all were. They were dressed as hooded monks, except Eddie, the bass player. He was in a blue satin dress, high heels, a blond wig. They still didn't have a name. They an-nounced a naming contest. The crowd was like the music, wild, alien-ated, discordant. A lot of old-time locals: six-and-a-half-feet, two- to three-hundred pound loggers drunk, stoned, stomping till the floor would seem to collapse. They didn't wear costumes. Neither did I. Matt Paoli grabbed me by both shoulders. "Wait you! Stand up to me. Look me in the eye." I pulled away. "I see you. You're not happy girl. *I'm* not happy." Matt was blond, physically like a god, grandson of one of the first loggers of Elk. The band was playing Leadbelly's *take a whiff, take a whiff, take a whiff on me.* I hated the song but now I used it to dance away from Matt. Then Johnny Barbata, the drummer for the Jefferson Starship grabbed me around the waist, stared expectantly into my eyes. I pulled back for him to explain himself. He just shrugged, lunged off. There was a scuffle at the bar, someone beating on Bixby the bartender, so dwarfed by the Elk men. Then Matt was be-ing forced to the front door, his arms pinned to his back by his bud-dies, his tiny blond wife cursing him, jumping up to slap his face as they dragged him out. The tune went on and on, sluggish, stoned, noncommittal. *Cocaine and horses are not for men. They say it'll kill you but they don't say when.* The guys of this band, Boyd, James, Eddie, and Jimmie D., had reputations for being great famous musicians, so much greater than those of the band Robin and Mickie had recently left but every time I danced to them I grew bored, sometimes finding myself at a complete standstill in the middle of a tune. They were too cynical and manipulative to be exciting. Especially Boyd, the lead guitarist. Every lick excused and covered the one before. See how clever I am. But if you've begun to know who I am, well, this will take care of you, *wham, chord, screech*. I missed their last band, the high expansiveness, the punkish youth, the electricity, Robin risen off his seat, the fiddle on fire between his legs. A witch went flying by, cursing the drummer. Mickie, his skipped beat. He has arrhythmia, I snapped back, indecipherable in the noise, he shouldn't be playing at all. That was probably what was bugging Barbata; he expected to play. This was Mickie's first gig since his heart attack in August. It had come right in the middle of a set at Caspar. A heart attack at thirty-two. Only Robin recognized what it was. Now Mickie's eyes were full of wild fear, his black shiny locks bouncing over the drums, his eyes dazed, *take a riff, take a riff, take a riff on me*. The tune turned into "Edge of the World" and Robin took his solo, the first magic of the evening, his bow pulled across the strings to sound like a small plane soaring off the bluffs out over the sea, the music building like a furious storm over the earth. When it was all over that night, Barbata and Matt left together. They failed to make a curve on the Comptche-Ukiah Road. Barbata's neck was broken. Matt Paoli was killed.

The following day I moved into my station wagon, Roses, until I could find a house to rent in Mendocino. I had been looking since August, had given my notice, my landlord expected me out. Darien stayed with friends. It took another week to find a rental, one I could afford, and then it was a one-room cottage. It was in the heart of the village though, only a block from the high school. Friends were incredulous that I would give up the bluff for the village, but we had always lived far from town, in woods, on deserted beaches, on bluffs, and once she was grown, I'd have the rest of my life to live in such places. David was gone, his first year in college. Now I wanted to make my daughter happy. Town would allow me a more active role in her life. She'd come home for lunch, bring her friends with her, they'd stay over night, just as now she stayed over with them to avoid the foggy coast highway, the long drive home.

It was not easy moving from four rooms into one. I sold and got rid of what I could and crammed in the rest. The boxes and furniture were piled to the ceiling. It took three weeks to arrange everything into a livable order.

On the first night I moved my grandmother's trunk to the foot of my bed. The year before I had pulled it out from under my parents' house in Ramona, rented a U-haul trailer and brought it the six hundred miles north to the Mendocino coast, conscious the whole journey of its having come by train across the continent in the forties. At Navarro Bluff I had stored it in the garage. Now that I was writing the Tennessee section of my epic poem I wanted to bring her trunk into my life. It could be used as a seat. I'd open it, read the diaries. My father's mother secretly aspired to be a writer, wrote poetry and kept diaries all her life, which, with the exception of her last five years when she lived with us, was spent in Tennessee. I was born on her birthday and was named for her. She had not been feeling well and I was sitting with her when she died.

Now, exhausted from moving, I lay down, my first night in this new cottage, this new life in town, wondering what it would bring, and in the instant I shut my eyes I saw my grandmother. When I think of her I don't "see" her. She died too long ago for me to easily visualize her. Yet here she was, in the back seat of a black limousine moving slowly by. She was looking at me through the window, her large silver-grey face, just like it was when I was a girl, but fierce. I bolted upright, her face even then staring at me through the limousine window. My heart was pounding; I kept blinking my eyes. I got out of the bed, got to the kitchen area. Then she went away. I was looking at the calendar I'd just hung. A week from Saturday, November 18, would be the twenty-fifth anniversary of her death.

The next day Moonlight was missing. I put lost-dog notices on the bulletin boards around town, called the radio station. Robin walked the streets calling him. I was sick for loss of my beautiful creature. Town must have freaked him. A tourist might have stolen him. He'd get into anyone's car. We walked over to Yvonne's and Jonah's new garage apartment to ask to use their phone number on the notices. When we knocked, Yvonne came out, quickly shutting the door behind her.

"It's not a pretty sight in there. Let's go for a walk."

As we walked toward the blowy ocean I thought of where my dog might be.

"He's gone home. Of course."

We drove to Navarro Bluff. With each of the fifteen miles the chance of finding him seemed more and more unlikely. It was a classic Mendocino fall day. The sky crisp, blue, the whales in their long winter migration to Baja leaping south out of the white caps, the trees arched against the sea and sky, cypress, redwood, eucalyptus dancing the crooked two-lane down the coast. *Blue Pacific, blue Pacific, blue Pacific, blue*. . . . chanting to myself in the wide back seat of Roses Darien's song while Yvonne described Jonah strung-out on Percodan. Pissing in his pants, falling down the stairs, a bloody black eye, throwing her around. Shooting up in his big toe, the veins in his arms ruined. And finally, long coming, her anger.

"I don't know how much more I can take. I'm sick of dying." Down into Dark Gulch, then climbing back out. "But I love him. He suffers so."

"What does he suffer from?" I asked.

"Guilt. Guilt for having been such a great guitarist and blowing it all on junk."

Judy Collins's "Send in the Clowns" floated through the car as we started the long flat stretch toward Albion. Jonah was Collins's bass player and arranger of her albums in the sixties. But he hated her music, did the albums for the money and prestige, to please his parents. He always said it was out of boredom that he began shooting up. Collins eventually fired him.

"He says it'd take ten years to get it back and then he wouldn't be as good as he was."

I watched the back of Yvonne's dark head, the side of Robin's face. Jonah and Robin had similar histories—both New Yorkers, both child prodigies of classical music, both now into rock music. As in so many ways Yvonne and I were sisters. Her poetry had always stunned me in its similar tones and themes to mine. But she was much younger than I, and, as she called herself, a workaholic, always putting her jobs before her writing. She had come to Mendocino because she was in love with Sky, who was at the time Cody's lover.

"Reed came over yesterday," she continued, "saw what was happening. He told me another story, how when they were nineteen they went to a guitar recital by Julian Bream. Bream unveiled this piece from a Bach sonata for violin known as the Chaconne. Do you know it, Robin?"

"Oh, yes," he said, driving. "One of the most difficult pieces to play on the guitar."

"After the concert," she went on, "Jonah was invited backstage to meet Bream. Reed tagged along. Bream asked Jonah what he thought of his performance of the Chaconne. Jonah praised it but gave a slight criticism of one section. Bream got pissed, threw his guitar at him, challenged him to play it better. Well, it so happens that was precisely the piece that Jonah had been practicing for months and he played it flawlessly. Reed said Bream announced the next day he was giving up the guitar as a concert instrument. He performed publicly only on the lute for several years."

"Does Jonah know how not to do himself in?" Until I asked this I had not thought he might die.

"No!" they chorused together. We were coming around the last curve, Navarro Head, the highest mount of land in a fifty-mile coast stretch. Way below on the beach, the Navarro River poured aquamarine, like a dream of Paradise across the silver-gold beach into the blue Pacific, and the white dog, running and leaping the huge trees thrown up as driftwood, chased the gulls who turned in V-formations and chased him, a fast moving streak like the white foam lines blowing on the sand. Oh, my Albion Moonlight, my hound of heaven, you are not lost after all. Dropping fast now in Roses like a gull from the sky all the way down to the white beach. *Blue Pacific, blue Pacific, blue Pacific blue.* . . .

On Wednesday I was still making curtains to give us privacy from the street, the houses on three sides of us. I was cutting a bright red cotton Indian spread for the kitchen window. Lorrain came by.

"I notice when you move you always put up curtains. I never cover my windows." Lorrain was my closest poet friend and severest critic.

"If you had had, Lorrain, as many Peeping Toms as I have had, you'd put up curtains." She always made me defensive. "And now I have a fourteen-year-old daughter. Shit! We're in the middle of town!"

"Jung says," she went on as I placed the red cloth into the sewing machine, 'Women who hang curtains are longing for the lost hymen,' And red curtains are particularly symbolic, don't you think?"

The next morning I was hanging the last curtain, a heavy dark maroon on the large north window over my bed. I backed away from it to see how it looked. On the street was a man in a bright blue down jacket. The window of my new cottage framed him in such a way that he stood out—or was it the dark red curtain? Or the huge black cypress trees towering the wet street? "Cypress is of mourning," Lorrain says in a poem. It had rained in the night, something, there was a man walking by on his way to the ocean. But he seemed too large, he seemed too old, he seemed to have just arrived in town, a stranger. His hair was silver, his skin was silver and blue. There was something of electricity. I thought *Libra*. I thought of my son. He looked like David will look when he is an old man.

The man walked on. The radio rang *many rivers to fall*. And here I am in town. The experience of my windows will not be of nature, but of people. The sight of this man had been like a slap.

An hour or so later—I was now attending to the first of the infinite boxes—there was a knock on the door. It was the silver man.

"This will sound strange to you, I suppose, but I met a psychic in Toronto this summer who told me to go to Mendocino and find you."

He was at least as tall as my son, six five. His name was Evan Bankwell. He was from Rutland, Vermont. I knew Rutland from the time I lived in Vermont. Jonah owned land in Sharon, Vermont. Vermont was one of the things Jonah and I shared. I invited the man in. There was hardly room for both of us. I cleared a space on my bed, gave him coffee. The psychic turned out to be Aurora, a friend of my sister's in San Diego. He said he could see that I was busy. Would I have dinner with him this evening? I'd love to have dinner with you, I said.

I surprised myself. Dinner? What would I say to Robin? He'll have a fit. But it had been months since I had been out to eat, we had been so poor and so driven, both of us by our work, he with the new band, me with the book. I wondered if it was wrong to accept an invitation to dinner for no other reason than to eat.

Robin arrived. Evan toured the flower garden in the front yard as if to leave us alone so I could tell him of my dinner plans. I pulled him into the bathroom to do this.

He was instantly alarmed. But he was always alarmed. It is why I presented it to him as I did, so as to leave him little room to object. I thought by being forthright I could curtail his jealous suspicions. Instead, my manner with him was so different from any he'd experienced he was more alarmed than ever.

"The guy's weird, One. I don't trust him. When I looked into his eyes I saw clouds passing by."

I assured him that my intentions were not romantic and then I refused to deal any more with his paranoia. He had practice, would be in Elk all night. I was going to dinner with the man. When Evan returned inside, I had the two of them move a mattress left by the last tenant to the landlord's house next door. The older man towered over Robin, who, cursing beneath the queen-size, kicked at the daisies in his path. I walked over to Yvonne's. Jonah's DO NOT DISTURB sign was hanging on the door. I wrote a note, told her to come visit whenever she felt like it.

We had dinner at The Fisherman on Main Street. We both ordered salmon. The candle shot silver sparks off the liter of Mendocino rain wine. Evan Bankwell, it seemed, had been a prominent man in the world, and very rich. His conversation was sprinkled with references to formerly well-known political people, his close friends, he said, Averell Harriman, Harrison Salisbury, John Kenneth Galbraith. Something about being on Lyndon Johnson's cabinet, or maybe, a special committee. He mentioned Harvey Green, the *New York Times* columnist, did not seem to know that his son, Reed, lived here, was one of my close friends. I ate slowly, not wanting the dinner to end, remembering the last time I had been in The Fisherman. A year ago with

Aurora. I had been depressed, still not over Max. He had been gone a year and a half and I was involved with Robin. "What is it that you want from Max?" she asked so simply and the answer, so vague before her question, came as simply. "I want him to tell me why he left. I keep expecting a letter." The next day Aurora visited me at Navarro Bluff. We sat on the bench over the sea. "I had an amazing perception of you last night," she said, her silver hair catching the sun. "I saw psychically how thoroughly you are a writer." Beyond her three whales spouted, breached, rolled south. "Even as I sit here with you in this most beautiful place, I perceive the greatest sorrow I've ever witnessed within a single body. I'm a Libra. When I'm sad, depressed, it lasts for as long as a half hour. Then the sorrow dissipates into the air. But in you the sorrow goes like a well into the earth. Your only release is through words." She was silent, watching the whales rise and fall. "You will be one of the great twentieth-century poets if you can cultivate the well, the bolt that goes from you into the earth. If you don't, the words will rot in the earth. In your body." When she left, I walked up to the cabin, sat down at my typewriter and wrote a forty-page single-spaced letter to Max. And then I did not mail it. I stepped off the wheel. I accepted his disappearance. I quit trying to communicate with him, wasting my words on him. And now I was in The Fisherman again, having dinner with a man who was, I slowly realized, in love with Aurora. I wished I'd realized this sooner. It might have relieved some of Robin's anxiety about Evan's motives with me. I wouldn't know until later that Robin was hiding in the wet, wild radish shrub on the headland across the street, watching us eat in the candlelight.

"I want to tell you about myself."

In an odd tone of urgency Evan Bankwell began his story. He had been, he said, the lawyer and spokesman for the *New York Times* during the typesetters' strike, December 7, 1962 to April 1, 1963. It was a time in New York City when no newspapers were printed. His closest friend was the editor of the *New York Times*. "It was business, I was the company's top bargainer, but I have to tell you, I loved that man. I loved him more than anything, more than my wife, my children, my work. We were inseparable.

"One day, near the beginning of the strike, Lester's doctor took me to lunch. He wanted to tell me that Lester's heart was bad, he would not survive if the strike lasted longer than a month. He appealed to me directly. What is most important, Evan, his life or beating the union? Well, I knew that the strike was going to last much longer than a month. I ignored the doctor's warning. I spaced on it. Lester died two months later. I went into a tailspin, from grief, from loss of my friend, from guilt. I began to drink. Very quickly I became an alcoholic. And I lost everything, my wife of twenty-two years, my children, money, home, career. In the next decade I married three times. I tried on many occasions to kill myself, but I failed at even that.

"About five years ago," he went on, "I was sitting on the Hudson River, getting ready to jump in, when something snapped inside me and I decided that I was going to get well. It had been ten years. I sought help, a New York psychiatrist famous for curing alcoholics. From that moment I have been undergoing and studying transactional analysis."

I watched him raise the glass to his wide, chiseled mouth.

"Yes, I can drink now. I'm no longer an alcoholic. You see," he put the glass down, leaned toward me. A movie star's face on the flickering silver screen. "In the traditional treatment of alcoholism, as in Alcoholics Anonymous, one is never cured. *Once an alcoholic, always an alcoholic,* right? The whole weight of AA's treatment is The Admission. Then the constant reminder that one is an alcoholic. You must never forget. You must remind yourself every moment for the rest of your life. *I am an alcoholic.* The catch of course is that you are programming yourself for the Fall. Just as with the concept of sin in the church— eventually, though you may go twenty years without touching a drop, the threat rides you, like the Devil, and eventually, most likely, you will succumb. The thrilling submission. After all, as you have constantly reminded yourself, you *are* an alcoholic. It's very Western, this attitude. It goes back to the Greek hero syndrome, *hubris,* pride, *harmartia,* the fatal flaw. Oedipus bound to marry his mother no matter how great the effort to avoid it."

He toasted me slightly with his glass. "I am no longer an alcoholic. Therefore I can drink. Moderately, of course. I am careful."

Then he said, "I want to tell you about Aurora. I hope you are not bored, this is important."

He was at a humanistic psychology conference in Toronto. He saw her in a group of spinning Sufi dancers. "Well, you know how she looks," he said.

"Yes," I laughed. "A crystal lavender." That's how she describes herself, the color of her aura. As is mine, she says. Crystal lavenders are neither male nor female. They are concerned with the psyche, which is without gender. Looking at Evan now I saw that except for age—he was thirty years older than Aurora—they were like twins. Aurora, six-foot, silver-haired, the same electric flash.

"Then later I saw her on the street in a crowd. Suddenly our faces were very close and I was looking into her eyes. I asked her to go to dinner with me. You know, as you and I are doing now."

He took her to the restaurant at which he and the *New York Times* editor had dined together the week before he died. Evan had not been there since.

"To Aurora, just as now with you, I felt compelled to tell my story. When I was telling her of the strike and the effect of his death on me—oh, how much I loved that man—a strange expression came over her face. She was looking beyond my left shoulder, her eyes trancelike. Then she described a man there, asked me if it was like Lester. What could I say? It was. She said, 'Then it is he who is here with us. And he has something important to say to you.' She concentrated. 'He says you must let him go. He says your grief and suffering have bound him here with you and he wants to go on.' I guess it sounds absurd but my reaction was objection and panic. I *can't* let him go, I said. I *love* him.

"'He will stay with you for a while yet,' she said, still in the trance. 'You should take a trip, you should drive west to the Pacific Ocean. He says he will accompany you and the two of you can talk. But when you get to the coast he will expect you then to release him. You will be able to do this after talking to him.'"

It was then that she told him to see me in Mendocino. "She said you would understand my attachment to my lost friend. And my sorrow. I first heard of Mendocino in the early sixties from Dean Rusk. He used to visit a woman here. And more recently from a couple, Cody and Sky. I met them one winter at Esalen."

Evan returned to Vermont, sold his retirement farm, bought a camper and began a slow journey across the continent, traveling sometimes in Canada, sometimes in the United States. "At nights I wrote the accounts of the conversations with my dear friend which will be a part of my book on transactional analysis. I've come to see, of course, that *he* was the real habit, the spirit behind my alcoholism."

In Seattle he visited his younger brother. They had not seen each other in thirty years. "My brother was the Cain of the brother set, a ne'er-do-well alcoholic from early youth. I was Abel. I had the highly distinguished career. Even after 1963, as an alcoholic, I wrote and published two books. My brother and I had never gotten beyond this programming. Our father was a strict, nondemonstrative Vermont minister. I was his beloved son; Chris, his No Good. That same system of duality, so fostered by our culture. Good and evil. We cried when we parted. It was extraordinary. Then I started driving south.

"I have to tell you this—though I wonder what you must think of me, this story I've told you is so fantastic—but this morning as I entered Mendocino, just as I turned west off the highway, I felt Lester leave."

It was a story as from one of my friends, not from the dignified, conservative gentleman sitting opposite me. The waitress was clearing our table. The musicians were setting up to play. I was missing Robin. What to do now? Out of nervousness I told him of Jonah, of his addiction, Yvonne's fear he might kill himself.

" Such people are in the process of killing something in themselves," he began sternly. "They may kill themselves in that process, or they may survive, as I have. But if they survive they will be a different person, a different spirit. The person is involved in a killing. It is their soul work. It is essential, necessary work. It is dangerous work. Friends of such persons have to understand that there is nothing they can do to help. Absolutely nothing. No one else is responsible. You tell your friend this. Only the actual person can do the killing.

"Shall we go?" he said suddenly.

I rose, and walked out, passing in front of the musicians in the middle of their first piece. Tom Lee glanced up. Too late I realized my social error. Shall we go? he said and I was gone.

We walked down Main Street to the headland, Evan talking. He told me more of the meeting with his brother. Unbeknownst to us, Robin was following, hiding behind bushes, fences, the old buildings. A story of mine had just been published in a monthly arts magazine, a story about living on Navarro Bluff and my 89-year-old landlord, Rollin Ormsbee. Evan had heard someone mention it that morning in the Seagull Coffee Shop. He wanted to read it. Still struggling for small talk I told him of my concern that the publication might disturb Rollin, mainly the part about his wife's stroke, though he had given me permission to print it.

"There is a book," he answered, "written about the newspaper strike in which I am the villain. I could never read it. It was a bestseller in New York, had a lot to do with my first drinking. But, you know, recently I read it. It wasn't bad. I could have even helped the writer, shared with him important information."

We were walking on the sharp edge of the land. The tide was low, the rocks exposed, the sky black and spectacularly starry without a moon. I pointed out Libra to him, the Scales sitting on the black water. I thought of Libra's love of the Other, like David's for his coach. Like Evan's for his friend. The sign of partnership, marriage. Good and evil, our system of duality. Then we turned and moved east, back up the land to town.

"There's one sentence I can't forget. 'When Evan Bankwell entered the conference room one wanted to turn up the thermostat.' That's the kind of person I was in those days."

Evan may have been successful in killing his demon but there was still ice in him. We came to his camper parked beneath the cypress that line Heeser Drive. I told him to see that old movie again, *East of Eden*. "This is where James Dean and his prostitute mother are walking in the fog. The road was unpaved then, but you'll recognize these trees." He invited me in. The space was very orderly, functional. He showed me his set-up for writing. "I drive during the day. Then at night I write." He showed me the row of books he was studying now. *A Course in Miracles*. The week before Sky had told me about these books. She credits them for her cure of cervical cancer. This sixty-eight-year-old man remained strange to me, but I was very impressed.

We came to my house but I said nothing and we walked another two blocks. I didn't want to be inside alone with him. I could see Yvonne's lights through the trees. Would it be insensitive to suggest that we go to the Seagull? Does he frequent bars? I could feel the music, the warmth, my friends gathered two blocks to the south.

"Where's your house?" he asked suddenly. "Have we gone past it? I want to read your story."

And so I took him back to my house, piled to the ceiling in boxes. Only the bed was cleared. He sat on it and read my story. I poked around in a few of the boxes. A current *Atlantic Monthly* magazine had been left in the house by the former tenant. It was lying on a box next to the bed. The cover story was "The Big Squeeze on Labor Unions."

"Look at this!" Evan exclaimed. "By Herbert Stein! He's the writer I just quoted to you. The one who wrote the book about the *New York Times* strike, who said when Evan Bankwell entered the room you wanted to turn up the thermostat. The man and the book I was so afraid of all those years. What a coincidence!"

When Evan finished my story he said, "I understand now why I was to look you up." And then he left. In two minutes Robin bounded through the door. He had been watching us through the curtain cracks! All week I had worked at preventing Peeping Toms and my first Peeping Tom was Robin. He hadn't gone to practice, I had frightened him, my energy, he kept saying, was strange, he had lain in the wet bushes watching us through dinner. As so often, his behavior was too outrageous for me to take seriously. I was still thinking of Evan. I felt disturbed about him, or by him, I wasn't sure which. His icy loneliness hung in the room, over the bed where he had sat. I felt I had used him to get a free meal. Robin was right. Normally I would not have gone to dinner with such a person.

We got into bed. He spread his marijuana onto the *Atlantic Monthly,* sorting out the seeds. I told him of the evening, how I had walked out on the musicians, and asked him to apologize for me if he sees them before I do. I told him about Evan's philosophy on addiction.

"It's what I've always thought about Jonah, that he's in love with his addiction, his fatal flaw."

When Robin and I first met and we were moved with the urgency to share our life stories, he had told me of o.d.-ing on heroin in LA, of being rushed to LA General Hospital. He told me this because LA General is the locale of several of my episodes. His story alarmed me, *heroin?* which in turn, alarmed him. He said he didn't want to talk about it. "Someday when I know you better I'll tell you." I had waited a year and a half for the right opportunity to ask him again about the incident, wanting him to trust me, wanting to understand him more. But now he said when I asked, "I don't remember." He passed me the joint. I was stunned. He had always made such a big thing about sharing everything with me. I could almost believe he didn't remember, him and his fucking musician's memory. I sucked on the joint, enjoyed its soothing ride down and across my shoulders, down into my pelvis. Him and his fucking lies. His secrets. While he *spies* on me.

It was a long time before I fell asleep. Evan Bankwell's presence remained in the room: blue. I considered getting up early, catching him before he left for San Diego, having him to breakfast. But I didn't really want to see him again. Something about him gave me the chills.

I was working on the boxes, trying to figure the right place for the bookcase. It was noon. Again, I had the experience of being visually slapped by a person's presence in the northern window. An electric shock. This time it was Yvonne and the electricity was like the dream of my grandmother in the black limousine. From the enormous '66 pink Dodge Jonah had given her, she was emerging; a tiny, dark child. She was wearing a charcoal-grey jacket and grey corduroy pants. Her face was the color of ash. When did she lose so much weight? I remembered her full, erotic ass, her abundant bisexuality. All that was gone. She seemed to be growing smaller and smaller as she came across the street, the black cypress hanging ominously over her. For the first time I felt real concern for her. Jonah was killing her.

She sat on the bed among the boxes. She was on her way to work at Cody's Deli in Fort Bragg, was just stopping in for a moment. Jonah was still at it. He had been busted by the Fort Bragg police. He'd bought a rabies vaccination kit from the Fort Bragg pharmacy, to get the syringe. It's illegal for a registered addict to purchase a vaccination kit. The pharmacist sold him the kit and then called the sheriff. She was incensed. "He got his money, *then* called." So Jonah was further demoralized by his hours in the infamous Fort Bragg jail. They ridiculed him, shoved him around. One deputy especially, the one with red hair, had always harassed him. She bailed him out and they spent the night in a Fort Bragg motel. It was the first time in two weeks that he wasn't stoned. They ate a little, laughed, watched TV, and even made love. The lawyer came by and talked Jonah into going back into the sanitarium in Sonoma. He called the judge who canceled his probation, ordering him back to the hospital.

"We're waiting now for the call so I can take him down," she said. "It better come soon. He's shooting up again. Fuck," she added, lying back on the bed. "I don't know where he got the stuff."

I showed her an article I had just seen in the paper. Someone had broken into the Mendocino pharmacy. Five hundred tablets of Percodan were missing. As Yvonne read she turned pale with rage.

"Jonah didn't break into the place. He's too strung out. But someone who knows he is, did, to sell them to him." She looked up at me. "If I knew who, I'd kill him."

I worked all day on the boxes. Robin was in Elk with the band. Darien was at a volleyball game. At 8:20 there was banging on the door. I had just washed my hair; it was wet.

"Help me. Help me, I think he's dead."

We ran. She had the Dodge started before I shut the door.

"I started calling around three. The line was busy. Or off the hook. I climbed the stairs. I saw him. I couldn't go over. I came and got you."

We climbed the stairs together. The room reeked of the sweet smell of Percodan. He was lying on his back, shirtless, his legs and buttocks spilled off the mattress onto the oriental rug. His head was tilted back, his mouth opened, his teeth bared, his skin the color of porcelain. The phone lay beside him, the receiver off the hook. O Jonah.

Will I know if you are dead?

I dropped between his thin, sprawled legs. I thought of Evan. I touched him. He's dead. The black eye in the skeletal face glared at me. To fight the revulsion I ran both my hands down his cold trunk. To warm you, Jonah. Then shouted, *Jonah!* Slapped him. *Wake up!*

He was so cold, the feel of porcelain, the icy feel of a toilet. But the left side of his chest, a circle larger than my hand, was warm, very warm. His heart—maybe it's still beating. Maybe it just now stopped.

I thought to put my mouth on his blue, sneering mouth. I couldn't. Yvonne. He's your man. You do that.

She knelt on the mattress behind his head, her wide black eyes dazed, took a deep breath and bowed to her lover's bruised face. His rib cage was so thin and brittle, when I pushed down on it, I was afraid it would crack. Yvonne rose up, inhaled, lowered herself to him again. His brown corduroys gaped around the hips, the sunken belly. Imagine making love to a man so thin. I thought of Robin over Mickie just two months ago. How hard it was for even the doctors to believe it was his heart. A heart attack at thirty-two. "He was so thin," Robin said, "When I lifted him to the van, it was like lifting a child."

I heaved onto his chest again. I love you, Jonah, come back. I almost called him Robin. His eyes were so dilated I thought, they are the holes he's left through. I remembered how the Nazis put naked Jewish girls on the bodies of dying soldiers on the theory that the sexual urge is the urge to live. *Flowers bloom when they think they're dying,* Mama always said. I put my hand to his groin. Come back, Jonah, come back. I wished for Robin. Evan's presence was strong. I thought to mention him to Yvonne, who was gulping for air. That's absurd. A cat sat above us, watching.

The warm circle around his heart grew smaller. His nipples were flat, colorless. Jonah. I almost called him Robin. How many times I had found Robin dead in my dreams. How many times he'd blown himself away. How many times I'd knelt to him like this. Oh, shit, Jonah, this is fucked! The anger churned through me. His arms were bruised purple. I kneaded his soft genitals. Urine came, a warm wash, soaking the brown pants, my hand. It felt wonderful, like a baby boy wetting his pants. River of life. James Joyce. My grandmother's face. Beginning to panic, starting to cry. Coming back. No. You can't. Yvonne. He's dead. Don't say it. Not yet. He might not be. He won't be until you say it.

"I think I'm going to faint."

"Fuck that," I snapped at her. "You gotta keep it up."

But I looked back across the glazed cheeks into the icy moons of his eyes—always I have believed if you look strong enough into the body of another you give life, always I have feared I will not be able to accept the death of this body I kneel to now—and saw to let go. I left him, came to the child's sweet face above him. Yvonne. He's dead. The expression on her face altered to something other than sweetness. Then Evan came rushing from my body.

"There was something he had to kill, Yvonne," I sighed, sitting back. "He was involved in a killing. It was necessary, essential work. Like a soldier in war. He was killed in battle. There was nothing you or anyone could do to help. Nothing. Absolutely nothing."

The sweetness came again to Yvonne's face, like clouds passing in Evan's eyes, and I knew what everyone knew.

"If *anyone* could have saved him, Yvonne, it was you."

The body is interesting in death. We sat around him without speaking, a peace between the three of us, a sort of friendliness. Jonah. He seemed more himself than he ever had in life. He seemed self-contained, fulfilled. Death must be the accomplishment of the self, when you are furthest from the influence of others, the gravitational pull that keeps you here, keeps you from succumbing to the self. He seemed a large hole, one of those black holes in the universe. He, who until now, absorbed light, has finally absorbed himself so completely, he has fallen into himself, he's disappeared.

The cat—I remembered its name now—Superfluous—jumped to the ledge where the fir panel ended and the peaked ceiling began. I touched Jonah one more time, to make sure. His fingers were grainy, heavier, each like a wet sandbag. The warm circle around his heart was gone. The thought that he had died just before our arrival was hard. The telephone sprawled around him, the line beneath the pillow.

"He must have tried to answer when you called."

"But this line's not connected."

Well, he would have forgotten that. A disconnected line as good as any. We both became aware of a noise that had been present all along. It was Moonlight, crying. Yvonne rose and went to the head of the stairs. The Alsatian was stuck in the cat entrance, his head, his right leg and shoulder, jammed through.

And so Albion Moonlight joined us. When he came near Jonah his head bucked up, he backed off about six feet, and dropped, stretching his white paws in front of him. He sat in complete stillness, as if meditating.

Yvonne laughed.

"Did I ever tell you about my dog, Persona? Raven was my lover then. She took acid and did the whole trip talking to Persona, trying to convince her to talk. She kept saying, 'Come on, Persona, I know you can talk. You just won't. You dogs took a vow a long time ago not to talk.' The next day Persona was walking across a high bridge in the Santa Cruz mountains and she jumped off. She was killed. Raven was convinced it was because Persona knew she was going to break the pact and start talking.

"Maybe you had better call someone," she added.

"Yeah, I guess so."

I rather liked sitting here. Soon the whole town would be involved. The cops. Then Jonah would really be gone.

"Call Johnson. The number's right there on the desk."

I dialed the doctor's number. He said he'd call the sheriff and be right there. I called Robin in Elk. Boyd answered. Shit.

"Who's this?" I asked, stupidly.

He answered as stupidly, "Who's this?"

His ego's as big as mine. And he's gunning for my man, I know it. But he's just a Pisces, in danger of being a little man. He used to be a bass player. This was always my way into Boyd, of humanizing him.

"Sorry, Boyd. Is Robin there?"

"That's okay. I'm sorry too." The apology seemed genuine. Will *he* be sorry, I couldn't help thinking, when he learns.

"Robin, Jonah's dead."

I would hear Robin's simple response for years. It held the essence of him, the sound and mode of his voice, how I could remember him later without putting on a tape. He seemed to fake the surprise and concern, seemed like a poor actor confronting a crucial, too simple line on the stage that is this strange world.

"He is?"

Now Yvonne was talking, a rush of words and stories as she watched him. She seemed astonishingly collected. Perhaps she was relieved, she had lived his dying for so long. On the desk beneath the phone were notes she had taken during the week, of things he had said in delirium. A dream of three old women. He is walking into the Rexall Drugstore and they are waiting for him. When the angels come down, he always said, and gather around you at your death you recognize them. You realize you've been seeing them all along. He always said if he started shooting up again he'd die. It would kill him. We talked about what I would do if he died. It was sort of matter of fact.

Last winter he was so crazy. We were living in that moldy school bus in the woods. I was working so much at The Well, Cody not paying me. For most of the winter we didn't even have the bus, just Sky's land to park the Chrysler on. It's large, though, for a car. I'd type in the front seat. Jonah would practice in the back seat. It rained so much I thought we were drowning. I kept thinking we were turning into dolphins. Like the whales that went back into the sea. They must have been like us, beings who got as far away from the mainstream as they could, lived as close to the water as possible. The first step in the evolution of going back. We were married in those woods. One midnight in February he hallucinated our wedding. It was in the bus. He was fantastic. He undressed me, painted my nipples red, draped me in veils, the curtains he ripped from the windows. He was the priest, he was brilliant, his rap about our eternal bond. *Death's dominion hath no power.* He sang and played better than I'd ever heard him. I would save his life. We would have children. He burned the vows into me with his eyes, *till death do us part.* He knelt at my feet, *here are some fragments of my hammer/ that broke against a wall of jewels.* Wright, I think, or Everson. He recorded it all. To make it legal, he said. He was insane. He flew up and down the aisle. Hiroshima, mon amour. He talked more about his past than he ever had. He made me talk of mine. Did you

know I was conceived in a fertility clinic? My mother was forty-eight.
Jonah always said he remembered the day I was conceived. It was the
day in 1952 when he finally succeeded at playing a tune on the guitar
that satisfied his mother. Everyone who knows his mother describes
her the same. Reed says she's beautiful, rich and very cruel. Veronica.
A professional singer. She pushed him from childhood to be a great
musician. Both Jonah and his brother, Richard. Richard's an ex-
addict. I've talked to him on the phone. The father's a writer, I think,
for the *New York Times*. Something like that. A songwriter too. They
own a record company. They disowned Jonah two years ago, the last
time he o.d.'d. That's when he came to Mendocino. Reed was here.
Reed and Jonah have known each other all their lives. They inspired
each other. Reed to be the poet. Jonah, the classical guitarist.

Her grey metal files towered over us. His Martin leaned against the
elaborate tape system she had just bought him. Her writing. His com-
positions. It'll take ten years to get it back and even then I wouldn't be
as good as I was.

I thought of the summer just past. Jonah always gave the impression
he was oblivious to humiliation, that he didn't care what the others
thought of him. Now I saw the whole descent to this moment. Yvonne
went to Russia with her mother. I went to Washington. Darien went
to San Diego. Mickie had a heart attack. Jonah met Nancy, Mickie's
lover, while both were visiting him in the hospital. They came home
with Robin to Navarro Bluff, fucked in Darien's bed the whole time
Mickie was fighting for his life. I was disgusted. Then Robin's turn.
Jonah's last gig with him. Jonah's last gig ever. "Tom Lee came by to
hear me play and Jonah kept fucking up. He was too stoned. I finally
got a good lick off but when I looked up Tommy was gone. I swore I'd
never play with Jonah again, I don't care how badly he needs me."

"Did I ever tell you how we met?" Yvonne asked.

I had the sense that Yvonne was racing to tell me these things before
anyone arrived. Jonah grew heavier, colder.

"At a party. I had met Sky and Cody at Esalen, followed them up
here. He was with Raven that night. Raven had been in love with me
for years. That's why she published my book, you know. Just as everyone says. We shared our first house here together. Someone asked him

what he was doing that night. He dangled his long finger at me and said 'I'm sleeping with her.' Later he climbed the stairs to my room, looking very sheepish, to apologize. I was in bed. I said, 'Shut up. And get in.' "

Then the accusation of theft from Reed's house in Little River. How furious he was. *He's a con*. Reed, the last person in Jonah's past to disown him. Remembering then my Woodland's descent with Jonah in August to see Gil Scott Heron. A con alright. He even fooled Smith, the most uptight paranoid fascist poet I know, standing guard to the whole affair. Jonah claimed the trunk of the Chrysler was loaded with perishables from Cody's Deli, the concession that Yvonne was running below, and so we dropped all the way down through the redwoods where no cars were permitted, to the front of the stage, right in front of the cheering thousands.

"When it was bad for him and he couldn't sleep I could always find him in the cypress up by the high school or in that grove on the bluff. Or down on Big River Beach. The water always helped him. So many nights we sat on the water, looking at it."

Doctor Johnson arrived. The town's sixty-year-old physician, born in China of missionary parents, a Capricorn as wonderfully crazed as any stoned musician, rumored to be hooked on a hundred different drugs, married to the other rock n roll violinist in town, the only doctor among all the hip young physicians my son would go to for his annual football physical. He knelt on one knee, put the stethoscope to Jonah's small chest, then rose, almost ran to the stairs. Then he turned and in a hint of his birthplace, bowed. "Goodbye, Jonah. Peace." And left. Without ever speaking to us. When we heard the front door bang shut we laughed, both realizing that he didn't want to be here when the police arrived. Jonah had been his patient, he had written him many prescriptions. His office was in the Mendocino Pharmacy building.

Now we sat listening to the town around us. Friday night. The high school teams returning from Ukiah, the sounds of victory. Darien one of them. Yvonne was almost as unused to town as I was, having only been in the apartment a month. The sheriff deputies arrived. Two of them. They came upstairs and immediately ordered us to leave. We hugged each other going down, jealous of leaving him with two strangers. They would search the room.

Robin arrived. Standing in the door behind him against the giant passion flower bush was Mickie. I was stunned, suddenly stunned by all the connections of this story, the twisted and terrible lines.

"What's *he* doing here?" I said to Robin, as if Mickie wasn't present. "What about his heart?"

"He was at Boyd's. He wanted to come. I asked him if he thought he could handle it. He said yes, I want to go."

The two men climbed the stairs. We stayed with the two officers who had come down to make their report. Robin said to me later, "When I looked at Jonah lying there dead, an ineffable bubble of joy rose from me and went out into the universe." As so often with him I was askance. He explained. "I praise death. You praise life, burning a yellow light. I've never seen such a light as in you that night. Oh, One, isn't it wonderful you were called?"

"We're waiting now for the coroner."

The larger man pulled forms from a briefcase, clipped them to a board. I sat on the piano bench, noticed the newly painted green walls. Yvonne's birthday: February 7, 1953. Just like Jonah, I remember the day. My oldest girlfriend's eleventh birthday. Yvonne graduated from San Ramon high school. Of course. These days I look for the name, Ray, Ramon, Ramona in any momentous event. It always shows up. Her religion: Congregational. Jonah's: Jewish. A little revelation. I had thought it the other way around, Yvonne so dark and wrought, Jonah blond and on downers. The officers were impressed with his Ph.D. from the University of Madrid. Were you married? I waited to see what she'd answer. No. His parents, then, nearest kin? His parents cut him off two years ago. They said they never wanted to see him again. I don't know their address. New York City.

Robin boiled water for tea. Humbly—his obsequious manner by this time so consistent and familiar to me I'd accepted it as genuine humility—he bowed his head to the seated officers and in almost a whisper, so as not to interrupt the interrogation, "Chamomile or Morning Thunder?"

They chose chamomile. I gave my statement, beginning with Yvonne's calling at my door at 8:20. I controlled the urge to begin with Evan Bankwell. Yvonne began at the beginning of the week. Her statement was like a brilliant documentary. Succinctly, graphically, she articulated the events of each day. The deputies seemed mesmerized. The night churned on, the room was cold and green, Jonah upstairs alone. There was the question of homicide. There was the issue of the stolen Percodans. There was the question: did they believe us? I rocked back and forth on the piano bench. Yvonne told of destroying a needle she found him with Monday. Every time I found him with a needle it was like finding him with a gun. The black eye was from when he fell down the stairs. The coroner arrived. The three men went outside to search the car. Yvonne, Robin and Mickie laughed. Fort Bragg rednecks. Their laughter irritated me. It was true their presence was obtrusive, ironic, the gap as great as it would ever be. But for me the night protested any lack of empathy. We are all the same, can't you see? The three men returned. They had found over a thousand pills in the door lining of Jonah's Chrysler, twice as many as reported missing from the pharmacy. The coroner stood near the door, his feet apart, holding a red sticker by both hands. WARNING. THESE PREMISES HAVE BEEN SEALED BY THE CORONER. We all reflected in the dark, undraped window. My hair had dried wild and uncombed. I couldn't stop rocking. There is that place in all of us where we fail the social, the demand of the others. It's what we die of. The hole, the great lack into which we finally fall. The place that is uniquely us. Life is keeping from the hole as long as possible. *Often I am permitted to return to a meadow/ . . . that is the place of first permission/ everlasting omen of what is.* Yvonne upstairs with Jonah calling New York City where it is the morning after he has died, searching for the father, brother, mother. Mickie so quiet. The room so cold. I rocked to stay warm. Why would anyone paint their walls green? I studied the art prints she had brought back from Europe. I saw a woman in a large sunbonnet sitting in a row boat in the impressionistic swirl of one. She's there if you see her, Yvonne answered my question. Robin looked at Moonlight who occasionally whimpered. "In antiquity," he said, "dogs could talk." Moonlight thumped his tail yes yes on the floor. The town grew quiet. The last kids going home. The bars closed. Jonah dead.

They carried him down the stairs on a stretcher. Yvonne rose. They were out the door, dwarfed against the coral passionflower bush. Wait. She went out to him. The tightly closed bell-shaped blooms swayed in the November night air. She lifted the blanket and, like a child in awe of a new discovery, touched his bruised face with her long, delicate fingers. She kissed him. Then she covered him. They carried him away. Like a heavy load of garbage.

Yvonne continued the search for Jonah's family in New York City. I continued to rock, ever so slightly, back and forth, at times conscious of myself, though not enough to stop. The rhythm seemed correct, like that of the heart that survives. You could feel the news spreading through the town, up and down the coast. Even at this hour. The phone began to ring. Reed, Raven, Cody. Yvonne called Sky. Mickie called Nancy in Oakland. "I have some bad news for you. Yes. It's about Jonah. . . . " Nancy, twenty years old, who fled her dying man for the arms of his close friend, now a dead man.

About three in the morning we left the house.

"Yvonne, you come with us."

Robin clutched my arm as we moved out past the passionflowers to wait for her to get her things.

"We'll put her between us."

His eyes widened. "Do we have to?"

"Well, yes. We have to. Where else would she sleep?"

He groaned. I refused to understand his reluctance. So much about him I refused to understand.

Out on the street we all turned to the silver-metallic Chrysler Imperial. The red streamers, WARNING . . . CORONER . . .were plastered across the doors, over the front and back windows like a car decorated for a parade. The Vermont plates glowed metallic-green under the lamplight. I thought of Evan from Rutland. All four of us seemed to sag.

"What a shitty thing," Mickie said. "To kill yourself."

He walked down to his car. The three of us walked west through the fog, Moonlight following.

"Look how beautiful it is here." Robin exclaimed, lifting his arms from our shoulders. "If Jonah couldn't make it here, he couldn't make it *anywhere*." Then he added bitterly, "this home of the Burn-outs, the Over-sensitized."

At the door of the cottage he added, "But sure. I'd rather die any day in Yvonne's bed, than go back to the sanitarium."

Darien was awake. Robin had run over earlier to tell her where I was, what was happening. She watched us, without speaking, from her bed that had finally been set up, her first night here. I gave Yvonne Patty Ferris's lacy silk negligee to sleep in. Patty, who had been shot to death by her lover's wife just six months before. It was all I could find.

"Where do you get such things?" Yvonne teased.

"I'm an insomniac. Silk helps."

I was in the bathroom when I heard Yvonne exclaim in a voice stronger than I had heard from her in a long time.

"I can't believe it! This is Jonah's father!"

She was holding the *Atlantic Monthly* with the cover article by the writer Evan had recognized. "E. H. Stein. This is Jonah's father! The man I've been trying to find."

I had felt Evan's presence through the whole night. It was his words that came to me in the moment I accepted Jonah's death and looked up and saw Yvonne beginning to freak. His presence remained through the whole interrogation. There were his coincidental connections with Cody, Sky, Reed, all close friends of Jonah and Yvonne. And Vermont. He had caused me to walk out on my musician friends at The Fisherman where I had last been with Aurora, the psychic. And now, it turns out that Jonah's father wrote the book that was partially responsible for driving Evan to drink.

"Do you think," Robin said from the far side of the now very still, very quiet body of Yvonne—her head on the pillow seemed so dark and small next to Robin's—"that Evan Bankwell came to Mendocino to take Jonah away with him?"

I kissed Darien, huddled so quiet and alone in her bed, turned out the light. When I lay down I saw the Lone Ranger and Tonto disappearing over the hill, the silver bullets and silver horse gleaming in the sunset, the town's people left behind in awe and dust. Beneath the blanket we reached across to each other. Our clasped hands came to rest on Yvonne's small silk belly.

II

My lover is dead.
He died in the battle of Ashan.
My lover is dead.
He died in the battle of Bashar.
My lover is dead.
He died in the battle of Asherah.
My lover is dead.
He died in the battle of Danjaan.
Died in a rushing run
died so suddenly
so gradually
died so long ago
died last winter
died this morning
in his new uniform.
Stark naked
denouncing America
died in silence
died hurting
died longing
died loving.
My lover is dead.
My lover is alive.
My lover Viet Nam.

ERIC BENTLEY

At the summer solstice in the coast village of Mendocino, *Father Time and the Weeping Maiden,* the giant redwood sculpture on the steeple of the Masonic Hall, appears as one shadow before the setting sun, a line pointing due east to all the continent and falling, in a symbolic number of feet, on the sculptor's grave in the Protestant cemetery at the entrance of town. Jonah's death was the beginning of a winter full of death, a winter far more difficult than I could bear to acknowledge at the time. I was in love with the place. I could not have dreamed that I would soon be in painful exile from it.

My son, David, Darien's brother, was gone, his first year in college. My journal from that winter is full of death images of him. *He's dead on the cottage floor beneath the Christmas tree. Then he gets up.* It was the death of his childhood. Darien died that year too, her childhood, that is. In California you can take a test and graduate from high school at sixteen. She wouldn't be sixteen for five more months when she took the test on the last day of her sophomore year saying vehemently she wanted out. I gave my permission remembering my own hellish experience with high school. She passed the test and within weeks received her high school diploma. The September before we had fantasized a trip together; she says she'll never forget where we were when it came up: crossing the Navarro River going home. Now such a trip was something she went to work for. When we went to South America the following fall and I suffered so deeply the pain of culture shock, I vowed to never again be so isolated from the world. I'm a poet. I maintain that I love the world. I must then be comfortable in it. To leave the Mendocino Coast became, also, a way of remaining faithful to it. A way of not allowing myself, in my inadequate humanness, to grow resentful of the place.

And Robin, my lover. Fickle, brilliant, crazy Robin. He was, somehow, in precisely these qualities, important, instructive to me. Under his influence I first dared to think I might write greatly. I dedicated my epic poem to him. *To Robin who has taught me the spirit of greatness.* I was healing from two long marriages, trying to change myself so as not to fall again into the same patterns, that is, into the same type of man as Maximilian and the father of my children. I had the self-image of being courageous, honest, but in looking back on Max and Sergei I could see how safe I had played it. Robin was unlike any man I had ever been attracted to. Confronting him was confronting myself. Curing a cellular addiction is not easy.

That winter, for the first time, marijuana was listed as the number one source of income for the county of Mendocino. Logging and fishing were two and three. It is said that money corrupts absolutely. Many rural Mendocino and Southern Humboldt County communities were experiencing economic booms—this in a time of growing national depression. The old-time locals, a decade into opposition, sometimes violent, to the back-to-the-land hippy movement were now strangely quiet. Many of their long-haired customers were paying cash for new items such as pickups, houses, land, appliances, fences, water systems. There were rumors and reports that some locals were beginning to grow the stuff themselves. What God-fearing capitalist in his right mind could (or should) resist the thousands of dollars profit from a single plant?

But in some ways the market was down, at least among my friends, the old-time users. The last harvest had been ninth and tenth generation. The next would peak in strength so potent that one puff would mean an experience almost like acid. Gone was the joint that meant relaxation, gentle bliss, sweet revelations. Farmers had to learn to cut their pure strains. Friends began flying off to colleges around the country to study horticulture, sometimes to eastern and southern farms as advisers. The phenomenon was becoming quite incredible. In another year marijuana would be listed as the number one source of income for all of Northern California. I kept thinking this is material for The Great American Novel. Here's a pioneer product with no advertising budget, no store fronts or chainstores, all underground distribution and dangerously illegal. Something to think about in a society totally dominated by the advertising world. And produced by that all-American character: the wildly independent, self-sufficient, capitalistic frontier maverick. One poet-farmer said to my urging her to write it as a novel, "Well, to begin with, marijuana is a woman's story." She belonged to one of the secret grower collectives of single mothers who had gone off welfare. It's the female plant that's so potent; the male is killed. Another poet-friend always became ecstatic in describing the weeks before harvest, how heavy *"heavy!"* it is just to walk among his sensimilla plants, the resin so thick you can see them vibrating. "They're *dying* to fuck," he explained. "Dying for it." I kept worrying about the discarded male, the female unable to fuck. There's something inherently sexist about this. Whatever happened to the old hippy value of balance? The male poet-grower said to me, "It'll take something this powerful, this female, this mindblowing, to overthrow the patriarchy."

Jonah died Friday night, November 10. Eight days later, the following Saturday, November 18, the twenty-fifth anniversary of my grandmother's death, the one she came back to announce, the mass murder-suicide of 913 people occurred at Jonestown, Guyana. People's Temple, before the move to South America, had been located in Ukiah, the county seat of Mendocino County. Many of the nine hundred were from Northern California. The entire Mendocino Social Services Department was implicated as the majority of the members had been on some form of welfare. One San Francisco headline screamed: 5 OF THE 9 KILLERS FROM UKIAH.

Stories were rampant that Jonestown was an experimental base for the CIA's MK-ULTRA program involving mind-control drugs. The visit by Representative Leo Ryan, it was said, had uncovered this fact, necessitating his assassination at the airport and the murder of everyone else. Certainly many prominent American legislators, including the President's wife, Rosalynn Carter, had been involved in some way with the politically powerful Jim Jones. Guyanese leftist politics had incurred a long CIA history, and People's Temple that fall of 1978 was negotiating resettlement plans to the Soviet Union. Whatever, by mad government or by single madman, people were utterly controlled—by their beliefs, their visions, their loves, their hatreds, their circumstances—to the point of enthusiastically surrendering, and taking their lives. Northern California, my home, was in shock.

But Jonestown, I believe, was a place that could not have been populated by coastal personalities, "The Coast Heavies," as the inland folks referred to us. As potential suicides, if such a thing can be projected, we were more like Jonah, too independent to follow anyone's path. The Pacific Coast Range demarcates two geographies as great in difference as the image of the orderly rows of 913 bodies lying face down for a cause is to the one of sardonic Jonah sprawled half-naked on the bed and floor, the disconnected telephone line wrapped around him. Solitary desperado: no beliefs. The dramatic moody coast is where the loners and artists migrate from the cities and suburbs. The inland valleys, with their cheap land and normal seasons and easy access to the cities, attract families, the settlers, the more collective and practical of the back-to-the-landers. Still, it's only thirty miles. All winter the nauseous stories seeped in, of who had known who and how. Next to a poem of mine in the *Mendocino Grapevine* from the year before I found a letter to the editor capped: PRAISE FOR PEOPLE'S TEMPLE.

During the week between Jonah and Jonestown we gathered at The Well for an informal memorial. Over a hundred people showed up. No one knew how to begin, what to do. I leaned against the wall, smiling largely. Finally Robin, anxious to get it over with, unfolded a metal chair, set down in the center of the room, began to play "Amazing Grace" on the violin. The crowd instantly hushed.

"Oh," Yvonne exclaimed. "That's Jonah's favorite tune."

I might have laughed. I found this hard to believe, such an old traditional tune. *I was blind but now I see.* I didn't know at the time that it was on one of Collins's albums. People formed a natural circle around the room. I began that rocking I couldn't stop the night of his death. And something else I wish I could rid from my memory. I kept smiling. Or rather, grinning. An idiot's grin that lasted throughout the entire event, except when Cody, in what seemed to me a typical move to control the whole scene, cautioned us. "Let's not get maudlin." If there was a potential master or guru, a Jim Jones, a Reverend Sun Moon on the coast (the Moonies lived in Boonville, twenty-five miles inland on the road to Ukiah), it was Cody. A young girl next to me whispered in adulation, "He reminds me of an old Indian scout reincarnated." I groaned. Cody was a friend but I did not trust his love of power.

"Jonah died a maudlin death," I blurted, my grin a sudden snarl.

"And *that* should not be forgotten."

I was a little crazed but confident that if any community could do an honest memorial it was this one.

Yvonne, still so strangely composed, told the story of the time Jonah cracked Women's Night at The Well. He wanted to watch TV upstairs. He came to the door, peeked in. The dyke standing guard said *"Oh, no!"* He said, *"Oh yes. TV."* and rushed past her. The separatists rose en masse. Jonah clutched his crotch with both hands, bent over, tiptoed up the stairs, crying TV, TV, TV! The gesture won him laughter, applause and what he sought: the television.

Reed waxed eloquently on his oldest friend, how they were teenagers together. "We encouraged each other, each believing we might change the world with our art. Jonah was one of those young men for whom it was easy to feel envy because he did all the things he did so well. He built lovely houses in Vermont, became accompanying guitarist for such personalities as Tom Rush and Judy Collins, performed in solo concerts at New York's Town Hall and elsewhere. He'd fix your car in a couple of minutes if it wasn't anything more serious than bad rings. He once even built a car from scratch."

Reed had a new story to explain Jonah's drug problems. "It happened that Jonah, after being mugged in New York and undergoing intensive hospitalization, became addicted to pain killers." As he went on and on, admonishing himself and all of us for our desire to play it safe, which makes us avoid people like Jonah, the beautiful and the frightening, which, after all, are the same thing, and so they die off, and how this society keeps eating alive its most beautiful children, I was again, in the self-generating sun of my grin, sitting with Jonah in the summer garden outside. He has just removed the old fence from around the place so as to have a clear view of the town to the west, the kissing cypress over Big River Beach, the dazzling sun and aqua-blue ocean. He wants to do my brakes before I go to Washington. For free. I don't know how to accept such an offer. A couple of years later when my brakes again needed work I was in Medford, Oregon. I pulled into a Les Schwab Tire Center. With Roses up on the hoist, her underside exposed, the mechanic inspected, then puzzled, then exclaimed, then raved about how they had been fixed the last time. He called the others over for a look. A marvel and a mystery. I was sorry to have them work on them. I had enjoyed driving around on Jonah's brakes so long after he was gone.

That week and the next, with the news of Jonestown constantly on the radio, I managed to get everything unpacked and more or less arranged. We spent Thanksgiving at Yvonne's with most of the band, Darien, Sky and her three teenage sons, Cody with his three teenage sons, and others who came and went. It was my first time upstairs since Jonah died; the smell of Percodan was still strong. Mickie, Yvonne and Boyd lay on the bed Jonah died on, and I guess Yvonne slept on every night since, eating turkey and dressing. Mickie, animated, "thankful to be alive!" told outrageously wonderful stories of hitching from Europe to India, rides through Turkey with heavy-duty truckers. A boy in India holding a fiddle the way Robin does. Wild dogs who live on sewage. A street called French Street in Katmandu where the hippies still hang out. Lorrain came late, very upset about Jonestown. A native of Los Angeles, from a Russian-Jewish family, she had been contemplating conversion to Christianity for several years—ever since she had had an affair with a married Christian fisherman. To say the least, she was in spiritual debate with herself. She waved a newspaper of Jonestown.

"This is what's going to happen to me, I know it! I'm finally going to give myself and this is what it'll mean. *Brainwashed!*"

I just shrugged my shoulders, said nothing. She knew my feelings; we'd had terrible confrontations. The most important poet to me! The one from whom I learned I could write like a woman! Behind her on the bed Yvonne and Boyd lay in embrace, whispering. Sky's and Cody's sons played Jonah's guitars, to Darien it seemed. Superfluous and Moonlight were again like sentinels over the whole room, its events.

On the following Tuesday I finally sat down to my epic poem. I had been unable to get to it since the move from Navarro Bluff—really, for most of the summer. I worked about half an hour. And I knew. For the first time I was certain I could do it. I had nine months to finish. In September Darien and I would go on our journey. I jumped up, elated, grabbed a pair of scissors, ran into the bathroom and without thought, whacked off my long blonde hair. It was the second haircut of my life; the first was six weeks after David's birth. Everywhere I went for weeks, months, all that winter, people seemed shocked, objected. Cody, it turns out, was conducting a Jungian Dream Symbol Poetry workshop at The Well that very morning and, as I was told so often, my hair and "what it represents" had appeared in a number of participants' dreams and was labeled as the community's "outlaw hippy flag." I knew then where the urge had come from, that I'd done the right thing. Not that I was leaving hippydom. I was acting intuitively on one of its basic principles: to change the energy of my body, what it means to the community.

The Linga Sharira is a fundamental structural theme of my epic poem. The Linga Sharira, translated as the Long Body of God, sometimes as the Long Body of the Dream, is an ancient name for the Milky Way Galaxy at the annual moment of the Scorpio –Sagittarius cusp, roughly, November 18 –23. The galaxy is a long tubular form—from inside it, as we are, a spherical cone—said to be the actual body of God. We, on Earth, within our solar system, are like cells of the body that cannot perceive the whole, though a functional part of it. Every year at this time our solar system moves into a right angle to these constellations, right between the Scorpion's stinger and the front hooves of the Centaur—the Source, the Beginning, in the Big-Bang Theory and many Creation stories, of the Universe. Astonishingly, this astronomical fact was known by many ancient cultures, that is, they knew the structure of the universe. This right angle, they saw, creates, structurally, a "Step," a Way Station, Change Station, the Crossroads of Time and Universe by which souls can leave this plane. Supposedly, too, at this time on earth, because of the angle, the music of the Universe can be heard: God's Voice calling. This is the time, most specifically the cusp, a moment between the twenty-first and the twenty-second, when those who have died in the year actually leave the earth. To die at this time, or to be born, is to be taken or given directly by the universe. The Linga Sharira is probably the origin of Halloween, though with the procession of the poles and our linear calendars, we are now off the real event by three weeks. There are many stories and events for me—they happen most Novembers—that make the Linga Sharira significant. That November, 1978, it was my grandmother, the woman for whom I was named. Near the unremembered anniversary of her death, itself the Linga Sharira, she came from some other realm, whether inside me or from the Dream, a sort of messenger, or perhaps, in her black limousine, as Charon (related etymologically, I am convinced, to *Linga Sharira*), to ferry so many of my home away. On November 24, her daughter, my Aunt Lucille, died suddenly in Georgia.

Even with short hair I rocked all that winter during my poetry readings. *The Jonah Rock* I called it. Sometimes: *The Jonestown Rock*. And danced to Robin's music three and four times a week. I loved it. I had always wanted to be a dancer. It was probably because I was in such good physical shape that I didn't realize the psychological toll everything was taking.

Now he was working well with the new band. He was a brilliant violinist, his lifelong classical training as a cellist, which culminated in an advanced degree from Yale, had been wonderfully enriched by five years of dropout experience. I didn't even know him as a musician the first year of our acquaintance. All his life he had despised rock and roll. He had gruesome stories of being beat up by street toughs in Schenectady to rock and roll blasting from their cars: the fat boy with glasses lugging the cello. Now he shaved, threw away the glasses, lost thirty pounds, wired the violin for electricity, listened to Papa John Creech, Stefan Grapelli, Jean-Luc Ponty, wrote a string of great tunes, became a very exciting rock n roll musician. The rest of the band was inspired, challenged, revived.

Its core had been the well-known Racoon Ma, backup to Jimi Hendrix in the sixties. When Boyd was just a bass player. People dropped out of some interesting situations to come to the Mendocino Coast. At the height of Racoon Ma's Eastern Seaboard fame, they just left, came to Mendocino, did no more recordings, played only locally. Maybe it was Hendrix's death, their own members strung out. I don't think it was a conscious decision so much as just what happened. On the coast the society is very insular; it is hard to remember the real world. Boyd had been busted twice for dealing drugs but got off; the original drummer, Colin Woods, was arrested the winter of this story for dealing heroin; he'd long ago, as Robin put it, lost his chops.

Now, with Robin, his musical genius and wired Yalie personality, the decision was to make it again. This time, Boyd as lead guitarist, what *he'd* been doing eight years as a dropout. They built a sound board and tape system in Boyd's cabin at the "Elk Compound," the string of tiny one-room logger shacks that hug the coast bluff. Along with the bar, store, post office, the old church, the graveyard, and an inn or two for tourists, the Compound makes up most of downtown Elk, twenty miles south of Mendocino Village. They began planning a promotional tape to take to Hollywood. They found their new name. *Horse Majorities.* James, the rhythm guitarist and band artist, was reading an underground bestseller, a sort of Sci-Fi cult book in which a rock and roll band named Horse Majorities is the president of the United States.

They drove around all winter in Jonah's '66 silver Chrysler Crown Imperial Yvonne had given to Robin. The "Limo" they called it. James's comic/cosmic drawing of all of them in it, floating out over a headland, is on the inside of the cassette cover. But in the spring a typical Robin thing happened—typical, that is, before he got too carried away with the image of himself as a rock star. He was frustrated with needed repairs and Jonah's mysterious mechanics. One day he picked up a hitchhiker at the Navarro River who, on the ride north up the coast, bemoaned his carless state. At Albion, Robin pulled over, pulled the registration from the glove compartment, signed the Limo over to the guy, walked away. Yvonne was furious. He looked at her with his Scorpio-steel eyes. "I see," he sneered. "It was a gift with strings."

It was the new name that gave the community its first clue: their greatly loved boogie band was about to take flight, not as representatives of the coast, but in desertion of it. There were near riots by the dancers the first few times the band said their name on stage. James's posters, celebrated and collected by local cultural historians, were ripped to shreds or felt-penned over with curses, protests. The name held no soul, no beauty, no feel of the place, no community respect—

just intellectual, trippy drugginess, obscure only-those-in-the-know elitist spirit. Everyone's similar dropout history from the real world cemented a great and rather fantastic bond. The audience claimed the band, believed it was almost as much their creation as the musicians. The band had always nourished, encouraged this notion, saying in interviews things like, "There's a real symbiotic thing there between the dancers and us musicians. They help us to see what we're putting out." That's James's voice. Robin spoke in his Yalie dialect of the dialectic of the dancers and the musicians. But now he just sneered at the protests of the name. "Too fuckin bad." And now instead of articulated praise for Mendocino, his speech was full of such things as I'd first heard from him the night Jonah died, mimicking Boyd I'm sure, whose longing to get back to the city was no secret, "This home of the Burn-outs, the Over-sensitized."

Forgetting the community out of which they evolved was ironic, however, and in the end, self-destructive. The lyrics and the sound was of the coast, intense, psychedelic, artist values. (I had suggested the names White Sugar and Hard Country. They rejected the first for its too blatant drug connotations—I was thinking of their skin, not their drugs—and the second for being just too general. I was thinking of their electric, American jugband sound.) I suspected all along they couldn't make it in the city, even though they'd become a really fine band. Punk was the rage, the world was not seeking the Jefferson Dead.

To make the tape, they holed up in the Compound. There was much pressure on all the members living with women to stay at the Compound to unify the sound, the energy. There was in fact only one man in the group not living with a woman. Boyd. The one who lived at the compound. One night there was a big meeting, supposedly to confront Mickie with the issue of his spacy, erratic drumming. ("He has arrhythmia," I pleaded with Robin beforehand. "He almost died a few months ago, *playing*. Give him a chance!") But Boyd demanded from each member a statement of his dedication to the band in terms of his woman. Jimmy D., the fabulous conga player who, along with the violin, gave the band its unique sound, was the one everyone said would not go on the road. He had a wife, children, land and a burned-out junky past from Racoon Ma. But when his turn came he said, "I'm ready for a change." This was a real shot in the arm. Rosie, one of the more legendary Mendocino women, about whom there are several well-known songs, had given James an ultimatum: "Me or the band." He had chosen her. But at the end of this meeting he said, "The music's too good. I can't refuse it."

I had known all along the lead guitarist was out to destroy the love relationships, but I didn't take the threat seriously. I had so little respect for Boyd, a lot of respect for the other five members. I couldn't fathom Robin, the great Romantic, the great articulator of hippy values, falling for Boyd's shit. Robin's whole story evolved from his burn-out from the cynical, divisive, commercial, sexist, capitalistic world; it had burned him out on the only love he'd ever known: music. Once in January in Cafe Flor in San Francisco, the three of us were having breakfast. Suddenly, Boyd looked at me and said, "Love and making it can't mix." He was speaking of Mickie's new love, Victoria, but he shrugged his skinny shoulders, dropped his dopey eyes even more, and repeated his statement, sort of apologetically.

"Yeah," I shrugged in my own dopey way. "Like if you masturbate you'll lose your edge." Then I opened my eyes wide into his. "Not to mention your sanity."

Was this guy for real? "Cut yourself off from life," I huffed out on the streets north of Market, as Robin and I tried to find where we had parked Roses and Moonlight in our haste not to be late for breakfast with Boyd, "you cut yourself off from your art." I was in total support of Robin's artistic endeavors, as he was of mine. Where was the conflict? If I felt sure about anything regarding Robin, it was of this.

But I watched him grow more and more infatuated, in love, really, with the band, especially Boyd. One night while they played in Elk, Bixby the bartender asked me, "Are you feeling better?" When I looked at him questioningly he said, "Oh, how crazy Robin is for you. He's so torn. He really loves you." Then he said, when I started off to dance, "Good luck," in such a way as to indicate I didn't have a chance.

Another night we slept in the cabin next to Boyd's. It was James's old cabin before he went to live with Rosie. Robin said James had lived here one whole winter without speaking to anyone. "Rosie brought him back." I once heard James refer to it as "my cauliflower year." How to describe the awesome beauty of this place? These old one-room cabins sitting right on the two-hundred-foot edge of the continent. There's a poster you see all over the United States of this spot, the giant egg-shaped rocks the Pomos believe contain the souls of their ancestors, pounded by one of the wildest seas in the world. This night was when I first came to really know James, his drawings, art books, shells and trinkets, even clothes—his aura still there. It felt almost like we were sleeping inside his body. But after making love on his bed Robin began to tell me, in the coldest, ironic terms, the process by which they would make it.

"I swore, One, *I shall not fail.*"

It was a confession and a warning. Nothing, particularly you, will stop me. It was his tone that was alarming; he had never been ironic to me.

"Robin," I said, wearily. "If you keep talking to me in that tone, I'll quit."

In the next second he slammed me up against the wall.

"I hate you. I want to kill you."

Robin was the first man I loved who had said to me, *I love you.* But every man I'd ever loved had said, *I hate you. I want to kill you.* When I finally fell asleep that night, his arms tight around me for fear I'd flee, I dreamt of Jonestown, between two freeways in Hollywood, my children Darien and David in the lines for their cyanide Kool-Aid. Frantically searching for them I saw that everyone I knew was standing in line to kill themselves. My screams woke us. We went for a ride south down the coast. The sun was coming up over Greenwood Ridge, Joan Armatrading kept singing " . . . *until we die, until we die* . . ." We passed a convoy of trucks hauling redwoods off the ridge so large only one tree fit to a truck. The last virgin redwoods. Robin said that Leland Deacon, the owner of much of the South Coast, had just sold a large parcel to a land corporation.

"Soon," he said, driving, "America will be just like Europe, completely developed and cultivated."

No more wilderness. We are in our suicide lines alright. We've lined up our children right behind us. The band was Jim Jones, the president of the United States. When love is absent power fills the vacuum.

"I grew up in Hollywood, Robin," I said as we floated out over the dawn sea in the Limo. "And I couldn't write. I didn't even know there was such a thing as a live poet. Only when I came here did I find my voice. I found it here because my voice is of innocence. Innocence is my only theme. It's the only theme left. The world is as polluted by our cynicism, our vision of it dying, as from any of the poisons or wars, or political, economic systems. I can speak here because this place respects innocence. I'm mute with your band because it doesn't. The band is like the city, the cynicism is so great I too quit having faith. Or, rather, I lose faith in my ability to counter it. To speak, Robin, to write, certainly to sing, is to have hope. Which is to be innocent. Or, rather, to *believe* in innocence. There's a difference. But writers of despair and pessimism never cop to that. They're liars. As are folks who make music and say they don't believe. Impossible!"

He always listened so well to me. Now tears were streaming his face as he drove the twisted highway.

"Oh, One, I love you."

As we rose up to Pt. Arena, he said, "Cynicism kills the heart. Conformity kills the voice."

But by summer Boyd's philosophy was Robin's. With their tape, their local popularity was very great, their name accepted. (Now everyone was in the know.) His personality changed. He hoarded porno magazines. "Deprogramming," he sneered. He bragged of breaking a feminist picket line protesting a porno film at the Fort Bragg Theater. I watched them both work on Mickie. But Mickie was in a different realm altogether. He had had a heart attack, death informed his life. He married Victoria, left Horse Majorities at the first worthwhile invitation from another group. And though, by then, the band had moved to the city, they couldn't find another drummer good enough. The drummer: that least respected, most important member of any rock band. The whole thing came tumbling down. One day Robin took me by the shoulders, looked deep into my eyes and said, "I gotta go, One." And was gone in two minutes. I never saw him again. Boyd gave up rock n roll altogether, relocated to Bangkok, Thailand. As everyone knows, there's only two reasons to move to Bangkok.

In December, at the request of the Stein family, Yvonne flew to New York with Jonah's ashes. They traveled by limousine up the Connecticut shore. At the end of a pier, Richard, Jonah's brother, played the flute, then opened the urn. Yvonne always put it in terms of *his* shock: Jonah's teeth, pieces of bone. His mother crying at the front of the pier, the father standing sternly in the sunset. Together Richard and Yvonne wept, embraced, then sort of dropped the ashes into the water. Jonah's teeth floated in the glob for a while before sinking.

When she came back from New York City she began spending most of her time with the band, mainly with Boyd. She was the only outsider allowed during the weeks of taping. Robin spoke of Boyd's taking her in, his compassion. It did seem a nice gesture; she was also by reputation, a great fuck. As a widow in shock, not very threatening. I still see her floating in the loft window above that room, the great sea churning into the arches and sea caves below. I still see her in the crowd dancing alone in a blue 1950s evening gown Boyd bought her. *Well, you can bleed on me.* She said "I've wanted a silk gown ever since I wore that silk thing of yours." "I have been placed beyond pain," she began one of her poems that winter. "If you don't respect me/I'll disappear." Twice I found her in Caspar Inn, drinking shot after shot of Jack Daniels. "To cry or to sleep," she said. "Either one. I walk that apartment all night screaming at him. But still I can't cry or sleep." By midwinter, rather than tears she developed an ulcer in her right eye. Isn't there a story of the princess who saw the lover dead on the ground and her eyes burst from the sight?

Eight days after Jonestown, November 27, San Francisco's mayor, George Mascone, a political supporter of Jim Jones, and supervisor Harvey Milk were assassinated by right-wing supervisor Dan White crazed by the mayor's liberal stance on homosexuality. This event, coming so soon on the shock of Jonestown, is I think, in the city's psyche, the same event.

In December I was drafted, as "the poet," into a group of four women wanting to write a screenplay about Patty Ferris, the original owner of the silk negligee, who had been killed the winter before by the wife of her lover. She was shot through the heart while she lay in his arms. Sky was in the front room of the house when the incident occurred. I think her wanting to write it up as a screenplay was mainly for therapy. All winter we met, pooling research and personal experience, to understand the events that led to the loss of two good friends. Patty was dead. Andrea got life in prison. Sierra, free of both women, remarried in a few months. In the beginning we were very sympathetic, even attracted, I think, to the poor guy. How do you live after such a thing? Sky used to swoon in describing him. But by Memorial Day, when we retreated together to Ten Mile River Ranch to draft the screenplay, we were all in a rage. In his dishonesty, fickleness, manipulativeness, he epitomized, so handsome, his blue eyes, his blond hair, his six feet, every woman killer, literal or otherwise, in history. The endeavor had become, for all five of us, much more than simple therapy. For me it was a devastating investigation into my own habits in love. There were times that winter with Robin I'd be feeling like one of the two women, the victim, the killer, when suddenly in a subtle shift of consciousness I'd see that I was like Sierra, the careless, duplicitous lover.

In December, I also became friends with a new poet in town. Howard visited the cottage often in the late afternoon when I normally took a break from my work. He knew as much about contemporary poetry as I did, but had different aesthetics so the visits were stimulating. But he was a growing irritation to Robin. I explained, and explained again, I was not and never would be sexually attracted to the man. Howard hinted of a dark past. As the winter proceeded he began to speak of seven nightmare years in the Atascadero Hospital for the Criminally Insane. This is where he had read so much, had become a poet, printed his first book. He had been a star runner for his LA high school, had gone to Berkeley in the mid-sixties on an athletic scholarship. Then came the drug years. He shot up acid and heroin together daily for a year and a half. He lost his mind, committed an atrocious crime. I didn't ask what it was. At present he was on probation and medication. I was not physically attracted to Howard—perhaps it was the medication which I could see in his body, or the insanity, the crime—but he did, just like a lover, hook me. He had, in growing degrees, my sympathy, my fidelity, my love.

Two days before Christmas my Navarro Bluff story appeared in the Sunday magazine of the *San Francisco Chronicle,* the holiday issue. At seven that night Rollin Ormsbee's daughter called. She was raging. "That A N Y O N E could be so insensitive as to write something like this!" She called it "poor taste, not artistic." "That stuff he shared with you was never meant to be printed. And there are inaccuracies." I wish I had had the presence to ask what the inaccuracies were but I felt one of the old dreads that had kept me from writing. The only art I'm interested in is of the intimate and personal facts of our existences. Most stories haven't been told yet. Sometimes I think the telling of these stories is the only thing that can save us. Privacy is essential to the integrity of the individual—we all need more of it, not less—but it's so clear that what has been kept "private" in the past has helped to create our dehumanized society, has served the status quo and its ugliest traditions. The structures can't accommodate what is kept from them! Still, though I know the nature of individual privacy is changing as the nature of society changes, I would not normally use another's story regarded by them as private no matter how good or important I felt it. I try very hard to be careful, to always check this, but I know it's a fine and dangerous line I write between the trespasses.

"What does Rollin feel?" I asked, upset, trying to explain. He had told me to go ahead and publish the story; no, he didn't want to read it first, and yes, use his real name. "Everyone's dead now who'd take offense." I bet she had no idea that the women now living in the place were a witches coven.

"It doesn't matter," she screamed, "what Rollin feels."

I am trying to recount here the events of the winter of 1978–79, how dark it was. On February 26 there was a total eclipse of the sun. It came at 3 P.M. I left my poem, walked outside to the headlands. The world turned a shadowy silver. It wasn't night, it was something eerie. Not even the birds chirped. Nor the gulls cried, nor the whales leaped. At four the earth and sun moved apart and the light returned.

That evening Evan returned to Mendocino. We walked the same headland, over Big River and the Pacific. The quality of his aura was as before, much like the eclipse. His talk was again personal, startling, full of the names of famous political spokesmen of the decade before. Averell Harriman, John Kenneth Galbraith, Lyndon Johnson. I pointed out the house Dean Rusk used to visit, the only house on this side of the headland. Evan seemed like a ghost from an ancient, conquering army, mysteriously humbled, reevaluating everything. He told me of a luncheon he'd once had with Johnson.

"He was a *feeler,* can you believe that! When he talked he kept grabbing my arm."

He gave a long, explicit account of an affair he had just come from with a young woman in San Diego. I can still see them fucking up against a chain-link fence. When I asked if he'd met my sister, Bridgit, he just shook his head, grinned, *"Amazing!"* When I asked about Aurora, remembering that he'd been in love with her, he said she videotaped him on a beach at La Jolla about his way of life now. She wanted it for her work with senior citizens.

We came to the Poet's Bench that sits on the edge of the headland, facing south, above where Big River pours into the sea. This giant bench was constructed years ago of a washed-up old growth redwood. He was telling me of a recent trip back East.

"There I was in New Haven with these two people, my age, whom I've known many years, and I was crying. I was talking about my father and I was crying. Later when I spoke of my mother it happened again. And I knew it was alright to cry with them. I said, *In California, I can do this. Cry in the presence of friends.* They said we have to go to Europe to find people with whom we can be so open that we can cry. Perhaps next vacation we will come to California."

South, over Chapman Point, a shooting star was falling into our atmosphere. As it fell, it grew larger and larger till there was an immense flaming tail. Then all was black. We sat speechless. A half minute later a loud crack came. Again, we were stunned. Then the silence filled with the ocean's roar.

"In the last six months something has happened to me in regard to money. I don't care so much about it. I've always been so careful with money, even though I've been very rich. I get $300 Social Security and draw $800 a month on savings." We watched the sky for more fireworks. "You know, I have to work some to spend a thousand a month."

"Me?" I laughed, a little nervous, when he asked. "Welfare. I consider it my government grant to the arts. My patriotic duty to write. I'm dedicating my book to the taxpayers of America."

Back in Evan's camper parked by The Well I thought I smelled Percodan. He showed me a carved antique wooden box that had been Bluebeard's, or some famous pirate's, explaining that once he had been addicted to Benzedrine. He showed me the secret compartment he used for his stash.

The next morning Rollin died. His granddaughter called me, waking me at eight. "I know my mother really put you down, but I wanted to tell you I think the story is beautiful. Only it and the Bible were on his nightstand when we found him this morning."

That afternoon Howard came to the house—to make his confession, it seemed later. He cried, his face contorting ghoulishly. I noticed, as he talked, his hand on the arm of my chair; it seemed separate from the rest of him. He said in 1967 everything he touched began to talk back to him. *You fucker!* It first began when he lived in Piercy with one of the first hippy tribes to leave the city.

"At first it was beautiful. *Good insanity.* I'd sit by the river for hours and it would talk to me. Birds landed on my shoulders. I'd think: *Hummingbird.* And one would fly up. In '69 we were moving from Piercy to Fort Bragg. The baby was seven months old. We came to the place on Highway 1 where the ocean is seen for the first time. The sea and the trees were singing to me like a high-soprano choir. I said to my wife, 'Do you hear that?' Well, she didn't. Of course she didn't. It was beautiful, but, oh, it frightened me."

They got jobs picking grapes. Then he could resist the voices no longer. It was his moral duty. They'd been whispering and screaming it in his ear from the day she was born. He killed his daughter to save her from *his* sins. *You fucker!* To not allow the continuation of his evil lineage. She was ten months old. He decapitated her in the vineyard.

He told me in great detail. His friend returning to the farmhouse with her head. The commune trying to hide him, the law bearing down so heavily on them anyway, these druggies from the city. 1969. He was sitting on my grandmother's trunk sobbing uncontrollably, how he wished he was dead. I've never been so overwhelmed with both horror and compassion. I remember thinking, this is the first story I've ever heard that I wished I hadn't. Then he began gruesome stories of the plots in the nuthouse to kill him, *the baby killer,* for seven years the most despised man in Atascadero Hospital for the Criminally Insane. Then the attempts to kill himself.

I was at a complete, dizzying loss as to what my function as his friend should be. How *could* you bear to live after something like that? My feelings of protectiveness of him were as great as any. But deep down, as deep as my horror, as deep as my compassion, I knew fear of him. *He killed her because she was female. Don't ever let him alone with your daughter.* I thought: *forgive, yes. But don't ever forget.*

"As terrible as it is, Howard, it's your story. It's all any of us have, the only thing we have. Our story. You're a poet. Don't kill yourself. Write your story so we can understand. Then write your future. A new story."

In March Max came back inside me. Sleeping, he took the form of dreams, and waking, worry. *Worry for him.* This was confusing because I was certain I'd gotten over him. One night I dreamed a phantom lover. He came and went and so did I before I could realize who he was. Then I dreamed of morning, of waking and remembering the lover, wondering who he could have been. When I removed my diaphragm I saw, deep in the cup of it, beneath a stranger's sperm, the words *I LOVE YOU.* I came out of the bathroom delighted, full of wonder and questions, *who* could have written this? The writing was similar to Robin's. At the door of the bathroom I looked out across a very large dance floor, and spinning on the cloud-lined horizon, so far away, was Maximilian Rainbow, dancing so beautifully, as beautiful as I remember him. His body. His grace. I watched him awhile, enjoying him visually as I used to, wishing it was he who had written this wonderful message that protected the deepest part of me. But then I turned away, smiling, knowing it wasn't Max. He never said *I love you* in the nine years we were together.

The next night Howard and Lorrain gave a poetry reading at the bookstore on Main. I was still having a difficult time with Howard's confession; it sat in me undigested like a bad meal. Before the reading I actually tried to call Max, fearing he was in danger. I knew he would cuss me but I was ready for that. I had to find out. But he didn't answer.

Reed approached me through the crowd when I walked into the bookstore saying he'd like to introduce me to some special people. The special people were Jonah's parents. Veronica, the mother, explained as we were introduced, that they had come to Mendocino to see the place their son had last lived, for some explanation of what had happened to him.

"If we can know his friends," she said, "just as you are, we will know him a little better."

She was in her mid-sixties, very attractive. She looked much like her son. Herb, the father, was embarrassed, retiring. All winter I had carried around his article on the obsolescence of trade unions due to automation, but still hadn't read it.

The reading was exceptional, in poetics, in passion. The subject matter of both poets was—what was Cody's word?—maudlin; perhaps suitable for the special people present, their quest. Howard was high on his confession now to the whole community. He seemed to be going for the legend of the tormented killer poet—although I doubted anyone else fully comprehended through the maze of his poetics, what exactly he was confessing. The daughter's decapitation was probably assumed as symbolic. This proved to be Lorrain's last reading. She had finally converted to Christianity, and after this night, she burned her writing, moved onto the Land, the Christian commune on Navarro Ridge. Her most apparent pain—*sin* was the word she used—was an abortion she had had of the married Christian fisherman's foetus, and with whom, it became quite clear in the reading, despite a long current relationship with another LA Russian Jew like herself, she was still hopelessly in love. In the poetry I heard for the first time Lorrain's sense that her killing this foetus two winters before karmically resulted in the death of her mother by cancer last winter.

Veronica's eyes were furrowed black with pain. This is the mother Reed and Yvonne blame for his addiction, his death. The famous singer who drove her son nuts with her demands for perfection. Here in this room that shook with every wave thrown by the sea she seemed delicate, fragile. There was about both parents a great air of nostalgia. They listened to the poetry well, as if for clues. So much imagery of pain, of self-mutilation, of guilt, of the burden of real and imagined crimes. The poetry of my generation is crazed, I think, finally, by the Bomb—the work of digesting *that* into art, into consciousness, into redemption, into the body, into the possibility of living. Our parents who created the Bomb can't acknowledge this. Though certainly my friends, along with their son, were giving the Steins a run for their money.

When the reading was over I sought them out again.

"You are beautiful," Veronica said to me, precisely my feelings about her. Then she said, as if we'd known each other for years, "It's terrible, getting old. I relied on my beauty all my life. It's a mistake I can see you are not making. You are cultivating another part of yourself that will insure personal power into your old age.

"Will you have breakfast with us in the morning?" she suddenly asked. "You and Robin? Reed will be there. Please. I want all of you to talk about Jonah. Please. Just stories."

"Of course," I said, feeling as if I was falling into her eyes. "I'd be honored."

Her wish was as mine would be in her situation. But what would I say? What could I possibly share with her that would meet her need? And it was not the sort of thing Robin would want to do. When they turned to leave, Veronica's colorful gypsy skirt a flying whirl over her high boots, their beauty, their age, their being Jonah's parents ripped the air. Through the open door I thought I heard the faint strains of that old tune playing somewhere down on Main Street. *Those were the days my friend. We thought they'd never end. We'd sing and dance forever and a day.*

That night I dreamed again of Max. *We are traveling in Florida with another couple.* (Florida is the one state I didn't know. Florida is where old couples like the Steins retire.) *We are in my car, Roses; the male of the other couple is driving. He bumps into a telephone pole which upsets me* (more than it would in real life). *We are not making any forward progress! So, the car disabled, we rent a motel room. I'm worried about Darien at home in Mendocino, alone, waiting for me. Max holds something in his hand, an object like a doll, and he says something about it. I respond, saying something myself about the doll and, instantly, we are in one of our old arguments. It's the argument we always got into, not the actual argument, but the pattern of our arguments. I say something, he says something. I say something. At this point, he responds to a small part of what I said, taking it out of the context of my statement. He twists it, "it" having little to do with what I actually said. I keep trying to straighten out the confusion. "No, you didn't hear me, I said . . ." but he will not let go of his reaction, which is not a reaction to anything I said or meant. He just keeps twisting it more and more.*

I always assumed Max wasn't conscious of what he was doing. In this dream I see that he perceives it all, that he always did, but out of his need to control me he never let on, certainly would never relinquish his power. He *uses* my compassion, my belief in understanding his side. And I see too the trap I lay for him by eating his shit. He has no reason to leave, which is what he always wanted to do, which he did the first time I seriously objected. I made it too good for him. Finally, in the dream, with great relief, I shout—am amazed that I find the words—*"You are unjust!" He begins to leave. Immediately I pretend I'm not as disturbed as I may have seemed. But as I eat the situation, the old anger and frustration churn in me, churns me over. I'm insane inside with the unfairness.*

I woke in a cold sweat. My first thought was Howard. I had to talk to Howard. Never have I known anyone to have to bear so much. Robin held me and I told the dream. He was wonderful in this way, always encouraging me to cry it out. I marveled that I had gone back into that most painful, familiar state, the trapped one of emotional blackmail. Why would I dream this at this time? I was sure I was free of such behavior. Hadn't I told Robin there were conditions under which I would not follow him? The dream seemed to come out of nowhere, about something long dead. Why was I crying? I must be crying for Howard. The images of his crime, renewed by his reading, were so awful in me. I had to talk to him. He must forget the past. He was trapped in it. His poems showed he *loved* his story, for all its horrors, for all his wishing his suicide attempts, the bizarre plots to murder him in the nuthouse had been successful. He had told me a surprising thing. Not a single person, his wife, his mother, his father, his brother or any of his friends turned against him. They were all good Christians. When his wife visited him the first time she said, "We'll have more children." *He* refused to ever see *her* again; he still hated her for that. "When I came to the first time I was in a strait jacket and my brother was sitting on the bed with me. In the most loving manner, he lit a cigarette, put it in my mouth." He said the only negative reaction he ever heard was from a friend who told him about attending an opening at the Music Center in Los Angeles with his mother. Afterwards, as they were leaving, the friend asked, "How's Howard doing?" She doubled over as if she had been socked in the stomach, collapsed. This man, I thought, is seeking someone to hate him. And he's so afraid for his sanity he won't allow himself, even momentarily, to forget. Like an alcoholic who reminds the self daily, you are an alcoholic. Most people, like Max, are trapped by their past because they won't deal with it. In Howard I was perceiving the opposite phenomenon.

When I mentioned Howard, Robin immediately lost his compassion.

"You're so close to him," he said, pulling away.

And so I shared with him what Howard had shared with me, hoping he would see what I was dealing with. Certainly not romance, sex. Howard had asked me not to tell anyone, but from the reading last night I knew he was now into spreading the word.

Robin was shocked. And concerned for me. We walked through the village to the Victorian, Moonlight romping behind and around every house. It had rained during the night. Everything was wet, clean, sparkling. The sky churned as I did. I felt terrible, like the beginning of flu. The sun was rising from the redwoods on the ridge east of town.

Again, I wanted to call Max. Again, I was afraid for him.

At breakfast I was awkward, stuttery—finally, mute. We had the dining room. Someone paid for everything. The silver, the napkins, the chandelier, the efficient, peasant-dressed waitress who pretended she didn't know us. I had my old nausea of class. Veronica sat at the head. We toasted champagne. Reed told wonderful stories about his youth, inseparable from Jonah, his boy memories of her. *How beautiful you were. And still are,* he quickly added. His chivalry maddened me. All the times he's blamed her for Jonah's problems. And Yvonne too. I saw her high Congregational background, all that proper puritanism that years of hippydom, pot, acid, vegetarianism, poetry, bisexuality, marriage to a junky Jewish musician, home in a Chrysler parked in the redwoods had not washed. Veronica's lashes were heavy in the oak-silled window against the heavy northern sky, sometimes heavy with tears. She talked and cried, highly animated, begged for more stories. She made me think of that song again. *Those were the days my friend. We thought they'd never end. . . .* Herb was silent, except for an occasional grunt, sigh of disgust, the murmur she should forget it. "You're wallowing in it," he said once. I'd look at him, then at her: the monster mother blamed for everything and wanted to scream B A S T A R D U P T I G H T H E A R T L E S S F A T H E R W E ' R E A L L D Y I N G F O R ! Robin, whose parents I imagined are much like Jonah's, whose mother, though I'd never met her or even seen a photograph, I knew physically in him, was chivalrous too. He even kissed her hand when we arrived. Well, I thought, popping a mushroom from my omelette into my mouth, I guess that is the whole point of chivalry and good manners: *hypocrisy.* It's thrilling, like pornography. At one point Reed, Robin and Yvonne were talking as if Jonah deliberately killed himself. I had not thought of this before. Yvonne said the thought of going back to the hospital or to jail really depressed him. "He was afraid he'd lose me." She laughed a little then, a high nervous laugh that enabled me, *finally,* to hear her—lusty heart and soul, true flower child—to hear just how much pain she was actually in. And how similar her facial bones were to Veronica's, the same white skin, dark deep-set almost hidden eyes. Just last week Raven's new lover had hung himself. Raven, who had always loved Yvonne, who had published her book. Raven, who had been in love also with Jonah. What the fuck is happening? Jonah, Patty, Howard, Lorrain, Mascone, Jonestown—something, Uranus? in the universe. I felt myself teetering on the cruel edge of it.

Veronica had just told a story of Jonah at three and tears were streaming down her face.

"If I'm getting too expressive, please take me back to the hotel," she said, emptying the last of a bottle of champagne into her glass.

"Alright," Herb said, rising, pulling her seat out. "Let's go."

She rose, obedient, humbled. Then she turned to me, his arm still guiding her out.

"Will you come this evening to Yvonne's? You've been so silent and I know you have something to share. Reed can't make it. Robin has to get ready for the gig tonight in Elk. Herb wants to try his hand with one of your Pacific salmon. It'll just be you and Yvonne and us."

I was afraid. I wanted to give to her, I wanted to acknowledge her quest, her mother's sorrow. How I hated the men this morning! But I couldn't imagine what to say, what to share.

"Of course," I said.

Back on the street, Moonlight waiting patiently at the gate, Robin pulled me under his arm, shouting to the town the same words from the night Jonah died. "Oh, fuck yes! I'd rather *die* in Yvonne's bed than go back to the straight world."

Once again, the formality of the meal. My body impatient, twitching to dance. Yvonne's ice-green downstairs. She'd found a long table in the garage that adjoined her apartment, set it up in the middle of the room for our dinner.

"That garage is packed," she said, setting the table. "No one seems to know whose stuff it is."

"Typical," I said. "Someone left, thinking they'd be right back."

With the piano and the table there was hardly room to get to the bathroom or kitchen. The salmon lay on its fat side, with round lemon slices all down it. Its eye watched us, even when all that was left of it was skull, spine, rinds of lemon. I kept wanting to turn it over, let it see with the other eye.

Yvonne told stories of her trip to Russia with her mother. I stared at the woman in the large sunbonnet sitting in the rowboat. They were swimming in the Black Sea when her mother's prosthesis floated by. Yvonne lunged for it but just then a wave took it into shore. The Russians, they noticed, were unashamed of mastectomies. She told me of Darien's progress on the piano, and how Moonlight opens her door in the mornings, comes in.

"The first time I was in bed upstairs. I heard him open the door, check out the kitchen, the bathroom, then slowly climb the stairs. I lay there paralyzed. I couldn't imagine who it was."

I had been hearing such stories all winter. Alsatians were bred for their instinct for opening doors, for getting into and out of locked spaces.

I drank the wine heartily. I wanted to get out of there, drive to Elk, dance. I wanted so badly to open, to give whatever it was inside me that belonged to Jonah, that was about Jonah. There must be some reason I was called, as Robin put it. Or maybe there wasn't, maybe everything is simple accident, whatever, only a fool would claim to know, I loved the mother, wanted to honor her grief, her seeking answers. I wanted to encourage her to not give in any longer to the men who rule the world: *forget it, don't dwell on it*. She told stories now of summer houses in Majorca, Mexico, of their penthouse in Manhattan. They had been a singing act all their married lives. *Herb and Veronica*. Thirty years on stage in Europe, United States. Colleges and nightclubs. They owned a well-known record company. It wasn't Herb who wrote the *Atlantic Monthly* essay but a life-long friend with the same name. I felt I knew this woman, certainly the profundity of birthing, raising human beings, their personalities and stories unfolding from utter mystery out of you. How does a woman ever survive the death of her child? This father so typically a pitiful lump of denial sitting outside parentage, outside heart, outside the woman who loves him. I knew it was he who had cut Jonah off. And she had obeyed the Patriarchy's law: *your husband before your children*. I saw Howard's baby in the vineyard, discarded like a headless doll.

"When the phone rang," Veronica was saying, "it was early Saturday evening in Manhattan and our guests were due to arrive. Well," she toasted the air with her wine glass, "the party must go on! And it did, didn't it, Herb? We performed our duties as host and hostess magnificently, into the wee hours. It was a great party. Then the last guest left, we cleaned up a little, got in bed. And then, only then did we cry. And cry and cry." She looked at me wildly, almost screamed it. *"Now isn't that corny?"*

I was telling my dream of the night before. It came pouring out despite my feeling foolish: *what does this have to do with anything?* All day I had been weighted with its images, Max's doll, a mindless puppet dangling from his hands. *How I eat his shit, pretending not to mind!* And the argument, the nauseating pattern of it, the awful entrapment. Blackmail! The neglect of my daughter in the sanctioned commitment to my lover. As I told it I began to see that I had dreamed the addict in myself. I dreamed of the situation where, like Evan, like Jonah, like Howard, like Lorrain in her obsessive search for the Lover and absolution from guilt, like the residents of Jonestown I am hooked on something that is clearly destroying me. But I refuse to see it that way, I see the love, I'd give my life, I'd risk it anyway, risk everything, to keep Maximilian Rainbow. I'm a *love junky!*

"Thank you," Herb said, startling me. I looked at him. Tears were coming down his cheeks. "Your dream is the first explanation of my son's addiction and death that I have understood. It was very clear."

And then an even more amazing thing happened. Those were, I know, the days of synchronicity, of a degree and nature that don't seem to come as often or as conclusively—at least, here, on the road where I live now—this whole story marked by something that has passed out of fashion, to be kept alive in the secret pockets of the populace, until the next outbreak. When Howard differentiated "good crazy," when the birds and rivers spoke to him, from "bad crazy," when the voices told him to decapitate his daughter, he was, I think, speaking of the most delicate law, synchronicity.

Anyway, Herb and Veronica were encouraged to the piano. Yvonne and I, unable to move in the crowded space, just sat there over the dirty china, the wine, the salmon eye. Occasionally, our eyes met, our lips curling in unison grins. They did a tune he had written in the thirties, then another. They were sort of Parisian cabaret tunes, of a victorious air, at the same time, sweet and nostalgic. The-party-must-go-on! tunes. The individual-sacrificed-to-society tunes. *We performed our duties as host and hostess magnificently into the wee hours.* Masochism! They were like the tune I had been hearing all weekend, humming, the lyrics of which I wanted to blurt out at breakfast, now dinner. *Those were the days my friend. We thought they'd never end. We'd sing and dance forever and a day.* Now the proximity of the piano, the chords, their singing bodies, something in the tone, the connections . . . I was thinking of being pregnant with Darien, of nursing her in the house in Ontario, David, three, playing beneath the window and the house filling with Edith Piaf that whole first year of her life. Sarah had given me three of Piaf's albums. I played them continuously, day in and day out. I wanted my children to grow on a triumphant spirit like Edith Piaf's. I didn't hear then the terrible groaning adult masochism. I played them until they were stolen, along with the stereo, by neighborhood boys. Oh, and when I first heard Mary Hopkins "Those Were the Days," it was around midnight in the summer of 1968, we were driving up the San Joaquin Valley, Highway 99, to Sacramento, to Max's brother's house. Max was driving, David and Darien were asleep in the back of the Falcon station wagon, our *Yellow Submarine.* It was very dark outside, the dank low of that valley, it must have been moonless. The song came, even then, that first time, like something utterly familiar out of the most urgent past. It took me in such a shocking way, the power of its nostalgia. I huddled into the dark corner of the passenger door, fought the tears that were building, so aware of the load of my children being hauled in the back, this man driving us. I couldn't help it though, the tears flowed. I cried, silently, on my side of the car. For the first time I saw: this was no different than my marriage to the father of these children. Nothing had changed—except the radicalness of my lifestyle. *We'd build a life we'd choose, we'd fight and never lose. . . .* This man was as unable to exchange with me as my first one. He may have refused to go to war, chosen prison to maintain his convictions, he may have grown long hair worn in spite of the violent reactions of his own gender, beads and pretty clothes too, he may see through much that is false and cruel about this culture—but he will not love a woman. I don't know if he knew I was crying, he was so dense, incredibly blind, deaf, unreceptive; it seemed likely I could sob aloud and he wouldn't hear. Even then, in all the misery of my revelation I still did not, could not consider that he knew what he was doing. I guess I was protecting my own vision. I would have really crumbled if I'd allowed the thought, that he was conscious of his cruelty. I certainly knew then that tears and reason were useless as petition, but it was the first time, hearing that song, *those were the days my friend. We thought they'd never end,* that despair overwhelmed my consciousness and I understood the trap he was for me, that I was truly caught. I loved him. I knew he loved me. I knew he'd never admit it. I was the woman with two fatherless children he had wanted to save when he grew up, when he himself was one of the two sleeping children in the back seat. He was the father he longed for then, the one he could someday be, but *never* one who actually loved the woman, his mother. His identity depended on not loving me, on being like his father who split. If he loved me he'd be the boy again, I'd be his mom. Oh, it was clear but all too late, I loved him too much like my own father as we wheeled north on 99, I couldn't get out, my own identity depended on staying, I was crying because I could see I was choosing the trap rather than lose him. I was crying too because the song was such a strange *déjà vu.* Then the d.j. cut in saying it was a new song by Mary Hopkins, promoted by the Beatles on their Apple label. *Why,* I sobbed, *in 1968 are we already singing about the days gone by, about our failure, all hope of youth and revolution gone? We're just beginning this life.*

When Herb and Veronica finished their second song, my eyes riveted to the play of his hands across the white keys, I clapped and said, "You two remind me so much of that song of the sixties. Do you know it? *Those Were the Days My Friend?*"

They looked at me, both suddenly very still.

"Oh, you are so perceptive," Veronica began.

"I wrote that song!" Herb exclaimed. The green walls rocked a little to the tune. "Veronica and I were performing it in a London nightclub one night when John Lennon walked in and bought it."

"You are so perceptive," Veronica said, staring at me.

Perhaps perception is the word, not synchronicity. Not my good crazy.

"I based it on Edith Piaf's 'My Lord.' Do you know her song?" Herb asked, seeming a different man now, open, filled with music, his cowardly male armor gone. He turned back to the piano, began the song.

And so then I knew why the tune, even in 1968, had filled me with such nostalgia, why it seemed of the past. It *was* the past, the music of my young motherhood, the music of my parents' generation, the music of World War II, the music of fascism, of heroism, of victimization, of genocide, of suicide. The Religion of Good and Evil, of Sadomasochism. Of Big Brother, of Mind Control, of the Bomb dropped, of Innocence lost, the Fatal Flaw. The music of all the repressed stories, of Bondage. The party must go on, *Hiroshima mon amour,* the Jonestown Rock! It was the first music my son and daughter passed their first days with, Darien at my breasts while I read *War and Peace,* David playing with his guns outside.

We are in our suicide lines.

We've lined up our children right behind us.

The poetry quoted on page 172 is by Robert Duncan.

Joyce

My last class in graduate school was a seminar in early twentieth-century English writers. The professor was "moonlighting" at our school, Cal State University at Los Angeles, from Claremont Men's College thirty miles inland. This man, in his personal tone and professional manner, seemed to go to great lengths to share his disdain for us, his *State* students. His disdain increased through the quarter, curious to me since I was impressed with the class, with the women students particularly. He caused me to remember a Shelley class I had been enrolled in at the beginning of graduate school. That professor was nationally recognized as the eminent scholar on Shelley; his latest publication was being hailed as the definitive biography. The first meeting was devoted entirely to a lecture on plagiarism. He gave each student a thirteen-page description of the sin. Before the next class we were to do a three-page textual analysis of an early Shelley poem, testing it for Wordsworth's "organic sensibility"—to find if Shelley qualified as a real poet—and for Aristotle's requirement that all parts of a work of art contribute to the "final cause." In some fashion I don't recall, we were each given a letter of the alphabet by which to identify our paper. During the week, before the next class, we were, surreptitiously, to drop the work into a special box outside his office. All this, he labored to tell us, would insure each student against the risk of his personal bias. I was named "P." During the week I wrote four papers. It was a hard week for me because my new boyfriend Maximilian was going on a caravan to Washington, D.C. to an anti-war demonstration. I wanted very much to go with him. I hadn't been across the country since I was a child, it was October and I had never seen fall colors, it was 1967 and by then I was crazed by my impotency in regards to Viet Nam. But finally I chose to stay and write my papers, to maintain my graduate-school status, not to uproot my kids for two weeks, not to endanger my National Defense Loan on which we were living. When the class reconvened the following Tuesday the Shelley scholar read my paper to the class as an example of a truly "brilliant" and "original" paper, the kind of work he wished but of course could not expect from all his students. Then he asked "P" to identify himself. When I raised my hand I felt a sort of trepidation and amazement too. I was in deep awe of the other students, especially for their oral skills of which I felt I had little. I remember, as the professor suddenly dismissed the class, of looking down on the rush-hour traffic of the hazy San Bernardino Freeway that I actually loved in those years, loved because it was the vast, fast road away from what had once been my housewife existence, as he, in the tone of a father, full of wrath and guilt, advised me to drop the class. There is no way, he said, that I can be fair to a student "like you." There is no way I can avoid my personal prejudices. When I walked out, his eyes, on my breasts and then on my bare miniskirted legs, were welling with tears.

There was one great redeeming feature of the Twentieth-Century English Writers Seminar. Dr. Days encouraged us to do our own reading and analysis, not to go to the critics unless we were unable to understand portions of a work. By that time I was disgusted with graduate school. It was an innocent's revelation, I suppose, to discover that an M.A. in English is a degree in literary criticism, that the study is of the men who study the men who write. I had chosen to continue my studies in order to get closer to the books, not further from them. In time I came to perceive the lowly status of writers held by these men, the teachers and critics. They regard artists as something akin to their naughty, but precious, children. And wives.

The work for Days' class consisted of doing two papers. For the midterm I did a paper on the socialist/revolutionary consciousness of Joseph Conrad in his novel *The Secret Agent*. I was at the time evolving my own revolutionary consciousness—as a tired, oppressed student perhaps subconsciously attracted, like Peter the Painter, to blowing up things—and so the work was not only interesting to me but inspiring.

I was pleased with the theme, as I perceived it in Conrad, pleased with Conrad, pleased with my paper.

Dr. Days returned my paper with a C grade. It was my first C in graduate school. Dr. Days reasoning for the C was more confusing than the grade itself. He told me that I had written such a complex paper that for him to understand it he would have to reread the book. The assignment was to give a more superficial analysis, a sort of book report. This struck me as odd, not to say absurd. Such a complaint as having to reread, or rather, a confession that a work is not well known by the professor who assigned it would never have come from a regular faculty member at Cal State. Moonlighting? His inferior students, indeed. My paper was too difficult for the professor!

He expressed concern for me, for my status in grad school, but then assured me that I would have a chance to make up the C with my final paper. I was not concerned myself. I hardly understood the miscommunication between us and assumed it would not happen again.

The second half of the quarter was devoted exclusively to James Joyce's *Ulysses*. Each student chose an episode from the book on which to report, both in an oral presentation and in a formal paper. Joyce's *Ulysses* takes place on Bloomsday, June 16, 1904 in Dublin, Ireland and has as its fundamental structure the ancient Greek epic by Homer. Leopold Bloom wanders the city as a present day Ulysses, his mind filled and filling with the stories, images, events and other bits of crazy data present on a modern city street. I chose the soliloquy at the end of the book by his wife Molly because I was attracted to its being in the voice of a woman—never mind that it was written by a man: in all my years of school I had never read a woman, with the lone exception of Emily Dickinson, the New England virgin with whom professors were so compatible in those days—and probably too because I could put off the work the longest; Molly Bloom is the last episode.

I sat through four weeks listening to oral analyses of the preceding seventeen episodes of *Ulysses*. I was not familiar with Homer so I had that great disadvantage and it was improbable that I'd get all of the 737 complex pages that precede Molly Bloom read. But I was delighted not to have to go the critics. I had a lot of time to absorb the story and Joyce's methods leading up to Molly, or Penelope as she is named in the Greek version, even though I put off the actual work until the final week. I had other far more major papers to write, namely a Jungian analysis of Kafka's *The Trial,* a Marxist analysis of Normal Mailer's *Barbary Shore,* a Formalist analysis of all the novels of Bernard Malamud. Typically, I knew nothing of Jung or Marx when I started these papers; as for Formalism, I had cut my literary teeth on the thing, both Arisotle's and the CIA's post-World War II, cold war version, though I did not understand it then as a "system." I was taught Formalism just like a religion: The Truth. The Absolute and Only Way to read literature.

Our last class session, indeed my last class session in college, was held June 5, 1968. I arranged the preceding week so that I could give maximum time to the project. I was newly living with Max, who, wonderfully, took over the care of my two children.

Forty-five pages. Thirty thousand words. The first observation that one makes of the Molly Bloom soliloquy is its complete lack of punctuation. The chapter is famous for this. Later, when I read them, the critics explained that this is symbolic of the sloppy, uneducated, sensuous, nondiscriminating, barbaric (a favorite, oft-repeated adjective) female mind. The Penelope episode is always cited as the first fully developed example in English literature of the "stream of consciousness," "free association" technique.

The second observation that one makes is that the forty-five-page episode, while devoid entirely of grammatical notation, *is* divided into eight parts or paragraphs. Later, I will learn that Joyce referred to these eight sections as Sentences.

The third notable characteristic is that the eight Sentences are highly uneven in length. It seemed apparent, given what I had learned of Joyce's method of constructing the other chapters, and being a Formalist by education, that is, like a scientist in a lab, observing only the given material, allowing no outside allusions or inferences or inside psychic/psychological states—it probably helped that I didn't know Homer; or Catholicism for that matter—that this was an important clue to comprehending the underlying structure of Molly Bloom. There must be a reason, for instance, that Sentence 2 is the longest of the eight, while Sentence 3 is the shortest.

I spent the week, which was primary week of the elections of 1968, trying to detect the differences in the eight Sentences. I set myself up at the kitchen table. The antique oak library desk my father had sanded, polished and given me stood in the dark living room corner with a pile of books and papers that had grown all year. It had my son's second-grade homework on it. David would bring the papers home everyday and throw them on the pile. This was the year I neglected him. This is the year of my guilt. He was dyslexic. He could not read. I knew it was going to take a lot more than nightly homework to deal with his prob-lem. So I just drifted with him, hugging him whenever he would allow it. Like most students I was in a state of severe exhaustion. I had not had a normal night's sleep in months. On top of everything else, I was newly in love, and coming to Maximilian was to be as major an adjust-ment as I am sure I will ever have to make. Soon, I told myself, I will have an M.A. degree, this will all be over, I will be a good mother again.

I had obtained from Rita Gomez, the mother of David's best friend, Miquel, an envelope of Ritalin. Ritalin is the drug the L.A. Public School District routinely prescribed to children diagnosed as hyperac-tive. In a child's metabolism, Ritalin appears to calm the child enabling him or her to concentrate. I had refused to let them give it to David. Miquel was a drug addict at seven. I think that as long as I live I will be haunted by his drugged eyes and the drugged eyes of other children I knew then. I could spot them anywhere. Within a few years some of these children were suicides; my own cousin tried to kill herself at ten. It is and was amazing to me that we allowed the schools to drug our kids, while I, an adult, could have been imprisoned for my discretion-ary use. As it is also amazing to me to remember that Miquel's father, Rita's husband from whom she was separated, was the hunted mur-derer of three border-patrol officers. This incident from the year be-fore was infamous: three guards shot to death on a lonely back road of San Diego County, one of the roads to and from Ramona, my hometown. He was contacting her about every ten days though they had not lived together in five years. They had five children. She was on welfare. I remember one evening she ran up the hill to my house with a can of Campbell's tomato soup that she had just swiped from the neighborhood store. By the time she got inside the door she was hysterical. She had been busted once before for shoplifting, her children taken from her and placed in foster homes. She was terrified she'd get caught again. But what was she to do? She could not feed herself and her five children on the welfare check. And she wished to hell he would quit calling her. She was terrified of him, terrified that she'd lose her children again because of him. Rita was a Chicana, five feet ten inches tall, mostly Yaqui. She weighed one hundred and four pounds. She was thirty-two years old but looked older. She's the one who pierced my ears. I paid her five dollars to do it. I paid her ten dollars for her son's Ritalin. My National Defense Loan. Later that year she had a stroke. I'm sure it was from malnutrition, Ritalin, her husband, her five young children, the welfare office. They took the kids away from her, put them in a school in Northern California.

Rita. Ritalin. Lovely Rita Meter Maid. Rita is Greek for pearl, meaning *born of moonlight.* I wonder about the etymology of the word Ritalin. There is the word retard, *to slow down.* Ritardando, the musical term, *with a gradual slackening in tempo.* Rita in the Vedic tradition is the cosmic moral principle of order that establishes regularity and righteousness in the world. According to the local dope lore and verified by my experience, Ritalin works on the metabolism of the adult in the opposite way that it does on children: as a central nervous system *stimulant,* but, and this is the wonderful effect, the power of concentration that it gives children remains.

I used index cards and made long lists of possible themes and motifs I detected in the eight Sentences. I listed images, adjectives, nouns, repetitive events and stories, likely symbols, Molly's mood changes. As the week advanced I began to detect a theme for each Sentence. Sentence 5 is concerned primarily with puberty and sex. Sentence 4, on the other hand, has no sexual references, is the only Sentence in the episode without them. Instead there is the dominant image of a strange, sort of other-worldly couple with whom Molly is riding in a carriage. Within certain Sentences I found recurring patterns of words, images and themes suggesting conscious ordering by the author. But then in other places these patterns would not hold. Obviously Molly Bloom was structured but the week was passing with the structure undetected. I worked hours and hours at my table, like a musician at practice, and outdoors under the sycamore tree while the kids played in their plastic swimming pool. My powers of concentration were very great; I could feel myself more and more seduced by the work. I worked almost all night every night after Darien and David were in bed. After making love with Max, I'd get up and go to the dark kitchen over Los Angeles that twinkled in its basin like a choreographed stage production. I shuffled my cards, meditated on the text, read and reread, thought on Molly and the whole story of Ulysses, on Penelope, on *"Moly the earth root to save us,"* the herb Hermes gives Ulysses to guarantee safe passage home; added up, again, adjectives, nouns, themes, subject matters; underlined, counted, blocked off in colored inks; tried to perceive what Joyce might have wanted to forge from this final chapter of a work that engaged him for seven years. Trieste, Paris, Dublin, Gibraltar, Wandering Jew, Black Irish, Daedalus, Woman, Los Angeles, epiphany, free association, stream of consciousness, the streaming consciousness of the race. The week rolled on with Wednesday, my deadline, quickly approaching.

During the week, while David was ending the second grade with all fail marks, Max carried four-year-old Darien around the city on his shoulders collecting signatures for the initiative to allow eighteen-year-olds the vote. Later he would be awarded for obtaining more signatures than anyone in the state. He too was working under tremendous pressure. He had been out of prison one year. His rage in this year of freedom seemed to be increasing rather than diminishing, as if it too had been held behind steel bars. One day during the week he came home and told me, sitting at the kitchen table working on Molly Bloom, that he had just driven past, near the intersections of the Pasadena and San Bernardino freeways, the cop who had busted him. Busted him after a year-long close friendship: he was the undercover agent. This man had continued to harass him through the year he did in LA City Jail atop the Hall of Justice and at the end of his time was responsible for Max serving two extra months in solitary confinement. Maximilian was due to be released in two weeks when he was caught looking over the wall of the exercise roof, the fifteenth floor of the old jail, looking down to the street, looking to the sea and south towards

Watts for which he had great nostalgia because during his first term he had watched it burn from his cell window. He prayed, he said, that the whole evil city would burn. He was spotted looking over the wall, an infraction of jail rules, by his ex-"friend," the undercover agent, and consequently put into solitary. He prepared himself for two weeks. He could hold his mud. He assumed that legally he couldn't be held longer. But the time came and went and he was not released. He was not told what was happening, or when he would be released. Now the man responsible for these "immoral acts," as Max called them, was pulled over on the side of the freeway bent to his state car engine, the hood up. Max fumed across the table, bitter that he had not followed his instinct, *run the fuckin bastard down. I would have,* he ranted, *if Darien hadn't been with me. All cops should be killed.*

June 4 was primary election day. I voted for Eldridge Cleaver for president and the Chicano New Mexico outlaw, Reis Tijerina, for vice president, both of whom I had helped to nominate at the Peace and Freedom Convention in Richmond, California the preceding spring. Cleaver was touching in his painful shyness. "I'm just a writer," he apologized, when he finally appeared to accept his nomination. "I'm not a politician. I don't know what to say." Tijerina was as flamboyant and colorful as Cleaver was retiring, so wonderfully typical of his people near or in whose neighborhoods I had spent my life, their oppression therefore more real to me than that of the more distant blacks. Tijerina stormed the convention hall with his Brown Beret troops in much the same way he must have stormed the New Mexico Courthouse, the deed for which he was famous. The poll for our precinct was the apartment beneath us, the home of a large Chinese–Mexican family. The building was a duplex, built into the side of Mount Washington in Highland Park, just north of downtown LA. Our neighborhood was mostly Chicano, though on the mountain above us, the oldest artist community of Los Angeles, the residents were more and more beginning to look like "hippies." Beneath, around and above, the city was becoming very colorful: banners, flags, balloons, piñatas; long hair and beads on men; women without bras, lipstick or hairpins; see-through blouses, funny painted cars and mailboxes; the smell of marijuana everywhere, for the first time not just from the Chicanos.

Something, as the song kept booming down The Avenues, was happening. That night before my last college class, after I fixed dinner for the four of us, after Maximilian bathed my children and put them to bed, after making love to me for probably the third time that day, he went off to the Peace and Freedom Party Headquarters to count votes and I sat down at the kitchen table for what I assumed to be my final work on Molly Bloom.

The class would meet at 9 A.M. I had to have a typed paper and an oral presentation prepared. Like Molly, like Eldridge in those days, I am not an articulate speaker; like my son, I now know, in fact, like all poets, I am dyslexic. To prepare an oral presentation would take extra time for me and special concentration. There was that unforgivable day at the beginning of my college career at Palomar Junior College when I found myself, a compulsive straight-A student, standing in front of my speech class, speechless. The assignment was an extemporaneous speech, the "subject" written on a tiny sheet of paper handed me as I walked to the front of the room. I opened my mouth and nothing came out. Not a squeak, not a monosyllable in the five minutes, it seemed, I stood there. The teacher was terribly disappointed in me; the year before I had won the campus intramural speech contest in an impassioned plea for an understanding of the Palestinian refugees. This speech was motivated by the combined contact that semester with two Palestinian exchange students and a woman who presented to me for the first time the philosophy of the John Birch Society. I was deeply moved by the passion of all three, but the reasoning of the woman grew in me as grievously mistaken and to this day I have not shaken the fear and horror she initially introduced to my psyche of how disturbed and tragically warped human reasoning can be. Presenting the award, the speech teacher invited me to sign up for his class. I don't think he understood that it was my passion and my concern for the subject that enabled me to speak, to speak well enough to win a speech contest, as I did not understand then that it is the free flow of words from the mouth on *any* subject that is the goal of a speech major.

I gave myself until midnight to decipher the code. Then if I still hadn't found it I would write the paper from a general, philosophical point of view, a book report, as Days in fact seemed to want, but which

I could hardly believe. By now I had a good understanding of who Penelope is, and so it would be easy, if I had to, to just let go of Joyce's compelling mystery. I'd let my week's work unravel from the warp just as Penelope does every night so as not to be forced to marry one of the suitors. But I wanted so badly to uncover the reason she waited twenty years for Ulysses to return and why he left and where he really went. Most of Los Angeles spread beneath me. Around eight the sun set behind Mount Washington, then its long afterglow, the Music Center and City Hall turning fuchsia, then, suddenly, to the intense ancestral silver of the moment before night. The kids slept. I was alone. How I loved my city, a love recently increased by my association with Max and his keen geographical and sociological knowledge of it, the world's largest town, this basin now of jewels, the long snake lights working toward every remote corner from the amorphous center, the spokes of a wheel that dazzled and disappeared, gold and red, LA spinning everywhere.

I turned on the TV my parents had given the kids for Christmas. Kennedy was winning. Of course. I wondered how the counting was going at Peace and Freedom Headquarters. As always I felt a little guilty in regards to my more politically active friends; it seemed they were doing important work while I was just a student. But then, as I've always told myself, who knows what the important work is? It may be as hidden as Molly Bloom. I was high over LA, high on Ritalin, high on the rising moon, high on my last work as a student, high on the unknown future, high over the foothills stretching beneath me, looking down the Arroyo Seco to city hall, which sometimes, in hard rain, the river floods.

Midnight came. I didn't have the code. With begrudging reluctance I gave up. I started drafting a simple philosophical paper on the Earth Mother symbolism of Molly Bloom. The phone rang. It was Rita. Have you heard? Heard what? Turn on your TV, Kennedy's been shot. I reached for the button. The Ambassador Hotel. Mediterranean. Pink. The palms swaying crazily across the racing moonlit clouds. It was true. Robert Kennedy had been shot.

They were describing the suspected assassin. About five feet, nine inches, dark curly hair, moustache, late twenties, gaunt. The description was of Maximilian. They had a police drawing. It looked like Maximilian. The Ambassador Hotel was one block from the Peace and Freedom Headquarters. The week before Max had taken me and Darien on a tour of the lobby of the Ambassador, the grounds and gardens.

I stood in the room, unable to move. I felt tall, my body too long in a vertical tube of silence. I think I was willing time backwards, unwinding the hour a half hour. I wanted Kennedy unshot. I wanted Max undone from this story. Even if he wasn't the assassin he was still in danger. If a cop came towards him in a menacing way I knew he would kill or be killed before being taken again. Max's arrest record was a long series of what seemed like cruel cosmic jokes, the source of so much of his rage. At twenty, during the Cuban Crisis, he had been drafted. He was excited to go. He would see more of the world than LA. He had two months to get his things in order, to report for induction. But in those two months he began to imagine the future: he is holding a gun on a Cuban who holds a gun on him; he must kill the Cuban or be killed by him. He is a father. What did you do in the war, Daddy? He refused induction in the army because he didn't want to answer his future children, *I followed orders, I killed.* Obviously, he was a conscientious objector but the court refused to recognize him. He was smoking a joint on the rim of the Grand Canyon, miles, he thought, from a living soul, when he was busted the last time. His hatred of Robert Kennedy stemmed from the time he did in Flagstaff's jail. The sentence there, in 1966, for one marijuana cigarette was twenty years. From his cell he waged war on Arizona and its marijuana laws. He pleaded an impossible "innocent" in a Mormon town to a Mormon judge with a Mormon sheriff and a Mormon defense attorney, on the grounds that marijuana was his religion. They threatened him with life. Life in Florence, Arizona's notorious desert prison. He petitioned Robert Kennedy and Allen Ginsberg to his trial. Ginsberg said he'd come. Kennedy wrote him a long, rather thoughtful letter apologizing that he was unable to attend his trial but affirming his position of support for the legalization of marijuana. It was something in the patronizing, "liberal" tone, his refusal to attend a trial in which a man's life was at stake, and the issue he claimed to support could be won, that infuriated Max. He told numerous people, anyone who would listen, of his hatred for Robert Kennedy.

But I was a student. It was after midnight. I had a paper to finish. Kennedy was already shot, whatever had happened, whatever happened now would not excuse me from my 9 A.M. deadline. I had to get free of school. If he was going to do this to his life then that was his choice. I couldn't stop him. I was probably in shock. My love for him was already like a river beneath and beyond his insanity. I saw myself spending the next twenty years visiting him in prison, being faithful. If that was my future I had to at least have a master's degree.

Finally I thought to call Peace and Freedom. John answered. They were okay. Yes, of course, they knew. He said Max was in the back room counting votes. He was too busy to get him. His voice had a condescending tone as if he was speaking to a child. I resented it, my own rage beginning to flare. As if how silly I was to be upset or excited. People had strange reactions to Robert Kennedy's assassination.

I sat down to my work on Joyce. The simple version. I couldn't seem to feel much for Kennedy myself and I felt bad about that. It was too hard to believe, harder in some way than any of the assassinations of those years, somehow preposterous, at the same time hardly shocking at all, sort of expected. Watching the television was like watching a movie rerun. At least he wasn't dead. Yet. The moon, stars and clouds strung low across the basin. Downstairs, the phone rang. I heard a sharp gasp and then the whole family getting up to watch the news. Carmen Lee, the sixteen-year-old girl, my favorite of the family, was crying, she who would be killed herself in three weeks on the first ride of her brother's new motorcycle at the bottom of the hill on the corner Max was always pointing out as the place where the man exposed his foot-long penis to him one moonlit night when he was sixteen. Kennedy. Another Kennedy. Why can't I feel more? Resignation. I was wrung out emotionally. I was on Ritalin. I thought of my mother. How hard she was going to take this. She loves him. I should call her. I picked up my notes. Words. What is it? Where is the key? Resignation. It's too late. I can't do it. Just go with what I know. Earth Mother. The TV suffers at a low moan. The lights are less now as the night moves deep into sleep. Into the politics of murder. It grows colder. I put on a bathrobe, can feel my mouth drawn behind the hours of study, of strain, of Ritalin. The Ambassador Hotel. Rosey Grier. Football. A woman in a polka-dot dress. It is a chore to write superficially; I have such contempt for the waste of papers that sing on prettily about nothing. A photograph keeps flashing across the TV of Kennedy sprawled on his back on the kitchen floor of the Ambassador. A young man in a cook's uniform is bent to him, holding his head, looking with great anguish into the camera. The young man looks Vietnamese. The image catches me, it's bizarre, the synchronicity of a poor Vietnamese holding the dying rich American political hero seems more like an artist's anti-war statement than an event that is actually occurring.

I looked at the text, my notes. The structure opened in my hands like a door, easily, with the found key. The structure of Molly Bloom. Of course. There she is.

I saw so clearly that Molly's eight Sentences embody two cycles, the first based on the evolutionary and historical stages of the earth and the second on the universal stages of human life, while both mirror the other. The structure, in the simple way I first saw it that night, is based on Greek myth (though the names of my ages here are from Giambattista Vico whose *The New Science* I would not be familiar with for another two years). Sentence 1 is *The Divine Age:* Infinity; Creation; the birth of the Mother Goddess; Gaea out of Chaos; the Castration of the father Uranus by the son Chronus, Time; the Rise of Venus, Love. Sentence 2 is *The Heroic Age:* the Birth and Evolution of Humanity. The longest sentence: the long evolutionary time before Western Civilization. Sentence 3 is *The Human Age:* Civilization, the Cities, Democracy and the contemporary human being, Dissolution and Corruption, Assassinations, Death. The shortest era in Earth's history. The Fall. Sentence 4 is the Underworld, the Afterlife, *Ricorso* or *Sandhi,* Heaven or Hell, Purgatory, the time of the soul between reincarnations, and in the human cycle, Childhood; the asexual time before puberty. Sentence 5 is *The Divine Age* again, the Return, Rebirth, Creation anew. It is puberty, the sexual awakening of the individual, the potential of new life. Sentence 6 is *The Heroic Age* again, this time in terms of the maturation of the individual: Marriage and Family. Sentence 7 is *The Human Age:* this time Death and Burial symbolized by the female menstrual cycle. Sentence 8 is *Ricorso* again: Purgatory, Chaos, Hell.

I worked feverishly through the remainder of the night, the TV at a low whine. My typing is dyslexic and therefore slow. Maximilian was all right. Another "loner," typical of all the accused assassins of our time, had been caught, this time an Arab from Pasadena, not a Peace and Freedom radical, not a Black Panther or a Brown Beret or a Vietnamese. Sirhan Sirhan must have driven right down the Arroyo Seco on the Pasadena Freeway to get to the Ambassador sometime while I sat there above it. By 9 A.M. I walked into the classroom ready to hand in my fifteen-page paper and to give my talk.

I was stoned. I was stoned on my discovery, the structure being very beautiful to me. I was stoned on Ritalin and the lack of sleep. I was quite out of my mind with the assassination, the cries and talk of which were all I heard as I hurried across my enormous campus. There was a large crowd in front of the campus Kennedy-For-President Headquarters. I was nervous about my ability to make the oral presentation. Many of the structural points of Molly Bloom pivot on her "obscenities." I was too far gone to speak academically, to substitute "defecate" for *shit*, "penis," or "the male member" for *cock*. I was too moved and inspired with the vision of affirmation and joy in Joyce's 30,000 words to say "fornicate" for Molly's *fuck*. To have done so, after my week inside Molly, would have been a real perversion and missing entirely Joyce's linguistic point. All I could do was trust the creative energy of the morning, mine and Joyce's, and the strong communal one arising from the political tragedy we were all experiencing and, as they say, go for it. Or perhaps it was simply survival energy given the low esteem in which this class seemed to hold me.

At any rate, with much energy, nervous and passionate, I presented "The Structure of Molly Bloom." Dr. Days said only one thing to me when I finished, the first time I encountered the universal consensus. "Of course," he spit, "there is no structure to the Molly Bloom soliloquy. The episode is stream of consciousness. Free association."

Maximilian met me after class, to be with me, he said, at the end of my long trip. My Daedalus, at the end of one labyrinth, the beginning of a new one. "Now," he whispered, "you'll be able to fuck me even more." "Max! He said there's no structure!" In the halls no one from the class spoke to me; they seemed embarrassed. And when the cop of the class, the lone police officer in the M.A. program, whisked by us Max cursed loudly after him for the gun hidden under his dark blue suit jacket. The cop had been in many of my classes and was as despised by some as I, the hippy, was. He always wore a dark blue suit, never spoke or walked with others, and sat in class with the air of a killer. Sitting behind or across from him I was always aware of the bulge that was his gun. It was rumored that he wrote literary analysis so conservative as to perplex even our professors. I first learned of The Fugitives from him in a class to earn the California Junior College Teaching Credential, which I suppose we were both taking in case everything else failed in our fantasies of the future. There was the time too I felt he was setting me up for a bust. But that's another story. The cop was Joseph Wambaugh a year or two before the publication of his first book, *The New Centurions*.

"Max, he said there is no structure!" I had too much energy to stand still in the slow-moving elevator so we walked down the seven flights of stairs. On the way off-campus we stopped at the library and I encountered for the first time the books on James Joyce. The Joycean Industry. "Fifty years of unprecedented exegesis." They all said the same: though all the other episodes of *Ulysses* have elaborate, often several overlapping structures dictating every word, the Penelope episode has none. The closest any of the critics came to suggesting a structure was William Tendal: "Whether these Sentences differ from one another in theme or character I am unable to say. . . . That some structure underlies apparent flux is what we should expect from Joyce. Why eight sentences? I have no idea. . . " And another said, "To Budgen and Gilbert, Joyce implied Molly had coherent form and argument 'achieved by means that are suspiciously both mechanical and ineffectual,' but to Harriet Weaver Shaw . . . he said it didn't."

We came out of the library to a huge TV screen set up outside the Kennedy Headquarters. Frank Mankiewicz was announcing that Robert Kennedy died at noon. People were weeping; most were silent. I felt sick. Someone screamed he asked for it. Mankiewicz had made many friends at Cal State/LA the year before when he debated the Muslim Ron Karinga on the future of revolutionary communities. I was impressed by his stories of South American peasants quietly moving onto land owned by wealthy absentee Europeans, setting up whole villages and communities. Karinga, on the other hand, who, to give his opening talk, was installed on something like a throne with all the pomp and ritual of an African Chief, while the hall lined with his intimidating warlords, was presently under attack for suspicion of being a CIA undercover agent.

We drove home, the back way, through the beautiful mustard-covered hills of El Sereno, LA's oldest neighborhood. Between news updates of Kennedy and Sirhan Sirhan the Chambers Brothers chanted and clanged, extolled and harangued one of the longest tunes ever recorded. *Time! Time! Time! The time has come today!* I felt Max cringe beside me and then listen. *Can't put it off another day!* While he was doing time his first love dropped him for one of the Chambers Brothers. I was having a hard time believing I was through. After eight years of classes. I was pregnant when I started in the summer of 1960. I had been a student for the entire sixties. Max had been in jail for most of them. It would be a year before I finished all the exams, incompletes, and actually had an M.A. degree. And it would be fifteen months before I would return to James Joyce. And then: five years of work on Molly Bloom.

The time has come today. Young hearts can go their way. I have often thought to name this story "Student," as I think my experience is typical of the chaotic, sometimes killing forces with which students have to deal. Perhaps these forces were particularly active in the students of the sixties, the ones who because they were students, or of the right gender, were not in Viet Nam. I had had some exceptionally fine, conscientious teachers. Jerry Farber wrote *Student as Nigger* while I was in his Contemporary American Poetry class. (I have always believed I am the one he cites whose mouth breaks out in cold sores just before every exam as I remember so well the time he looked at my blistery mouth and lost his train of speech.) Another was on the graduate committee for a UCLA anthropology student, Carlos Castaneda. Dr. Watson alluded to the unpublished as yet unfinished *Teachings of Don Juan* in nearly every lecture in his myth and lit class. Another important teacher, Peter Marin, was the first to introduce to me the concept of no grades, the first to introduce Charles Olson and the "New American" concept of poetry as, first and foremost, energy, the first person to say *"fuck,"* deliberately in my presence; he said fuck to the whole class and challenged us on what constitutes a "dirty" word. He told stories of a friend and poet already being named by some as the greatest living American poet, a man at UCLA named Jack Hirschman. (Peter was, of course, fired for saying fuck. As was Jack fired from UCLA.) And there was my friend and fellow student, Neeli Cherry, now the poet and Ferlinghetti biographer, Neeli Cherkovsky, who told endless stories of his friend in Venice, Charles Bukowski. It would take moving to Vermont four years later before I would learn that Bukowski was a serious writer, and not just a dirty old man someone had taken pity on and given space for his "notes" in the *L.A. Free Press.* In hindsight, the total maleness of these influences is glaring, and I will add, these wise men were outstandingly guilty of sexism. In my faith in the non-gender of student, in my own culturally induced sexism, I worked very hard to ignore this. But most ironically, it was the linguist and later right-wing reactionary, S.I. Hayakawa and his book, *Language in Thought and Action,* assigned by the poet Gerald Locklin during the Watts riots, that most deeply had influence, that forever changed my mind. How Men Use Words and Words Use Men. The book, though obviously meant for men only—after all, a linguist, particularly this one, would understand his use of the word *men*—taught me *how to think* through the emotionally loaded clichés and false reasonings of my culture. Sometime that last spring, what proved to be the spring of My Lai, I understood, in a moment like a Joycean epiphany, while walking across campus, the terrible but very real connection between the law and order of the army and the law and order of poetry. Formalism. A deadly principle of exclusive left-brain Anglo maleness. (Being dyslexic I was very familiar in 1968 with the phenomenon of the right and left hemispheres of the brain though it's only recently that this understanding has entered our mainstream thought. Traditionally, in art, the phenomenon is labeled Classicism versus Romanticism, and the other way around, the history inevitably viewed as a violent slamming from pole to pole; the notion of balance is not much part of the tradition.) I sat on a bench in the smoggy green landscaped center of the place, beneath the ever-growing skyscraper classrooms and the cars stalled at the intersection of the San Bernardino and Pasadena freeways, right in the middle of East LA, the largest Mexican population in the world outside of Mexico City, though there were no Mexican students in the many walking by me at the moment, nor had I seen but a few in all my years on the campus, a fact which only later I considered as possibly an affirmative one, and I understood: *I am not a poet.* After eight years my education had its effect. I understood. I must not allow myself to write from my roots, my class, my sex, my heart, my body, my mind. My education had made me ashamed, that is, aware that what I wrote, especially the rhythm by which I wrote, would be scorned and ridiculed by the middle class into which I had somehow, innocently risen. And I must *never* allow myself to write by their values, like a killer, with the anal fascistic principles by which they were waging war on Viet Nam. I vowed never to write poetry again. I had to vow it; the instinct was very strong in me.

I have no place to stay. My tears have come and gone. Now I have to roam. I have no home. Now the time has come.

As for the future, for me and Max and David and Darien, there were no plans, no ideas. The only image I had was the recurring one, as I walked through the halls of my brick and glass skyscrapers, of tumbling down green rolling fields. We were driving away from our campus blind, as once on that same road I had gone totally terrifyingly blind from my first marijuana brownies which I had gobbled down, loving chocolate, as if they were my mother's. We had only our bodies to feel the way. Max was one unit short of getting his degree in sociology, a unit he swore he'd never work for. He had taken acid his last school test and seen a similar truth as I had about poetry. Together that spring we had taken a mini-course at the new career center on the campus. But we couldn't find a single career that did not require immoral work—the best paying jobs were directly related to killing Vietnamese and other Third World people, or destroying nature. The most refined career, the lowest paid, the only possible place for us seemed to be the profession of teaching. But I knew I'd never last if I managed to get hired. I could never sacrifice the well-being of *any* person for the overall good of the institution, which was, even as a young child, and always will be, my politics. There are good teachers but I have never encountered one, in the public schools at least, that did not smell somewhere deep in the being of moral compromise. I didn't want that to happen to me. I felt that my life was a work of art. I felt very protective of it. Despite everything that was happening around me, or perhaps because of it, I believed in life, I believed in the good of it. I had spent eight years trying to rid myself of such corny thinking; at least, testing it. But I had also birthed two human beings in that time and I believed absolutely in their goodness. I did not want them to grow up seeing negative compromise in their mother and therefore succumb to it themselves as inevitable, as the whole world insists. They were the ones to teach, the only ones I had a real chance with. Max did not understand sexism, the state having done to him what it does to all its males, but he was still raw enough from prison and from being a forties welfare kid in downtown LA with his mother to detect that something of the souls of the men we most admired had been co-opted.

Now the time has come. There is no place to run. I am a problem son. There are things to realize. The time has come today!

The task of our future had to do with money. Money and the money maker, the state. How not to be co-opted by it. How to raise the kids in such a way as to show them that money is not all-powerful, that it robs one of personal power, that they can do *anything* without money being the central focus of their lives. *Time! Time! Time . . .* there is that buildup of drums in the middle, the thumping pounding beating hitting clanging of cymbals and cowbells, the screaming, hysterical laughing, the clouds tumbling over the LA mustard hills, the whooping calling crying begging and finally after forever the guitar unwinding out of it OH! *I've been loved and criticized. I've been loved and shoved aside. I've been crushed by the tumbling tide. And my soul. Has been psychedelicized.*

A week or so later I was at my sister's in San Diego trying to come down off my Ritalin high. Actually it would take another two months before I would have a normal night's sleep and the fierce headaches subside. We were on the north end of Mission Bay, a block from her apartment. We had my two children, her daughter and our brother's daughter from Ramona,—three preschoolers and David who had just passed second grade even though he still could not read, write, add, or subtract, and had received Fs all year. LA school board policy. I longed for the ocean, for its pounding waves, its great cleansing tidal action, but Bridgit, who was six months pregnant, had persuaded me that with four small children it was wiser to be here. We spread out our blankets, the kids' things and the food, laid ourselves out to the sun. The cousins paddled and splashed in the water and climbed on a six-foot drainage pipe that opened onto the bay. Bridgit and I, like always, jabbered away at each other our news since we'd last met. I read my mail forwarded from LA by Max. There was my Molly Bloom paper. I was given a C- for it and a C for the entire course. In Days' note he informed me that I was too emotional for graduate school and although I may not realize it he was doing me a favor by making me ineligible. I guess he assumed I was at the beginning of the whole process and his C would prohibit me from going on. But I had a near-perfect grade point average and his C, being my last grade, hardly made a dent in my As. It was only there in the hot sand of Mission Bay that I realized the professor had all along had me on his own personal graduate school probation.

Darien, as I read his note, was saying to me, Mom, Shelley is acting funny. I looked to the water. My brother's four-year-old daughter was floating face up with her mouth open, just beneath the surface of the water. I ran through the deep sand, past people who stared at her, who stared at me. Bridgit was screaming, coming behind me. Shelley's arms were floating languidly out from her side. Her face was blue under the blue water. Her mouth was even bluer and open in a garish grin, her eyes staring wide. She was only about six feet from the shore but as I plunged the last step, reaching for her, suddenly I was going under myself. We were in a deep hole. I came up beside her, grabbed her, struggled back to the edge of the hole, then the shore. As I did, I was again aware of the blank faces of people who were gathering to watch, as if at a television screen. No one came forward to help. I was filled with an extraordinary rage. This is San Diego. You live your life on the beach. You know what to do for a drowning person. Someone help her, please. No one came forward; I could see that no one was going to come forward. I was still emerging from the water. This was all in my mind. There was not enough time to beg them. Bridgit was standing on the shore in that tall silent tube of stopped time. From what I could remember it seemed I should lay Shelley on her back and blow my breath down her mouth. But a strong feeling told me no, no, no. If you blow into her you'll blow the water further down her. I slung her upside down, held her by her fat ankles and with all my rage shook her. I kept thinking this is a waste of time, I must lay her on the sand, put my mouth over hers, give her breath. But something else told me, though she wasn't responding, to just keep shaking. I shook her and I shook her and then did not allow myself to think of anything but her coming breath. After a long minute or so, she coughed and a large gush of water flew from her. I held her blue cold body in my arms, sobbing as she sobbed and sobbed. All of us in a huddle, sobbing. My anger was as great as any I'd ever known. That the city could be so negligent and stupid as to put a large drainage pipe on a children's play beach, that these nice residents with their many children would allow such a hole to erode from rain and lawn water, a hole hardly significant when we arrived that morning at low tide. That there was no lifeguard—though several arrived within a few minutes, their sirens wailing—a few minutes too late if Darien hadn't come to me when she did. That the people were paralyzed, how I've seen through all these years a woman's leathery wrists attesting to the fact, just as she said, I've lived on this beach all my life and nothing like this has ever happened. But most of all I knew great anger at myself, for being ignorant of the bay's tidal changes, of artificial respiration, for taking my eyes off my children to read a fool's judgment that I was too emotional, without giving a single comment on the paper I had done. Not even a denial that Molly Bloom is structured.

II

YES BECAUSE HE NEVER DID A THING LIKE THAT BE-FORE AS ASK to sleep with me on the beach because its Bloomsday because its Bloomsummer a hundred years he begged forgive me and

sleep with me yes because now he sleeps like an egg in the night of the
sand the water only inches from us and the tide still coming in sleeping
like Sinbad the Sailor and Finbad the Failer and Albion Moonlight in
the bed of all the auks of the rocs of Darkinbad the Brightdayler where
the last question he asks after who and when because Molly Bloom is
materia the Earth slipping off the whome of your eternal geomater and
the eternal now of this bed ground zero I answered and that old faggot
Mrs. Riordan so symbolic with her methylated spirit like methyl-
aphenyl Ritalin but Molly with a New York accent with the soft lap of
the waves behind her and a gulls scream in the night these words from
so long ago that held me for so long amazing I can still feel the structure of her song do re mi fa so la ti do the song beneath the words of an
opera singer the run through the wheels of the old memory of her
structure the five years of daily work still inside my body though shes
reading the words wrong they must still be ignorant of the structure
and how sexual how obscene even it sounds now her creation out of
chaos Vico's Divine Age I was writing Beauty and The Beast on the
boat when he came running down do you know what day this is yes its
ten days since I left you its June 16th its Bloomsday 1982 the
hundredth Bloomsday since Joyces birth doesnt that excite you the
radio has two readings of Ulysses one from New York one from
Dublin Ive been listening all day oh sweetheart its fantastic Ive never
read Ulysses did I ever tell you that so I lay out on the deck all day and
just listened yes he came somewhere Im sure now thats 1 of 2 of 1 oh I
want to write like Joyce he ranted though shit how can anyone write
anything after reading Joyce well Im hardly the person to ask that because I quit writing entirely in the five years I wrote on Molly Bloom
the five years I kept my vow not to be a poet because someone said no
one need write another novel for a hundred years and I agreed though
now I know literature and art so differently more as energy than product they all said the epitome of female psychology and the creation of a
man but I was so starved for the female in myth and literature to work
inside words the critics wouldnt read what a real woman has to say
theyd treat her like Williams did that womans letter in Paterson or
HD a sort of embarrassing curiosity too close to what theyve heard all
their lives and have banned together to ignore their mothers and sisters

and lovers and daughters and wives yes because I loved it working on it everyday I knew early on that the whole structure could be done in a few days on a computer I could have gotten Sergei to do it at his work but I didnt want that I wasnt looking for an answer I wanted the process inside me I wanted to immerse myself into something fantastic I needed the education I needed to be inside a great writer though stream of consciousness it is not because if hed really believed the system he was proposing would be there naturally beneath her words how did I put it like a rivers meandering course that reveals the inexorable law of the universe it can go no other way and the ancient Chinese poem the deer that lives on the evergreen mountain where there are no autumn leaves can know the coming of autumn only by its own cry poor little pussy he teased walking me and Moonlight back tonight from the tavern down Water Street pulling me close when we got out on the highway please let me sleep with you on the beach please you must forgive me I didnt know it would hurt you so bad I love you Ive realized I really do love you yes and because searching for a smooth place high enough up from this afternoons high tide line finding our bed between these two huge logs I want to live on boats from now on I yelled pissing down the beach from him off the land that so pulls me down like a magnet you wouldn't believe the epidemic of masturbation thats got me since I left you I think its dry dock my broken heart in dry dock three four times a day its the only thing that makes life bearable do you know the Egyptian myth that has the demiurge creating the world by an act of masturbation but he only responded wake me if the tide comes up with Molly going on and on into Puget Sound eternity above the waters whoooooooosshh echo slap on the sand where it meets the waters of Juan de Fuca my favorite sound in all the world and the moan of the fog horn and gurgly squawk of some two am bird dozing off yes because Im a Joycean Molly Bloom floating in and out though I never did like his main motif yes because his four cardinal points the female breasts arse womb and cunt expressed by the words because bottom in all senses bottom button bottom of the class bottom of the sea bottom of his heart woman yes and Banana yes because is not the eternal present not Present Indicative yes because it sets it up too much too linear as if a rerun like last nights nightmare of the mass murderer Patrick caught and held in custody in the back of the church but then was so careless with almost intimate with putting away his gun and sitting very close to him he seemed drugged or hypnotized because he paid no attention to my concern so I went into the dark sanctuary of the Church not knowing where else to go reminding myself I cant think for him if he wants to live this way it is his choice I have to let go it has nothing to do with me but in a few minutes the murderer was there behind me very close clean shaven in a dark blue business suit oh Id recognize him anywhere what are you doing here I think I just bought my freedom he whispered very deliberately very coldly which filled me with great fear for Patrick and I saw that he was preparing to kill me I slipped through the cathedral doors but was caught in a wild beautiful wedding party rushing up the steps in the beautiful blue dawn with thick rushing snow blowing everywhere I managed to get out of the path of the brides gown and veil blowing like an iridescent white river behind her to be greeted by a priest coming out from the back of the church who announced to me very formally your husband is dead I was screaming and screaming no no no please no not him not him though for all my hysteria the wedding party kept charging fast and beautifully into the church unnoticing of me and the murderer coming through the cathedral doors making his way through the procession and I fled down the stairs to a getaway car with him right behind me planning to drive to Bolinas though it seemed I could never make it until I woke understanding I would make it but just not wanting to go through the ordeal again of escape the fear in my body was so great I woke soaking awesome in that it was only a dream at times I think I am dying how I was walking yesterday through Uptown and suddenly feared I was going to collapse from the pain of his betrayal and I was so far from my dark boat where no one can see me and who was the murderer so familiar Id recognize him on the streets how can the betrayal of love be so powerful it starts destroying the body the center gone the breath knocked out of you so that you cant breathe cant walk I keep trying to understand work it out to grow I cant bear not to I cant bear to keep making the same mistake I even listened to the tape of the psychic reader from five years ago in Mendocino after Max left how I scoffed then at her no-tions of past lives that I of all people dont have enough earth energy so I never listened to the tape but I had to do something now whether I believe in reincarnation and coming from another world or not Joyce called it metempsychosis and sandhi and ricorso and I accepted it in him yes because no one has enough earth energy we are all so afraid of Her and what she says of me is true like a metaphor or dream though hard to accept that I get my earth energy entirely from my men through their sexual emotional chakra their second chakra into mine like a penis a chord she said Ive been assassinated in every past life the first time in Atlantis as the political leader of the people in opposition to the dictator but when I gained power I sold the people out and it happened again in Egypt and in every subsequent life and this is why I am so afraid of my own power and why my dreams are so full of violence the last time I was a total recluse hiding far away in the woods of an East European village but the people knew I was a witch and came out and got me and burned me at the stake she said Ive been spiraling for centuries the body personalities Ive incarnated in the past two or three thousand years have been attempting to work out this spiraling which is so dizzying I ground myself through my lovers rather than grounding my own body directly into the earth my body she said is made stable through sex so that then I can bring cosmic energy down and through but when the connection is broken when Im suddenly without my grounding cord Im like a helium balloon theres no grounding no stability in my body my energies start fluctuation vibrating at a very high rate my body goes into survival that produces great emotional pain my body says Im going to die I have no earth energy my work in this lifetime she said is to learn to draw up the earths current through my own feet and legs to take responsibility for grounding my own body rather than being dependent on a lover yes because it is an accurate description of Max and me Maximilian my Boylan my giant boy of the land my rainbow my Leopold Bloom my Wandering Jew my Daedalus my artificer of labyrinths we were such great pals cosmic pals I always said he gave me the earth this world and nature those three incredible years on Topanga Beach in Malibu in our tiny little shack where I began Molly Bloom in the strong winter light my first coming to beauty where the kids became the real kids of them-

selves full of gritty sand enormous waves and teeming sealife like that
swordfish leaping out the first day we moved in just as in the Chumash
myths though we never saw a swordfish again she must have been the
last one greeting us and the wild wild mountains of the Santa Monicas
Los Angeles falling away the beginning of everything I can hardly remember myself before then the years as a student and before that with
Sergei in Ramona like another person the war raging on the city so evil
and corrupt with everyone mindlessly working at their immoral jobs
producing only waste and machines of war but the beach and the
mountains the vast sea and the sky and the light seemed infinitely mag-
nanimous full of destruction and death and yes terrible things but part
of some structure or scheme that portended life full of unexamined
knowledge we were trying to find another way of life from the programmed one so clearly bent on destruction we sat on that winter
shore looking back on Los Angeles looking deep into the glassgreen
breakers meditating on the movement into the land the waves great
folding over on themselves the violent and beautiful dissolution we sat
every night on the beach after the kids were asleep trying to find a way
into the world we had never known or been taught trying to know the
force of the seasons the moon and sun and planets the paths through
the stars and the lines connecting them to our place on earth we sat
seeking a new way to live a new way to eat a way without money a way
to raise children in witness of the earth so that they would not grow to
be soldiers but lovers capable of thinking and living as close to the inner self as possible to live their life as a story as a creation the most difficult of all I think trying to love ourselves to care for our own time the
only time of our lives to regard the time as sacred the only given to
open our bodies to earth and to each other to understand the drive and
force and ecstasy of sex and spirit in everyone we encountered yes because Darien started first grade the week we moved in Max said I
should try and write something maybe to sell everyone left and I was
alone for the first time in my life the beach deserted during the week
the rich neighbors working all the time to afford their luxurious beach
homes they never had time to stay in and voted Reagan as governor because he promised them he would save their private beach from becoming public while we lived in the condemned shack I was there

alone every day Max rode his bike seven miles the Pacific Coast Highway to Santa Monica to janitor those apartments across from the high
school coming home full of images of braless barefoot rebellious teenage golden hippy girls and fucked me pretending I was one of them
riding the bike to not use gasoline and because of the warrants out for
his arrest I dont think he wanted me to go to work he wanted me to
stay home where I was safe and his I realized this in the end when I
cocktailed at the Foghorn in Mendocino but all those years I felt guilty
not helping out with the money he worked so hard and hated it so I
thought I could write an article on the psychic trauma of abortion for
McCalls even though abortion was still illegal how absurd I was to
think I could sell them such a paper but I wanted to write it I needed
the excuse Ive never been able to write anything but what I want to and
Molly it had been fifteen months since old Days class I thought I
should inform the critics of the structure that it should be known I told
Max I could do it in a week or two just clean up my old paper find out
where to send it so I checked out all the books on Joyce at the Santa
Monica library I thought to write a critical paper I had to know something about the critics hitching with Max downtown to LA City Library his knowledge and love of the city so fascinating I wanted to
know it as he did a native of downtown a welfare street kid hitching
with him back to Cal State to UCLA where Darien was born that time
during the Kent State strike standing on the edge of the crowd as the
student leader like an arrogant Army Commander harangued us his
followers his pawns his army and I had to turn away for wanting to
vomit on his ego or start screaming his artificial male and campus
world go into the library and get my books on Joyce sick with the war
for so long and it was still going on nothing had changed for all the
protests how many had been killed since I quit counting the only solution seemed in building a new life that countered the murderous one
like that famous Hollywood writer I met that foggy morning on
Topanga Creek who had seen me writing in the window he said he
heard my typewriter across the beach and followed it he seemed sincere
so I told him about my Joyce paper and he said I should submit it to
Playboy or Esquire and he told me to use his name and he gave me the
name and address of the person to send it to and then he said I should

be sure to send my photograph along with my submission how sickened I was how deep in those days was my humiliation and paralysis for the crass exploitation and commercialization of everything why I could not enter the brothels of the world as Meridel says to make space an enemy deterrent and the body a surface commodity I was a pacifist I would not trespass on anothers psyche though his words like so many did violence to me for years I hardly understood but it was crucial not to do to him what he was doing to me how could the worlds imbalance ever be corrected I didn't say anything back to anyone in those days though that didnt mean I wasnt depressed by his ignorance of me or that I didnt say to him under my breath Ive always refused to pose for Playboy and for the same reason I will always refuse to write for Playboy and Patty says pity the ugly woman writer fuck hes so stupid sometimes like all men about sexism pity the woman writer I couldnt believe any man who told me I was good I wouldnt let them publish me because of the times Id been made a fool locked in the professors office lets talk about your work its good let me get inside your panties its good yes because I was falling deeper and deeper into Joyce and Irish history the three hundred years of colonization by the English and still they are not free Parnell and the 1916 Revolution Joyces first book written when he was nine a terrible beauty is born Yeats Easter Rising poem finally reading all of Ulysses both Joyces and Homers and then again with guides and the books Joyce was reading when he wrote Ulysses and here comes the history of Everybody and Everything Eastern and Western religions the great secret doctrines volumes of Helena Blavatsky the Caballa sometimes entirely absent of punctuation eleven volumes of The Golden Bough all the metaphysical renaissance writers of the Middle Ages Vico and Bruno and Yates and Yeats secret structures received through his wifes automatic writing the night they were married I think Greek and Roman and Irish and Catholic myth I knew nothing of being Southern Baptist Jesus born from the ear of Mary because she was made pregnant by the Word and Gurdjieff and Ouspensky and Collins and Suares and Wallace Berman painting Hebrew on the rocks at low tide the first person to take me seriously as an artist and Jack Hirschman and Jim Gill and the Cipher of Genesis The Hundred Years War the Rosicrucians the Hero With A Thousand

Faces The Theory of Celestial Influence In Search of the Miraculous
and Isis Unveiled and The Tales of Don Juan and the Dictionary of
Symbols and HD and Pound and Olson and Meetings With Remarkable Men The Linga Sharira November 22 when John Kennedy died
and Ramonas brother killed himself and Brunos Coincidence of Con-
traries Marxs dialectic and Davids dyslexia everything Joyce wrote and
everything written about Joyce and everything verifying the structure
of Molly Bloom which is not my theory but a fact I found when Robert
Kennedy was assassinated like the poet who said the death of even one
rabbit releases enough energy to write a thousand poems and Patrick
said today make the connection between Joyce and the Kennedys yes
because Joyce knew Joe Kennedy when he was Ambassador to England and he was writing Finnegans Wake Id return the books to the li-
braries to find that in the two weeks new books on Joyce had come out
the Joycean Industry to keep the critics busy he said for three hundred
years and to insure my immortality one source said except for the Bible
there are more books published on Joyce than any other subject yes
and starting again with Sentence 1 falling into Gaea out of the small
god of gas Chaos and the sky Uranus the third god laying over her oh
Sweetheart May Id rather die 20 times over than marry another of their
sex thats 5 of 8 of 1 until she and Chronus her son castrate him for his
oppression of creation and from the genitals thrown into the sea arose
Love and the profundity of the structure its movement into my life my
consciousness my children and Maximilian into my body Maximilian
and marijuana Maximilian and acid and peyote and MDA and mes-
caline Moly the earth root to save us yes because Maximilian said you
never get over the first person you take acid with the same Topanga
day he found the name Maximilian Rainbow and his epitaph He Was
In It For The Colors and I discovered that my thumbs bear the perfect
prints of the yin yang symbol the Tao the Seal of Solomon the Star of
David the very structure of Molly Bloom and my index finger a perfect
spiraling circle Blavatskys circles within circles Blooms wheels within
wheels my spirit spiraling for centuries and the earth breathing in and
out in an 8 minute rhythm as the ancient Hindu astrologers knew as
the pelvic platform pulses eight tenths of a second in orgasm

such a long one I did her bowel movement the birth of Earth and the

heroes the long evolutionary time before civilization Sentence 2 is
echo and shadow and time the bisexuality of all things the body as the
vessel the Hebrew letter Boyt the spirits transubstantiation into flesh
the transmigration of souls through the bodies of time voyeurs and
duality the longest sentence before the disassociation of sensibility
when mind and body are one and you can feel your mind and Jack the
second time I saw him though I had known his name around LA for
years posters in Topanga Canyon whats a poetry reading I wondered
and drove all the way into Hollywood with that private detective
whose name was Jack too who lived above us to the Bodhi Bookstore
in his black cape and his wife who looked like me who was the program
director for KPFK that Max said radicalized him made him a conscientious objector and his son David who could know then he would
die and his daughter Celia named for his grandmother who went to
Mexico turn of the century to have an abortion and died reading Black
Alephs and Aur Sur that afternoon lying on the mouth of Topanga
Creek he had just returned from Europe where he slept on Joyces grave
and now his words were really Joyces he said and that is why his lines
are spaced as they are they are breath spurts Joyce on the vehicle of his
breath Jack always wonders how it was we knew each other those LA
years he cant quite remember me but in those years I stayed in the back
of the crowd I never introduced myself I couldnt have matched his social or literary power and a UCLA professor where Darien was born 8
days before Kennedy was killed I had wondered all that week why I
had named her the Irish name for John and Darcy was in his lit class
when he announced to them the President has been shot and then she
said he laughed the strangest sort of laugh she will wonder for the rest
of her life what that laugh meant yes because UCLA was going to in-
stitutionalize him the ambulance was on its way when his students kidnapped him to save him some very blessed students for a blessed
teacher only finally introducing myself so many years later in
Mendocino and he told me Wallace Berman had been killed in a car
wreck in Topanga Canyon on his 50th birthday the very weekend Max
and I ended and I started my epic poem because I kept seeing across
everything that was happening a car accident at first I was so afraid it
was my children who were in Paradise that weekend and then when

they were safe waiting 3 weeks for the news of who it was who had
died and sometimes then I thought if I am from a past life as the
psychic says it must be Joyce who died 3 months before I was born yes
because then I was trying not to see the Manson Family trying not to
read of the trial all that winter though an Olson poet was reporting it
how they swam on our beach that Friday night after killing the
LaBiancas before the next nights killings at the Sharon Tate home
hitching back there coming down our steps three weeks before we
moved in running naked into the moonlit sea what was the moon in
that night washing the blood from their acid high bodies and Sharon
Tate pregnant and high too on MDA as were all of them everyone in
those days victims and killers alike protesters and soldiers the hairdres-
ser whose name Jay Sebring was on that beautiful sign hanging outside
our door painted by that San Quentin checkforger friend of Maxs who
had been a psychedelic sign painter at the Whiskey A-Go-Go how I
wrote in my library book Tales of Beelzebub GURDJIEFF
IS CHARLEY MANSON never to this day being able to
forget the man who was crying in the philosophy section of the
downtown library crying and crying of a grief too terrible to overhear
though Ive heard it ever since yes because the waves that first October
as we walked my first acid rushing in across my feet obliterating the
footprints of my children who ran ahead the waves bringing in unaccountable sealife but crushing them in the force of waves hitting the
beach seeing begrudgingly the impersonal beauty of death and rebirth
in nature as I was studying it in my Molly Bloom books Persephones
principle like language the perpetual de-creation and re-creation like
dyslexia the tongue slips no one knows why words break up combine
with words mysteriously coming from other languages and play tricks
upon themselves in accordance with the laws of phonetics following a
crab scooting along with his right claw torn off by the wave and seeing
suddenly Max is a crab a cancer the one who at summer solstice suddenly stops the 3 months spring into the future stops turns and sees
from the greatest light the coming of the dark and knows then more
than anyone the greatest fear and so in the slow fall back to winter
builds walls to protect the self because the soul of cancer is in the skin
Rudhyar said and that is why the crab builds its shell and the cancer is

domestic learning astronomy and astrology with Ramona in our letters the full moon always opposite the sun the new moon setting with
the sun Venus and Mercury so close to the sun and earth they are always in the morning or evening such simple facts imagine growing up
without them having a Masters degree without them and Dane Rudhyar Henry Millers astrologer who lived on the palisade above us I had
that picture of Henry riding his bike on Palisades Road past Will
Rogers ranch I always hoped to see him Max urging me to write him
and say Ill fuck you just let me get to know you everything beginning
to connect the correspondences the J Paul Getty Mansion perched
high above our beach once the home of Rita Hayworth lovely Rita
Meter Maid and that starlets body found there when it was a Jesuit
Retreat I was so haunted by her murdered blond nude body I could
never get over it and we would go to his archaeology museum of ancient Greek and Roman statues of Venus rising from the thrown genitals and someone told us that Getty who bought the place in 1949 had
never been there but still demanded that the sheets on his bed be
changed daily in case he arrived from Paris unexpectedly where he had
a payphone for guests and we thought we should bomb the place in
protest of the war it seemed the only moral thing to do until we were
picked up hitching once by a gentle little man who was the caretaker
and we realized he would be there Gettys unlived in mansion wasn't
just of expensive bricks and stone and ancient statues bought with
blood money so instead we made runs in the middle of the nights
spraypainting the outer walls with N I X O N spelled with swas-
tikas nightruns painting all the lifeguard stands S T O P T H E
W A R from Venice to Malibu Colony 30 miles of stone walls of the rich
the white mansion of Peter Lawford where Marilyn Monroe and
Robert Kennedy fucked I painted W H O K I L L E D M A R I L Y N
M O N R O E ? and answered down the wall T H E C I A and we fucked
too right in their archway and again under their windows they never
dreamed we were coming right there and laughing and running on to
the next very famous and very rich and Daniel Ellsberg looking out the
window at us that demonstration we circled the Rand Corporation
those FBI guys taking so many pictures of me we waved and he walked
out with the secrets and finally during one national antiwar effort bar-

ricading the coast highway and spending the night in the Santa
Monica jail until Walters got us out Maxs lawyer in Arizona when he
was busted on his bike for not coming to a complete stop when he
turned right from a residential street onto a residential street of course
really because of his long beautiful hair but then giving a false name
and then arrested again in court for refusing to salute the flag yes because the first time he was in jail for refusing to go to Cuba he was so
young the summer Marilyn died and how even then they all said cops
and prisoners alike she was murdered they claimed a special closeness
with her Max always said because her first husband was an LA cop and
the Chief of Police thought he was going to be the head of the FBI and
one cop bragged to Max hed seen her naked body in the morgue and
put carrots up her that was the first time I ever heard of Noguchi and
his autopsy report how she was born in my old hospital LA County
General where my grandpa died and baptized in Aimee McPhersons
church and Bridgit in Italy that August the Italians thought she was
Marilyns ghost they would run up to her on the streets and collapse at
her feet praying did Robert Kennedy kill her the Mafia they always described him as ruthless was he killed because he knew who killed his
brother and Mary Jo Kopechne was Teddy's Marilyn Monroe and
Marilyn Bobbie's Chappaquiddick and thats why I knew she was
drowning because Marilyn is my Muse she always comes to me out of
the walls of the universe comes exploding like orgasm through her face
large and incredible in the world pulsating wildly around me yes yes
yes she is chanting write it write it you must write it I was murdered I
was murdered it wasn't psychic that night on the beach near Chappaquiddick so terrifying even now when I remember not like you
normally think the mind the spirit in the air yes because I was on the
sand like now near the water and I felt her calling through it it was
kinesthetic yes and why doesn't Arthur Miller say something probably
after hes dead some great work or Joe DiMaggio who just this birthday
quit sending her roses he said hed send for his lifetime O all our heroes
murdered Janis and Morrison and Hendrix and Lennon and King and
Malcolm X and Hemingway and Richard Wright and Che and Francis
Farmer and Jean Seberg a real Joan of Arc and all those Mendocino
people they say poisoned by the CIA in Jonestown though it was the

kids and ourselves and the mountains and the beach and Molly Ive
never been so happy as then I thought I could never write anything so
beautiful as the sound of that roaring ocean all day the noise of water
making moan sad as a seabird going forth alone he hears the winds cry
to the waters monotone Ellman said Ulysses is an epithalamium love is
its cause of motion yes because its one thing to seek but another to find
because you search within the boundaries of your ego but when you
find the ego boundaries give away like dams in a flood and you pass
from your own life into the other lives and world and someone else
said the soul is called a circle because it seeks itself and is itself sought
finds itself and is itself found but the irrational soul imitates a straight
line since it does not revert to itself like a circle my children growing so
strong around and into themselves with that place of great energy and
beauty though the eggs of the Brown Pelican didnt hatch that year on
Cabrillo Island because of DDT pollution in the fish chain the pelican
in her piety I read in one of my books is a symbol of Jesus because it was
thought pelicans fed their young with their own blood and David on
the beach fishing every day and Darien playing house on the beached
catamarans hiking in the Santa Monicas fucking high on the palisades
above the coast highway watching the cars like ants inch toward the
city fucking in Lee Marvins Moonfire Temple with peacocks screaming for guards watching all of the LA Basin the desert the mountains
the sea fucking out on the Malibu dock in the mist and fog and crashing tide in the mud slides and hot Santa Ana Winds like Mollys
levanter on The Straits of Gibraltar that would nullify the waves till we
went into the sea and fucked to see the hills ignited with fire and the
house shake from earthquake fucking in Castanedas holy spot fucking
standing up in our little shack watching the light change across the
water how Molly thought she lost her son she was carrying when
Poldy fucked her from behind like the dogs in the street they were
watching but that time when Max was fucking me from behind standing up I saw a Chumash for the first time he was coming down the
beach he was pissed as hell at something he was 1200 years old he was
so real I can still see him we were fucking in the very place his child was
drowning which crazed his heart enough to leap from time like Vico
said all history is to be deduced from any part of the created universe

but it is found most completely in the mind of any human being finding then Kroeber on the Chumash and the Zuma but there were so few
books on LA history because I realized it is still such a new place
Bridgit gave me Whos Who In Los Angeles in 1929 I found Gettys
picture as a young man and Cabrillo landing at Maliwu in 1542 the
most advanced coastal people with their red boats they rowed all the
way to Santa Catalina and the myths of the swordfish the waves taking
everything back the crippled crab the grunion runs at spring full moon
the waves so fundamental to their fucking to the source everything the
language and the imagery and themes of Molly Bloom death and
rebirth 8s within 8s the ideogram of the Seal of Solomon the sign of
the Virgin the Star of David yin and yang the lingam and the yoni as
above so below the union of opposites the male and the female Molly
and Mother Dana weave and unweave our bodies because you never
know whose thoughts youre chewing so that I finally saw that each of
the 8 sentences is constructed in 8 parts and that each of those 8 parts is
constructed again in 8 parts so that in the longest sentence Sentence 2
each phrase is a count off of the 8 parts and in the shortest sentence
Sentence 3 each word is a count of the 8 part score again because all
that exists from the smallest imaginable atom contains within itself all
the elements of the entire process of the whole universe and thats why
its been so difficult to crack Joyces code because a 2 motif will appear in
2 of 4 of 7 why the pattern is apparent in some places but doesnt hold
in others and then in the third winter of Topanga I finally read Finnegans Wake and all the books on it and discovered it has the identical
structure as Molly Bloom a 3 part circular progression of humanity
and society combined with Blavatskys 4th part from Eastern religions
making it even more perplexing that the scholars have not discovered
Mollys structure especially since they debate about when Joyce became
involved with Vico and give much critical attention to the endings of
his books how they lead into the next book but of course the reason is
sexism and elitism because even though Molly Bloom is the creation of
a man she is to them what they want a female to be and so just like a
woman they dismiss her they said a long time ago with relief she has no
depth no underlying meaning and staked their careers on her being
stream of consciousness free association and therefore uneducated and

ignorant and unimportant not to mention their great fear of her
femaleness her copulation and masturbation her menstruation and
pregnancies and defecations on which the structure turns though they
delight in Leopolds fantasy of being pregnant yes because Virginia
Woolf said Joyce was not welcome in her home because he had married
a peasant Nora Barnacle and so Ive never never read Virginia Woolf
because I cant forgive her for being so stupid about something so fundamental though Joyce said worse things about women and Im programmed to forgive him programmed to spend my life with him oh
shit Jamsie let me up out of this sweet pooh of sin this sand pit between
2 drowned trees we lie in the water even closer now its going to drown
us oh sweetheart how can you sleep how can anyone sleep trying to get
comfortable again shape the sand around me if I fall asleep well probably be so soaked firecrackers popping somewhere on Water Street 4th
of July coming still he is so beautiful so asleep oh so much I love him I
could love him if hed let me with his mouth slightly open 2s always
have lots of mouths in them mouth almighty and his boiled eyes he
came to town so excited I was writing Beauty and the Beast and listening to the tape lets get a 6 pack and find the highest hill so itll come in
good arent you excited its fantastic yes but the pain of his taking that
girl into my bed in our beautiful cabin if only it had been somewhere
else and he hadnt lied to me for months and all our friends knew but me
only a couple of weeks after I wrote my love poem to him about the
cabin I cant do anything for seeing him driving her down the long path
through the woods just as he drove me 2 years ago pulling her up the
stairs taking her clothes off oh each piece blouse skirt bra and panties
and laying her down where I sleep and putting his mouth on her
breasts his finger inside her the way he does to me so that Ive lost my
home again cry and die again my love again the hurt and Monica said I
could stay on her boat in dry dock listening all these days to the psychic
on Albion Ridge say Ive been assassinated murdered or burned in
every past life my body still being fed from the astral level the pictures
of earlier incarnations and this is why I am so afraid of my own power
afraid to speak write publish I see two spirits at your throat she says one
is green and good the other is evil is he named dyslexia I joked on the
tape in one life she saw violent trancing a foaming at the mouth from

spiritual grief the image of a person I can relate to easily a person who is
an oracle at the post office letters from April of dreams of the beast that
is the refinery her father built when she was little and from Mama and
Meridel and Carolyn and Maureen and Alma and a bill for $3423.39
from my 1968 National Defense Student Loan that I vowed Id never
pay because it would be supporting the Viet Nam War that moment I
finally understood about honesty and responsibility the epiphanal moment I was totally radicalized driving around Peoples Park and that
time in Mendocino James Joyce from Payco in Oakland called me is
your name really James Joyce yes it really is and you owe us $2749.27 I
laughed and said this is wonderful but you must understand I took a
vow and if I have to fight you all the rest of my life you will never get
that money though it means of course that I can never own anything or
have a serious job or have a bank account though Ive learned from all
my moving around it takes about a year for them to catch me a moving
target is hard to hit Lew Welch said that loan had nothing to do with
the Vietnam War and I laughed well I can see you are not really James
Joyce or youd understand how connected everything is but still Ill
compromise if my book on James Joyce is ever printed and you James
Joyce not Payco still want the money what ever it is by that time the interest $32 a month Pounds usury about that he was right you can
have it that is if it sells and that other time Robin and I were making
love in the G Road cabin on Albion Ridge he was looking in the
window I knew it was James Joyce he seemed so sinister a bill collector
yes because when we got to the market I couldnt get out you get the
beer Patty Ill get the station clearer remembering then the plans Id seen
somewhere for all the Joycean scholars to meet today in Dublin the
whole industry flying in to celebrate the 100th Bloomsday since his
birth and for a moment I felt left out I can just see them in the pubs following Leopolds trail the digital professors with their irrational souls
imitating a straight line Stephen and Bloom are somewhere in Nighttown but I cant tune it in well just screechy static and Im too depressed
to keep trying rock and roll is so much easier and soothing couldnt you
get it he asks when he comes back here have a beer so now we wander
this northwestern town trying to find a high place we can receive
Ulysses up the hill to the highschool where she lives somewhere the

night he went there after I left the cabin so crazed so out of my mind when I found out trying just to keep my heart beating all the rest of the long terrible night on Cape George beach until the light finally came that he would go to her when I was so shattered and across from the Catholic Church that always makes him shiver because he is still fleeing the priesthood why did you leave the priesthood my mother asked him for women he answered I wanted to get laid he told me he went to her house they went to the Uptown Tavern he said he even hoped Id walk in what was he thinking how unreal he is then he went home with her fucked her slept with her and in the morning fucked her again when you left he said so crazed your screaming forever piercing my soul I could only think of myself what am I going to do now I see everything through myself in the streets I see people looking at me wanting something I even used to see the whole world as just an extension of myself its terrible to be a narcissist because youre never in the world it wasnt until the third day I went out in a boat with Joe and I was looking back on Port Townsend that I thought of you I realized what it meant that you were gone and I almost cried right in front of Joe I crawled into the back bed of Psyche then following Stephen and Leopold through Nighttown from a corner the morning hours run out golden haired slim in girlish blue you may touch my May I touch your O but lightly Oh so lightly he is so beautiful the back of his neck his boyish head in the window driving this town he has such an affair with his little boy quality Christina called it accusing me of mothering him what does she think that its mature to love old men like a father the authoritarian father I do love boys the male before he gets fucked up the boy is my muse my brother my equal imagine having been in one of my towns for 10 years well Mendocino for six his love of all the little houses his Irish Boston love I think and yes all the queer little streets and pink and blue and yellow houses and rose gardens Port Townsend even looks Mediterranean from the ferry I wonder if he knows Joyce at one point changed Daedalus to his name from the Greek to the Irish to be more authentic moving back to the front seat do you remember what my novel is about he says its about betrayal I wanted to kill my girlfriend that night I took acid theres the path I was running up when the cops stopped me and now we drive down a very narrow street up the next

hill around the cedar and fir woods of Morgan Hill the Vico road goes
round and round to meet where terms begin over the Straits and the
Sound where they come together at Wilson Point the ferry coming in
from Whitbey the tugs going out this tight narrow convoluted peninsula Quimper even its name is like the clitoris as George wrote me
when I moved here I looked Port Townsend up on the map he said and
it looks like the clitoris of the Olympic Peninsula because he is saying
the problem is how to write well and clearly and seriously about acid
about what happened to us I want somehow to suggest that we really
have started another species our cells are different now so I tell him of
Barbaras dream that all of us from the 40s and 50s are aliens from another world we have a high pain tolerance which is why weve gone
through so much and why well be the only ones to survive nuclear war
and I try then to tell him about Joyce and me because he has always
thought me crazy youre too crazy for me he said when we met me and
my rock n roll dancing me and my love of sex me and my astrology me
and my lipstick me and my LA but its been 10 years since I left yes he
sang the song you can check out any time but you can never leave like
that first Halloween you were here I was so free and freaked I lied my
way into the Sea Galley as a bartender I didnt know bourbon from beer
but the sexism really began to get to me those short miniskirts so for
Halloween I shaved my pubic hair and glued it to my face a perfect
blond goatee my merkin and dressed as the male bartender and all
night after work I went into the mens bathrooms in every bar in town
how wonderful it was though I could never do that now Ive become so
tight here like everyone else and yes I said youre a product of the cynical northeast where everyone makes themself feel important by doubt-
ing and now you are of this place 10 years which is so conservative
stingy of its heart though it thinks itself so hip so convoluted and
whimpering tight and dark and wet and hidden like the clitoris the
screams pitched too high to hear of the land being cut by the melted
glaciers what resists what gives away to the sea so full of lost ship-
wrecks a puritan ethic that denies it has a clitoris an aesthetic so to
blending in to acceptance never a loud blooming bursting protesting
or beautiful orgasm but tasteful passive washes of fineline perfection
the rigid rectangles of the poems that only whimper little paragraphs

soaking in the vision of calm domesticity in Curtises still blue Indian shadows of film

   yes I said and then I sang to him the ballad of Finnegans Wake did you know Vico fell off a roof too when he was 16 and woke up like Finnegan at his own wake and out of that rising from the dead came his circles and cycles of history his death and rebirths of civilizations his theories of the origin of language and poetry and myth he said imagination and art is always memory there is nothing new under the sun all history begins in the transformations of the human mind and the structure of language is the history of the race he said what is not yet in the mind is in the body words are carried over from bodies and from the properties of bodies to express the things of the mind and spirit he said a human is only mind and body and speech and speech stands midway between the two and Molly is a Virgo I told him Sept 8 1888 the Seal of Solomon is the symbol of Virgo the earth sign ruled by the mental planet of speech Hermes who protected Ulysses from Circes spell that turned his men into pigs with an herb named Moly the gift of meaning she is the perfect resolution of Body and Mind because you enter her body and experience her mind its processes within the body rather than her mind as a result of process the third human stage Vico called the degenerated intellectual mind that is no longer in touch with the body trying to tell him of those years sitting on the beach like Molly sitting on the chamber pot looking back on LA in exile with so little recorded history as Joyce looked back from Europe on Dublin with so much too much history the cities as a symbol of the third stage blood and urine pouring from her at the same time you are running the streets of Port Townsend afraid youll kill your girlfriend because youve taken acid we were all crazy because we needed to be it was healthy in a terrible time with Viet Nam even in Vicos time the 17th Century we were well into this short third human stage weve been spiraling for centuries yes because I told him of Shelley almost drowning when she was 4 of pulling her unconscious from the sea and imagine he said shes 18 now and Darien how he met them both this spring when I took them to San Francisco because they wanted to live in the city and it was when I was first gone that he met her and first fucked her he said maybe we should go to Sean and Kates they would love to hear Ulysses yes al-

right but please not if your girlfriend is there shes not my girlfriend Im
sorry you had to lose her Im sorry you had to make a choice though
you really didn't have to thats why I moved out immediately though its
true you would have lost me Im sorry Patrick that Joe is with her now
that must hurt you now hes looking at me watch the road Patrick I love
you I was lonely fucked up you were gone Im sorry that I hurt you

frseeeeeeeennnng a train somewhere whistling the trains coming
into the Boat Haven at high tide to be loaded on the barges for Seattle
how funny to see a train floating across the water how nice for those
guys to go to work by the time of the tides it must be close to 3 now
every morning the Seattle North and Gold Coast right there ten feet
from my boat where Im trying to sleep like Joyce I think Im afraid of
losing consciousness of waking up in the grave though in his 18
episodes from the 18 letters of the Irish alphabet all named for trees
Mollys 18th IDHO is the yew that grows around the cabin protector
of sleep and graves and also the wood from which bows are made oh
but oh shit Guy Davenport and his deep Southern elitist sexist analysis
of Molly his prejudices getting in his way of objective criticism typical
and as soon as I do fall asleep screeching and screaming and jarring the
boat till I think its another earthquake and I wake thinking how funny
to drown in dry dock and turn over and sleep some more remembering
the phallic train of Molly the vehicle on the path of pralala the return
even so waking over and over to the bodies of males over me under me
boys and men even old men and baby boys and Sean telling me tonight
he plans to hop the train to Port Angeles with Erinn and Jody so young
the water doesnt seem to be getting closer only inches from him so
beautiful the stars in it the boat I saw today Marry Me and the drone of
her voice on and on for two more years in Vermont with its four seasons David becoming a star athlete highest scoring jr high free thrower
in Vermont though he still couldnt read and beautiful Darien 9 skip-
ping down that stone wall through the red and yellow falling maple
leaves and homesick dreams of the crashing Pacific across the deep
fields of falling snow that guy I met in the snow who said so seriously
Plainfield Vermont is the center of the universe walking every day the
two miles to Goddard through the 30 below woods through deep tun-
nels of snow piled on both sides of the highway the faces coming at you

masked so you cant tell who anyone is so you hardly know even yourself its so cold yes and a VW slowing behind me do I want a ride God-
dards Joyce scholar his specialty Finnegans Wake syllable by syllable
the class catalogue said and so yes hurtling down the snow road in his
little car so removed behind the wool scarf across my mouth I cannot
share with him my own Joycean self the deep secret work I cannot
share that I too am spending my life within this man and re-creation of
the world for despite the absurdities and contradictions there is something important here against the terrible enemy the biggest lie Meridel
says the linear the oppressor of space and time it was in Vermont when
I understood Davids dyslexia as being joyfully correctly and truthfully
nonlinear all the ancient natural languages written from right to left
Hebrew Arabic Chinese when Mao came to power in 1948 he said we
must enter the Western mind we must become straight from now on
we will write from left to right as every child learning to write must
learn to go against his nature and I know too what men such as the professors think of women like me because he never dreams the source of
my question I ask to get him started its a book of prophecy he answers
everything is there that will happen in the 20th Century after Joyces
death Hitlers suicide after killing his favorite Alsatian Blondie
Hiroshima and Nagasaki the founding of Israel and the United Nations Korea the Kennedys in America Russias domination of Eastern
Europe the Common Market the present IRA Viet Nam and Ireland
names of current leaders all over the world and movie stars the Beatles
Marilyn Monroe and Jack Kerouac are named and so is Chappaquiddick and Woodstock and the date of the first moonlanding the age of
psychedelics and hippies and acid peyote marijuana yes I know but he
ignores me and tells me my favorite story of Lucia Lucy In The Sky
With Diamonds who when informed of her fathers death screamed
whats he doing under the ground that idiot when will he decide to
come out hes watching us all the time yes because beautiful crazy Lucia
though wild horses couldnt pull the truth from me to embarrass the
professor now that hes gone on and on that I know Joyce named his
daughter for his eyes the girl with kaleidoscope eyes though she was
born before his eyes went bad yes a prophet and that is why he hired
Samuel Beckett to be his secretary after one of his operations yes be-

cause Thomas à Becket is saint of the blind though Patrick said tonight
that Becket was denied sainthood because when they dug him up when
he was nominated to sainthood they discovered his hands sunk into
the eyesockets of his skull which means he had that disease where you
appear to be dead just like Finnegan and Vico but Becket woke up too
late in the grave and so was denied sainthood because clearly from the
position of his hands he despaired something a saint would never do
and Lucia Our Queen of Lights with burning candles for a crown lost
her mind when she fell in love with Beckett present everyday in the
Paris apartment crazy crosseyed daughter Lucia patron saint of the
blind and Blind Poet Homer who wrote the first Ulysses and now
Howard like Oedipus pulling his eyes out I keep wondering where
they are his eyes in the Pygmy Ive got his eye Ive got his eye the Jefferson Airplanes song about Joyce Rejoyce but the professor is uncomfortable and lets me off at the snow path snow being general all
over Vermont I sigh walking away from him to the library to look up
faggot in the OED seeing the footlong penis of the man on the
Highland Park moonlit corner twirling at the 16 year old Maximilian
Rainbow the very corner above which I found the structure of Molly
Bloom 12 years later and Carmen Lee died on the back of her brothers
new motorcycle but the OED example sentence is Molly Blooms the
very one Im trying to find the etymology of I never have found much
worth in the OED that old faggot Mrs Riordan because shes the beginning of creation because in the beginning men and women are one
Riordan like Dante at the beginning of The Portrait like Stephens
milkwoman symbol of Ireland the Cosmic Hag at all Joyces begin-
nings the androgynous angel though in the 3rd stage they are called
faggots and Ophelia in Vermont did my horoscope on a computer and
found it is a perfect Seal of Solomon the Star of David and all your
planets in the 6th House of Virgo right as the sun set youll be known
after you are dead the yin yang structure I told him tonight and he said
Jung called that synchronicity yes going east to Provincetown because
all four of us natives of LA we wanted to know a different part of the
country but the same country I won that 9 months residency at the
Writers Workshop but the kids hated the town an eastcoast version of
Malibu and we had promised them snow and my vow never to be a

poet and I wanted to finish Molly which they said was not creative work though I was looking forward to working with Louise Gluck whose First Born along with Galways Book of Nightmares I had just found in the basement of the downtown library on a special shelf entitled Small Press Poetry poems like I had always heard inside and the beginning I guess of my slow journey back to poetry and yes he says synchronicity because Louise was living in the apartment beneath us when we got to Plainfield after the kids in the backseat took the map and found the place with the most ski symbols we want to live here and so we drove off Cape Cod to Vermont and Rita Mae Brown was there too and so many I went to a poetry reading every night and discovered Olson poets I could hardly believe it a community of Olson poets the first modern poet I ever understood the poet who first awakened the poet in me but the same old problem even maybe more severe there at least it hurt more coming from people so much closer to what I was seeking Tyrone once actually introduced me as an LA Blonde that time standing with him so close in the apartment over the Winooski River with the broom in my hand trying to protest his categorization of me but in his streaming monologue that keeps sucking me in he is saying but where does the image come from as if I project it and he is a complete innocent and the book he wrote while I was so drawn to him he confesses and celebrates his male superiority his Jewish disgust of women and that night after his reading we were all at the party in East Calais and I couldnt tell him how fine his reading was because of his stupid arrogance sitting on the couch with John who is telling me of his uncle in Ojai where Maxs mother now lives because just before we left I found the house for her from Krishnamurti near Blavatskys Krotona and that fabulous old woman walking against the great horizon of Meditation Mount its Annie Besant someone whispered to me on the silent path or was it Alice Bailey who was born on Bloomsday 1880 and he told me of his cabin without electricity on the Canadian border and next to us Barry was describing Iowa as a school of the very brightest from all over the country and I asked him about the local kids wondering what if there had been a college in Ramona and he said you get occasionally a local bankers son enrolled the first hed ever known there are redneck intellectuals I remember my ears

ringing my throat catching looking away for horror and embarrassment for him and then someone asked from across the room how I can
work on something like Joyce without the structured discipline of a
university program I didnt know anyone knew of me and Joyce I
blurted what does the university have to do with it what does the university have to do with anything though in the window the moon was
on an old Maple with buckets hanging off her and I was filled with a
strange grief the lecherous sucking off of someones vital juices and I
wondered if it was me sucking off of Joyce Stephen said hed always be
a student and I will too but of the universe not the university and Molly
for sure is my phd yes because that Bloomsday that June 16 was
wonderful it was that scholars theory that Finnegan can be read in 24
hours that Joyce wrote it with this intention so each of the 24 hours
was assigned to a reader and the reading took place in the old town Inn
across from Lona Beans where we lived the second year from quiqui
quinet to michemiche chelet and a mambebatiste to a brulo-brulo how
I was falling in and waking back to the river words the great amazing
Amazon river flow of Here Comes Everybody and his wife Anna Livia
Plurabelle and Shem and Shaun all Livias daughtersons a little un-
nerved at the intimacy of the student bodies around me and the fire behind the reader who changed at the end of the hour quickly so as not to
waste a minute so as not to interrupt the river flow the echoing voices
down and down and back up into ones dreams and HCE the sound of
the water beginning to recede Molly from Dublin and New York and
Paris and Trieste and a palisade over the Pacific from which I am
watching Max fuck another woman waking to the church bell chiming
3 am walking across to my bed up the stairs to the maple bed where
Lona Bean has slept all her 82 years setting the alarm and Max waking
oh thanks be to the great god I got somebody to give me what I badly
wanted to put some heart up in me youve no chance at all in this place
like you used to long ago and out of the bed at 5:30 the silent cock shall
crow at last the west shall shake the east awake walk while ye have the
night for morn lightbreakfastbringer back across the misty Vermont
road through the blooming foliage about to burst into the cozy lobby
where Norma is reading enunciating precisely with great dignity syllable by syllable to no one but the walls my beautiful crazy blind Norma

who danced her thesis for the Finnegans Wake class oh what has ever happened to my beautiful Norma though the reading took 30 hours

Mulveys was the first under the Moorish wall Rubio like Riordan like Dante attending her in bed ah horquilla disobliging old hag shes half way now shell finish at 4 the new beginning 5s always the exact center puberty the number that occurs in animate nature yes triumphant growth yes he was the first man kissed me my sweetheart when a boy it never entered my head what kissing meant till he put his tongue in my mouth O the mouths of 2s this is 2 of 2 of 5 how well I remember I hope I sleep because in another hour itll be light because we are so far north because my life I told him in the tavern is moving around trying to find the geography trying to find the real stories and languages of the land that Communist who wrote me this week protesting my writing saying geography has nothing to do with it fuck you wonder where on Earth he lives he said we need a proletarian international criticism god how I hate the way they fall under the language like that embarrassing like falling in step like following the leader why cant they think inside the language so that its new and genuine Patrick said thats the mistake the Communists always make they deny the reality of geography yes and the reality of the peoples language and Marx rid Hegels dialectic of its mysticism the other thing thats wrong with Communism Mendocino was at first a compromise between Vermont and Los Angeles how little did I understand what it really is protruding so far west into the Pacific washed in air cleansed of all humanity by its long sea passage association with the sea Steinbeck said does not breed contempt in Mendocino I became the real woman of myself what I had always avoided in order to keep Max and sure enough as soon as I became myself he split O the very very worst pain of all that he didnt love me after 9 years God how I loved him and believed that in time he would trust me he would know me and then not be afraid for me to be myself what else is love but he said he only loved his control of me oh fuck to learn he was conscious of this how crazed it made me I just let go of Joyce I fled Molly became the real poet of myself in Mendocino where I finally understood the mistaken foundation of my vow I am a poet what I had learned in school was not poetry yes Mendocino and the courage of the heart the courage of innocence in

this terrible everyone is guilty and coopted world I found my true
voice of innocence I sent off my 500 pages my 5 years work to the
James Joyce Quarterly and to Ferlinghetti who loves Joyce the way I
do I think the quarterly sent back a standard rejection slip with a note
added by a student reader but this is fantastic this is important Ive tried
to no avail to make them see and Ferlinghetti was interested but he
wanted me to cut it to 60 pages which really was not unreasonable but
it would have been cutting myself back to 1968 and I didnt want to be
seduced again it would take me a year to write a whole new book of 60
pages I wanted my own writing I knew better than to toy casually with
James Joyce fucking Aquarius just like my father and grandfather ruler
of the 20th century and my own crazed Mars right there in 18 deadly
degrees Aquarius in my 3rd house of words and siblings Ferlinghetti
sent me all the books City Lights has published on Joyce one I loved especially the Key to Ulysses a map of Dublin yes because Jack gave him
my epic poem to read 5 years later he said I was expecting Finnegans
Wake instead I found Headstones she should try a long Joycean prose
Bloomwork yes and if I ever do my Bloomwork will be of Mendocino
six years of cypress clinging to sea-torn bluffs that undid me from Max
but gave me myself and grew my children like redwoods rare prehistoric awesome strong like Topanga and Vermont inside them now
Albion Ridge and Navarro Bluff the Pacific from Japan and Robin
crazy crazy rockin Robin who left his woman P for me I always
thought betrayal of synchronistic genius P we are the same woman
Robin in my children too such a beautiful man though at first he actually thought he could get me to leave my kids for him the fool but
then he figured me out as if thats all he is the response to the music
coming at him where and when to take his lead how he gave me his
teachers book Richard Ellmanns autographed Joyce from his class at
Yale and now hes written another version one could spend ones life on
that man and when I was moving out of Patricks cabin grabbing things
in my hysteria the dried red rose of me and Robins first lovemaking in
Roses fell out that he bought me at Davids basketball game in Eureka
and kept kissing me in the stands in front of the Albion postmaster
who never could look at me again no matter how much mail I had and
David so embarrassed trying to play the Northern California Small

Schools AAA Championship his mom making out in the stands I just couldnt resist no man had loved me I was so hurt his coach throwing the 2nd place trophy at his head yes I must write about that man and my terrible failing then as a mother and we slept in Roses that night under the I-5 underpass in the mudflats and he said we were married and I said yes yes I marry you even though youre a musician Id always vowed Id never love a musician but he explained what I could never find out about the octave the unequal mathematical intervals of do re mi fa so la ti do Mollys 8 uneven sentences yes because finally I can begin to remember him too without so much pain because more than anyone he is the lover of my psyche as Sergei is the father of my children as Maximilian is the brother of my body and Ramon the lover in the land and now Patrick still how I dream of Robin and then find out the dreams are what really has happened to him in Paris and Bangkok and Hawaii and Utah and San Francisco like the last night in the cabin when I flew home from Minneapolis and 3 hours on the ferries from Seattle with Ward his woman freaking out when she picks us up because of Carolyn thinking its me fucking her lover and when I finally got home to the cabin Patrick was like a tall dark cedar so still and ingrown and centuries cold alone in the woods and the emergency message to call Jack in North Beach about Darien he didn't want to go with me so unlike him and he hit the cedar with Psyche my vans first dent as we pulled out when we finally got in bed we were like strangers and I buried my head into his chest and for the first time in so long cried a great relief though each sob was like pulling teeth and then I saw so clearly Robin looking at me from Patricks heart which I could hear beating looking at me the way he used to when he was trying to be genuine it was always so hard for him to break through the barriers of his mental powers with his electric eyes in his Scorpio porcelain face and he was saying to me I love you One and Darien wrote me the next day saying she and Shelley had seen Robin and his girlfriend playing at the Hotel Utah the first she had seen him since we went to South America she said he looked so different Id never have recognized him except for the same piercing eyes but I know from the way he looked at me we will always be friends we will know each other through our whole lives and thats why he was looking at me from Patricks chest he was in fact that very moment looking into the eyes of my daughter and all that week I kept throwing up the first time with Carolyn in Minneapolis I never never never vomit but for Patrick lying to me fucking a secret love betraying me he wouldnt tell me what was happening I just couldnt stomach it though I didnt know yes because he had fallen in love with another how she had just left the cabin when I arrived and thats why he hit the tree and thats why I saw Robin in Patricks heart my lover the unfaithful one until I finally knew from the way she looked at me that night we were introduced in the tavern hello and she said hello and my name so pointedly and told me with her eyes your man is mine now and I the fool all sweaty from dancing said when youre happy and you dance the blues you just get sloppy and Sean and Patrick groaned in unison like twins and Robin maybe more sexist than the rest with his Yale and Catholic education though he was smart enough to hide it and dancing arm in arm with Jack and Moonlight down Ukiah Street outside the Seagull singing Kalinka in Russian and when he left me that morning I came home with the groceries he said with them still in my arms his beard smelling of a womans cunt I gotta go One and he was gone with no explanations I never talked to him again so haunted still by the last terrible things he said I couldnt ask what he meant when he started doing coke he got so straight no longer wildly blooming as with marijuana and me now the crazy one he said he wanted to be straight and clean and coked I was in shock for so long after he left he had been so in love with me until I said yes and then he was gone the groceries molded in the bag all that week I never ate a thing and Sarah In The Sun trying to help took me to that old man in Booneville and we passed Robin and a woman on Highway 1 I didnt see that it was him until they had passed going north who had just had his 3rd heart attack and wanted to tell a writer the history of prostitution on the Mendocino Coast no one will take down this information he said its important its the early history of the coast as important as the logging camps he was born in a Eureka whore house in 1904 the year of Ulysses he had that photograph on the wall above his head as he fed the fire redwood chips the kind called beauty bark in Southern California for landscaping and he actually kept the cabin warm with them all winter long he said I just go out and pick them up Robert Kennedy had just been shot as he makes his way through the kitchen of the Ambassador Hotel and a young man with dark hair is knelt to him bleeding looking with great anguish into the camera I saw again in a way so hard to believe he is Vietnamese O the heart ache such a sexual old man and just before I fled Mendocino David and Darien both grown and gone Ferlinghetti came to Casper to give a poetry reading and the invitation by someone to do a hot tub with him and snort good cocaine which I declined he said how can you say no to a hot tub with Ferlinghetti thats easy the last time I was in a hot tub I got pregnant how Jonsey said City Lights hasn't published a feminist yet but someday they will have to when I went back to the bar and sat down Jonsey was reading an article in Harpers entitled The Computerized Ulysses Some of the Bloodiest Pages in Textual Scholarship and out of the blue just confessed to me that shes really a woman as if I hadnt known asks if she can take me home on her Harley and when we got back to the village she wants me to get stoned with the pot she bought to seduce me she never touches the stuff herself and then after that she pulls out Jack Daniels I tell her about my Grandpa from Lynchburg who was a hangman in Arizona how it wasn't till I slept over night in the Jack Daniels parking lot in Lynchburg Tennessee and woke straight up in the night next to Darien on our way in a driveaway van to Miami to fly off to Bogota Lynchburg no wonder he was a lynchman but she was smoothing out the sheets and fluffing up the pillows on her bed behind me what are you doing and she said so matter of factly dont get worried I just want a piece of ass is all when I got out of there without hurting her feelings too much beautiful beautiful Jonsey the world will be saved by people like her and in my own bed on the floor of the pumphouse that had no locks that always reminded me of Joyces Martello Tower waking every morning to the invasion of banana slugs I found I had the Computerized Ulysses still in my hands and fell asleep reading of the galleys in the margins of which Joyce wrote 9 consecutive sets of proofs in which elaborations were further elaborated on a third of the final text handwritten onto the proofs and sometime in the night I wrote across it my dream Jonsey and I carry the heavy leaded plates the one hundred thousand manuscripts of Ulysses dutifully like workers down to the sea and throw them in and on another

page sometime in my sleep I wrote in huge letters H Y P N O G O G I C
A N O T H E R W O R D F O R M O R N I N G W A K I N G and then I
dreamed the pumphouse my Martello Tower fell on top of me I found
myself outside naked screaming no no no no no no no no so on the 4th
of July in red white and blue clown face the stars and stripes forever on
my face marching in the parade down Main Street with Reed and
Yvonne costumed as giant pencils to Robins rock n roll electric hard
country blues band on the generated float Power To The People somewhere behind us on the next block his music so far away from me now
except turning corners I could hear him real clear and we 3 poets marching for freedom of the press reading through the Mendocino streets
American Alchemy and that night driving out in Roses with 4 poets
for Port Townsend and never going back

   5 is Molly standing silently above the windy straits waving goodbye
to her lover she has promised to wait for though his return be 20 years
6 is 20 years of waiting in her house my house your house everyones
housewife in her skekinah 2 plumes of smoke from the housetop of 7
Eccles Street the Holy Ghost metempsychosis in her fart the whome of
your eternal geomater and boyt the archetype of all dwellings the triol-
ogy of her orofices the perineum as passages as doorways 6 is of Mollys
double her daughter Milly 6s have lots of wind horses running to the
West Wind to get pregnant and Ulysses coming home aided by moly
the earthroot to save us and slaying the suitors blood and parts of
bodies victoriously strewn everywhere yes because Homer was shocking when I finally read him the foundation myth of Western culture
and now we have Trident nuclear submarines coming to the Hood
Canal the patriarchs dildo in the holy female waters the myths of the
patriarchy like Mary Daly says have all been reversed men do the birthing creating life Adam births Eve from his ribs Zeus births Athena
why don't they try and create something Molly says and the Holy
Ghost in her fart rising through the chimney the all male Trinity imagine Freuds penis envy when the clear tragedy of our culture is womb
envy the Navy birthing nuclear subs men birthing death to compete
with women who birth life as it was written tonight on the blackboard
in the Town Tavern War is Menstrual Envy and Lawrence says the
same thing in The Man Who Died men love death because they are

afraid of women who give life the notion I have always rejected as anything more than cultural because it wasnt true of my baby boy though I
suppose it could be true now all these years a football player what
could I do but shout yes yes yes youre a great athlete and believe what
he learned in his childhood was good would last would make him even
greater drinking Guinness on tap for Bloomsday hours at the tavern
talking finally talking yes because yesterday in the meadow I told him
more than anything I want to know him so tonight he told me of all the
women he has loved how he fell in love with this woman and then he
fell in love with this woman and then he fell in love with her how misty
from his guilt he would get when he described certain women as nice I
couldnt believe it when he said I am his longest relationship a year and
a half no wonder love has such a bad reputation how can he say he
loved these women if his love is of such short duration like a crush
though at least he does remember them as important well I told him
you are my shortest relationship which means maybe we have both
learned something about relationships and drank my Guinness and
forced myself to say I never want to live with you again it is so hard for
me to say such negative things hell think I dont love him I just cant go
through it again move back in as you keep begging me now and then
once there I must know again your regretting it I look at him and see so
clearly the priest the tendency to just go away from the world to be
celibate the instinct not to mate is so strong in him at puberty he
wanted God not a woman its a great life without a wife the Salesian
motto he is single solitary alone and interested really in pursuing only
that when I ask him how he sees himself as an old man it is as a single
old man I should learn this for myself to be single thats why hes writing
a book about wanting to kill his girlfriend Christ killing the female and
that priest in Nova Scotia the last time I checked about 3 years ago in
Berkeley was getting close to finding Mollys structure studying the 7
original manuscripts how the lines and words seem to be color coded
because Joyce composed them in different colored pens to represent
the structure and Paddy thinks of me in terms of not wanting to hurt
me he said in the meadow where we walked it was such a beautiful day
the scotch broom all blooming birds and sun and ferns the huge cedar
and fir surrounding us the sea so blue he was tired of trying to protect

himself from himself tired of trying to proect me from himself so I said
why did you want to kill her I dont know its a novel about unfaithfulness do you want to know what the plot is I brought her to this town
yes I fell in love with Morgan the first time I ever saw her I think I
brought Dana to this town to fuck Morgans husband so I could have
Morgan do you really want to know me I think Im going to write this
novel I think thats what this has been all about Im sorry it was a shitty
way to do it but to write this novel I need an extraordinary amount of
solitude the kind of solitude I had when I wrote The Owl when I
moved out of the cabin into my tepee and stayed up all night and didnt
eat just drank tea and got crazy it was awful for Morgan for the kids
and for me I wore a long black cape haunted the bluffs roamed around
all night I couldnt talk to anyone words wouldnt come that way I went
crazy until I heard the voices in that poem I mean I actually heard them
I didn't know what they meant but I wrote them down sometimes
Morgan would come to my tepee I didnt care whether she came or not
besides Im tired of putting your book first imagine he said that putting
my book first the way Ive had to struggle for every inch of space and
time from him to finish my book and everytime Ive settled into it hed
create another crisis but they were playing Toora-loora the tune my
mother sang to me at her breasts making Moonlight howl in the door
Sean requesting all Irish tunes for Bloomsday why do men cherish the
part of themselves that can only do one thing at a time they cant love
and write at the same time they have to think of themselves as isolate
the sullen male tradition the male right I love myself I think Im grand
when I go the the movies I hold my hand singing his school song to
Sean he loves the trait of unfaithfulness in himself I was even unfaithful
to God he said his self-identity and watching her down at the other end
of the bar slept and fucked him in my bed and then slept there all night
she seems so young so blondish red full of light and greed with dark
Water Street moving through her hair and Moonlight watching us and
Israel bombing Beirut she is nice he said why do I always choose men
whose first requirement in a woman is that she is nice yes because I am
very nice to them oh she seems very nice and very unevolved stupid in
regards to men the kind of stupidity I have had a nice girl love to the
point of loving being killed yes because I cant be her anymore I have to

change grow but what kind of man will love a woman who isn't first
and foremost nice Oh Danny Boy its you its you must go and I must
stay the worlds oldest recorded tune and Beirut left like a shell the sick
obvious karma the first bombing June 6 exactly 14 years from Kennedy and Molly and Djuna Barnes died today I thought she died years
ago drinking Guinness and toasting the IRA with Sean and Kate feeling high and noble with Patrick we can be clear Im sure we can be clear
really love each other have the great friendship we both want without
getting bogged down the friendship of writers he says I hope we have
more than that I say Justine says the goal of every love affair is deper-
sonalized love what is that I guess its the kind of love like the psychic
reader says of the heart not the emotions and genitals love without
possessiveness compulsion want jealousy but shit Patrick I told him in
the meadow as we walked back down the drive I know about that kind
of love how do you think I stayed with Sergei for 7 years who never
spoke to me or with Max my task in this life is to learn to love the other
way to know the love of this earth this time I want to claim my lovers I
want my lovers to claim me we must learn to claim the earth possession
passion yes commitment the lack of this is somehow what is wrong I
dont believe like the psychic reader that we are just here as a step to the
next life and personally I write best when Im mated theres peace inside
me I am not looking for a lover I am not horny or hurting or wandering in that worst way I can work Im secure committed but then I realized I was saying just what the psychic reader said I ground myself
through my lovers their penises give me earth energy and she said thats
not good oh Paddy I want to learn to love you as you love me no more
than that I didnt say it to be cruel when I can look at a man and know Id
fuck him if I had the chance then I will know that I love you as much as
you love me how she looks so different everytime I see her hair up
down braided pulled back I feel guilty about her he says I just want to
be able to talk to her normally when I meet her on the street I called her
a girl once he said you want to know how old she is I said no no no
please dont tell me I wanted him to tell me everything what they talk
about how it felt how she looks with her cotton print blouse off is her
pubic hair the same color as her golden red long so very long hair spilling over the bar and her small high ass I see myself making love to her

or rather I am just him trying to know the experience when we make love how he made love to her to understand how good it was that it was worth hurting me so Durrell says you always fall in love with the one your lover loves Ward said at the party the other night I find myself loving men my women make love to but I understand this is sexism because women are regarded as property and so theres this sense of moving the property around among the brothers with women theres the code dont mess with another womans man because it is understood that women have much more to lose it is a more serious infraction to threaten her with the loss of her man shes caught something good but I begged him not to tell me her age no no no that will hurt too much I dont want that to be an issue too maybe shes older than she looks that he was so eager to tell me 18 to 30 it is hard to tell 18 yes because Darien and Shelley are 18 now Shelleys birthday as we were leaving San Francisco after being there all spring sleeping 6 weeks in Psyche in 2 hour parking places in North Beach until they found their jobs and I bartending at Gullivers seeing Jack and Kristen everyday just a month after his son died and then staying at their apartment when Patrick came on my birthday and Jack gave me the chapbook Anna Livia Plurabelle Faber & Faber 1930 Work in Progress and a birthday poem now if foal the fauns of the deerest lefted their airs they wood be toned air on the whesper of a dayhip cullextive sounding the birdday greetings to you in a saladearity of calmreds like Robins last birthday poem to me Direst Won massed wander field pear sun hive fever gnome sail or break ewer press us ours hot penis owl weighs oil a few now what did that mean oil a few something wonderful oh yes oil a few I love you and hot penis was happiness like Patricks Hopping Burstday Puoyme for Dylan if on the fly bridal of ya breed day ahfta year foist woids foist throusanth stepita shtepida schlepitha weigh brink ya a drink of zu kigger uv da beerio even thou yaint gotcha no thirst fert no liveriver in ya wee ripe golden grapefruit of a boody and Jack bought me Tertium Organum and said this book and Joyce were the major books on which Crane built The Bridge this book The Bridge and Joyce were the major influences in my life and the girls hotel room in the Entella how much Id forgotten what its like to be 18 because I still take abuse on the streets but its nothing like what they take old men

and young sailors reaching out and touching their breasts standing in
the alleys and exposing themselves that mailman that had Shelley
trapped for hours inside Psyche 18 I never even thought to ask them if
they are registered to vote and Milly as Mollys teenage daughter as
Mollys double the double motif of 6s the theme of generation Joyces
spermatic flood of creation I was so old when I was 18 strange and
pregnant an alien if I ever was caught in those stands over the Ramona
Baseball field while Sergei knocked balls into the dust and blinding sun
against the Barona Indian Reservation team secretly studying for my
first English lit test the poet with 2 names George Gordon and Lord
Byron and his poem was another name Don Juan there were so many
names Id never heard of trying to memorize the name as Walt Whitman not Walt Tennyson at 18 I had never heard of Walt Whitman
trying to find ways to remember tricks and clues to find ways to these
names memorize only one name George Gordon or Lord Byron with
Sergei making a homerun David kicking from inside the Barona Indian women so fat drinking beer and cursing and booing from the hot
dusty sidelines my mother always said in this country we are a democracy we dont respect titles thats why we came here so I dropped the
Lord and on Tennyson too wrote on the test George Gordon wrote
Don Juan Lara and the Corsair in which the Queen disguises herself as
a page to follow La Fitte into battle even now on the Monica J I have
that old picture Mama got at a garage sale in Ramona the Funeral of
Shelley Ive carried it with me ever since Ramona Shelley smoking on
the pyre on the Mediterranean beach July 8th Maxs birthday and the
real Maximilians birth day 1832 and Lord Byron stands beside his
drowned friend about to snatch his heart from the flames or was that
Trelawny Molly said Byron was too beautiful for a man she made
Byron and Jesus the Adonis son-lovers of 7s he made me a present of
the Lord Byron poems I was too brilliant or too blonde or too female
or too flashy too something in that class I was named P and wrote of
Shelleys heart his harp I wanted to be demonstrating against the war in
Washington looking down on the rush traffic the freeway life of those
days Mary Daly says theres a Background of everyone and theyre
trying again to cut California into 2 states for Southern California to
be named Ramona Mama I never saw her influence on me as a writer

because when I look at her she always directs my attention to Daddy but shes the one who told me the stories and encouraged me always and shes even a writer shes written me a letter every week at least since I left home she is really extraordinary and Ive never even told her it is she who kept me from being locked away insane in the house of marriage the mother is the muse HD said when I was huge and pregnant and so dangerously unhappy I didnt know what a muse is unless like Jesus Sergei hadnt spoken to me since the night we married I couldnt figure it out I was paralysed with hurt I had taken a vow to stay with him for better or worse I kept thinking he would come out of it if I didnt freak if I maintained my great love for him Paul just yesterday said thats Oblomovian a common characteristic of the Russians they start re- treating they retreat to the living room then to the bedroom finally to the bed which they never leave and never speak so I started taking classes at Palomar because Mama took the baby 2 days a week and said I had to do something else besides just be a mother or I would become ill like her Dr Boehm speaking a language I did not understand though I did understand the poetry or most of it I was the river merchants wife at 14 I married My Lord you I never laughed being bashful called to a thousand times I never looked back at 15 I stopped scowling I desired my dust to be mingled with yours forever and forever and forever at 16 you departed but I was intrigued and sometimes what he said was so funny though hes the one who told me not to use so because it is a fem- inine adjective it took my breath away and made me cry and scream all the way back up the mountain whats wrong with a feminine adjective Id see beyond my ignorance and laugh at the amazing connections he weaved because the name Penelope means with a web over her face the most popular girl in highschool and her husband castrated what did she ever do and hed look over at me sitting sideways in my schooldesk my son so large inside me and Id realize that I was the only one who laughed the only one who got it and he in his Harvard accent and pipe would nod his head at me sort of ironically and when on that last day of class he who everyone was terrified of the hardest grader at Palomar gave me an A- for the first paper I ever wrote Emily Brontes Psycho- logical Identification With Heathcliff In Wuthering Heights oh how I wish I had that paper now like Molly I wouldnt mind being a man and getting up on a lovely woman and Boehm died of a heart attack after that so young I never told him thanked him like the girl in the desk behind me that first class so vivacious and alive who reminded me anyway of my dead Bobbie Sue in her fiances car at 19 and how crazed my Uncle CD was and this one killed on Highway 78 over 4th of July weekend her empty desk behind me and I stood there in the doorway of his office in my early hours of labor the day before David was born and said as if to reassure him Ill be back and he said the first encouragement maybe the only I ever received to go to college though Mama encouraged me to do something anything for myself in what seemed to me an English accent which was really only high Boston Brahmin yes in his funny professors suit you had better I was so ashamed then because I hadnt read Wuthering Heights since I was 14 called to a thousand times I never looked back certainly never reread the only book besides The Black Stallion books and the Bible I read as a kid so I went in labor to the library with the determination to start reading and found on display a poet named HD like CD because now I understand she had just died though Ive never known who at Palomar was responsible for that display I checked out all her books and read them cover to cover every painful grueling mysterious word of Helen of Egypt while I gave birth to my son and began to nurse him O patience above its pouring out of me pregnant as big as he is O Jamsey let me up out of this pooh sweets of sin she said you can read my work in 2 ways she maybe the secret mother of Lawrences child Perdita HD and DH the real Lady Chatterley my mother read in the 20s before it was banned with a flashlight under the covers at the orphanage and HD was into Vico too as megalomania or as an extension of the artists mind I didnt understand a word of it but I didnt let that stop me

who knows is there anything the matter with my insides sometimes I have thought to name this story Free Association though mine is so much shorter than Joyces like that old rock group who sang Here Comes Mary Max said was marijuana in the tavern Sean hanging over Patricks shoulder citing Marco Zorro poems everyone drunk and the Dead singing what a long strange trip its been and Kate urging me again to come up and see her she knows I cant for fear Joe will have brought her there its awkward these days for everyone Sean says how bad I feel to make everyone feel bad how I cried this afternoon on the boat oh Paddy shes my sister too why am I the monster in this I didnt do anything wrong anything to hurt anyone I love her too I love you how could I not since you love her I dont like her for sleeping in my bed with you and I wont just dismiss it she had no regard for me and now she wants to be my friend well a friend is something more than that and so she must find what it is if she wants to be my friend but we were doing better tonight even with her standing at the end of the bar so beautiful and looking at her I thought of how he has shared so little of her with me only what she said that night dancing to still crazy after all this time O Patrick you are my only friend in this town I am so lonely and maybe once or twice he said how lonely she is we were even laughing and making jokes but then he asked me if I didnt think I was oversexed images flooded my eyes of the men Ive loved who were yes oversexed like Joyce begging Nora to beat him Nora his whore his Virgin his Goddess his Wife shit and then tears simple tears no no my sexuality isnt perverted is it I dont use it it doesnt control me I dont hurt others with it Ive never been adulterous not even with my young husband who didnt speak to me for 7 years thats perverted that I stayed I went into the bathroom to wipe my eyes because he made me cry O Molly your words and in the light checking what the moon is in Aries maybe a new beginning things are going pretty well I sit back down on the stool tell him he says I wish I could believe in astrology we are so different that way but leaving her there I begin to fall I feel the moon under the earth in Aries pulling me down I feel the old betrayal and rejection I cant bear to make the same mistakes again keep taking him back ignoring the implications he brought Dana to this town to fuck Morgans husband so he could have Morgan it is going on 2 now as we walk through the town down to the Boat Haven walking with Stephen and Leopold through the streets of Dublin on the portable and Grace Slicks ReJoyce the only Jew in the room and Mollys gone to Blazes Boylands Scotch of Maizes any woman whose husband sleeps with his head all buried down at the foot of the bed singing I got his eye I got his eye all you wanna do is live so sell your mother wars good business so give your son I tell him of the young women I watch who come down to the beach on these warm days they all have little boys the young women and the little boys wade in and out of the gentle waters of the Straits in their bathing suits their bodies so bright and real they wade just as they did not very long ago when they came to this beach with their fathers throwing stones and skimming objects across the water their loneliness against the Olympics is very great and very real I want to shout to them from the Monica J where are the fathers oh where are the fathers you are the ones who took love seriously you gave your body to make a child and then he disappeared do you ask why arent men more serious about love and do you teach your sons about love because the country will take them from you and turn them against you and make killers and rapists of them unless you teach them to be lovers husbands fathers Ward told me of the poster he saw at Bangor when he got inside the Trident base he came to a pair of double doors marked off limits and on each door was a poster of Poseidon God of the Sea standing in water up to his waist holding his trident in his hand a crown of kelp on his head and coming out of the water right where his penis should be is a missile and scientists and critics and computerized Joyce and Trident the mind that created this system what a triumph of technology the paper said hot penis is happiness though there a few men like Sean who are raising other mens children stumbling then through the deep wet sand he hugs me close again poor little pussy youll be a dyke yet and we laugh and cry and Moonlight barks through the driftwood and big soaked logs the smoke stack from the mill bursting into Scorpio dragging our bags from the boat looking for a place high enough from the high tide to sleep and just as we climb into them Molly Bloom is coming live from New York City YES BECAUSE HE NEVER DID A THING LIKE THAT BEFORE AS ASK to get his breakfast in bed she was 34 in Los Angeles so much older than me older than I could imagine ever being though I loved her for being 34 and still viable still sexual still plausible orgasmic and even now after all this time all the things that have happened I can hear shes reading the lines wrong ignorant of the structure which reverberates the world on a thousand other levels shes ignorant of 7 was always my favorite sentence always the most female and mysterious and strange 7 years it took him to write it I used to think 7 years an outrageous amount of time to spend on a book now I marvel that he

did it in 7 and 7 is pain and the moon the mind in the uterus and 7 rules
the heart and Molly sitting on the chamber pot blood and water flowing from her O the return to the earth the 3rd democratic stage of corruption death and burial the purge of the old so life can continue and
we return with it passing through the opening of the womb as blood
and urine through the vagina and urethra into the Holy of Holies the
vessel the cracked chamber pot like a throne I have paid homage to that
living altar where the back changes names like the cup of Ulysses like
Finnegans coffin Charons ferryboat like Shelleys little Ariel like Trident Submarine and Patricks boatman has a light canoe like Demeter
at the well for Persephone the mysterious box of Finnegans Wake that
contains the universal secret of humanity Stephen said the soul is surrounded from the start by liquids urine slime seawater amniotic tides
though she does sound a little obscene O holy Goddess I never
thought so before Ive been in the north the puritan north too long
dont you think youre oversexed fuck Ill lose my vision here my vision
he calls crazy my expansiveness my knowledge of love why am I always
going further north away from the celebration of the self in San Diego
light having to apologize here everytime someone asks me where I am
from and why I use California hippy cliches yes because I was born one
and beautiful is the most beautiful word and you are all so afraid of
fucking what guess Ill go to Utah in the fall and watch David play football and spend time with Una though the thoughts of it are grinding
hard to be so far from here I think its for love of child land self language
and story I want the continent the earth for my home I get so claus-
trophobic in one place so suspicious of everyones even my own belief
this place as the only place how the wisdom profundity of place in the
human psyche and body is so real powerful so obvious but when it
makes you provincial and prejudiced against other places their ways its
evil still I love this place rainy and dark and cold and soggy so soggy its
beautiful the power the purity the pull I get sucked down I think everyone does you can see it in their shoulders so self conscious its all the
water making mirrors a hard place the clitoris of the peninsula secretive
hidden down in the terrible folds of her exquisite blue watercolor song
so unlike anywhere else she even has a tiny town named Joyce beneath
Mount Olympus and one named Sappho and Pysht Bill just told me

was really Psyche but the original mapmaker spelled it wrong which is funny because I couldnt decide whether to name my van Sappho or Psyche waited for my first trip in her to know which one treeplanting out on the West End and I chose Psyche even though we were parked in Sappho I think its true that this was all a setup to get rid of me over and over he wants me when I pull away from him he doesnt want me when I want him Im so tired of that game I cant bear to make that mistake again that nightmare I had on the boat last night of having plastic surgery to remove the scar on my belly looking down on the fresh red incision and seeing that the sewing hasnt been done well there are terrible gaps not only will I scar again in the exact same way but I am in danger of breaking open of losing all my insides from this I have to get away from him for whatever truth there is in Meridels objection to Crazy Horse that Im looking for a man to save me the Cinderella Complex when I defended Crazy Horse as the lover in the land and that women are read differently than men its sexist to accuse a woman poet who presents a vision as being in a state of desire in relation to what she presents she wrote I guess you are Ariadne but you must not give Theseus the clue of thread I really dont know what she meant I wonder if Im giving it here she was 4 years old that Bloomsday in 1904 when Joyce met Nora Barnacle in Dublin with a name like Barnacle his father said shell stick to him forever she was the first socialist as Bloom says of Jesus who is mentioned in all 3s and 7s I dont know where I can go she wrote to finish my 3 circle novels before the grim reaper Id like to just go west and camp out and finish them and then pour blood down the nuclear sub and pass away from this violence and my periods here I could write my history here in terms of bleeding Goddess hemorrhaging sweet holy fine wombblood gallons of it more than in any place Ive ever lived all the water in the air I guess and living without electricity and there is real love I know it I am not wrong perfect love is possible HD says for what is given cannot be entirely lost it is transferred or translated displaced it finds a new form and to find it again in a new context is to begin again though Ill never forget the first time I fully understood sexism that day at Goddard standing in the cafeteria like an epiphany like the racism in the film I had just seen I understood why after all my trying and loving after all the years Sergei and Maximilian the reason he doesnt love me as much as I love him is because Im a woman he sees me not as another person soulmate whatever but as a woman first and foremost Max even said it when I asked him he such a radical and sensitive to others its one thing Ill never get over sexism yes because its his sexuality the pleasure hes learned as sex to dominate how sick I was sick to my very soul I wanted to die no revelation could ever match that one vomiting in the snow wanting to bury myself in the snow all the work I had done for him to overcome my programmed sexism our 2 babies I aborted for him because it seemed only right that he have equal say how I grieve still for them I who at 15 looked around my sophomore history class we must have been studying woman suffrage or something and I knew again and again as I had all my life as I thought everyone knew that gender is an adjective as is the color of ones hair or skin adjectival to the basic person who has mysteries and characteristics far more essential more fundamental than an adjective I considered the social ways the differences in our clothing and behavior he opens the door for me as just a game a hangover from the past that you go along with because things run smoother that way all social mores so silly and awkward I had such total faith then in my brothers that I was not really betrayed by them like Marilyn must have believed acting that way what they demanded of her the dream I had of her on Kalaloch that night we camped there such an odd surprising place to dream of Monroe and tv so wild and far from civilization the last beach in America she was on a tv talk show she was 53 years old and very beautiful she was explaining to the world that she disappeared because no one had understood that she was a comedian and April said in her letter today I cant believe how I overlooked the obvious in my marriage just like my parents my father would say outrageously shitty things to my mother and my mother simply ignored them answered with something else something from her body her intuition her body language whatever she ignores what he says to keep the family together to keep him with her to avoid a confrontation but he keeps saying even more bizarre and cruel things because he wants her to hear him I cant believe how Ive overlooked the obvious Ive perpetuated the old relationship of my parents it changes everything when you start taking men at their word responding to exactly what they say I dont love you

means I dont love you I want to kill you means I want to kill you I hate
you means I hate you yes because this is what I learned most from Maxs
leaving from now on I will hear what is being said to me my responsibility in whatever hope there is in changing this though Patrick goes
into shock when I take him at his word no thats not what I meant even
though he said it everyone must have this ingrained in them and Alma
wrote because I wrote her of how beautiful and extraordinary she is
through all shes gone through having her baby alone in the Sierras after leaving her husband in the city and she wrote yes I thought exactly
this about you when you came Im always amazed to see this rebirthing
in the women I love which brings me to why aren't the men I know exceptional in terms of deep feeling and the courage to love to surrender
to love not romantic love but naked love that has diapers distance
death she said romantic love seems to love all these terms fidelity good
sex etc when what we really want is to be known it is my goal as a
mother to evolve my sons to this oh the worst despair it seems hopeless
I cant just be nasty and shallow and clicheish like Molly about it and Ive
always believed you must not become like them how will anything ever
get corrected though these days I come to understand that as long as
you take it as long as you dont object you contribute to the problem
though still you must not become narrow like them when Darien said
that morning in Cuzco Peru before the altar on which the Incas sacrifi-
ced 16 year old virgins there arent any good men are there Mom I
didnt know what to answer I still dont know how to answer how could
a mother tell her daughter you are right there are no good men and
how could a mother say to her daughter yes of course there are good
men just keep looking deception Mary Daly says is not one of the 7
Cardinal Sins of the Christian Patriarchy and yet deception is the cardinal not to say the most common sin of men there are only 2 forms of
love in the world Joyce said the love of the mother for the child and the
love of the man for lies such a stupid Catholic though when you look
into the nightsky like this O fuck the magnificent heavens that tell such
another story I wrote around her body all the bodies of time are
gathered the earth the solar system the galaxies of far extending space
all swell within her womb and Doug who came from Utah the same
time I came here he showed me the plans for his house as we walked on

Point Hudson that first week and now its completed he calls it the
Northern Cross I designed it on the exact scale of the Northern Cross
oh you know he said there was a time in my life when I thought I had to
know the constellations in order to get out of this life he is so much like
me with his hard time here with these cynical nonbeliever Northerners
2 years he said not a single pat on the back its a strange place man the
Quimper Peninsula and Alice Walker said if we have any true love for
the stars planets the rest of creation we must do everything we can to
keep white men away from them they who have appointed themselves
as our representatives to the rest of the universe they who have never
met any new creature without exploiting abusing or destroying it and
what of Joyces Lucia how men change when their daughters reach puberty become men again first not fathers sexism stronger even than
their love stronger than parental love Lucy In The Sky With Diamonds
thank god for acid and my generation and Molly wanting to make love
to a statue like Pygmalion I often thought I wanted to kiss him all over
his lovely young cock there so simply

no no no no no no no no 8 nos he doesnt know poetry from a cab-
bage 8s are madness murder prisons poison passion men as big brutes
women trapped in big holes sandhi and ricorso 4s and 8s and war between the sexes though I hate dismissing it in a cliche that they can slip
out of without thinking the war between the sexes and generalities
about gender as if it is all inevitable or natural and not the state the culture that will be changed if we are to survive it the Church The State
and its holy Trident 8 in its shape is the 2 interlocking serpents of the
caduceous the balancing out of the opposing forces the eternally spiral-
ling movement of the heavens the way Molly and Poldy sleep his head
to her feet 8s are dirty jokes my uncle John has a thing long my aunt
Mary has a thing hairy 8s are like Jonestown in New Guyana the CIAs
experimental drug lab that Mayor Mascone knew what Ryan had
found out and Hemingway and Cuba and The Man Who Cried I Am
about Richard Wrights possible death by the CIA in Paris the Russian
Secret Police nothing to ours and Marilyn Monroe murdered 48 cap-
sules of Nembutal and Chloral hydrate though Noguchi stated her
stomach is completely empty no residue of the pills is noted that one
policeman who was at her house in Brentwood first and saw that it was

bugged and thought it was murder from the start why was there no
vomit around her no glass of water to swallow the pills and her red
diary he looked at with its writing of John and Bobby Kennedy how
she wrote she was going to blow the whistle and tell all she knew of the
CIAs plot to kill Fidel Castro which seemed preposterous then but
years later the plot was verified and the diary listed in her personal ef-
fects at the morgue disappeared the next day and then was crossed out
from the inventory and how John Kennedy was first involved with her
until she embarrassed him when she sang Happy Birthday too sexy to
him on tv and so he passed her on to his little brother Bobby who she
really fell in love with talking with him nightly on a private phone in
the Justice Department and he told her he was going to leave his wife
for her but then he dumped her had the phone she called him on disconnected and the deputy coroner said he always believed it murder
but that he signed her death certificate apparent suicide under duress
under the threat of losing his job you wouldnt want to lose your job
shit people and their coveted jobs that justifies anything murder what
about your soul and now the one cop says he was in the ambulance and
she was coming to when the doctor pushed him aside and plunged a
long needle directly into her heart and pronounced her dead just this
week I read of the private detective this is a jigsaw puzzle with missing
pieces I just didnt expect it to take over 10 years like me with Molly but
the part of the picture we see is that Monroe was murdered possibly
politically assassinated there was a kidnap plot to take place days before
her death she was to be taken from LA to Virginia where she would
have been kept it would have been leaked to the press that she had suffered an emotional breakdown to discredit any press conference she
might hold later he and an ex lover petitioned the FBI for Monroes
files but most of the material was blacked out and under orders of the
FBI director Webster half of the pages were completely withheld for
national defense and foreign policy Id like to know he said just what in
the files of a 2 decade dead movie star still threatens national security Id
like to see those files and Id like also to get Monroes body exhumed because the autopsy shows a bruise on her left hip would could be an in-
jection site oh god to think of her body preserved 20 years in a vault
they wont even let us go back to the earth when were through better to

be trapped in a big hole where youll eventually dissolve into the earth
than trapped in a plastic and chrome vault the nightmare of our modern civilization and why doesn't Arthur Miller say something or Joe
DiMaggio who just quit this birthday 2 weeks ago such a Gemini Leo
she was fuck sending her roses he said hed send for his lifetime 8s are
karma and those nuns committed to throwing themselves in front of
the sub when it comes in here who havent understood yet the connection between their male gods and nuclear war though theyre willing to
give their life to stop it and that one priest at the meeting kept calling
the submarine a she when she comes in hed say it was sickening just like
mens attitude of maneuvering a big old dumb awkward broad I
wanted to scream at him how dare you refer to that motherfucking
dildo as a female even in Ulysses they say the last day is coming this
summer 1904 sea serpent in Royal Canal safe arrival of the antichrist
and they say theres a Russian spy ship sitting out at the mouth of the
Straits at Neah Bay waiting for the Ohio too I said Patrick lets go look
at it imagine the Russians and he said I bet thats why Sergei couldnt
talk to you he must have been torn without hardly knowing it between
Russia and America we were training him to kill Russians what could
he say you were like his soul he couldnt consult this whole summer of
our waiting for the most destructive weapon ever created absolute evil
the United Nations said yes imagine that we are going to accept the
presence of that evil thing in this most holy place I cant believe its really
going to happen Fuji said when they were constructing their Buddha
temple at Ground Zero with no money all found materials coming all
the way from Japan to New York drumming walking and chanting
across the country to Bangor the nations producing these absolutely
evil weapons can thus be called absolutely evil only harmful without
benefit to the world and the first of such countries is the United States
the second the Soviet Union it is taught in Buddhism that those who
sow the seed must reap the harvest the law of causation the United
States he said which planted the seed of dropping the atomic bombs on
our country will eventually be subjected to nuclear attack in order to
prevent this let us give rise to the nonviolent movement to change this
world of ours to a peaceful Pure Land Heaven 8s are of the murderer
and the murdered I must remember to pour my blood into the Straits

before I leave its the blood soaking the earth gives new life thats in the
Hades episode I think like voodoo death like the apocalypse we are
programmed for and Alice Walkers reading at Grace Cathedral last
spring with Darien and Shelley irradiating ourselves may be the only
way to save others from what earth has already become she began with
Zora Neale Hurstons ancient Black curse prayer from the Deep South
let the earth marinate in poisons let the bombs cover the ground like
rain for nothing short of total destruction will ever teach them anything O Man God I ask you all these things because they have dragged
me in the dust and destroyed my children broken my heart and caused
me to curse the day that I was born now she is remembering Hugh
Boylan her lover that afternoon with his huge cock though not so
much spunk in it as Poldy Hugh Boylan meaning the mind in the boy
of the land or the mind in the boyland I like to think of the land as the
boy the 2nd Sentence the terrible division of the land into Male and
Female she tells of Remus and Romulus of the 3rd Sentence and all the
3rd sections sucking her tits titties he calls them making them firmer
and western civilization the strange Stanhopes of the asexual 4th
sandhi and ricorso the great fucking on Gibraltar of the 5th the
depressed housewife of the 6th Molly sitting on the chamber pot of the
7th blood and urine of the church amor matis gushing from her as a sea
will I ever get it published there could be a fire I could lose it all and
over and over the excruciating images of his long beautiful hands un-
buttoning the back of her cotton blouse of the words he said to her
over and over of bending his extraordinary Jupiters mouth to her
breasts and inserting his penis deep into her you are such a good kisser
I said tonight when he kissed me at the bar and he laughed I know its
always been my downfall oh shit he can stick his tongue 7 miles up my
hole O Molly let me see if I can doze off to the tittering daughters of
sleeping to the waters of the chittering waters of all the liffeying waters
of a tale told of Shawn and Dan of who was Shem and Shaun oh tell me
tell me tell me a tale of all Livias daughtersons 8s and the nights and
dream I am alone in a boat drifting the beautiful northern seas trying to
get home waking over and over to the bodies of men over me around
me under me waking to Molly calling from all the ends of Europe my
name outside Larby Sharons waking to her awful deep down torrent O

and the sea crimson like fire waking on this beach the eternal Now of
ground zero and the iodiney smell and shall I wear a red rose or a rose
of sharon or Rose Rodriquez then yes I asked him with my eyes to ask
again yes a crescendo crashing wave coming in and then he asked me
would I yes to say yes my mountain flower and drew him down to me
so he could feel my breasts all perfume yes and his heart was going like
mad and yes I said yes I will Yes to the thunderous celebratory
winedark sea aflame applause in New York City waking me and Ireland where they are still fighting and dying for independence how
everyone in the world loves that ending so affirmative yes I say yes I
will Yes the church bell ringing 1 2 3 4 first light spreading across the
sky we are so far north and Indian Island the Navys stockpile of nuclear
weapons yes because someone said here on the peninsula the Makahs
like the Navy perfected the art of war because living here is so easy is
that why its so hard to live here with the light coming over the town
here we come together wayfarers I used to whisper to Max from Pomes
Penyeach here we are housed among intricate streets by night and silence covered by anonymity we rest together Patty and I in the seaweed
and driftwood folded by night we lay on the earth how incredible how
amazing the moon must be coming up too right behind the sun to
wake here from sleep to come from the stomach of the sky to the day
like this to her words and the waters monotone and yes I said yes I will
yes her song as my life I always say yes I marry you on a boat named
Marry Me yes because Robin said yesses is Greek for Good Eye if only
he had not stopped loving me and Sergei and Max why do I become so
unlovable in the end when I love them more because Meridel says our
words are more dangerous than any linear action her silvery soft wet
sand under me her funky iodine of a million years dead digesting all the
sand through the shells of crabs and snails and sand dollars the million
unseen thoughts you are chewing youll never know whose nor the
wash of the sea over your childrens footprints and the girl in literature
Im trying to save from drowning in everything I write the screams of
gulls the gargly squawk of the blue heron standing there looking east
to the sun coming the morning hours running out goldenhaired slim-
blue like a girl named Sunshine on a dory waving to us from Oak Bay as
she sails in front of the Ohio to stop Vicos 3rd stage its 24 missiles each

with 17 nuclear warheads 408 cities its 2040 Hiroshimas here in the
curled and difficult clitoris washed by the vaginal waters Sarah In The
Sun soon my own blood but now I must get out of this bag this sweet
pooh of sin to shut off that static yes Moonlight yes I love you more
than any man good night from New York and Dublin and Parnell and
the prisoners in the Maze and my hunger strike yes with the IRA for
only 6 days because I grew so weak I was dependent on him and
dreamed my father is black when Bobby Sands and Bob Marley died O
what a relief its off his 30000 words my 23000 words though both my
parts together add up to his and the sound now of just the chittering
waters of receded 30 feet already Paddy stretching out of his bag and
rolling over on me dont you want to make love yes I say yes I always say
yes to his hands O Patrick I love you that cup my breasts my hands that
cup his ass his golden haired ass the length of our long bodies mouth to
his mouths kiss to his long limbs pushed into mine and long tongue far
into my throat our hearts going like mad the tense full call in and
within so phallic the way he and I fuck the best nipples through the
deep center of his palms I could come through the pulsating room at
the core of my being the call and echo up the walls the turn and throw
and pull and twisting 8s over the land curved and curled tight and slip-
pery hard and secretive teased and hidden in the mysterious folds uncommitted unknown unfound unexplored little piece of wilderness
convulsing and uncurling land banging vagina walls bursting dystole
and systole throbbing open banging shut the mathematics of love do
re mi fa so la ti do my bloomwork exploding vaginal orgasm deep base
organ falling off a bluff and hitting the beach below and now the stillness heron call for peace laughing in my ear sum fuck Ill never forget
the first time we made love how surprised I was you were singing a
little song when you were coming lalalalalalalala turning me over I
havent come yet oh I thought you did I felt your penis go thrum thrum
thrum my face half off the bag in the sand my stars and stripes forever
face in the Mendocino 4th of July parade do you know the famous
Arab proverb I read it in Justine today life is a cucumber you have it either up your ass or in your hand yes and Molly tried with a banana a
capitalized Banana at that I never could figure that out out except its in
5 I think in the beginning hot penis shut up both of us giggling the

light on my wrists where I see the sun and years those deep down creped wrists of the woman that morning on Mission Bay who said shed lived on the beach all her life and Shelley was the first to almost drown no I was that time with Jason in Paumo my brother O and Bridgit O Bridgit Irish Goddess of poetry where are you my sister the healer who bridges everything to heal people all you were ever meant to be all the changes youve been through too Tahiti and Ashland and all its psychics and healers the safest spot in the US in case of nuclear attack because of the north south Siskiyous the most incredible spot to be north of Mt Shasta on the Oregon border looking down California from your funky old church and your girls and Shakespeare and lithia water a book and the Masters Report saying you cant come in your vagina how funny when I first read that I wanted to fly myself to their clinic to have them test me its always where Ive come the most certainly the best where are your earrings he is asking in my ear O Ive lost all my earrings I lost them all Rita Rita a Greek pearl born of moonlight slow down and her children shes probably dead and Reis Tijerina and Cleaver my god his rapist name and Ritas murderer for a husband the drugged eyes of her little boy and Carmen Lee and the Chumash and Plainfield and Topanga and Darien and David and all the murders of our time how many weve never suspected the 913 killed at Jonestown to keep the world from knowing and poor little pussy he says and Yesses the Good Eye watching us penis in Egyptian is Good Eye in Greek yes I say yes and Emily Dickinson theres an awful yes in every female constitution I think I was trying to uncover the reason Penelope would wait 20 years for Ulysses and why he left in the first place and I wake in the body of myself in 1963 1965 1968 in 1971 in 1974 and in the places of those years and though everyone says I look so young when I wake in my young body I know the difference I can hear my children call me from their beds I love it that they are all around me and then I know my children as adults gone far from home what will happen to them male and female such different crosses still theres so much more light and joy and innocence now everything and everyone is interesting maybe its the joy of a survivor I was so afraid Id die before I got them raised I didn't trust anyone else to raise them but me and I wanted to find out who I was I knew it was a journey and now they are

so beautiful and I am free to take more chances though I keep thinking
of having another one and Ramona O Ramona whatever happened to
you you could be dead your new husband cutting us off the last time I
saw you in Taos with a black eye I love you how incredible how
enormous how fantastic it feels when he puts it in from behind the
Chumash I saw that time the dogs Molly saw on the street my bottom
soft this month of no dancing all crying Ill tighten my bottom Molly
says and let out a few smutty words smell rump or lick my shit O I love
even more than the sounds of the waves lapping the shore the sound of
his coming his low then high breathless helpless man moan I love you
Patrick forever and forever my dust to be mingled with yours O am I a
fool to still believe in love how Robin said Im sorry Ive made you bitter
and I said with the groceries molding in my arms and his beard smelling like cunt you cant make me bitter that he assumed bitterness would
come so easily that he assumed he could cause it he didnt understand
that if you know love you grow more innocent with age and that moment of great silence and peace afterwards I saw my face buried deep in
the cross of my arm staring into the sand at moly the earth root to save
us O Patrick where are we going going so fast and then in the dream
Im trying to get to Utah but we break down half way in a strange
mountainous land which is green and beautiful god of heaven theres
nothing like nature the wild mountains but I hear many reports of a
monstrous man who rules the land he is like the king he resides at the
far end of a long palatial suburban hall behind expensive thick rug
hangings like a sheik when I enter I am warned he is a killer and utterly
unpredictable I notice 2 small children a boy and a girl huddled against
the wall they are so small and passive in their personalities as to seem
deformed perhaps they have been starved the king is grossly fat he sits
at the head of his hall on huge thick pillows like a buddha I kneel in the
proper fashion as I have been instructed to by the door attendant to the
small aqua pillow before me I am to place my knees on the pillow but
because Ive heard that this mans special pleasure is the torture of children I fear theres a childs body inside the pillow I fear its full of bones I
will crush with my body crush in order to pay homage to this monster
but cautiously I kneel if you kill these 2 children I will kill you I say this
quietly but with absolute resolve Im surprised Ive said this because

from what Ive heard of this man he will now do something very horrible to me not just kill me but torture and maim me as is his custom his
pleasure yet I mean it I keep looking back to the small girl and boy
huddled up against the wall the terror is very great the air thick with his
suffocating power his cruel unpredictableness but then suddenly I am
next to him with an overwhelming desire to kiss him my mouth is
opened by spasmodic waves of sexual desire a part of me protests what
are you doing this man is gross but it doesnt matter I want to fuck him
terribly we grope and push against each other begin to make love then
he offers me cocaine he has a large amount of it in a long glass vial my
body feels utterly at one with his but the sight of cocaine makes me
afraid how will I refuse he will be offended and I know if I snort it he
will have seduced my mind too I will be totally his I take the vial in my
hand as if to change the subject as if forgetting the cocaine then accidentally as I carry on a bright conversation I bump the white powder
over the pillows I apologize profusely feeling very bad about my clum-
siness knowing how expensive the stuff is though thinking he of all
people can afford more I assure him that we can just snort it up from
where its spilled which I proceed to do so as to show him nothing has
been lost and I am one with him it really was an accident I snort even
the pill size chunks unground on the mirror the deep brain beauty
comes completely over me my brain being fucked by this monstrous
powerful ruler it is very sexual haunting the cocaine pervading everything the rest of the dream I am in a real coke high my brain and body
having released the chemical that simulates cocaine and we are making
love fucking it begins with my fondling his genitals moving under him
and over him and moving into incredible powerful sex and it is then I
see another person with us a small hard to see person a young girl then
I perceive the most amazing thing from his genitals his penis and his
testicles which are hanging from his giants body above me hanging the
way they do off the male body as if separate from the body he is able
more and more as the act proceeds to extend his genitals from his body
until I see that his penis is a boy about 4 feet long that he is manipulat-
ing to fuck me and the young girl with us O that is so beautiful I moan
yes so beautiful my excitement unbearable my awe of this mans ability
to do this tremendous and O rhythm I am O yes rhythmically fucked

by the long horizontal purple submarine shadow of the first boy I loved the beautiful boy Im still in love with and the boy who comes from the man though he is only a memory manipulated by the man this boy killer on top of me I still fuck

Part IV

A Rolling Stone

By night on my bed I sought him whom my soul loveth:
  I sought him but I found him not.
I will rise now, and go about the city in the streets,
  and in the broad ways I will seek him whom my soul loveth. . . .

SONG OF SONGS

The world stands out on either side
No wider than the heart is wide;
Above the world is stretched the sky,
No higher than the soul is high.
The heart can push the sea and land
Farther away on either hand;
The soul can split the sky in two,
And let the face of God shine through.
But East and West will pinch the heart
That can not keep them pushed apart;
And he whose soul is flat—the sky
will cave in on him by and by.

Edna St. Vincent Millay

Vets

I can hardly remember his approach. Would you like to dance? A little redneckish. Out on the floor, that moment of stiff awkwardness. So many eyes on us. I say I forgot how to dance. Then, suddenly, it's magic between us. We are brand new, unsure, scary, and at the same time, it is as if we have been dancing together forever. He dances me. He swings me. Western. I feel emotional—sweet, girlish, shy, stirred. Still, I keep it together; when he swings me under his arm like a man, I swing him under my arm like a man. He sort of resists, then goes under laughing. In my boots I feel myself turning into a cowgirl. I can *feel* the West. I dance with a couple of other men who ask me, but come back to him. Like some sweet adhesive. I recognize the syndrome. My loyalty to him. Already a little test. Already a little married. We talk some. Helicopter pilot. Spraying, logging, seismic work. Viet Nam? Yes, when I finally ask. I'm sure he's married.

On the wall are giant posters of the moon landing. I know where I was that day. Yeah, I know where I was too. Where were you? Viet Nam. I was at Chappaquiddick. The drowning happened the same weekend. Yeah? Ole Teddy really did himself in with that one.

We are standing beneath giant photo murals of Castle Rock and Delicate Arch near Moab. On the opposite wall a woman in a black evening gown with long white sashes orchestrates a herd of elephants, her long arms with the sashes like trunks and tufts. Going there next, he says, indicating Delicate Arch. Near there.

We dance every tune. Sweaty dancing. In western swing the man just stands there, twirling you. So macho. My toes begin to hurt in my new boots. He steps on them. We crack up laughing. He swings a lot. I break away. Rock n roll. Then he catches me. We swing.

It gets hot. He won't take off his wool shirt. I'd look like a bum, he says. A T-shirt underneath. Blue. I become aware of his large belly. He introduces me to Casey. His co-pilot. Casey and I dance. He says Casey never dances. Once between the three of us he says his mother gave him fat pills. He clears his throat often. He's nervous, high-strung. I say I ran away from home. The Olympic Peninsula. He logged last year in Port Angeles and Forks. He liked that job. Do you know those places? He's originally from Downey, Norwalk, Southern California. My brother and sister were born in Downey Community Hospital! Is that right? His name is Rusty. He says, German. He has to get up at six. He's tired. He's uptight. He mentions his heart. During the evening he mentions his heart three or four times.

Slow dance. I ask him questions, afraid not to talk, afraid my body will say too much. He was born in LA General. Must have lived in Norwalk, Downey the same years I did. My mother is a crazy old lady. Very simple. From Arkansas. The kind of woman who arrives to the stoplight and shouts at everyone because it's red. Or they're in her way. I didn't like my mother much. Three brothers. When my father left, I was thirteen. So all five of us left her, went to Lake Shasta. He was a caretaker there. I grew up on Lake Shasta.

He describes the seismic work for Mobil. To see if there's oil. I don't follow well. Then, the magic: I see smoke shooting up from the veins they detonate. They were last in Kemmerer, Wyoming. He hated it there. Boom town. People greedy, ugly, prices sky-high. They have two weeks left here. He hopes it'll rain tonight so he won't have to work in the morning.

There is such instant and great rapport between the three of us. Like old friends. I love Casey too. Long, skinny, from upstate New York, a little comical looking, no chin. (Later at his trailer there's a picture of the crew. Both of them have beards.) Me and the boys. Toi and the Boys do it twice. I could almost be home in Mendocino with Bonnie Raitt up there singing. I've been so happy since I got here, like coming home. A kind of elation. Well, you know what you have? You have Rocky Mountain high. It's the altitude. You're kidding. No. Its a fact.

Description. (I will see a man two weeks later from the left profile and remember his deep-set eyes. Cancer rising, I bet. Or moon.) He is not much taller than me in my boots. I laugh, explain the boots. My girlfriend Una bought them for me at a garage sale down in Provo. Two bucks. He has dark curly hair; in the morning light: reddish. Rusty. I'm a little embarrassed to be falling in love, at least feeling like I am, shy and touched, eager and reluctant, eyes a little closed. Keep them open.

Scorpio. I just say it.

He just answers. I like to get in my trailer and pull all the curtains. Hide. And you?

Scorpio. Grins. (In his bed, later, watching the constellation of the Scorpion rising on the Wasatch.)

We stand hypnotized by the dancers. He says I like to watch people.

Yeah. Laughter. Actually, my Scorpio is rising. Opposite my sun.

So what does that make you?

How can you fly and not know the sky? I tease him.

He's telling me about growing up in downtown LA. Only other person I ever knew who grew up there was my ex. I'm telling him I just ran away from the town *An Officer and a Gentleman* was filmed in. I'm even in a shot or two. I was the bartender in that restaurant on the water where the parents of the guy who hangs himself are eating.

Slow dancing. Keep talking. Toi is singing *I know a heartbreak when I see one.*

As the night proceeds I begin to dance more and more like my real self.

Where did you learn to dance so good?

Oh, I'm not! I'm off balance. Must be my Rocky Mountain high. I've only danced at sea level.

Sometime I said oh I used to hang out with a band. Did I say this? I don't think I told him anything about myself. Just where I'm from.

When you first see the Southern Cross you know you can't despair. You know how small this ship is.

I was in Chile six months. '79.

I was in Peru, Equador, Columbia in '79!

Terrible work. But interesting. In Santiago the men wear shirts and ties to order ice cream from a stand.

Did you see *Missing?* That movie?

No. But when you're in Chile you stay out of politics. Only a fool would get involved.

I say nothing. Just do your job. As in Viet Nam. As in Forks, Port Angeles. As in spraying. Logging the old growth.

He told me he sprays.

I say nothing.

He's going next to some place near Telluride, Colorado, the road east from Moab. In two weeks. Robin used to live in Telluride.

He's scared. I can see it. He feels a lot of pressure. I can feel it.

Was it the second night I asked him about geologists? He sneered. Called them neurotic.

The last set. I'm already feeling nostalgic. He and Casey point out a short old man in the crowd. They've been watching him the whole time they've been in Park City. He always has young girls hanging off him, he pats them on the behind. They tell a story of encountering him and a young girl in some real odd out of the way place and even there she was hanging on his arm, he was feeling her butt. We all stand there watching the guy. Short, cuddly, but at the same time, gritty like sand. Looks just like a poet I know, an orphan from Utah. I say Daddy. He says, you think? I watch. Yeah. Daddy. My father. Una's father. Old, rooty. The poet I know. Utah Patriarch. I'm not being political. That's what the Mormons call their men. All males at eighteen get the priesthood. The women pray to their husbands. Women can't stand in the prayer circle for their newborn. While I'm saying this the old guy pats the pretty girl on her very high ass. We all crack up. *He* doesn't worry about *his* heart.

A song about Tennessee. Oh dance with me, my Daddy's from Tennessee.

What?

My Daddy's from Tennessee. I say this so he knows that I'm from simple folks myself.

Sweaty. Last dance. Ten minutes. Then he's bought me something. Coffee and bourbon. No, that was the second night. First night, a Bud.

Moonlight is waiting at the door outside. He's very happy to see me, then bounds off, down Main Street. Psyche's parked in Swede Alley behind Main Street. I will think for weeks it's Sweet Alley, my Rocky Mountain high. The spot, under a large tree, will be my home. I keep asking what is that tree I'm parked under? A cottonwood. He points out his jeep, parked a few spaces away. We were bound to meet, he says. Come home with me. Home is a trailer out on the highway. There's a swift, sweet kiss. How shocking the first kiss always is. The Unknown of a stranger's mouth. You know how familiar it could become in your life. I say no. He doesn't leave.

We are sitting on the curb around a small patch of grass under the cottonwood tree next to my van. You live in it? Yeah. The cars rumble down the hill that is Main. Are they really going all the way back to the city? Already I realize the Utah liquor laws cause people to drink more than they normally would. I'm going to get a room to rent for the winter, either here or in Salt Lake City. I drove up today at noon, having been reluctant to come when I first got to Utah two weeks ago. I knew coming here would be coming home. I like the idea of trying a city for awhile. But when I got here, it had me instantly, I didn't even get out of the van, just let Moonlight out, it was pouring down rain. My dog hates the heat as much as I do. All that heat down there, the thousand-mile crossing. He just flopped down in it, raised his face to it, shut his eyes and never asked to get back in all afternoon. I had planned to drive my girlfriend Una to Moab to haul back her great grandma's table, but at the last minute she changed her mind. (I didn't tell him why. God.) Stayed in the van until six, just enjoying myself. Reading. Proofing my book. For the first time since I left Washington I felt comfortable, relaxed, cozy, the rain outside. Peed in Moonlight's purple bowl, now my piss can. I checked out a place to rent just as I was leaving Salt Lake, a two bedroom $87.50 house with garden, to share with female student. Great price, great location, nice house but it was oppressive to me. I didn't want to put myself in a house, then get a job to pay for it. Guess I'm addicted to the road!

Now on the curb. In the dewy wet mountain night with him, knowing I will not go home with him, but he is here. How deeply quiet the first feelings of love make you, how profound and beautiful and sad somewhere down some long corridor of your soul, how moody, dreamy, beautifully emotional. Memories. Lots of memories. How it keeps you awake though. I'd never sleep if I went home with him.

Remember that place, he says, near Norwalk, you'd sit in your car and roll *up* the hill?

Oh! You're the first person who's ever mentioned that place since I was a kid.

Yeah. It was in *Ripley's Believe It or Not*.

What was that, anyway?

Some sort of earth vortex.

We'd go there on our Sunday rides, turn off the motor. Then roll up the hill everytime! That's where I began to know about the earth.

I think they bulldozed it for a housing project.

Yeah, sure, that's what happened alright.

He tells me about his twenty-five foot trailer. Tells me exactly where it is. Out on I-80. I think I saw it. Those trailers just before the Mormon church, that old farmhouse with the horses.

He looks at Psyche. How long you been living in it?

Oh, this time, six months. Psyche's the name for the human soul.

What do you do for exercise?

Dance.

Finally I say very clearly, sternly, no. I'm not going home with you. You have to get up at six. It's after two now. You had better go. Suddenly I am very sad, knowing my oldest hangup. Unable to fuck a stranger.

Kisses me several times, standing on the asphalt in my cowboy boots, the strangeness of his tongue flicking in and out, his full lips, the taste of whisky. Something.

She floated out of the rain forest of the Olympic Peninsula, drifted east across Washington, Oregon, Idaho, the whole way spinning the dial for Willie Nelson. She'd never liked Country Western before but now suddenly it spoke of her soul. In Idaho she went north out of her way to see a town named Eden, her maiden name. It was almost a ghost town. Then she came down into Utah, taking a back road through the Sawtooth National Forest to Albion, Idaho. She wanted to see a town in Idaho named Albion. Her dog, a white Alsation, was named Albion Moonlight and once she had lived a long while in a tiny town named Albion on the Mendocino Coast of California. Albion, Idaho was not much larger than Albion, California but the old woman in the store had been to her Albion for the same reason she had come to hers. This woman advised her to go back to the interstate. Dangerous, she said. Terrible things happen down there. It'll turn to gravel and there you'll be. Out in the sage. But she was into it, the back road into Utah.

When it turned to gravel she came upon an old pickup, stalled. The meanest looking longhair she'd ever seen. His eyes so light blue in the dark leather of his face, they caused a glare. A boy about nine. Can I help you? Too soft. They tied a chain around her hitch, she pulled the pickup with the mean man and boy ten miles across the border to a station in Utah. She waved goodbye. Too warmly. They just stared.

Utah was her karma. She rode her first horse in Utah when she was nine. St. George. As soon as they crossed the Nevada and Arizona lines her father just stopped the car, asked a farmer if his daughter could ride his horse. She had written an important poem named "Utah." I want to go there: *the first line. A breakthrough for her in learning to be a poet: it was honest, direct, and in subsequent years, prophetic. When she wrote "Utah" she was living in Albion with a man who later moved to Utah, fell in love with a woman in Utah. When they returned to California they lived in the Hotel Utah in San Francisco, were employed as musicians there. Each week she saw their faces in the* Chronicle *beneath the big words* HOTEL UTAH. *She took a long time healing from that man.*

And then there was Una, her oldest friend, born and raised in the wild southwest of Utah, Moab. When they met as teenage mothers, Una, a Jack Mormon, had just been released from the Utah State Mental Hospital in Provo. Una was her first acid trip, her first psychedelic experience. Una's consciousness was as if she was from the moon. Una questioned everything she took for granted, assumed as the Truth. Una taught her to think. It was later that Una found the Church. Now for years Una had been giving her The Book of Mormon, Doctrine and Covenants, The Pearl Of Great Price *with inscriptions like* Mate of My Soul, *or* To the One Who Has Outlasted My Husbands. *She felt blessed to have this access to the only white American religion. Her karma, perhaps. This time Una would give her a book explaining the history of polygamy in the Church,* The Principle of Plural Marriage, *Wife Number One is always first. But to get into heaven the door must be held open for One and her husband by Wife Number Two. Wife Number Three . . . At this point in the study anger would blind her. The correct word is* polygyny. *Polygamy would mean that women could have more than one husband, too. She was convinced, given how independent and rebellious the older, rural Mormons are, and their doctrine—in her mind, the best part of Mormonism—of individual divine revelation, that there must be somewhere a Mormon woman practicing polygamy or polyandry, that is, a woman with several husbands. She told Una she was coming to Utah this time to find that woman. She wanted to write about her.*

She had had a number of husbands herself, though only in spirit and only serially. In the eyes of the law she was still married to a man she hadn't seen in fifteen years. In the eyes of her spirit she was still married to each of these men. One had even named her One after learning from Una its Mormon meaning. All her husbands had left her.

And so, at this point in her life, in the eyes of her soul, she had to change herself. She was on the road, she had come to Utah to rid herself of her monogamous nature. In her life many men had professed to love her but she had married the ones who professed not to love her. What is the Achilles' heel in a woman? She had always believed they did love her. It took their sudden and complete disappearances to finally convince her of what they had tried to tell her all along.

She was a fool for love, yes, but she was also, genuinely, a lover. She loved the world. She loved people. She loved herself. Her course was not to quit loving—she couldn't have changed herself that much—but to love more. She wanted to learn to love as she had never been able to with her great virginal—twin to her monogamous—nature. Many men. Physically.

She had learned from her husbands how to be nourished on very little, she had learned to be self-sufficient, to gain sustenance and love from hidden sources, to gain love in loving. She figured she was old enough now, wise enough, to learn to do the same with many men. She admired her sisters who had always done this. Now she wanted to find her brothers. She wanted them to find her, though she knew when they did they'd refuse to recognize her. This had always been true. Her greatest sorrow. But she could handle it, she was reconciled to never being loved as she loved. And secretly she still believed love is exchanged.

To change herself. But at every turn the road seemed to give out. What now? She had never slept with a married man. When she was very young she had taken a vow. Probably as a result of her best girlfriends' husband's hitting on her. Usually, almost always, when the women were in the hospital giving birth. This was such a pattern, so shocking and nauseating, she couldn't help but take pity on the men. Perhaps it was more than just the wife away from home, a chance to screw around. But why with the wife's best friend? Even though she rejected the husband it meant the two of them had a secret against her, her beloved friend, his wife. She knew something important about him that the wife didn't. This was wrong! And galling! That he could count on her not to tell. That the bonds of sisterhood were so weak. In the future she would tell, she would not be his partner, however passive, in the betrayal. Even if it meant she lost the friend. What kind of friendship, what kind of marriage is based on lies? And with this kind of knowledge at the core of her passion, how could she now sleep with a married man?

To change herself. At every turn, the road seemed to give out. For all her embrace of her generation's story she had never slept with a veteran. The gulf between herself and such a man had always been too great. She had a deep fear of being killed by her lover. She was an insomniac but when she did sleep this was the most recurring nightmare. To actually sleep with a real killer always struck her as stupid.

The next night, Saturday night, I'm standing in the same spot at the end of the bar watching the dancers and Toi and the Boys. Then he is there, standing a little in front of me, looking at the band. A punk couple, she blonde, long-waisted like me in her pedal pushers. He's Indian and weirded out.

He looks more handsome than I recall. In a black leather jacket, curly dark hair.

Hi.

His silhouette, the dancers behind it. Me behind him. Casey. Flashing lights.

Only the punk couple dance and one very drunk or more likely stoned-out-of-her-mind girl in Levis, boots, rhinestones across her breasts, cowboy hat. Toi and her ten-gallon.

How are you?

It was hard. A hellish day. Got a hangover. Took a nap. Should never take a nap. (Never heard a man say this, my feelings exactly.) I feel awful. It was close today. You know we spend most of it on our sides, studying the ground. Hard on the headache.

Explains to me the whole thing. Because I want to know.

Porcupine Prospect, north of here, east of Coalfield, the largest crew, the largest seismic prospect in the entire country. It's a survey area where seismographic data is being gathered and recorded to determine the underlying geological formation and structure. We measure the echoes from energy put out by explosives. We do portable work. All explosives.

I wrinkle my nose. So he tries again.

We measure the blast, the energy beneath the ground and by it we can tell the formations under the ground.

But why?

Oil.

You never hear an explosion. There is virtually no evidence that one has occurred. But the environmentalists would shit. The explosions are occurring all around here with precision regularity.

I'm surprised by his intent to explain it to me. He's really into telling me. I try hard to follow.

The prospect is divided into half-mile swaths. There are sixteen lines per swath. Drillers come in with portable rigs, drill 120 feet and plant a small charge. Crew come behind them and lay out lines. Geophysical phones are put in place, then the seismic geophysical recorders or boxes are put on line and tested. Crews are pulled out and the charges are electronically set off, in sequence.

The boxes are receiver points. The seismic information or earth vibration produced by the explosions underground and picked up by the units is fed into a central computer. The resulting information produces a 3-D picture.

They read the echoes on a tape. We haul around half a million dollars worth of computers. They record the data. The cost to drill one hole is phenomenal but if this prospect finds one structure that's never been played before it'll pay off.

The oil company hires the seismic company who hires the helicopter company. One hundred thousand dollars to pay for the helicopter.

We dance. He tells me more. He's possessed with an urgency to tell me.

All the helicopter pilots in the country are thirty-three to thirty-eight years of age. Yes. They're *all* Viet Nam vets. There aren't any younger pilots because they're not as good. It was great training, Viet Nam. The best.

You're sort of a geologist.

Geologists are neurotic.

He drinks bourbon and coke. The pilots in the Rockies are in the top ten percent. Because of the altitudes. It's migrant work, though. Did you know more vets have killed themselves than were killed in Viet Nam?

We are standing under the mural of red Castle Rock east of Moab in the La Sals again. Delicate Arch. The largest natural arch in the world. Johnny Lookfar took me there the first time. I can't remember his name but again the automatic linkage, connection, our two bodies standing side by side, like we are married or something. He's telling me this stuff like a wife. Now the Priests and Nuns are marching into the ancient valley. I have to hold myself from falling in, I feel him holding himself. This man is immoral, dynamiting Utah. Again, his words of worry about his heart. Some reference to the Andes. Chile.

You graduated from Redding High School?

Yeah. His eyes darting at me, suddenly paranoid. But he names the high school.

I'm beginning to like it here. Just as I knew I would. I'm going back down before I make a decision but I like it here. I talked to someone today who told me of living in his van all last winter in Evanston, Wyoming. Forty below! He used a Coleman stove for heat, had it on the front seat, kept the windows cracked so he wouldn't die. All winter. Comfy inside, he said. He said the Sioux did it in tepees. A van's nothing.

What do you want to drink?

Oh, I want wine. But they say I have to buy a whole bottle. And drink it. Can't take it out. Utah! You can't get a glass of wine anywhere. You can't be a stranger. You have to be a member. Just to get in a bar.

We dance again. Didn't wear your boots this time. I'm wearing my Chinese red cloth shoes. Rhinestone ragged Hawaiian shirt, the one I left Mendocino in. Too tight blue jeans. Later he complains of his boots. I say you should get some of these. He looks. I feel it rising in him. First resistance (resentment) to me. He says nothing.

Shasta's so beautiful. You make me homesick.

Yeah, it was a great place to grow up. West of Redding, all those lakes. Then the hippies went in, ruined it.

My brother lives in Modesto.

Modest, he says.

Yeah, I grin. (Oh, Sweetheart. Don't you recognize a hippy when you see one?)

Again he says Chile. When he was there. Where did you learn to dance so well?

Oh, I'm sloppy these days. When I'm happy I'm sloppy.

We three are standing there, end of the bar, watching the dancers. He says to Casey, you notice how there aren't any black people here.

I rush in, claiming the space. (Don't tell me you're racist.) Yeah, really. There never are in these towns.

He complains again about his hangover.

You should go home.

I don't want to leave you here.

My sister lives in Ashland. You know where that is?

Hundred thirty miles north of Redding. North side of Shasta. Oregon border.

A geographer. Like me.

Two cops standing in front of us. Nightly check of Main Street bars. Even they have gold chains around their necks, two a piece, in fact, in their uniforms. Their guns. He says, *So?*

Look. You want to have a date tomorrow night? My heart is in my mouth, but I said no last night. I say this so he can go home to bed. I'm surprised at my boldness. He doesn't strike me as the type of man you can be bold with.

OK. He jumps at it. Yeah. What time?

Well, time enough for you to have a nap after work.

Eight at your van.

Smiling. Touching the small of his back.

This boy must get some sleep.

I dance the rest of the night. Dance good and hard. By myself. With guys bold enough to ask. With arrowheads at their throats. Turquoise and silver on their hands and wrists. *Poor poor pitiful me!* Blue anteater boots. My pants too tight. Gained weight that thousand mile crossing. The crack in my pudendum showing. *All these boys won't leave me alone.*

(A boy from Texas. Works the oil fields in Kemmerer, Wyoming. He's foreman on the job. He keeps saying I can come up there. He'll get me a job. Good pay. Stringy-type boy.

I met a boy down in Yokohama. He picked me up and pulled me down. Please don't hurt me Mama.

Another guy says you remind me of Raggedy Ann.

Raggedy Ann?

Yeah. The way you just flop around like you're happy.

Ha! I hug him. And you should see the heart tattooed on my left breast. It says I love you. *Please*

don't cut me Mama.

I write on a Black Pearl napkin, Remember the Town Tavern graffiti in the women's room just before you left Port Townsend.

WHAT TO DO ABOUT TRIDENT SUBMARINE?

Sleep with the crew.)

Sometime in the night it begins to snow. It's only September tenth and it is snowing. I can hear it, feel it, the white stuff, filling up the world. Softening it. Moonlight moans a little for it. Helicopter keeping me awake.

Work on the proofs to my book in Psyche all Sunday morning, into the afternoon. Over and over again the oldest story. How I ended up here. Then walking up and down the mountain streets with Moonlight, trees turning to fall. Old houses perched haphazardly on the sides of the canyon, streets zigzagging up. Mouths of old mines. At the top looking over the pretty town, studying the land, figuring out where I am. Highway 248 to Heber City and the Uintas, rare east-west

mountain range. Can't see the van, canyon too steep and narrow.
Moonlight barking. Echoes. Can't help but run back down, the street
so steep. Jogging in your cowboys. Go into The Alamo. Read the Salt
Lake Sunday paper about a woman who's running for district attorney. She's wife number five to Isaac . . . They don't give his last
name because then he'll be harassed. If she's elected she'll work for the
legitimization of polygamy. She says it is not illegal now in the state of
Utah, only bigamy is. The reporter keeps commenting on her intelligence and physical beauty.

A guy named Skip talking at me. A helicopter pilot. Chartered tours
for real estate companies, helicopter skiing.

Yeah, it's hot.

Pool players. Levis. Levis through everything. My whole life. The
juke box. *If you wanna hang out you have to take her out, cocaine.* Football
on the big screen. Three beers in front of me. Alamo special, Skip explains. Six beers for a dollar. Only catch is, you gotta order all six at
once.

Ever been in a helicopter? Listen, I'll take you up. An eagle's eye
view of it all. Nothing like an airplane. *We fly em low and we fly em slow.*
Helicopter tours convince people to buy condos here. He says this
ironically. When folks drive up they get the feeling it's an isolated
town. But a chopper ride gives them a new perspective. A bird's eye
view of the density of ski facilities here. They can see Alta and Snow-
bird are just over the ridge. Last week we had a couple from New York.
Fondness now in his voice. They weren't sure they wanted to buy a
place up here. Took them up for a half an hour. When we landed they
had their checkbook in hand, bought a condo for five hundred thou.

She's gonna go, man. There's no holdin her back. Might as well get
in on it. Make some bucks. There's a plan to build a tram from the airport in Salt Lake to Park City. It's easier to get to Park City from LA
than to Mammoth, if you can believe that. Major airlines. And the
snow's the best. The best, man, *in the world.* That's why the U.S. ski
team is here. Powder, man, pure powder. The clouds come across that
basin out of the Sierras, the salt flats just suck the moisture right out of
them. By the time they dump here, they're pure powder.

Are you a vet?

Oh yeah. For sure. We all are. He downs a glass in one chugalug. Left some of my best friends over there. Flew in missions where choppers went down all around me.

You ever get hurt?

Nope. In two years I only had one bullet in my copter. Came in right behind my seat and exited out the top of the cabin.

Second beer, I'm getting talkative myself. I met a helicopter pilot the other night. Sheepishly, clinching my teeth, I sort of have a crush.

He names a few guys. No. He doesn't live here. Migrant work. Couple of weeks at Porcupine Ridge.

He's scared of you.

But why?

Why shouldn't he be? It's survival, man. He pats his heart. Nurture or torture. Whole helicopter crews came back in body bags. He talks to a little girl a minute about the inlay in his boots, then says they fly off, helicopter pilots.

How did you become one?

A draft dodger. Remember that term? He tells a long, elaborate story. Chicago. Canada. Running. In love with a girl named Candy. The sixties. A real cute little blonde. Turned out she was fucking his best friend all along. Blew him away. Signed up the next day. Because of his college they gave him helicopters. My best friend, he signed up the day after that. They said we'd be together in Nam. The Buddy System. We're still close.

What happened to Candy?

Who knows? We disappeared into Nam.

He points out the woman at the end of the bar. As if I hadn't already been caught by her. She's waiting for her old man. Bringing a bird in from Wyoming. Romney's legendary through the whole Rockies. The best. The Hippy Pilot, they call him. He's crazy. Really crazy. He flew his last mission over Nam naked. Said he wouldn't wear his uniform to do the shit. Said he couldn't do that to the American flag.

She is small, blonde, Utah tough, probably young, though her skin is already desert parched. The four-year-old girl is her daughter named Bell crawling all over her and on the floor. The floor covered in peanut shells. Guess Utah liquor laws don't include kids. Oh, they do everything to encourage you to have kids in this state. Let the saints come down! He signals for La Rue to move down. Like tingaling, he says when he introduces Bell to me. Heavenly white curls spilling down her faded Levi vest, her faded flannel shirt, her faded Levi pants, her scuffy cowboy boots. Cowgirl, she corrects me. For sure. A saint come down.

In '66, La Rue says. Romney was in Nam in '66 when he saw it was fucked. He was already decorated, the DFC. The Distinguished Flying Cross. He was brilliant. Grew up in these mountains. Other side, Denver. Grew his hair long, smoking pot before anyone. He saw it was fucked.

They talk about something that happened in Borneo. I'm here, I want to help out. A street without joy. Or named Joy. Viet Nam, Skip says, the most beautiful place in the world. Only two places have white beaches, Viet Nam and Florida. Did you know Teddy Roosevelt went tiger hunting in Viet Nam?

I really love that guy, La Rue says. '66 when he saw it was fucked. He marched into his commanding officer, stripped, stood there stark naked, said he wasn't flying anymore. He was the first hero over there.

Love is what we came here for. Who's song is that?

Proposed to me at This Is the Place Monument. Now she's talking directly to me across the corner of the bar. You'll really dig Romney. He'll dig you too, I can tell. You're his type. You ever come to Moab? You can always find us at The Poplar Place. Come there. You'll know you're home.

Skip's getting a little drunk. He keeps saying I can be his roommate. You *can't* stay in your van for the winter. Gets too cold. He lives out in Kamas. A condo up on the side of the mountain. Talks about the stars, the quiet. There are nights when you're with a woman and you wake up in the middle of it hearing choppers and shaking.

Helicopter pilots were the real heroes of Viet Nam, La Rue says.

The Grateful Dead: Truckin.

We could bring in the moving girl if you want to go that far.

Skip's telling me about shooters and linemen and juggies. I say I gotta go. Maybe I *will* move in with you. If you get a third roomie and I get a job. I couldn't afford half the rent. I tell La Rue and Bell I will see

them in Moab sometime. Skip walks me to the door. Be careful. I love
that guy too, but they're into group sex. She's just one of Romney's
wives.

I'm in the van at eight, searching for a needle to sew on a button. Give
up when he knocks, look for a pin. I hand him my manuscript. Here.
Want to hold the original? I'm done. I'm fucking done with this thing!
I've been working on it since 1975.

I know somehow it will hurt him, hurt us, but how can I not share it
with him, this wonderful moment, he here at the very end. I want to
celebrate. I want him to love me for it, not fear me. I want to say all this
to him but I don't.

I don't think I told him I'm a poet. Maybe one brief reference.

And I want him to see my last name.

Sitting in the door, pulling on my boots. His jeep parked next to my
Psyche. Feeling very sexy.

He's standing there in Swede Alley I still think is Sweet, looking at
the front page. Just staring. Not a word.

It's damp, wet. Stepping down into the parking lot I say now that
you know I'm a poet do you still want to have dinner with me?

Clearing his throat. Hard time saying well I'm sure there are other
things about you that are interesting.

He actually said this.

Up on Main Street, old Park City. Where to eat? Listen, I asked you
to dinner but I don't have any money.

I have lots of money. We look in a few places. Walk up, around.
Closed.

I refuse to eat in a place called The Eating Establishment, he says. It
turns me off when a place names itself that way.

We are coming down the street, the two of us and Moonlight, he is
telling me of Robert Redford's favorite place to eat near Heber City.
How he and the crew went there. How small it was, cotton red-
checked tablecloths, maybe six tables. He thinks this strange.

I take his arm.

We go in to Car 19. No, don't worry about Moonlight. He'll be

okay. He's never been leashed. A large place. We're the only customers.

I keep trying to see what he looks like. I can't quite. It's the feeling.
Beautiful, wonderful, tender feeling, falling in love. It puts everything
on edge. A love on things.

We are seated at the table far across from each other. After the
waitress takes our order, he steak, me shrimp, I up and seat myself on
the corner next to him.

Well, hello, he says, just as he said it on the next Sunday morning at
the cafe when I did this again.

The waitress is sort of amazing to me. Strong. Hard. Masculine. We
keep eyeing each other.

Suddenly I need a mirror. Some privacy. I have no idea what I look
like. As I get up he asks me about wine, remembering my rant against
the liquor laws. Anything you want, I say.

In the bathroom, the harsh light, my rags, my ugliness, my age. My
hair washed in cold water in the Memorial Building basement, didn't
get all the soap out. My nose broken out like a kid. But I look old. Try
to do something. Hard to dress without a mirror. Take off the pink
top. Too short. Then suddenly, in one angle, glance, all this has
helped, I look beautiful.

When I climb the stairs he is looking at me. I feel like I'm entering
the palace. I think he's stunned by my beauty.

He got the small size wine. Called a split, I think. We eat delicious
vegetables. His steak is mammoth. Bloody.

When she brings the check he looks, I try to see, smiling, tease, he
won't let me see. But I plan to pay you when I get my job.

Not bad.

He puts a twenty-dollar bill on the tray. I pour the wine. I'm going
to drink the rest. I can tell you don't care for wine.

We talk, laugh, stare. The wind never stops blowing on Porcupine
Ridge. The toe of his boot slides into the arch of mine. Then the
waitress and he are exchanging.

I'm waiting, she finally says, for enough money.

Oh. He looks again at the check. Pulls out a fifty-dollar bill. Clearing
his throat.

Let's go get drunk. Annoyed. Rising. A unique idea, he adds, ironically. Something different.

He's afraid he's going to die. He's afraid he's crazy like his mom.

Climbing Main Street. Well, the boys are here.

HELICOPTER PILOTS KEEP IT UP LONGER. Crew trucks. He's excited they are here. Though he's been with them all day, all week. Their dirty, red mud, high-sitting pickups lining both sides of the street, grabbing you right in the cunt, the heart, the eyes. Beautiful. Intimidating. The boys. So macho it's funny. Moonlight pissing their tires.

Walking in. The Black Pearl. Of Great Price. *Once upon a time in the West*. The high wind of the guitar across the mountains. Then the lope of the horses down. We each bought a two-week membership. All of them turning. Big screen. Football. Brotherhood. Nervousness. Camaraderie. The news. Train strike is on. Patrick and Sean hopping a freight here to visit me. *No use feigning you don't know nothin. Still gonna get you if you don't do somethin.*

Introduced. Dark-haired, strange and beautiful young man. My mechanic. *Sittin on a fence, that's a dangerous course. You could even catch a bullet by a peace-keeping force.*

He buys him a drink. I was a bad guy today.

To the bartender: I want to buy all that man's drinks.

Even the hero gets a bullet in the chest.

Again, to me: I was a bad guy today.

Some of you mothers outta lock up your daughters.

Turning on my stool to watch TV.

Turning back to watch his crew.

Turning back to talk to him.

Once upon a time. In the West.

My life with the boys. The bars, the bands, the teams, the guys, the hoboes, the hippies, husbands, hitchhikers, treeplanters, poets. Sometimes I think I'm more boy than they are.

The mechanic saying once you survive the bullet.

Lady writer on the TV. Dire straits, alright.

Turning back to watch the bar. Horseshoe in the center of the large room. All the glitter of the mini bottles. Mirrors. Two male bartenders. White dress shirts, vests, lace garters on their biceps. They hold two, three, four mini bottles in the palm of their left hand and in a ballet sweep with the right, off all the tops in one twist, snapping the bottles over into set-ups, while the right flies around the back, caps into the trash, then the left flies out with the bottles. The best performance I saw of this was at The Sundown in Salt Lake. The gay bartender shirtless in his dance, muscles rippling, ass high.

Just the way that her hair fell down around her face. Then I recall my fall from grace. Another time, another place.

Come in next week to apply for a job. When Andy's here.

He orders me another split.

She knew all about history. You can hardly write your name.

I'm trying to learn about football.

He never asks why to any of my comments.

Something about playing football in high school. Linebacker and offensive tackle. In those days we went both ways.

Talk about the Virgin Mary. Yeah I know. I'm talking about you and me.

Casey comes over, arm around his shoulder. You know who the Rotary Club elected for its man of the year?

The ironic rises all the way up his face. Vic Morrow.

Great laughter. Even I get it. That actor killed on the set last year. Chopper accident. He and two Viet Namese kids.

He seems so depressed. He apologizes. I'm depressed. And tired. How neurotic he seems. I keep the joke to myself. Casey is saying the crew was crawling all over the mountain. The wind blowing like a mother. The mechanic says I hung around till the birds pulled them out.

Do you have any kids?

Head nodding, yes, three.

How old?

A boy, fourteen. Just started high school. Susan and Sarah, ten and eight.

And a wife?

I'm in the process now of divesting myself of her. I hate her.

Looking at him.

She won't communicate. I can't get her to communicate. She just won't talk to me. I've tried everything.

I know he's lying. I know it's the other way around. What a line.

Do you have any kids?

Finally. Here goes. Yes.

How old are they?

Head ducking to my arms on the counter. They're grown. Eighteen and twenty-one.

His turn to look at me. Creedence Clearwater. *Rollin' on the river*. You must have been ten years old.

CCR saved my *ass* in Nam! Casey.

And you went to Viet Nam when you were seventeen.

Not me. I was twenty-four when I went into the army. I'd gone to several colleges. Got married. She was pregnant. They said I could have helicopters.

Turning on my stool to watch Casey and the black-haired mechanic shoot pool. *Holiday in Cambodia and we're all dressed in black*. The Dead Kennedys.

How can you divorce kids?

Men do. They just disappear.

No. No, no, no.

The mechanic is a great pool player.

Yeah, he's good. My life's in his hands.

He's afraid he's going to die.

Once years ago I was having an affair with someone. I won't tell you *who* she was. I was living in Pasadena and I felt myself going crazy. I remember flying over the Rose Bowl and feeling myself losing it. It was the only time I ever felt that.

I wanna start a forest fire, the Dead Kennedys.

Now why am I telling you this?

Because you're about to have an affair with me. Because you're falling in love with me. I don't say this.

I don't know anymore what's right.

He orders another coke high.

And that fucker wind is getting to me. You know just the rustling of leaves of a tree can alter the seismic reading. That's how sensitive the equipment is.

I was trying to cheer him up, but it was a bad joke. You should be a geologist. I put my arm around his shoulder just like Casey did. Just like the buddy system.

We sit there with the guys till closing. When Dylan sings Like a Rolling Stone I tell him Park City's the town Joe Hill tried to organize. You can still see his signature other side of this wall, the jail where he carved it in adobe. Wrote that IWW song in there, "Joe Hill's Last Will." *My will is easy to decide. For there is nothing to divide. My kin don't need to fuss and moan. Moss don't grow on a rolling stone.* When the Rolling Stones come on I say it was down in Salt Lake where he went before the firing squad. Sugar House Park. He says and that's the magazine too. I say I always liked it that he pulled the blindfold off the last minute to watch his killers. We walk to our vehicles parked side by side in Sweet Alley. *No one ever taught you how to live out on the street.* When we kiss Moonlight whines. Jealous, I say. He knows I love you. I'm so unlovable he says. He says you know where I live. He drives off.

The very week she met the helicopter pilot the headlines screamed FIRST MAN TO WHIRLYBIRD AROUND THE WORLD. *Ross Perot circumnavigated the globe in a helicopter named* Spirit of Texas.

The very week she met the helicopter pilot White River opened bids on construction of a decline that will take it into target oil-shale ore zone 1,150 feet below the surface. White River's underground mine will be the largest in the world.

"With an earthjarring thud, some 20,000 pounds of ammonium nitrate blasted a rock shelf into 30,000 cubic yards of rubble.

"It all began eight years ago in March in Salt Lake City when the White River partners put in the top bonus bid of $120.7 billion, to lease the tracts. That was after the Middle East Yom Kippur War triggered the OPEC price hike and embargo."

Four months later in July, Una's second husband, Johnny Lookfar, died from this contract. A car accident coming around Strawberry Reservoir after working a seventy-hour week.

All week she read of boom towns with names like Parachute, Rifle, Battle-

ment Mesa going bust. The bubble burst May 2. Black Sunday they call it. *In Parachute forty percent of the apartments built for the boom are empty. Many refugees from the recession-ridden Midwest came to this rugged piece of Colorado high country and staked their hopes on oil shale. In Rifle where mirrored glass and steel buildings shot up over the past year entire floors are finished and empty—70,000-square feet of vacant office space. Snow-covered mountain peaks in the mirrors. On a lot midway between Rifle and Parachute about 100 pieces of heavy machinery—bulldozers, dump trucks, backhoes—sit idly now. Colony, a magnificent mountaintop effort to mine oil-bearing rock and extract petroleum was to have been the centerpiece of the nation's synfuel program. But costs escalated, the blip in the petroleum shortage disappeared. So did gasoline lines. OPEC prices, though rising, seemed gauged to staying just within the flashpoint that would have triggered a domestic shale oil industry. Exxon called it quits.*

"It's so pretty up here. I can't believe people won't want to live here," the mayor of Parachute said. Parachute, where boom-or-bust cycles are as old as the history of the rugged pioneers who homesteaded here, where people like the mayor have seen oil companies come and go.

Alarm grew in her for the earth. Someone told her that somewhere in Utah they had punctured a hole through the earth's mantle. The earth's mantle! *he kept shrieking. She wasn't sure what this meant. She visited Hansen Planetarium. "To Worlds Unknown." A star show that takes you to the rings of Saturn and to witness the violent volcanoes of Jupiter.*

That very week kissing for sexual pleasure was declared punishable by 100 lashes in Iran. "Under the new law, sexual offenses could only be proved if four men were brought as witnesses. In the absence of a male witness the court would accept two women substitutes."

But the news stories that really caught her were of polygamy. POLYGAMY—BEST OF TWO WORLDS? *Photographs of his nine wives dressed in white in the feature section of the Sunday paper. One of them is thirteen.* A *prepubescent thirteen. Photo of the patriarch. Jacob. Alex Jacob. His beard, his crinkly eyes. The women, the article says, are all intelligent, attractive and independent.*

Several of the wives have professional careers. Others assume the domestic, educational and construction responsibilities at "Long Haul," the family's home in Glen Canyon City. All consider their marriages more successful than monogamous relationships.

"*The polygamous relationship is simplified with more wives,*" *said Margaret who married as a third wife, just as she had always wanted.*

"*I grew up hoping I would be a third wife. I just had it in my head that that's what I wanted to be,*" *she said. She is the only wife who was reared as a child of polygamy.*

"*I could have taken third on down, but I would never want to be a first or second wife.*"

"*There is a tremendous amount of respect and willingness of Jacob's wives to meet his every need,*" *Bodicca, wife number two, said. "Even so, polygamy is largely to the advantage of the wives. They have the freedom to pursue their own interests, yet have a large family that is supportive and well cared for.*"

"*The drawback is that polygamy works too well,*" *Jacob said. "That's the sadness of it. It works too well. You get rid of the oppression and you enjoy your wives' company so much, there isn't time enough in the day to spend as much time together as you want to spend. But that sadness is easier to endure than the other, not wanting to go home.*

"*The more wives you have, the easier it is to be in love,*" *Jacob added.*

The limited amount of time and attention has been cause for some jealousy and insecurity for some of the wives in the past. They learn to overcome those feelings early on; to accept them as "imaginary" rather than intrinsic.

"*There are a lot of personal feelings you have to get rid of because you just can't have the conventional notion of a marriage relationship that you might have had,*" *Bodicca admitted. "So it's a choice; you can be married to one guy and sleep with him every night, if you want that. There are times when you may really want to be with Alex and he might not be there, because a lot of things take him away from home, or he's with another wife.*"

Jacob has been married more than twenty times. He considers himself a political activist and as such is trying to restore the political atmosphere of Israel's ancient kingdom. "Our government is a patriarchy, one of the many in a confederacy of patriarchies," *Bodicca explained. "Every man is head of his own family: Alex Jacob is Alexander, leader of the Kingdom of God.*"

The children of the patriarchy are educated through a private school on the Long Haul compound. Young boys are members of the government's "Royal Guard," a military academy. Youngsters enter the guard at two.

They live in a segregated area furnished with bunk beds, a lounge and kitchen area. The boys are provided with guns and are taught how to use them. "The reason for the Royal Guard," Jacob said, "is to promote discipline and respect above all."

She noted that in the group picture Dawn, the thirteen-year-old, was standing in his arms. She noted that the little boys in the guardhouse were all acting tough, unsmiling, hands on their hips. Names like Stonewall, Maness, Manson. The six-year-old girl was smiling, burping her three-month-old brother, Vallis Christian, on her shoulder. Everyone except Vallis Christian was wearing white.

The oldest question rose in her. How is it that through all time women have handed their children over to all that is the opposite of the miracle of birth?

She remembered something she had read years ago. Over the long haul, polygynous marriages rarely produce more children than a large monogamous one. This is due to the fact that women are fertile only forty-eight hours of the month and the odds of the "polyg" hitting one during ovulation is greatly reduced if he's not sleeping with her nightly, if he is having to hit a dozen others also. To let the saints come down, to populate the Kingdom of Deseret was a main motivation in the Church's doctrine of plural marriages, but, rationally, it should have been the women taking multiple husbands. If a woman has more than one husband the odds of pregnancy are greatly increased. The patriarchal line is quickly lost, however. Discipline and respect also.

In my Psyche, curled around Moonlight. All night. Waking to him. Then, loss. Holes in the earth. All around here, explosions regularly. The cottonwood brushing her roof.

Helicopters are like butterflies. Like Psyche, the soul.

All I ever wanted was one man for life.

Apply for jobs all week. The Cowboy, The Branding Iron, The Ore House. With each application I drop my age a year. How can an astrologer lie about her age? Anyone with knowledge of the planets can see I couldn't possibly have been born that year. But the Club won't even take one from me. We hire only inexperienced twenty-one-year-olds. Wrote an outlandish essay for The Black Pearl (WHY DO YOU WANT TO WORK FOR THE BLACK PEARL?) All my work history. All those bars and hotels and restaurants. Sea Galley, Sea Gull, Brass Whale, Fog Horn, Tip Top, The Surf. Having to conjure up the names of those men, my bosses. Just the thought of them, *still*. You sure do move around a lot, a young Mormon manager says. I can see his pink undergarment beneath the fitted white shirt. The young ones so programmed. Lost the wilderness of their parents, their land.

In The Patriarchy now, got the blues bad. Trying to write it out. How I keep looking for him in everyone who walks in. How my lips long to kiss. And kiss. How horny I am and no one turns me on. Does that word come from Karen Horney? Never seemed right for a woman. How *desirous* I am.

And I hear how they speak of their wives. Wife is worse than nigger. Worse than anything. That guy called his wife my blister.

Why do women have two sets of lips?

So they can piss and moan at the same time.

I get up from my corner, order a beer. No. No glass. I like to *suck it* straight from the bottle. Guy at the bar says there's only two women I've ever seen with a face like yours. Melina Mercouri and Vanessa Redgrave. You won't be offended, will you if I tell you what I see in your face? You have a totally frightened look but it's masked by a totally cool one.

So I sit down on the stool next to him. That's pretty good. He introduces me to his friend on the other side of him. He says, Jeanne Moreau too. What were you writing over there, your diary? Yeah. They are owners of the newspaper here. Need any writers? They landed here because of a broken crankshaft. This town's full of such stories. People cashing in the return portion of their tickets to help come up with the first and last month's rent. They were on acid when they got the idea to buy the newspaper, still tripping when they bought it. Seven thousand dollars in 1976. Now it's worth a hundred thousand dollars. Now, the guy who saw my face says, I'm president of the Chamber of Commerce.

I look out the window. A man is trying to put a long hypodermic needle into Moonlight's butt. I turn over a table charging out of there. The dog catcher! I'd have killed that man if he'd drugged my dog.

I'm in the Hilton Hotel, the Room at the Top, overlooking Salt Lake City, the Wasatch Front, and all the desert west, north and south. The gleaming lake way out there. Every place I walk into I look for him. I expect him. Applied for a job. I like what they wear, I'd look good. Fuchsia Danskins. And they're all blondes, my age. I should have a good chance. Decided I'd better go over my galleys one more time. It's 2:30. I'm drinking Coors, breaking a ten-year political ban. Afraid of all the chemicals I've been drinking. Men, as always, watching. They rarely approach though when I'm working. There's one in a black suit, moustache, sleazy thin, leaning back on his elbows at the bar. Very strange dude. I keep working. When you're closed you're closed. Men are pretty smart about this. When you're open, boy, do they know.

Pages go by, I'm not concentrating, just remembering, not really seeing the print, thinking of the pilot, wondering where Porcupine Ridge is, how to get there. I find one typo, a big one. The whole poem is about a woman named Geneva but she's only named twice. And here, one of those times, her name is set as Genevieve.

The thin man is standing now above me.

What are you doing?

I look up. Really slimy. Drink in his hand, bolo tie. Glance to the clock. Three. Have to get these in the mail by five.

I'm proofing the galleys of a book.

Yours?

Yes.

That's what I thought you were doing. I'm a writer myself. I recognized what you were doing.

So rare for me to be unkind. I don't know what it is. Perhaps feeling the triumph of myself in this last moment with my creation.

What kind of book is it?

As always, the hesitation. Look right into the wrung-out face. It's an epic poem.

You publishing it yourself?

No.

A vanity press?

No.

He stands there over me a long time. I look to the incredible turmoil of sky coming over the mountains. Just staring at me.

Do you ever write prose?

Yes. Yeah, I do. Trying to soften myself.

I write mysteries.

My only smile. I write mysteries myself. Always searching for the clues.

Look. I'm only trying to be helpful. I'm a mystery writer. If you ever write prose and need any help you should get hold of my editor. He's a great man. He'll help you. For years I wrote in a closet. I just couldn't get started. You should contact him. He's responsible for who I am now.

He writes the names on the napkin. Dr. Benkins, McGraw Hill, Chicago. He says this as he writes.

I am so cold to the poor man. Later I look up and he is gone and that's when I feel bad, very bad.

I go down in the streets, the wide wide streets of Salt Lake City Una says proves Brigham was a prophet. He saw in his vision of the city *automobiles!* I let Moonlight out of Psyche, mail my epic poem to Minneapolis. We wander around as the fashionable people pour out of the offices, Temple Square. Funny, how in all cities I'm in Lima, Peru, now. Always looking for my husband. Except here my eyes search out the lines of their undergarments, the silky pink one-piece they receive when they marry in the Temple, worn always next to the skin, that is, *under* their bras, panties, jockey shorts. In the old days they didn't take them off for baths. Years ago Una told me the secrets of the Marriage Ceremony. She wasn't supposed to tell and now I carry the burden of the secret, wanting so badly to write it. The ceremony so sexual. Brigham Young in the middle of the street, ass to the Temple, hand out to the Bank of Deseret. Everyone says this. Walking by his house, never could bring myself to go inside. Forty-eight wives. I don't care how you bring 'em, just bring 'em young. Before the Saints fled Navoo and he was martyred, Joseph Smith had the dream of polygamy. It shocked him. He said to Brigham Young you won't believe what God showed me. It was the only vision he didn't have the balls to instigate. Crossing the country Brigham took over. He had no trouble at all. But the widow, Mrs. Joseph Smith, hated Brigham Young. She said that in *that* way her husband was weak like all men, it wasn't God, a Divine Calling, it was a wet dream. So at the eastern base of the Rockies, they split up, she took her group down to Missouri and founded The Reorganized Church of Latter-day Saints.

When I walk along your city streets and look into your eyes. When I see that simple sadness I see lines, lies.

Two cute missionaries trying to get me into the Temple. Moonlight pissing on the wrought-iron gate. But your dog can't come. Rooms up there sealed until the Second Coming when Jesus will descend the east side of the Rockies on a white stallion. Then two more missionaries (I'm sure) trying to hand me a free ticket to see Reagan in the Salt Palace at nine in the morning. I'm laughing are you kidding? I am awash in haughtiness.

I go into a bookstore, telling Moonlight to stay, and see the blurb on a pyramid display of a book about Sal Mineo's murder. It is the poet Diane Wakoski. "No writer since Ross MacDonald has captured the spirit of the land of Southern California as well." I look at the Room at the Top napkin crumpled in my back pocket. *Ross MacDonald.* Rows and rows of mysteries. I've never read a mystery. Two mystery writers named MacDonald. One is the man in the Hilton. His photo. The man I was so cold to. Why do I feel so sad?

Because I only felt him after he was gone.

Wonder if he knows Arthur Conan Doyle's first Sherlock Holmes book takes place in Utah?

It's been a long way from anywhere like heaven to this town. Your town.

The weather fluctuated wildly between extreme heat and snow, hail and rain. Sometimes in the basin she'd watch the lightning run all down the Wasatch Wall. She had bad moments of not knowing where she was. Her intent to change herself seemed not only absurd but tragic.

She thought she would live in the little town. She had never lived in high mountains. She liked her Rocky Mountain high. On the other hand, maybe she'd go to Kemmerer, Wyoming. Work in the oil fields. Make some money for the first time in her life.

Late one night she went to Una's in Provo. Her oldest girlfriend had just become a grandmother. She was sitting in the dark mobile home. Just sitting there in the dark.

What's the matter, Una?

I lie down, close my eyes. But I can't find revery. I'm telling God if he doesn't give it to me soon I'm giving up.

A long quiet. The two of them sitting there. On the wall she knew was the painting of Jesus meeting Mary at the well. Una believed, like many Mormons, though it's unofficial doctrine, that Jesus married the Mary he met at the well. How could he have not? she always said. Marriage is the sacred purpose of Terrestrial Life.

You know what we did today? We filed bankruptcy! *She started crying. It was so humiliating. The Church teaches that material prosperity is one of the sacred purposes of Terrestrial Life. She cried some more. They say I have to go to court with my husband because I signed the contracts. I don't think that's right. The Church doesn't either. A wife is to be protected from these things.*

But Una you bought this shit, not Blackie. She thought this but she said Una I'll go with you. I'll dig a bankruptcy trial. You know what I feel about all that. I'll take notes for my book about money.

After awhile Una said I'm going back on my medication. My doctor keeps saying I must.

Mormons are not to ingest mood-altering substances: coffee, tea, alcohol, drugs. Hot soup is considered a stimulant; one is to sip it lukewarm. On the other hand Mormons believe scientific advancement is a sacred purpose of this life and the Nineteenth Amendment, which gave women the right to vote, should be repealed. And so, statistically, more women of the LDS faith are on tranquilizers and speed than any other group in the United States.

He says the synapses of my brain just need extra help. It's not the same as being a drug addict. He tries to convince me of this anyway. You love stories, listen to this one. He told this at General Conference to introduce new by-laws. He said that the bishop's ignorance of psychiatry in this story is sinful. It is as if an apostle had performed open heart surgery without any training.

He had a patient who was the wife of one of the twelve apostles. She had been hysterical for a long time, several years on heavy medication. Finally, the truth came out. She had found in her husband's things an extensive photo collection of pornography, S&M, homosexuality, the whole bit. After a long time she confided in her bishop. The bishop told her that she had grown so unattractive to her husband that he had had to resort to these means of sexual pleasure, sexual pleasure being every man's terrestrial right. The bishop counseled the elderly wife of the apostle to buy a new wardrobe, paying particular emphasis to her lingerie. He even counseled her to take off her undergarments!

At this point Una burst into more tears. She bought sexy lingerie! *She choked out these words like gunshot. You know what happened? Her voice now spits and whispers.* The woman lost all her hair! She went completely bald!

She put her arms around her friend, held her. She could feel the grief at the core of her being. The Patriarchy. And something else. Husband number two. Johnny Lookfar. The Temple Recommend for Una's and Johnny's marriage to be sealed in Eternity had come two months before he was killed. As far as Eternity goes death is a small matter, but as far as marriage goes, life, this terrestrial existence, is the only chance the soul has for finding the mate promised at the Beginning. "For in the resurrection they neither marry, nor are given in marriage." Matthew 22:30. Mormons believe in resurrection but not to this earth. And so marrying (and baptizing) the dead is a common practice. One goes through the ceremony with or as a stand-in. In every Temple there are full-time workers researching the names and dates of the dead and then baptizing them. Blackie, though he was not sealed to anyone in Eternity had agreed, so great was his love for Una, to act as Johnny's stand-in. But at the last minute, Una married Blackie, not Johnny, sealing herself off from Lookfar, stranding him in Eternity without his promised mate. I just couldn't do that to the living man, *she said. Over and over. It was the first and only time the poet ever witnessed the Latter-day Saint stumble on the avowed code of her soul.*

Then Una mentioned the famous princess who died that morning in a car accident.

It's affected me too, more than I would have thought. I was in Scaggs and somehow got caught in an Enquirer *photograph of her and her daughter climbing out of the Mediterranean onto a yacht. I kept staring at her, the backs of her heavy thighs in the dog-food aisle. When I got out to Psyche the radio was announcing the bulletin of her death.*

It's us, you know. It's us.

Una, we're not that old!

It is long past midnight and they are curled together beneath Una's homemade quilt on the sofa that has just been repossessed. Johnny Lookfar's sons are asleep down the hall, fourteen-year-old Dede, the last child from Una's first husband, Rulon, is in juvenile hall. Blackie, a highway patrol-man, is out on duty. I'm always afraid he won't come back. Car accidents, she shivered. You never get over the shock.

Una collected elephants, all kinds, stuffed, ceramic, brass, photos, pillows. She had found a postcard of the woman herding the elephants at The Black Pearl, sent it to her. In the dim light from the street outside she could see it propped on the TV. The woman reminded her of Una, her dramatic dance with the cosmos. Beneath this woman and herd of animals she had met the pilot.

I know what I'm supposed to do about Dede. Become totally selfless, think only of her, her needs, move into her. But when she says I hate you I just feel anger and weariness. I know what it is to hate a parent. I hate my father.

I look at Eagle, we've been so close. He's almost twelve now. I look into his face and I feel this anger rising in me. In a year, it'll be over, he'll hate me too.

She thought that's because you tacked those rules of the priesthood above his pillow, you gave him Dede's room the hour they took her. First rule of the Patriarch: Hate your mother. Second rule: Obliterate your sister. She thought these things but wild elephants couldn't have pulled them from her, not even the fear that her greatest friend was dying from them. She had learned this lesson a long time ago. Either keep your mouth shut or lose your friend. Una was the rare love for whom she kept her mouth shut. The ex-ample of her life was the only argument. Una probably thought the same thing, their friendship being something profoundly other than doctrines. Objecting to the other's path was the taboo but sharing was the heart of their love. Each recognized the spiritual quest of the other. Una's stories of the nuthouse had been constants in her psyche for almost twenty years. The most creative, psychic mind she had ever encountered had come within eight days of a lobotomy. She was under age, they couldn't find anyone to sign the papers. Most of the women in the hospital were polygamists hauled back from Mexico. They weren't crazy at all, Una used to say, just crazy in love. They liked being one of many wives, they liked all those sisters. They believed it was God's will. So the state lobotomized them.

And now, she thought, you gave them Dede. The most perplexing thing for her in growing older was witnessing her friends whose most oft-told stories were of being victims of their parents now betray their children in the same way. The despair, the sense of futility that washed through her was almost as bad as when her husbands deserted her, as when again she fell for the same type of man. Where, oh where is the future, is vision, is progress?

Una blew air through her teeth when she asked about The Poplar Place in Moab. You be careful, shaking her head, laughing a little. You think you're so immune.

She told Una that Patrick was coming. Hopping a freight with Sean.

Over and over the same pattern. He wants me when I leave him. The minute I move back he asks me to leave again. I just pray I won't give in again. But I love him so much, I believe him. How come, Una, I only love the man who is unable to love?

Your parents, Una said. You're trying to redeem your father. Your mother having stuck with your father through everything and she's passed that value onto you. If you fail at this you'll fail your father, your mother, your whole childhood. You'll have to admit they didn't love you.

It's true, I can't admit I've failed. The woman holds the marriage together. How often they said that. They blamed me, my sister and my sister-in-law when our marriages failed.

They laughed. Snuggled closer.

It's true. I'm trying to redeem my father. She was struck by the revelation. Prove my love. No matter what he does to me.

She told Una that she had met somebody. A helicopter pilot. And if I let him inside me, the same old story, I'll be hooked forever. And if I don't I'll be guilty of being just like him. A fuckin coward! Those poor guys, Una they need redeeming! Now it was her turn to spit words. Why is love so frightening to men, Una? They're supposed to be brave. What is it that they are so afraid of?

Una said remember when we were virgins. How we'd do everything else but let the man inside us. How hypocritical that later seemed. But it's true, just as the Church teaches. A man inside you is life and death. Out of here, she said, raising and spreading her legs, clutching wildly at her cunt, came six human beings, from Rulon Hatch and Johnny Lookfar inside me!

Remember when we became friends? She laughed. When we discovered how similar *our marriages were!* How crazed and lonely we were. *I thought* no one *could* ever *believe about me and Sergei. That's why I've never written about him, you know.* After a passionate three-year court-ship the man quit speaking on their wedding night and she stayed seven years and had two babies though he never spoke another word to her.

You knocked on my door. A newborn on your hip. Was that David or Darien? You said I've been watching you and I want to know you. Una always laughed uproariously over this, like she still couldn't believe it.

Yes, and you were six months pregnant with Joli. Stephen and Blanchie were toddlers. You'd walk by my apartment window, your face like Botticelli's Venus. Your '57 baby-blue Thunderbird with Utah plates parked right there by my door for months. But it wasn't any of this. Oh, Una, I could see *your soul.*

I'd just gotten out of the nuthouse, married Rulon a second time. In Las Vegas as we went down to California. A new life. Joli, our love child. The laugh was terrible. When I think of Rulon now I can't believe I didn't succeed at killing myself.

But you did kill something, Una. You killed the demon, you broke the pattern. Johnny and Blackie are not *new versions of Rulon and your father. Johnny and Blackie are exceptions to most men. That may turn out to be the miracle of your life—that you broke the pattern. That you found these two. I thought it was just me and my men. You and Rulon. But Una, it's the Big Secret. I'm finally getting it! The Secret of the Ages. Fuck! It's the apple Eve ate. The banishment from the Father's So-called Garden because she ate the Fruit of Knowledge! Now that we're ready to blow ourselves to Kingdom Come the Secret's coming out again. A new book every few months on the best-seller list.* Men Who Hate Women, Women Who Love Men Who Hate Them. *They say there's nothing—NOTHING!— in the psychiatric literature that describes this kind of man. The most common husband. No one wants to believe it. Men or women. No one can, really, all of us needing,* so badly, *to redeem our fathers. Our terrible childhoods. But, war,*

Una—you know how I've been trying to figure this out forever, it's my soul's work—war, *the destruction of the earth! Turns out to be the war between men and women.*

Writing It Out:

  Climbing the Wasatch. Psyche losing power. The barren hills. Wanship eight miles. Always want to drive on to a town named Wanship. His trailer over there but no jeep or helicopter. Across from The Church of Latter-day Saints. Built right on the massacre spot. Too many gentiles coming into Utah. Brigham dressed his men up as Indians, they snuck up in the middle of the night, killed every last soul. Kids and all. Brigham Young's Avenging Angels. It's a violent place, man. In the beginning it was a cult just like the Moonies, like Jonestown. Kidnappings, wifestealing, dictatorial iron-rule. Park City was always heathen though. You notice there's no Church there. Never was one. Only town in Utah that doesn't have an LDS church. That's why it's out here on the interstate. God can't see over the Tetons, they say in Jackson Hole on Mormon holidays. He can't see into Park City, either. And Salt Lake's the only American city ever guarded by federal troops. That's right. Fort Douglas, the only federal fort that overlooks an American city. That's why the pass between Park City and Big Cottonwood is called Guardsman Pass. The Saints were going to secede. They would have too. The Kingdom of Deseret.

  Did you ever read that Sherlock Holmes book, how he comes from England to kidnap a daughter back from the Mormons? Just like today, the Moonies. Indoctrination.

  Did you hear how Miss Wyoming kidnapped and raped that Mormon missionary in England five years ago? Handcuffed the poor guy to the bed three days, had her way with him. Arrested again today in Salt Lake for watching him. In the land of the free and the home of the brave you can watch anybody you want, her lawyer said.

  Mormons believe in Blood Atonement. That's capital punishment. Some crimes, murder and adultery, are so grievous, Jesus' dying on the cross doesn't save you.

  LDS. LSD. First time I ever talked to Max I thought he was talking about Latter-day Saints.

The brothels in Park City closed in 1960. Same month the last mine closed. There's more miles of railroad—700—beneath Park City than under New York City. The mountain is riddled with shafts. Sometimes Main Street just caves in.

Introduced one night in The Leather and Lace Club to another writer. He's writing the book on Jim Singer, the polygamist who was killed near Kamas a few years ago by the Utah Liquor Commission. Singer wouldn't send his kids to public school. Built a schoolhouse on his own property. But the thing that did it, halfway through the whole mess, which had this state rocking, he took another wife. With his first wife's approval. A young girl with a teaching credential. So they killed him. He was just coming down his drive to get the mail and they came up over this rise in snowmobiles. Shot him in the back. Ain't no such thing, man, as real freedom in this country.

But why the Liquor Commission?

Shrugging his shoulders. The state I guess. Utah almost lost statehood over this issue.

Song I think I hear: *Every time I touch you I travel inside.*

Meeting young men whose name is LaBaron. Raised in Canada, Mexico. Una in the nuthouse with lots of women named LaBaron. Photos on the front pages of the *San Diego Union,* years of assassinations in Baja of LaBarons. My mother was the second wife. She always said she was glad not to be the first. It's a great life. I aim to have it myself.

Why do you ask? Moving closer. Recentering to his groin.

Reading *He Walked the Americas.* Meaning Jesus. That's why it's a sacred place, man, saved for the latter days. And so Mormon walked it too. Took him twenty years from South America after his people destroyed themselves. He was the last man alive. You can follow his book like a map. Saw not a living soul the whole way. Twenty years. So he kept a journal, wrote as he walked the history of his people. To the Saints, writing is a sacred act. In the beginning was the word and the word was God. But before the beginning was chaos and even before that was the letters. Our basic task on earth is to take the letters and form words, find the words, to send back to God. When the last king, realizing the end, spoke to his people, books instead of words came out of his mouth. Mormon buried these volumes somewhere on his walk. These buried books are what make the Western Hemisphere holy land. When Mormon finally reached Cumorah in 421 A.D., the hill in what is now New York State, he buried his journal, to be found in 1823 by Joseph Smith, a twenty-three-year-old digger from Vermont. The angel Moroni led him to the cache of gold plates and helped him to interpret the hieroglyphics etched on them, thereby producing what is known today as *The Book of Mormon*. Moroni is the angel depicted in the gilded statue atop every Mormon temple.

Reading Zane Grey's *Riders of the Purple Sage*. Kidnapped by the Mormons from Missouri, taken to Utah and raped, she gave birth to the baby who grew up to be the Lone Ranger. But behind the mask when Lassiter finally shoots him, beneath the shirt he removes to inspect the wound, the Lone Ranger is a woman. He falls in love with her as he nurses her back to health in the sacred Utah valley guarded by Balancing Rock.

Left at the Salt Lake City-23/Reno-548 sign. You know where I live. His trailer over there, his orange jeep. A *chartreuse* helicopter! How does it feel? Heart pounding. Into the throat. Nurture or torture. Down, down, how all the mountains, all the lines go down. To be on your own? This is the place. Where they put a plastic heart inside a man. R U N A W A Y   T R U C K   L A N E! First time I saw that coming back from Vermont and those hills they call mountains back there I knew I was home. A *meadow* of mountains. Emigration Canyon. They walked across the continent pulling hand carts. Photos of old women showing the scars on their shoulders. We could bring in the moving girl if you wanna go that far. Oh shit. A cop behind me.

Psyche's a good name for a Dodge.

Park for the night in the avenues, deep tree-lined street.

At least I'm not thinking of Patrick.

The sun sets behind the low mountains, the Oquirrhs mirrored in the Great Salt Lake.

Curled around myself. Holding on. If you're not with the one you love, love the one you're with.

Coming back over Guardsman Pass. Nine thousand feet. Keep climbing and climbing and climbing, gearing down, the road dirt. Moments of fear to be so alone, to be so high up. What if Psyche can't make it? Back all the way down. Moonlight moaning. Eye in the Sky, the radio crying. At the crest a lone guy there, watching hang gliders. Afraid, but can't really drive past him. Out here in the middle of nowhere. He pets Moonlight, hands me a beer. We watch together. Men just hanging there on crosses in the sky. Moonlight barking and barking at them. Invasion of New Zion from the sky by flying saucers from Lucifer's City of Enoch. His car cassette blasting the Beatles, *I'd rather see you dead little girl than to be with another man.* He's twenty-two, just got here from New Jersey. There's nothing like this in the East. That song's as old as he is. Leaving. *Why wait any longer for the world to begin?*

Telegram to Bill Haywood in Chicago from Joe Hill, November 19, 1915. *It is only a hundred miles from here to Wyoming. Could you arrange to have my body hauled to the state line for burial? I don't want to be found dead in Utah.*

Walking into The Alamo, Neil Young. *Welfare mothers make better lovers.*

Hey you got one hell of a good body on you!

Into his eyes. Thank you.

Later. You're too pretty to live in your van.

Later. You're too pretty to live alone. Then a sudden flush of anger all through him. Afraid he's going to hit me. Picks up the bar stool. Quit pulling my leg you bitch.

Age. Telling depends on whether you want to give or receive. If you want to give you tell your real age. They will be full of awe and wonder. Also fear. You will be a spectacle. If you want to receive, if you need them to love you, to not objectify you, to accept you as one of them, you don't tell. You lie.

The off-season. Soon skiers from LA. Skiers from all over the world. Pure powder.

I like the cowboys best. The real people here. They're like the Indians now. Losing their land. Way of life.

Cowboys Against Nuclear Power. A group going to Moscow for Christmas. We figger the real people are just like us. It's the leaders that want to do us in.

That Church booklet I saw once at Una's. How to raise your adopted Lamanite child. Lamanite is the Mormon word for American Indian. Cut off all connections to his tribe.

Darling. Even the women call each other darling.

Beautiful. Beautiful is the most beautiful word.

You know that expression in your country, the man from New Zealand says, the little woman. I have to go home to the little woman.

Yeah. Like I have to go home to the little man.

Stone the crows! Roaring.

What? Looking at his mouth.

Stun the crows. It's like strike me dead. Fuck me gently. Tie me down kangaroo now sport.

Heavens. And then I add boney maroney.

Coming down steep Main Street with my dog, wearing my boots, feeling like I'm growing spurs. *Coming home to a place I've never been before.* Coming down the street and little laughs coming uncontrollably. Sometimes Main Street just caves in. The whole mountain is hollow now. The frantic search for gold, for silver, for oil, for God, for the lover. I pass that old man, the one who pats girls on the bottom, he's the bread delivery man in town someone told me. Wood, too. He grins as we pass.

Hard body.

I ask about him. Oh, Caleb's harmless. He'll put his hands on your ass but don't be offended. He's the town hero. He leads the Nightriders.

The Nightriders?

Yeah. Lady riders. We ride at night. Caleb is our leader. Mostly his horses. We ride all night over the mountains. The only time we come out in the day time is for the Fourth of July parade. He leads us down Main Street. You know those stables out on the highway, near the church. That old farmhouse. That's where he lives. With the Captain.

Where've you been anyway? Guys from all over Hades been calling here for you. A guy named Joey is flying in from San Francisco to see you. The train strikes over, some guys named Patrick and Sean will be here any moment.

I go down into the Silver Spoon. I was just walking by and a guy said

I should go down there on his membership card. Basement of the oldest hotel in town. Dark and funky.

Caleb is the only one down here. Shouts to the bartender in the other room I'll buy whatever she wants. I'm dying for a glass of wine. So for the first time I order a split.

Ain't no sunshine when she's gone.

So I sit down at his table. Put my boots up like him.

Only darkness every day.

I like your altitude, he says.

He's grieving. I see it instantly. His oldest friend just died. The man who always played Santa Claus in town. Tears down his leathery face the whole time we talk. I've been sent down here to console him.

Tell me about hard bodies. My sweetest smile.

I'm too old for you. But you don't know. You just think I'm an old fart. 'Scuse my language. My mother down in Panguitch, she's a writer. Writes the local history. Genealogy. It's important. She's the only one keeping track down there. Me, I'm like my father. The heathen, the Gentile. I just can't *see* what's *in* the words, you know what I mean? I can't see what's in them. That's immoral, I know. But let me tell you a story. I had a heart attack in '67. By all rights, I should be dead now. The Captain, that's the wife, that's what I call her, the Captain. She come down to Salt Lake where I lay down dying, she was outta her mind for fear I was gonna kick off. She got down on her knees and prayed and prayed and prayed. I thought I was dead too. Trying to be a good husband to her and the kids and the Church. We got ten kids you know. Ten that are counted. You know what the doc told her? He told her you gotta take *all* pressure off that man. He's got to be free or his heart will break. You got to let him be free. No matter what. And so ever since the Captain's never asked me once about what I do. Blondie, let me tell you, *truly* you are looking at a free man.

I'm laughing. Or is it crying? Tears almost down my own face. I believe him. I also believe he's the lost father of the orphan poet I know from Utah.

You're like Spider Woman.

Spider Woman?

You don't know who Spider Woman is? Where you from? Spider

Woman was at the beginning of time. She was everywhere. Weaving her web. Like you, I can tell. You just happen to be in the important places when they happen. You don't plan it. It just happens.

Dylan wailing *just like a woman*.

> Moon in Scorpio
> September 20
> The Week You Are A Grandmother
> I-80 Rest Stop

Dear Una,

I cry to think of you and Monad. Son of the son of you. It's truly amazing this time passing, this knowing people for years and being witness to their lives. I am incredibly fortunate and blessed to have you and Sarah and Ramona and Bridgit as life mates. Yes, as you say, a kind of marriage. The husbands not making it.

An honor. A miracle. I love you, Una. For all Eternity.

A baby boy. I remember all our little boys. David, Stephen, Joshua, Billy, Patty, Erinn and Jody, oh so many beautiful boys. What true lovers they were! It's the greatest love there is—the little boy's for his mother. Remembering, seeing it in every mother and son I encounter, I just will never be able to accept that the adult male is less capable of love than the female. So what happens by the time they grow up? Every mother thinks with my son things will be different. I will love him enough. I know it's the culture that has hurt them. Or something universally psychological—the culture just being a product of the human psyche. Sometimes I think it has something to do with the mother–son relationship. But I just can't seem to crack the mystery. *How could our love fail so?* For all these eons? How do we make killers? Why do they hate us? Why can't we stop this? These days I begin to see every man as his mother's son.

Una, you're the only one I can tell this to, you're the only one who knows me well enough to understand.

You told me once that our basic task on earth is to take the letters and form words, find the words to send back to God. Well, I'm finding these and sending them back to you.

Last week in Park City I met a man, Rusty. We danced. He was a good dancer. But I know a heartache when I see one. He said he didn't like his mother! I said no the first night. To going home with him. We danced again on Saturday. On Sunday we had dinner. Then drinks with the boys at The Black Pearl. He didn't invite me home that night and oh, I was ready then, I'd fallen in love. He said, you know where I live.

Una, you're the only one I can tell this to, you're the only one who knows me well enough to understand.

Tuesday. The moon was in Leo. Fiery crashes and the heart, I woke in the middle of the night somewhere in the Avenues in my van *worried* about him. Reason enough for me to go flying up the mountains in the middle of the night to find him. But I know that's a trick of my psyche too. (I'm sick of mothering men who won't mother me.) And I was glad and a little thrilled to dare fate when you needed me to babysit the boys so you could help out with Monad. Kept me out of Park City Friday night. Somehow I knew he was looking for me. These straight guys, you have to be so crooked, just like when I was a girl and my mother told me you have to play hard to get, you have to make them wonder where you are.

But then you came home suddenly Saturday morning so I went up the back way, through Provo Canyon that will always be for me Johnny Lookfar. Every twist of the road, every escarpment, every geological feature I can hear his voice explaining. I can see him, too, that white spot on Timpanogos. The granite the first temple was cut from. The vaults tunneled into the mountains to hold the Records, the Genealogy. David and Stephen fishing as boys, the beautiful day. And as always every time up that canyon a tragedy: this time a drowning, a little boy, rescue crews walking the river all the way up, looking for him.

And I felt pretty cool, pretty much *over* the helicopter pilot.

I was hanging out at the door of The Black Pearl, waiting for someone I might hit on to take me in on their membership, I could hear wild electric violin music inside like Robin, I could hardly keep from dancing in the street, when suddenly he was there.

Guess what, he said. I don't have to work tomorrow.

He led me through the throngs of people. I put my hands on the back of his shoulders to get through.

I'm so *glad* to see you again! How sad it would have been to have never seen you again.

His shoulders tightened! So there I am signing in, insisting on paying my own cover (though deadly broke), rushing to assure him oh I don't mean anything by that. I mean it's just true. Looking at him. I just mean it. (Why am I apologizing?) I'm glad to see you.

Meanwhile this electric violin music, sounding just like Robin, is coming from the dance floor. After sitting down with him and the helicopter crew at a table in a window on the street (did he choose the table to watch for me?), furthest from the dance floor, grinning and touching Casey, I'm glad to see you too, and the violin is screeching like wild gypsies, I excuse myself to go check. *Conceivably.* After all this *is* Utah. It turned out to be David Laflamme, the electric fiddler of It's a Beautiful Day who wrote, played and sang that great song, "White Bird." So besides everything else (falling in love, being afraid to fuck him, preparing myself for Patrick's and Joey's arrivals—I haven't told you about Joey yet), there's this music identical to Robin's, the gypsy soul of it beneath the elephants and the moon and Delicate Arch, beneath Utah the cries, aches, shrieks of those years with him, the gutter so low with blues and white bird must fly or she will die. It's a beautiful day, the violin so low, so high, behind these eyes, just like an old lover, tambourine man, David Laflamme, his bewildered clown face, the straight blond hair, Utah native, his blue violin. A wild punk female vocalist two weeks out of Brooklyn.

So I went home with him. Or rather, my Psyche just followed his orange jeep down here to I-80 to where his trailer was parked near the church.

Before asking me though to come with him we were out in the parking lot and he was kissing me. It was fast, speedy, not sensuous or erotic or emotional, his tongue flicking in and out like a snake's, my mouth too intent. I couldn't figure out if he was kissing me that way for himself, or for me—if he thought that would turn me on—so following him the eight miles down the mountain, knowing this was to be a real one-night stand and so, how to make it worth it, how to get what *I* need from the experience? I thought very clearly how I must not be solely passive, accepting of whatever he wants, as I might be, expecting an affair in which we have time to get to know one another. How to direct him, how to get him to kiss me as I want to be kissed (after all Patrick and Robin are the world's greatest kissers, I'm spoiled, I've thought much on the virtues of kissing).

As it was in every way with him, it was easy and beautiful and natural to take my clothes off, to get in bed with him. In his twenty-five-foot travel trailer beneath the rotary blades of his chartreuse helicopter. I kept my hand on his face. I kept thinking remember Rusty how Richard Gere kissed Debra Winger in *An Officer and a Gentleman*. I've fucked in that very room, the Tides Inn Motel on Water Street in Port Townsend, Washington.

He kept saying over and over as he touched me what a beautiful body you have. Oh it both thrilled me and terrified me.

But alas neither of us had any contraceptives. At first I thought I'd truly die from disappointment. I really wanted to be *fucked*. But I was so broke. What do you usually do? Oh, the pill. I wanted to say do women still use the pill? Or throw caution to the wind. I'd get pregnant. This very moment. See how red my cheeks are? That's it. That's fertility. Everytime I've ever thrown even a tiny bit of caution to the wind I've gotten pregnant. I pulled him down on top of me, we can do other things. But what do you like? He mumbled the word, embarrassed (even in heavy love making he'd clear his throat if he had to say something intimate), that ugly word when I asked what to do, *manipulate*. He came in my hand. To his surprise I manipulated myself. Do you mind? I whispered.

How do you do that? he said.

Same way you do it, I said.

Vagina banging walls when you manipulate the clitoris, *thump-thump-thump-thump*.

Then he went to sleep. I-80 whizzing by, Cheyenne, Wyoming to Salt Lake City on to Reno and San Francisco. Moonlight outside. My old insomnia, dreading morning and the light. It was Rosh Hashana and the moon was gone in Libra. I crawled over him, went out to my van, hoping for sleep, lay there an hour or so. Must have dozed off because I woke to a helicopter taking off. I thought oh no he's flying away.

I got dressed. Outside Scorpio was sinking down in the south-western hills, the Milky Way was so close it looked like a cloud churning out from the feet of Sagittarius. I crept back in—a real evolved move for me, to choose to *sleep* with him. He was sound asleep. I crawled back over him to my side by the window, fully dressed. It seemed too brazen to undress at this point. I watched the shooting stars, Moonlight chasing something. The Nightriders?

I slept until eleven. Dreamed of my father turning into a woman in a dress like a float in the Pasadena Rose Parade, a dress of all yellow and real flowers. World War II planes flying over his head.

Naked in the morning, heavy set (the closest to a fat man I've ever loved), but very beautiful in the morning light, oh, his skin, his dark reddish curls, the thick black hair on his chest, like a big bear!

And your mom's a crazy old woman? Well, not exactly. Do you ever see her? Oh, sometimes. Snuggling into him I said that's what I'm going to be. A crazy old woman. He said nothing.

Is your father alive? I asked this after telling him I was dreaming of my father in a dress crossing a street in Park City, so alive, all the flowers were yellow and alive, as on a float, like a joyous funeral procession.

Oh yeah. What does he do? He doesn't do anything. He's on Mount Shasta.

He got up and made me coffee. On the short shelf above the foot of the bed were very interesting books. One by Lucy, the archeologist. Another: *American Indian Life* (1924, University of Nebraska). Where did you get this book? I had the feeling these books were put out for me.

Sipping coffee in bed. Looking out his window. Joe Hill's ashes in forty-seven states, South America, Europe, Asia, Australia, New Zealand, South Africa. Bill Heywood and Meridel LeSueur stuffed his ashes in envelopes, mailed them to every place in the world. But Utah. Terrestrial. The hardest thing about growing old is the losses. Losing the world. Losing your life. Your self. You've loved so. Such a short time you have to learn it. Love it.

We went to Sunday morning breakfast in Park City at the Mountainaire Cafe with the crew. Oh, you know Una, how I've always loved being one of the boys. I didn't even mind when somehow, I can't remember how, he let it be known to the boys that he knew my body and approved. Great body, he said. My mind drifted to the ski slope, Joe Hill was killed on November 19, the Linga Sharira, I've told you what that means Una, remember? It's God calling, three months before my father was born, and came back when Casey said the phrase "burnt out Valley girl." A wave of paranoia. Was he talking about me? When they left I got up and moved into the booth with him. He said, oh, hello. We both spaced awhile.

Want to come to dinner tonight? I'll cook. My long pause. O.K. We both laughed. If you'll show me your helicopter.

He was going to spend the day packing. I went into town, bought some diaphragm cream, was in another aisle when I saw him come in, go to the same shelf. Condoms. I hid out until he left. I wrote some in Psyche, parked in Sweet Alley, took a road up into Deer Valley and felt so good, a little triumphant, it was so beautiful climbing up, up, and up, the fall colors so brilliant, rain turning to snow. *The clouds blow high the earth turns slow the leaves blow across the long dusty road to the darkening sky to the range up high. But white bird just sits in her cage unknown.* Went back down for a job interview at The Cowboy Bar (I start Friday night!), read the sports page and the book section of the *LA Times,* went back down for dinner. *The sunsets come the sunsets go. White bird in a golden cage alone on a winter day in the rain.* The dinner was delicious, I eat so few home-cooked meals. His job is over here. He has a two-week break in which he's going home to Redding near Ashland and where Bridgit lives now. Makes me homesick to think of Redding, the Sacramento River, I-5 down through central California, down from Shasta. Then they'll all meet in Nucla, the road from Moab to Colorado. We watched TV, the Emmy awards. Una, I haven't been near a TV set in a million years and only know Bob Hope. He said I can't help it if I look like. . . . Well, somebody who won an award. Best actor. Dark, moustached, probably a cop. I looked and he did look like him. But you know, for me it's hard to look at TV, (I think its ions or something; does TV have ions?), I mean I find myself looking away, out the window to the starry lightning-streaked night so much more eventful and thus losing track of what's going on. Bob Hope is in his eighties! Bob Hope is entertaining the troops in Viet Nam years ago. That's the Twenty-fifth Division. My division. There's a flash of guys, heads at stage level looking up to Hope. Three awards for the Third Reich, for several World War II films. He said nothing on Viet Nam. I said oh just wait. It's the most important event of the second half of the twentieth century. It's taken forty years to do the Third Reich. Yeah, I guess. The most important what? Then he said, when they were awarding the writers—I enjoyed looking at them—no one's written about Viet Nam. I tapped the center of my heart. I'm going to.

December '68 to December '69, he said, far away.

Do you have flashbacks?

He's quiet a moment. Well, there's a scene that I wake up from sometimes, over and over the same scene. I'm looking from the chopper right into the eyes of a Vietnamese guy on the ground. Guess I killed him. I don't know for sure. I can hear so vividly the sound of it. It's weird. Like I'm right there low in the chopper and he's right there on the ground. He's looking right into my eyes. A moment out of a million just frozen like that.

The Emmy Awards did an Ed Murrow Special, of Murrow confronting Joe McCarthy. Did you know McCarthy died in an insane asylum?

He told *me* this. But that's also when we had our one little fight. I said they age the film intentionally. TV didn't look like that in 1960, 1969. They have a chemical that does it, so we have the impression we've progressed, so we'll think the future will always be better. It's to make us despise and forget the past. He got a little pissed. Forget it he said.

He'd switch the channels saying things like "intellectually stimulating" which made me know that he was in part intimidated, or at least, cognizant of our differences. This would make me feel better about the fact that he never asked me a thing about myself. Sometime during the night I became very aware of the fact that not only did he not know my last name or have an address for me but that it was really true, we would never see each other again. I had thought a lot about this during the week. A painful edge it gave to everything.

We watched a documentary on gorillas. A woman in Santa Cruz lives with two of them. Her roomies. She's convinced they are as intelligent as we are. She taught them to sign, so they can communicate. The gorilla tells the story of the men who came when he was a baby in the trees in a land far away and how these men, *bad men*, killed his mother and his father and all his brothers and sisters and only he is alive now to tell. Bad men, he keeps signing. Bad men.

You know what this means, I said, shivers running through me. It's proof animals have moral judgment. It means they have memory, story, history. They know how they got there, they know what was done to them.

It's like Big Foot, he said. Big Foot is something we share, both of us from Big Foot country. I think they've evolved, he said, to the point that all they have to do is look into our eyes and we know in the instant not to shoot them.

I looked at him. Looking from the chopper right into the eyes of a Vietnamese guy on the ground, a moment out of a million just frozen. Robin used to say the same thing about Big Foot. Way back in their evolution they started working on this one thing. That's why no one's ever shot one, brought a body back.

The gorillas hugging and wrestling, so physical, when I was a girl with Sarah riding our bikes everyday to the county farm to watch the monkeys fuck, the gorillas like football players, the greatness of the physical, the whales in Newfoundland, like our sex, like gliders at 9000 feet just hanging there on the current, arms outstretched in the sky. Utah is a physical team, the Texas team is saying on the news, this is important, gorillas like football players, how you could get caught in your evolution fixated on the physical, what a place to be, hypnotized into the cells and never want to leave, never get up to leave. How like our sex, he and I, the gorillas, the bear sucking my foot. He makes me understand that for even a one-night stand you have to find the right man, you have to find your husband. I never knew this before, you have to find the ones you were promised in the Terrestrial Kingdom, how he kept wrinkling up his eyes when he was on top of me, I can't tell, I finally said, if you're in pain, or angry, or just feeling lots, lost, so deep inside me.

I'm trying to keep from coming, he said. Clearing his throat.

Oh, it didn't matter that he didn't know my name or address, that I'd never see him again, I was truly, as I said to him at The Black Pearl, delighted to be with him again. In this alley of our sweet eternity. To fuck and fuck and fuck and fuck. My tongue all along his straight teeth and far back. The hitting of our teeth together, the slight bang, so erotic. Will you show me your helicopter in the morning, going down on his silk cock, the chartreuse chopper rising and rising through the trees, this road we're rolling up and up and up, the white bird must fly or she will die. Riders of the purple sage. Kissing for sexual pleasure a hundred lashes. We fly em low and we fly em slow. Books coming out of my mouth. Coming and coming and coming. Once he mumbled you're really a little lover aren't you? Once his head was on my belly, how good it felt what he was doing, something with his tongue and finger, and then he said scar and I said yes, scar (Una, as soon as I get a job, make some money, I'm going to have a rose tattooed on my scar.). God, it's been since Maximus I mean Maximilian that it *hurt* to be fucked, to bang away like I like. He was *long*. And I asked him to fuck me in the ass which he obligingly did. By this time I think I no longer shocked him. I had been wanting him to fuck me in the ass from the very beginning. I held off, trying not to shock him. (Now I recall that I had Patrick fuck me in the ass that first night; he used his hand because he'd already come several times, but I thought all along it was his cock. He only told me the next day when I was bartending at the Sea Galley. I couldn't stop laughing. I always thought with Patrick it was because I was so so so crazy and so so so needing and so wanting to be fucked, good and fucked, by that I mean I wanted a heavy physical encounter because of my broken heart from Robin, I wanted something to overwhelm it.) Last night afterwards, lying there so sweetly, exhausted, sweaty, I found myself explaining it quite clearly:

Most of all I like to come in my vagina. But that takes awhile to happen with a new man, until we know each other well and my vagina adjusts to his penis and then it happens all the time, easily. So I wanted to be fucked in the anus so I would really feel you deep inside me. It's emotional. When I leave I want to feel really fucked by you.

Only rarely in our encounter did he seem moved or genuinely interested but there was real response, almost gratefulness, that I told him this. Then he went to sleep. I lay there. Lightning was attacking every mountaintop, every hill and meadow. Cars whizzed by from Cheyenne, Wyoming, rain slicing their headlights. Five hundred fifty miles to Reno, where Max lives. Finally I went to my van, naked in the rain. Smell of come and cunt and shit. Sore. But I couldn't sleep there either. I missed him. I went back. This time in my soft, that is worn-out pink nightgown Patrick always says is tan. My first Port Townsend garage sale. It was hanging on the clothesline. Twenty-five cents. Crawled in and lay there until light. How I loved his warm chunky body around me, like a gorilla. How I loved his old bear body around me, the football holds and cuddles. I don't think Max ever cuddled, and loving my father in the flower dream, yellow flowers, *real* flowers. Dahlias.

Waking, happy mountain high, his beautiful skin, the smooth smooth skin of his penis, like silk. Una, I'm not kidding, like silk (Oh, how I love men, their pokey Adam's apples, the black hair on their toes, their droopy testicles.) His was a beautiful color, a reddish pink. *Rusty!* Don't you want to fuck? Real quick, I assured him. A quickie, he said, rolling over on me. By now he knew my favorite position. Missionary, he laughed at me. That went on for an hour, banging our teeth together, erotic pull between us like a stretched rubber band, pulling my legs up over his hips, both of us on our backs, and inserting his penis so long. The way he played with my breasts, both of them at the same time. He'd pull them together under his hairy chest, hold them there with his chest and work both nipples. *Oh, die,* when you touch me I travel inside. That is, come, I was a little afraid of all the light, but fucking and coming three times when he "manipulated" so well my clitoris, my vagina sore, my anus sore! He got up to make coffee, turned on the TV (both mornings from the bed), I'd look out the window to the fall-colored mountains, the little snow that had fallen and the cars coming from Cheyenne, Wyoming thinking how much I love the westernness of it all, how the first night dancing in Park City I felt myself turning into a cowgirl, growing spurs and a ten gallon.

How I want to learn to ride a horse. How you have to come eight hundred miles east to get to the west.

What are you laughing about? I was reading one of his car mechanic magazines, "The Lone Ranger of the Oregon Dunes."

This ranger is complaining about the treeplanters like gypsy caravans bring in dogs and women and children and camp out in the dunes! So? Well, I'm a treeplanter. I've been a wife too with children on the caravan. And my parents live in the Oregon dunes. I know those dunes. Lots of quicksand. Funniest highway sign I ever saw was in those dunes, first time I hit Oregon. WATCH OUT FOR WATER! You understand, I'm a Southern Californian. I read aloud to him about the dune that sunk last year. Highway and all. My father talks about it on the phone. So he told me of a phenomenon in Alaska that he saw, north of Juneau, drew it on the dune but I was distracted by him, didn't follow. Something like a mountain sunk and became a lake. Then he looked at me in a funny way and asked me if my teeth were real!

I didn't have a cent, worried about gas. I asked him to cash a fifteen-dollar check made out to me from Port Townsend. His eyes darting. Paranoia. Like Robin's for a moment. Afraid of getting caught. Scorpio. Wild fear.

Oh never mind. I can get someone else to do it.

Showers and breakfast and the crew in and out. I lost my panties. Searched for them high and low, tore the bed completely apart. In the trash a huge stack of *Playboys*. I said something about not wanting anyone else to find my panties. The only time I made reference to the possibility he's not really divesting himself of his wife. He didn't even know what went into a diaphragm. Or have any condoms in his wallet. Could I be a rare encounter? I see myself years from now coming down I-5 out of Shasta, looking over to my left and he's passing in a jeep. He looks surprised. I nod, grin, hi, mate of my soul. Later in the day I found my panties in the back pocket of my Levis. Now when did I put them there?

I'm ready for Patrick now. I just had to have some such experience before he got here. But it was hard, it hurt to drive away after breakfast. He never did ask my name or address. I got the feeling that he may even have a real love somewhere. When one of the crew, the black-haired mechanic, asked him what he was going to do on his break, he stepped out of the trailer to answer so I couldn't hear.

Actually the real love somewhere only occurred to me writing this letter. I assumed his wife and kids are his real love. I remembered the affair long ago in Pasadena that made him crazy. All my questions must have frightened him. I was just trying to know him in the short time that we had. Though, you know, for all this, I could see the girl deep inside me who has always fallen in love with the man who cannot/will not love her, falling falling falling into the oldest trap. Trying to win her father's love.

So I drove away. I wish the parting had been more joyous. It wasn't. It hurt. Dylan on the radio. No one's ever taught you how to live out on the street. I said, well, I'm going. You say you never compromise with the mystery tramp. He said see you later. As you stare into the vacuum of his eyes. I didn't look into his eyes. I didn't want to do that to him. Or to me. I never looked back. How does it feel to be on your own with no direction home a complete unknown like a rolling stone?

They were standing at his helicopter. He was telling her about logging, his favorite job with the helicopter. Because she wanted to know he told her in detail, not all of which she followed. She was distracted by him.

The hook. They pick the logs up by weight not length.

She remembered Gary, a poet she knew in Port Townsend, how he had the job of attaching the tree to the chopper hook.

The loggers don't know how tired you get, all day leaning over. And it's hard to stay alert. There are no sounds, no smells, to tell you what's going on. A log can be smashing into something, kill someone just like that. It's so far away it's hard to stay alert, to understand the danger. All day you're leaning over watching. It's like watching TV, or playing a video game. It's like in Viet Nam you're a pilot so far above, you don't grasp what's being done below.

And again he was telling her about Chile. He was there for six months. He flew in the Andes. Landed at 21,000 feet. Chile. More than anything, more than Viet Nam or Porcupine Ridge or her or himself he spoke of Chile.

She asked if he ever wanted to go back. Too cold, he said, touching the chartreuse. Too hard.

She looked at him, her wide face to his wide face. The helicopter perched like a wasp ready to sting. In her boots, in his thongs they were the same height. They had both been so far. When he touched her she traveled inside. She wanted to ask him but she knew she could only have what he offered.

She said I'm going. He said see you later. She called her dog, probably an Alsatian-Lab mix, got her things, got into her slant-six 1977 blue Dodge Van, turned the key. Willie Nelson wailed out the sweetest thing I've ever known is loving you. She backed out to this tune and though she was looking in her rearview mirrors she saw that he never looked up to wave goodbye. Telling the guys how she begged him to fuck her in the ass. Earth seen from the sky. So never leave me lonely. Tell me you love me only. She turned north toward Cheyenne, Wyoming. The last sight she had of him from out on the interstate, he was bending to the hitch of his travel trailer, her home for two nights. Hooking it up to his jeep for the trip to California. Each time we meet love I find complete love.

ABOUT THE AUTHOR

Sharon Doubiago grew up in Southern California and has spent much of her adult life traveling the North and South American continents. The mother of two children, Doubiago is the author of *Hard Country*. She is currently at work on *Son,* a book-length feminist narrative on raising a male athlete.

The cover art is *Delusions of Grandeur* by Rene Magritte.

Text and cover design for *The Book of Seeing with One's Own Eyes* is by Tree Swenson.

The Galliard type was set by The Typeworks, in Vancouver, B.C.

Book manufacture is by Edwards Brothers.

Library of Congress Cataloging-in-Publication Data

Doubiago, Sharon.
    The book of seeing with one's own eyes.

    (The Graywolf short fiction series)
    Contents: Ramon/Ramona — Raquel — Chappaquiddick —
[etc.]
    I. Title. II. Series.
PS3554.O814B66   1988   813'.54   87-81373
ISBN 1-55597-101-6